C000081656

FATHER OF ONE

FATHER OF ONE

Jani Anttola

The Book Guild Ltd

First published in Great Britain in 2023 by
The Book Guild Ltd
Unit E2 Airfield Business Park,
Harrison Road, Market Harborough,
Leicestershire. LE16 7UL
Tel: 0116 2792299
www.bookguild.co.uk
Email: info@bookguild.co.uk
Twitter: @bookguild

Copyright © 2023 Jani Anttola

The right of Jani Anttola to be identified as the author of this
work has been asserted by them in accordance with the
Copyright, Design and Patents Act 1988.

All rights reserved. No part of this publication may be
reproduced, transmitted, or stored in a retrieval system, in any form or by any means,
without permission in writing from the publisher, nor be otherwise circulated in
any form of binding or cover other than that in which it is published and without
a similar condition being imposed on the subsequent purchaser.

This work is entirely fictitious and bears no resemblance to any persons living or dead.

Typeset in 11pt Minion Pro

Printed on FSC accredited paper
Printed and bound in Great Britain by 4edge Limited

ISBN 978 1915603 982

British Library Cataloguing in Publication Data.
A catalogue record for this book is available from the British Library.

For Mersa and Smajo
and for all those
who did not make it

PART ONE

WEST OF THE DRINA

ONE

IN THE SUMMER of 1995 the young woman lived in Munich, in a block of flats along Dachauer Straße. The street was an orderly thoroughfare in a nondescript suburb, lined by residential houses and neighbourhood shops that always gave her a sense of normalcy; in the mornings she would catch a streetcar in front of her building and, riding to work, she looked like any girl in the city, comfortable in the early sun. But it was always the evening that reminded her of who she was and where she came from.

Her apartment was on the third floor of a four-storey building. She lived there with her family. They shared the flat with two other refugee households. Each group – Bosniaks, Serbs, and Croats – had its own crowded chamber from where they spilled over into the cluttered kitchen, living room and the single bath. They were over twenty people, in total, more than any building code allowed, but they got along and never caused trouble to each other or their neighbours, cramped though it was.

Only the young woman's husband was not there.

That night she lay awake in her bunk. In the dark, she could hear the others' steady murmurs all about her. The cloth curtain

3

was drawn over the window. From a gap, a beam of moonlight lit up the door. She listened to the evening traffic on the avenue die down, the voices of the people returning from the games in the Olympic Park trail off. After the last streetcar passed, the warm summer night fell silent. And there was nothing to be done.

She tried to shut her eyes, but only managed to see the clear image of a burning town. Plumes of thick black smoke were rising far beyond the roofs of the town centre. In the foothills she could see the people fleeing. Then it was too much, and she gazed at the strip of moonlight, wondering how long it would take to cross that little distance. She'd have to get up at seven anyway. She wouldn't get any sleep. Not when it was like this. How could anyone sleep when it was like this? She was thinking of her husband. There were so many people she was thinking of, as she lay in the darkness, but her thoughts always revolved back to him, then to the town that was on fire.

It must have been past midnight when the phone went off. She had managed to doze off into a thin sleep, but now the sound entered her head from somewhere far away, urgent and growing louder. She knew, instinctively, that the call was for her.

Stumbling into the living room she saw the phone, ringing insistently next to the television. The streetlamps outside cast a yellow glow across the ceiling. Suddenly she felt scared to touch it.

She lifted the receiver.

"Is this Amelia?" a male voice asked. The tone was tense, nearly hushed to a whisper.

"Yes."

"Who are you living with?"

She glanced around, her head still foggy from the sleep. Her brother and mom appeared along the corridor, hair askew, they too arranging their nightgowns.

Who am I living with?

Three families – but it was hers that had spent hours over the past few days facing that television set, terrified, hollow inside, watching the news unfold as the Chetnik offensive consumed Srebrenica.

"Well," she said, "with my mom, dad, and brother, but—"

"Do you have children?"

Her brother came to her side. "Who's that?"

Amelia gestured for him to hush up. She pressed the phone's loudspeaker button. A low, crackling static filled the room.

"Yes, I have, one. He was born in Croatia. Why? Who are you?" She sat down on the corner of the television table, still light-headed from the influenza she had endured two weeks ago. And, for God's sake, she knew the past few days had drained her... she pushed open the window to the street below and took a deep breath, welcoming the fresh scent of the summer night. It was very quiet outside. The half-moon was high in the sky.

"Maka asked me to call," the voice said.

"What—?"

The mention of her husband's name made Amelia jump to her feet. "Listen, it's from Maka!" she cried out, and her thoughts started racing. Was this a phone relay from the radio amateurs? She'd sometimes had contact through them, with Maka talking into the handset in the barracks in Srebrenica, while somewhere in Macedonia someone held a phone receiver to a ham radio. But Srebrenica was lost now? Maybe his unit fought its way out to Tuzla or Žepa? Either way, he was alive! *But why didn't he call himself?*

"Who are you? Where are you calling from? Where is he?" She saw her mother standing in the doorway. Grasping the wall, the old lady had that troubled look on her face again.

"Near Srebrenica," the man whispered.

"In Žepa? Is this what you mean?"

For a moment, she could only hear her own breathing.

"Look," the caller hesitated, "I'm from the other side."

The other side. The word hit Amelia's insides like a sudden, cold vacuum.

The *other* side.

The phone just slid from her fingers.

She found herself sitting on the floor, the small of her back against the table's leg. Somebody was trying to prop her up. Her first thought was she needed to get up, get on her feet and help Maka, but her head was drooping, limp like a ragdoll. Why the hell did I faint? she thought. Through her long black hair she saw the receiver lying on that faux Persian carpet, then Nirzo, her brother, picking it up.

The man's voice crackled through the loudspeaker:

"Hello? Hello? Are you there?"

"Please, don't hang up," Nirzo pleaded. Amelia saw his hand trembling. Somehow she noticed it, that little shaking of his hand. "If you let Maka go, we can pay you. We're in Germany, and we all work here. We don't want any trouble. We're just ordinary people. We don't have much, but we all go to work. If you could only let him go! We can pay you, and—"

"Listen, it's not about money!" the man interjected. "I'm trying to help him! We need to figure out how to get him out of here. Have you got a Yugoslav passport?"

Nirzo glanced at Amelia, his face the picture of confusion. She didn't get it, either. *Help? What's this person talking about?*

"No, I don't," Nirzo said. "I mean, we don't have. You know, the authorities, back home, they insisted everyone swap those for Bosnian ones. Why are you asking?"

"We could've met in Serbia." The man was again whispering, his voice disappearing into the static. "You could've taken him across the border to Hungary. But you don't have the right passport. We'll need to find another way."

"I understand," said Nirzo. "What can we do?"

"I've got to go. I'll call you again."

"Wait, what's your name? Who can I thank for this?"

"Never ask for my name! I'll call you again."

"No, wait! I want to ask you..." Amelia started, reaching

towards Nirzo and the receiver. What she really wanted to say was that she'd missed Maka these long, terrible years. She wanted nothing more than just for him to be there. But the phone clicked, then there was just the repeating, monotone bleep of the disconnect signal.

She did not know what to say. They all looked at each other, all silent now. She felt her shoulder. It seemed she'd hit it on the way down. Amelia rubbed it and moved the arm. It felt all right. The bloody flu, she thought. The window was open and the air was still. Somewhere in that moonlit night, a thousand kilometres away, her husband was alive.

Just then a child's voice said, "Mommy... I had a bad dream..."

A little boy, still a toddler, stood in the corridor. He was in pyjamas a size too large, hugging a grey plush bunny and rubbing his eyes, as if something had just frightened him from his sleep.

Amelia's eyes widened and she began to climb to her knees. Her mother helped her up, saying, "Easy, *draga moja*, lest you'll pass out again. Don't you worry about Maka. You know how he loves you. He'll get through, by God, I know he will!"

TWO

Five days earlier, near Srebrenica

THE NIGHT WAS cold but Maka Delić was sweating. The roots of the trees felt solid and slippery under his boots. On every step, the rifle's curved magazine bumped lightly against his thigh. The weight of the ammunition was gone.

The trail, jam-packed with what must have been hundreds of men, winded its way upwards through the pitch-dark forest. Only from the laborious sounds one could tell how the wounded and the sick were being hauled. Some groaned and begged for water. Before Maka went a man carrying someone on his back. Up ahead, he could hear a platoon commander searching for troops. The officer's calls to regroup disappeared into the night, just like his men had. There were hardly any fighters left.

Maka was a young soldier who had survived three years in the siege. Now, as he marched on, with the sporadic gunfire and the thuds of artillery sounding in the distance, he knew the enclave had fallen. With it, his home was gone. Gone like everything. He'd never been in a retreat. He wasn't sure if one could call this a retreat. But when you had the whole population running for the hills, you knew it was over.

There was a small clearing in the forest. At the edge of it, by the path, the officer who had lost his platoon was calling for soldiers.

"Anyone with a rifle is okay! Anyone with a weapon, come!"

Maka stopped and looked at him: he was tall and young but gaunt beyond his age. He could see his eyes, devoid of any expression. The man leaned against his rifle and held his army cap, motionless as a statue.

"Second Brigade, First Company," Maka said. "Anyone else make it?"

"No, nobody from the Second yet... but come on over."

Maka sat down beside the path. A handful of quiet soldiers rested on the slope under the trees, some leaning on their assault rifles, others with only hunting guns. One was an old man with no weapon, perhaps a civilian who'd lost the courage to carry on. In the absence of moonlight, Maka couldn't tell if he knew any of them.

He took off the light, half-empty backpack and ripped open the front of his flak jacket. The white T-shirt underneath was soaked. The night breeze made it cold on his chest. His feet were throbbing. He started loosening the boots' laces, then turned to the others.

"Anyone know Edin Delić? The garrison mechanic?"

The men stared back at him.

"You're his brother, aren't you?" asked a short man with a sniper rifle.

"Yes. Anyone seen him?"

"We were in Potočari," replied another.

"I heard there was a group that left from Jaglići," the short one said. "Maybe he was with them."

The men fell back into silence; they seemed to know the Delić brothers' story, and there really wasn't a great deal one could say about such thing. So they all sat and waited, watching the dark silhouettes of the townspeople pass by. What struck Maka now was how everyone seemed so eerily resigned to losing all they'd ever had. Simply lean, ghost-like figures fleeing through the darkness, with nothing but their bones and clothes to salvage.

When the enemy drove their tanks into Srebrenica, a week ago, Maka knew he was in for a battle. Seeing that the Chetniks, the ultranationalist Bosnian Serbs, had been building up forces around the enclave for many weeks, he understood that his side stood little chance. It had been two years since the United Nations had dubbed Srebrenica a "safe area" and the Dutch peacekeepers had confiscated the Bosniaks' heavy weapons and bulldozed their trenches over. You can't fight like that, besieged, with no guns or dugouts and weakened by starvation, not against an armoured enemy that enjoyed full logistics from Serbia. A civil war, they said. Maybe it was. Names made no difference to him. What did matter, acutely, terminally, was that they'd always been mortally outgunned. In the free territories the Bosnian army had been reorganised and armed. Maka knew, at least he'd been told, in many battles the *Armija* was giving a beating to the Chetniks. But Srebrenica was and always had been a pocket, defended by a guerrilla troop, rather than a real army corps. Then even that was gutted by the UN and their "peacekeepers".

There was no peace to keep, of course. When the Chetniks smashed through the Dutch checkpoints the blue helmets simply fled.

Maka and his platoon fought for six days. The whole division fought. Anyhow, they stood little chance. First they lost the hills of the western flank, then the southern suburbs, before the town centre fell. At noon of the sixth day they got the orders to retreat to a village north of Srebrenica.

It was there Maka understood the full grimness of their situation. The whole population of fighting-age men, from teenagers to the elderly, had evacuated to the fields behind the farmhouses. There were the army units, too, close to five thousand soldiers, many of them weaponless. It had all happened so brutally people were bereft of belongings. A sea of boys and men – the women folks and the younger children had fled towards Potočari, to seek refuge at the Dutch base. Stupefied, he watched as a police officer stood on top of a root cellar to shout over the noise of the crowds with a megaphone. The division commanders and the municipality leaders were organising a breakout column, the cop announced. They were assigning large groups to each army platoon. The troops were to protect the civilians. It would all go well. They were all to march across the hills to Tuzla, the nearest free territory. That was the plan.

The policeman's voice was taut with anxiety. The forests rose into the hills behind him. There was a stubborn sound of combat to the east, where the remains of the Fourth Brigade slowed the enemy down in the river valley. Everywhere around, Maka saw distressed men and the wounded lying under the hot afternoon sun, with flies swarming on their bandages. How in the hell would they do it? Tuzla was dozens of kilometres away. It was all Chetnik territory, with minefields, rivers, uneven terrain.

Maka's company, what was left of it, was assigned near the tail. The tail meant roughly a thousand men. By nightfall they had all entered the woods. They travelled in bouts, crawling through the hills like a giant caterpillar, in the darkness between the strips of white paper the pathfinders had tied in the trees to mark a narrow mine-free passage. Maka was aware that the column was stretched over ten kilometres head to tail, at least twelve thousand scared men.

He and his group pressed on through the night and that morning. The sun came up. They still didn't have to fight. Then, in the sweltering afternoon, word came over the radio: the head of the column had crossed an important waypoint, the Vlasenica highway.

Maka remembered he'd felt a certain hope – felt as though they could all make it. But the enemy cut off that route at sunset. The sound of combat, coming through the dusk, was nothing short of a gut punch, and it continued into the night with a sporadic, dying quality of a lost battle. The column had been hit severely. They could not break through. Yet they marched on.

His section was ambushed in a deep valley. He couldn't tell how many died in that forest, in the dark, but it was grim and chaotic, and he'd been separated from his unit.

Now it was midnight and he was back on the trail. He'd found the stragglers the gaunt officer was collecting. The moon had not risen yet. Tuzla was as far away as ever.

Sitting back against a tree, Maka could see nothing but darkness. The numbers of the passing civilians had dropped. A cold breeze came wafting through the forest.

The officer gave up and sat down, heavily, next to him.

"*Jebemu*... what a great idea," the man snorted.

"To have them mix with us?"

The man said nothing.

There were no more volunteers, no more men with weapons. After a quarter of an hour the commander put on his cap and they all got to their feet, stiff and clumsy from the cold, and with the others Maka joined the slowly advancing column.

They had marched no more than two kilometres when there was a shrieking roar in the dark and a hot flash blasted through the vegetation. When the shrapnel hit the trees, Maka was already flat on the ground. More shells exploded in the high ground. Up ahead someone screamed like an animal and Maka could smell the acrid fume of the explosive and the splintered stone. The column around him dispersed. He could hear people dashing into the forest.

The commander was there, with his handful of men. They all lay flat like lizards, looking for advice from each other.

"Let's go here," a voice called out. "I know the way!" A shadow got up and went scrambling up the slant of the hill. Maka, with his legs heavy, could not force himself to move. He knew the rumour about Serbs infiltrating the columns. It was absurd. Just one of those things people started inventing. You didn't run amok with your own artillery, or strut wittingly into an ambush. Then again, he thought, with those lunatics anything was possible.

Think, he told himself. Think before you run. There was no one here. But behind him, he was sure, on a hilltop to the south-west, was a Serb tank and it was firing at the trail. It meant the Serb troops were there, too.

"No, everyone stay put," said the officer hastily. The man sounded like he was tired of losing his troops. "Everybody good?"

Nine soldiers, that was what he had left, and roughly a dozen civilians.

"We need to get off this trail," Maka said. "That tank will fire again."

"Up or down?" the sniper whispered.

"Down," said the officer.

"And if there are mines?" one of the civilians asked.

"There won't be any."

They skidded down the forest slope. The ground was soft and the solid trunks of beech trees made for an easy descent. Maka could see the valley and the vast, black night sky through the canopy. The stars were out. He knew the moon was rising behind the mountain. The tank fired again. Maka saw a flash where it was on a hilltop in the distance. He heard the report and the shell went screeching through the sky like a giant drill bit, and far above them an explosion shook the night.

THREE

T HE GROUP ADVANCED quietly in the forest. They had worked
a good way, through the floor of the valley, then up another
hillside and around it, putting the crest between them and the
tank. The mountain from which Maka had descended showed
through the trees, cold and dark and massive across the valley,
against the glow of the rising moon.

It was very dark under the trees. When the commander
stopped to read the compass, Maka saw the phosphorescent dial
hover in the night like a cluster of tiny fireflies. He waited and
listened to the night around.

There was something unsettling in it, something Maka at first
could not understand. Then, concentrating, he could make it out:
muffled cursing and twigs breaking underfoot, people speaking in
whispers.

The officer looked up. He had picked it up, too. Now he
stood up and started towards the sounds. Maka could barely see
his back as the tall man pushed into the vegetation. Why is he so
sure these are ours? he thought.

On ahead, someone yelled to them: "Identify yourselves! I

swear I'll shoot, *u pičku materinu!*" The sentinel's alarm triggered panicked shouting that spread in the forest.

"Identify with what, you smartass?" the young commander snarled. The man spat on the ground. "Gostović from Two-Eight-Four. That good enough?"

Maka, cursing in his mind, slid behind a tree. Out of everybody he'd managed to stumble on one with a Serb name! Now, trying to make himself as small as he could, with the solid mass of the tree trunk against his back, he was about to shout *"We're Muslim!"* when he heard the watchman say, "Gostović? Third Company?"

"Damn sure, if you say so."

"Platoon? Tell me your platoon! The names of your squad leaders!"

Maka heard him say them. Judging by the little metallic clicks that ensued, this sufficed to convince the sentries. They were switching their guns back on safety.

As they got closer, Maka knew there were at least a hundred people clustered on the slope. He could sense them rather than see them. Nearby, in a spot illuminated by the rising moon, someone sat on the ground. The man was in a raggedy camouflage uniform. He had his face buried in his arms. A machine gun stood on its bipod next to him, with a stub ammunition belt hanging from it.

"Tell me," said Maka, "is there anyone from the Second Brigade?"

The soldier looked up. His face was like a death mask in the moonlight.

"I don't think so. I'm from the Fourth."

"How did you get here? Were you up on that trail?"

"No, we came from Jaglići. We got hit in the Kostraća pass. You can see, there isn't much left…"

Moonlight now came through and Maka discerned the shapes of people scattered on the slope. Most seemed unarmed. So these were the ones that had left from Jaglići?

15

"Do you know the mechanic from the garrison? Was he with you?"

"No idea..." the fighter said. "We started with more than a thousand. You see what it is now."

Maka could, sort of, staring into the darkness. All about, amidst the trees, people were whispering, as if sensing the proximity of the killers. Somewhere a man was sobbing and crying. So, this was it? Maka could feel it in the air the way one feels static electricity. The Chetniks had decimated the columns. They were coming after the remains. No need to fool oneself. This was the end of the line. The hushed talk and weeping and coughing sounded to Maka like an anomaly in the nocturnal forest, some terrible mistake of nature. He could make out a teenage voice, too. Even the children were trapped in this madness. "Has anyone got water?" he heard the boy plead.

With a sudden jump of the heart, he recognised the voice.

That was his nephew.

Scrambling up the hillside, Maka called out, "Hassan! Are you all right?" Then he saw him: the boy was kneeling in the shadow of a large tree, alive and delicate-looking. At that same moment Maka realised his own brother Edin was also there, and he went cold all over.

Edin, the eldest of the four brothers, sat against the tree and breathed heavily. He looked up and tried to speak. A bout of coughing shook him and Maka knew he had been shot in the chest. He was in the same greasy work coveralls he wore when the Chetniks had steamrolled through the Dutch positions. His son sat next to him, holding him by his shoulders. Even in the dark it was obvious the boy was exhausted. He was only fourteen and he must have half-carried Edin all the way here.

Maka put his rifle and backpack down and knelt beside them. The ground was cold and soft with the leaves of the previous summer. Edin was coughing.

"I'm so sorry, Maka," Hassan started. "Dad got hit..."

"It's all right, guys. Don't speak now. Was it a bullet or shrapnel?"

"Bullet," the boy said.

Lifting the coverall breast, Maka saw that the wound was on the left side. Most of the blood had already washed away with sweat, but Edin's breathing crackled and Maka knew it had bled into his lung. He felt his brother's back to see if the slug had gone through. His fingers met wet fabric. He couldn't tell if it was sweat.

Edin started coughing again. "Goddam bastards... where's Nermin?"

"It's okay, don't speak," said Maka.

"I swear... the bastards..."

Maka took the canteen out of his pack. It was the same one-litre soda bottle he had carried throughout the war. There was only a little water left. Edin stared at him. His face was strangely pale in the darkness.

"What do you want?" Edin's voice was loud now. "You look like a Chetnik. Just kill me. Go on, kill me, if that's what you want!"

"Shh... don't you worry, we'll make it," Maka whispered, confused, as he helped Edin to drink. He clearly didn't recognise him. And Nermin, their youngest brother, had gone missing in combat three years ago. This wasn't a good sign. This wasn't good.

Maka passed the bottle to Hassan but the boy did not want it.

"Come on, sinko, you've gotta drink some."

"No, give it to Dad."

"Why is he like that? Why does he talk like that?"

"I don't know," said Hassan. "They shelled us with some kind of gas. A lot of people went all crazy. Some started shooting at others. I don't know what it was. I saw some men kill themselves. Maybe it was that gas. Then he got hit. I don't know. It's all crazy."

17

Yes, it was all crazy. It had been lunacy since 1992 and Maka had thought it couldn't get worse and now they were here. And how to continue with Edin?

Hassan was taking it well, though. He was taking it better than many of the adults. He'd just turned eleven when the war started and he'd grown into it. But what the hell, Maka thought, that a child should go through this. Only fourteen, but the boy was tall for his age. Maka knew the Chetniks would kill him, too. And for what?

"Did you hear anything about your grandmother?"

"No… from the hills, we could see all these women on the road. There must've been thousands of them. Did she join them, do you think?"

"I told her to try for Potočari. Don't know if I should have," said Maka, feeling sick inside wondering if his mother had made it through the shelling.

"You think the Chetniks have done something?"

"No, I don't believe so. You can never tell, though."

The boy said nothing, then, "You can never tell about the Chetniks."

"No. But she'll be all right, I'm sure."

Maka got out a half loaf of buckwheat bread, broke it, and gave it to his brother and the boy. They sat quietly, chewing the bread and passing the bottle around. Edin had calmed down. Maka could still hear the froth in his airways. More people kept coming from the dark, scared and tired, and each time their arrival stirred a wave of alarm in the forest. A hint of light had appeared in the eastern sky. Nearby, Maka saw Gostović the officer slumped on the ground. The man probably hadn't slept for days. None of them had.

Maybe Edin would feel better after a doze. Even if it was short, it might make a difference. Maka did not like this son of a bitch of a forest, or the darkness, or the waiting like sheep to be slaughtered, or their ever-growing flock. But he knew, with the three of them, they might run into Chetniks or get shot by their own people. It would be difficult to clear out before dawn. He wasn't sure how far his brother could walk. They'd find out, though.

"Let's have a snooze," he said. "Daylight's coming soon. *Sinko*, can you help me?"

They helped Edin lay down, holding him by his shoulders.

"No, on the left side," said Maka. He did not want the blood running into the good lung. "You got a jacket?"

Hassan was only wearing jeans and a T-shirt.

"Then lie here between us. Get close to your dad. It's gonna be all right."

The three of them lay on the ground under the old beech tree, pressed to each other. The air felt bitterly cold. But the layer of leaves was soft and Maka so tired that as soon as he closed his eyes he felt the sleep coming, as if he was falling, falling and spinning into some bottomless chasm.

They woke up to gunfire. Maka cursed and rolled over to check Edin – he was still breathing. It was dawn now and there were Chetniks approaching from the high ground, through the forest. They were calling to the Bosniaks and firing their weapons. Maka could see the trees and the people, now visible in the morning twilight, everyone crouching low in the brush. There were at least two hundred men in that forest.

Gostović was on his knee, holding a carbine rifle. He scanned around for his men, looking unsure of what to do. With these people, they could not return fire. The Chetniks, though, were firing into the trees as they advanced, shouting as the bullets zipped and cracked through the foliage.

"It's no use running anymore," someone cried out. "Let's just surrender!"

A sense of sudden and cold logic came over Maka. In that suggestion lurked nothing less than death.

"Quickly, get up," he said to Edin and Hassan. "Let's hide in the valley."

He grabbed his pack and rifle and helped his brother up. Just as they started to run, the fire came in: volleys of machine gun rounds and rifle grenades' explosions ripped the air and instantly there was a white flash and a stinging hot blast of dirt that punched Maka's whole body and blew him off his feet. He tumbled and rolled down the hill and the air was filled with dead leaves and bullets and he could glimpse others running past him; he managed to get on his feet and run, taking big, flying leaps down the steep hillside. He fell twice more, scrambled up and ran, lungs burning and ears ringing from the detonation, until he reached the bottom of the gulley and dived behind a tree.

Breathing heavily and hands shaking, he checked the rifle. With a quick swipe he brushed dirt off the gun's breech, then looked around for Hassan and Edin.

It was just the group of stray soldiers again, now reduced to seven. Gostović was there, staring uphill. His thin lips were working as though he was praying. The sound of the gunfire and grenade blasts uphill rocked the forest like a lightning storm. Sons of bitches, Maka thought. They were mowing down civilians.

"Everyone, count your munitions," said Gostović. The words came out hesitant and for the first time Maka could sense his fear.

What should I do? he thought. What could I do? He detached the magazine and pushed on the top cartridge with his thumb. It went down lightly against the spring. Five rounds, max. Up beyond the edge of the gulley, the shooting went on sporadically. Then he could hear someone begging for his life and a sudden, bloodcurdling scream. It was the sound of a man being butchered with a knife, like a calf, so unbearable that it made the others start to run again.

Maka dropped to his knees. He closed his eyes. He took a deep breath, trying to think.

In his mind his saw his father. He remembered his deep, good voice. It's too late, it said.

Save yourself.

Maka stood up and dashed towards where the rest had gone. Now he was sprinting through the forest, zigzagging between tree trunks and rocks. He fled, and his heart was heavy with grief and his lungs were burning. He ran what he thought was at least a kilometre, with a metallic taste rising to his mouth, and by the time his body made him stop he had caught up with the others. They were all leaning against the trees and their rifles, panting and coughing and spitting.

"What we gonna do?" one asked.

The commander looked around. He was badly out of breath. "Can't go back," he said, gasping for air. "Too many. No ammo."

"*Jebeni šupci*," someone cursed.

"What to do?" said Maka. "It's just us."

Gostović, holding the compass, wiped the dial. His hands were shaking. He pointed where the sky was growing blue as the sun rose behind the hills.

"On that side, there's Kravica. Everybody was killed there. That's where I lost my platoon." He turned to look towards the mouth of the valley. "Earlier, I saw a large group in this direction…"

Maka felt it coming now. He'd done the most shameful, gut-wrenching thing. They'd killed Hassan and Edin.

But he knew there wasn't anything else. There wasn't anything. And certainly no strength in numbers. He now saw that one of the men didn't even have a gun but carried a rusty old axe. *A goddam axe, for fuck's sake.* How could they fight? Or haul the wounded? It was pointless, deadly and pointless, to be in a crowd. In the end, it was every man for himself. If he were to exit these woods alive, he'd have to go by himself. No group could survive this.

And what excuse did he have? He was still supposed to be under command.

Gostović, looking as sour as ever, snapped the compass shut. He slipped the device back into the pouch on his belt, then turned around and, with the semi-automatic carbine on his shoulder, started into the gulley.

Feeling hollow and sick, Maka took one final look into the sloping mountainside where he had left them. The alder trees already stood out from the grey daylight. No, there wasn't anything, he told himself. It was done.

FOUR

IT WAS DAWN and soft light had begun penetrating the leaf canopy. The seven men walked through the forest cautiously in file, in their faded and patched uniforms. Maka came the last. He now saw three of the others were wearing civilian clothes, smudged enough so that in the night he had taken them for fatigues. One had his pockets torn and a length of rope for a belt. Ahead of him went the short sniper, then the man with the axe on his shoulder, like a woodcutter, and another who carried a battered, Second World War–era Schmeisser gun. The underbrush was difficult and their trousers and boots were soaked from dew.

They arrived at an old, abandoned trench line. Maka could observe the rotting logs and weather-broken sandbags in the shadow of the trees. Gostović and three others went ahead to inspect it, while the rest waited in the bush.

"They said you found your brother," the sniper said to Maka.

"I did. Him and his son."

"Those Chetniks never gave us a chance," the short, unassuming man noted regretfully.

"Do you have anyone here?" Maka asked.

"Just cousins and friends. I'm from Blječevo." This was a village north of Srebrenica that the Chetniks had razed in 1992. Maka looked at him. His face was hapless and friendly, and he spoke in a way that made him sound a little simple.

"What about the others?" the man asked. From the way he said it, Maka knew he meant his brothers.

"One died on the front. The youngest went missing in action."

"Hell, I don't know what to say."

"It's all right," said Maka. But in his mind was the image of Edin and Hassan disappearing in an explosion. The more he tried to push it away, the harder it kept coming: sharp, acrid and brutal.

"It's so senseless," the sniper went on. "I'd just built a house. My wife had the Party membership, so she got the loan. You know, she believed in Yugoslavia. My daughters even went to the Youth Relay."

The man spoke confidingly, having unexpectedly found a companion in misfortune. Maka looked towards the trench line and saw the others on all fours on the forest floor, pushing what looked like sharpened sticks into the ground, probing for landmines. He could hear the little rush of the wind in the foliage and he felt like moving on.

"What happened to your wife and daughters?" he asked.

"Oh, they're in Srebrenica," said the sniper. "They went to Potočari, like everyone."

"Like my mother."

"How about your old man?"

"Died a while ago. Struck by an eighty-two shell in the backyard of our house."

"So, you're the only one?"

It was the one with the axe who said this. He was sitting some distance away and had listened in. Maka looked at him and smiled.

"No, I got married before the war. She left in the last convoy, pregnant."

Maka had put Amelia on that bus. He knew she had given birth to a baby boy.

He would soon be three years old. Maka had never even seen a picture of him, but he missed him and he missed Amelia and he wanted to hear their voices. He was desperate to hear all three of their voices together. That was all there was left to fight for.

"We must get to Tuzla," the sniper said, "then this will be over."

"If we ever make it," said the one with the axe, "they'll only send us back to the front."

"We mustn't think too much," said Maka.

"That Gostović, he's a radical," said the one with the axe, looking towards the trees where the others were still clearing a path through the line.

"How come? Is his father Serb?"

"Both of his parents are. He's a real Serb, not just in a name. A good Serb, all right."

"Why did he stay?"

"Who the hell knows? Wanted to fight for his town? He's a radical, and a strange one."

"How come?"

"Well, you know," the man said, shrugging his shoulders. "I know I love my hometown and all that. Grew up in one place, don't know much about the world. But what's a town? Or a city, or a country? Just strangers that don't give two fucks about you or your family. Serbs, Croats, Bosniaks – all the same! Makes no difference who lives where, does it? How we pronounce our names. Which building we go into for worship. I never cared about that. It's the same earth under our bloody Western-made, cousin-in-Germany-sent Adidases!"

"And now you're hunted like a beast anyway?"

"Exactly. It's preposterous."

Maka heard the man, he heard him well. If he, Maka, could, he would fight back. He'd help people make it out of these woods alive. But, above all, he wanted to see his son, and he wanted to see Amelia.

He'd been so lucky to meet her. His pretty, cool, rational Bratunac girl. What was she doing now? What day of the week was it, anyway? Maka hadn't had any days or weeks for three years. But if it were a weekend, she was somewhere cosy and reading. A hint of calmness touched him as he remembered her and her passion for books.

No – not that. She must be watching the news. Watching the news and calling Sabina, Maka's cousin in Tuzla. Worried out of her mind. She didn't even know he was alive.

Someone whistled to them from the trench.

"Well, let's get moving," he said.

They crossed the old positions and some distance beyond, going down another slope, came to what looked like a road. Maka kept his eyes on the line that showed through the trees and his rifle ready.

It was a fresh logistics trail bulldozed through the forest, parallel to the hillside: just raw earth, ripped-up tree roots and crushed stones, though it was wide enough for vehicles. On both shoulders the ground had been flattened smooth by something big that had driven up the mountain. As they paused to observe for signs of the enemy, they heard a distant, rusty rattling of tank tracks. They were far from government territory and Maka knew it was a Chetnik tank, and that a tank meant infantry.

"Should we change the bearing, uphill?" one of the men suggested.

"Anywhere but there," said another, gazing nervously towards the sounds.

Gostović looked up into the adjacent hillside.

"Perhaps," Maka said, "from that top we could see where we are?"

"Right. We'll figure it out from there."

The sun was rising above the forest and the slope had become steep. The seven of them climbed it, grabbing tree trunks and shrubs. Now and then, the young commander looked back to see that the others were keeping up with him. Somewhere, far-off sporadic dull cracks of gunfire disrupted the morning air. The slope they were ascending felt safe and when they reached the crest it was flat and the forest was scrubby, but it did not make a good vantage point.

They waded deeper into it and came to a large meadow. Now, out in the open, the grass and bracken were up to Maka's waist. The bracken waved gently in the forenoon breeze, still wet with dew and bright green in the sunlight. Near the other edge, they found a small clearing. Surrounded by the ferns, under the high and clear sky, it gave a feeling of a little hideout.

"Let's rest here. Have the clothes dry a little," Gostović said. He held seven blades of grass in his fist. "Pick one each. For the guard shift."

These were not his men, and it occurred to Maka that Gostović probably did not feel like he was in command. There had never been full command in the Srebrenica division, not in a military way. They had all been ripped from their lives and dropped into the trenches, with their rag-tag fatigues, unshaven faces, and wind-blown hair. The command was cooked up from the early defenders of the enclave; anyone educated or with a rank in the Territorial Defense or the Yugoslav National Army, now with vague titles such as "squad leader" or "company commander". Orders were rarely refused, yet often discussed and grumbled about. In this predicament, with men he did not know, Gostović probably would have preferred to simply walk, alone, into the woods and disappear, just as Maka wanted.

They drew the lots.

"Make it just fifteen minutes each," said Gostović and handed the first sentry – the Schmeisser-gun man – his wristwatch. The others put their weapons on the ground and lay down along the clearing's perimeter.

Maka lay on his back, with the rough fabric of the rucksack and the contours of the empty magazines inside the pack under his head, smelling the moist fronds. He looked straight up at the blue, infinitely tall sky. This hunger, the heat and the thirst were wearing him out, he now admitted to himself.

And what if I will die here, too?

He knew he shouldn't harbour such thoughts. If he wanted to come clear of these damned hills, he needed to stop all that.

He turned on his side and closed his eyes.

It was hot and Maka awoke with the sun in its zenith, blinding him. There were voices speaking. Sitting up, he saw the meadow had filled with people. It was a motley gang of civilians and some in army clothes. His own group of soldiers was fast asleep around him. The sentry had fallen asleep and slumped over his vintage submachine gun and backpack.

Maka watched the gathering, still sleepy and vague in the head. The attacks on the columns must have left dozens of stray groups like this scattered in the hills. Now the Chetniks were corralling them for murder.

The enemy must be trailing a pack this large, he figured. He did not have much time.

The others were asleep. If he were to decamp, he knew he should do it now. He began, quietly, so as not to wake up Gostović, lifting the rucksack on his back.

Just then he could hear panic erupt in the crowd. There was no better way to describe it, though nobody was scrambling like a flock of birds. But the enemy was again in the forest. Sure enough, that Chetnik platoon had tracked them.

"Can't bloody believe this," Maka cursed out loud. He was wide awake and could hear them. "Come out! Give yourselves up," the Chetniks yelled, as they moved towards the clearing.

This time they held their fire. People began to obey, hesitantly. Maka could see some of the men start walking towards the skirt of the forest where the Chetniks were. He watched them wade, his heart pounding, stiffly through the ferns towards the waiting executioners, as if they were already dead.

Maybe this was it. That was the thought in his head. His brain felt like jammed in some fog. Hiding in the bracken, Maka took off the flak jacket and dropped it next to his backpack, then grabbed the rifle and thrust it further into the weeds.

"I will go," Gostović said numbly. He stood up. Maka saw that he was hiding a hand grenade against his thigh. He grabbed the man's arm and wrenched the grenade from his fist.

"No, don't do it. Maybe we'll make it."

The Chetniks continued shouting commands. Maka saw the first five of them emerge from the bush, spread out in line. They all had camouflage uniforms, assault rifles and full webbing gear, and they advanced with the air of malignity of men that had committed themselves to a bloodbath. These were pure Chetniks. He rarely saw them, not like this. He had seen shadows dash across a street in combat, or some tiny movement in the lines up a distant hilltop in the binoculars, or sometimes the dead and mangled bodies at the bottom of a trench. But they were his old schoolmates, people he had worked with on the construction sites, young men he had bantered with at the cafés, and the older ones he had respected in bureaus and stations. Seeing them this close, oozing the vengefulness that he did not understand and dressed for murder, something cracked inside him.

"Run!" Maka shouted. With the grenade in his hand, he started sprinting the opposite way, across the grassland and into the forest. Again, gunfire whizzed past him and he heard the bullets smash into the trees around him. The terrain started sloping out and he knew he was running down the other side of the hill.

After a few hundred metres, he stopped and looked back. There was no movement or sound in the forest above him. He hid behind a fallen log and tried to calm his breathing. Remembering he was wearing a white T-shirt, he quickly took it off and tucked it into his trousers' cargo pocket.

A mortar shell exploded up the hill, then another, and the shrapnel buzzed high above him. The sound made Maka duck his head and he smacked it painfully against the log. He lay flat on the ground, holding his forehead, underneath the tree trunk.

A sense of stillness settled over the forest. Soon, he heard someone calling him.

"Delić! Delić! Come on over! The Serbs won't do anything to us!"

It was the young officer. The voice was distant and it echoed in the forest with an unreal coldness. That was a dead man calling. Maka knew the Chetniks had caught the group. They had made Gostović try to lure him in.

No, he told himself. What fool did they take him for? Slowly, first backing up on all fours then crouching, taking cautious steps to avoid dried branches, he started retreating deeper into the valley.

FIVE

Maka was alone now. He was bare-chested and holding the hand grenade he had taken from the young officer. He had descended through the undergrowth to a dell that cradled a dry stream bed, hoping it would offer protection if the Serbs started shelling the forest again. He sat on a rock and wondered what to do.

In this part of Bosnia, there were hills after hills. Maka had lost his sense of direction, and he was not sure about the sun's position, and did not know what time it was. He needed to go north. He was not sure where that was. All Maka understood was that this was Chetnik territory and Tuzla was fifty kilometres away as the crow flies. In this terrain, with these enemy-infested hills, he did not know how he was supposed to make it.

He stood up and looked around. All he could see was trees and more trees and the sunlight filtering through.

Maka started ascending the other side of the valley, away from the danger. Should he reach the crest, he figured, he might get a view around and some idea of his position. He cut into the undergrowth, always climbing, trying to avoid areas in the hillside where the trees opened up and where clumps of bright green bracken grew under the sun. He was still afraid to wear his shirt and the branches brushed roughly against his skin.

At least he had his boots. Nobody knew the value of good boots better than a soldier. Boots and water. He was thinking of this to keep his spirits up. As he was climbing, he had grown thirsty and he hoped to come across a spring or a stream. But the forest floor was dry and he figured he was out of luck.

As soon as he had thought this, he felt a certain remorse. No. He'd had a lot of luck. He'd had everyone's luck. He'd need to find water soon, though. What if the Serbs sent a patrol after him? He was a witness to a mass murder. They'd go to any lengths to destroy him. Still, he thought, they probably wouldn't send a patrol. He'd hear them coming, and trying to root out somebody in this terrain was just too daunting. And there were dozens or hundreds of others. No, they wouldn't go after a lone man. They'd set a net and wait for him. Or simply let him starve here.

Those were the options. He could hide in this bush and starve, or try to get to Tuzla and walk into their traps. *Their nets must have large meshes, though… just look at this country. What a jungle.* When it was like this, a small fish might swim through.

When he was nearing the top, the ground spread out to a woodland of old beech trees that rose from a sea of ferns. Through the forest, Maka heard people talking. The voices were loud and carefree. He crouched in the ferns and tried to see. About fifty metres ahead were two olive-drab flysheets tightened between the trees, and under the sheets he caught glimpses of men, in uniform, with uncut hair and guns slung on their backs. A group of Chetniks was making a camp.

They were here probably for the same reason he was. The hilltop did make a good location for an observation post. Maka imagined they kept a watch not far from where he had just struck the ridgeline. Had his course been fifty or a hundred metres more to the left, he would be dead now.

Maka had come so near to the enemy he was afraid to move. Even the dry leaves on the ground could give him away. He lay down in the brackens and waited.

He lay still until night fell. The soldiers made a campfire, and he could see the shadows dance in the trees. He heard them talk and laugh. Some started singing: "*Molim se u džamiji*... I pray in a mosque... pray there were only Chetniks in Serbia," they hollered, mocking the Bosniaks. Maka could hear more troops arrive at the campsite.

Now I know, he thought, how rabbits must feel in the dark... He had an urge to back off, but he knew that in the night all sounds became monstrous noises.

He tried to sleep. Afraid of donning the T-shirt, he was half-naked and swarms of mosquitoes attacked him. He tried to wrap himself in the bracken fronds, shivering in the cold and weak with thirst and hunger. He wished he could have just a sip of water. The hard roundness of the hand grenade pressed against his chest.

Then, for the first time, he felt it: it came with sudden clarity, like the chill of the air on his back.

He would never make it out of this alive.

He had always managed to push the image of his own death somewhere underneath the preparations, plans, attacking, retreating, ducking the shells, foraging and plain surviving. He had refused to believe it would one day come to this. It was always somebody else's death, his platoon members, his relatives, his friends. He had shoved it into the back of his mind where it lay buried under his will to one day start everything from anew. But he could no longer push it aside: he now understood he would die in this forest.

He curled his arms and knees into his chest, shivering. The dew was already coming heavy and the ground was cold and moist. *Three summers, three winters*... How on earth did he get through?

In his mind he saw the house. It was a simple, pretty Bosnian house, with white plastered walls and an auburn tile roof. It was on the slope of the valley, which was beautiful in the evening sun. From the upper floors you could see the road leading up to the house and, over the orchard, the stream and the thoroughfare and the town that lay between the hills. In the summer the hills were lush with green, and turned fiery in late autumn, then ash grey and then the snow would blanket the roofs of the buildings below, and the Holy Virgin church's tower and the two mosques' minarets stood out from the white townscape.

The houses in the old quarter were ancient and the alleys between the houses narrow and deserted, with black footsteps in the snow leading inside the doorways. In winter, all the sounds were muffled by the snow, and the smell of burning firewood and cigarettes would drift into the alleyways. But at night it was very dark, even under the starlit space; soldiers would walk back to the barracks with hands tucked deep into the pockets of their field coats, breath steaming and hunger lingering in their stomachs. The streetlights were out, it was midwinter, and the cold bit their faces.

Then it was summer again and the shelling was worse and a mortar round fell right behind the low concrete wall that separated the yard from the road. Maka's father was sitting on the stairs of the house cutting plums for šljivovica and was shaken and deaf from the blast. The wall had saved him from the shrapnel. Five weeks later, he was out of luck.

Maka remembered the day they were told to demobilise. The UN declared the safe area, their heavy weapons were confiscated and the worst fighting abated. But the encirclement continued, and nothing was ever confiscated from the enemy.

And they lacked everything.

For three years they had scraped together daily necessities, from building a generator out of a washing machine motor and extracting hydropower from the Križevica, to fishing that same stream, to scouring the woods for mushrooms. They dismantled the town's transformers to get oil for the lamps. Like cavemen, they used flint stones to make fire. They had to continue incursions into the Serb areas, just to pillage food and supplies, with half the team armed only with an empty pack for carrying the loot. Once, Maka's squad burgled a Serb doctor's clinic to take bandages and medicine, six kilometres behind the enemy lines. At the time they laughed about it, because a week later, when they went back for more, with the clinic building standing forlorn in the steady grey November rain at the skirts of the village, there was a note on the door saying: *To the fuckers who stole from me, I've reported you to the command.* The medicine man thought it was his own people ransacking him.

One thing they had, though, and it was time. They had time, and they spent it smoking homegrown tobacco and swimming and enjoying the sunshine the best they could. Days were never easy with the gnawing hunger, but somehow they scraped through.

Most of all, they missed their loved ones. The Serbs had cut the power lines and the phone cables. The radio relay opportunities at the barracks were limited. Red Cross messages would occasionally arrive from outside with news of relatives. It was via such a letter that Maka learned about his son's birth.

He knew Amelia had named him Dino, and he thought of him now as he lay in the ferns amid the buzzing insects. The sound of his son's name soothed him. Then he thought again of Amelia and the winter five years ago when he first met her in Bratunac. One thing in life led to another, he figured. If he hadn't gone out to push that car in the snow, he would have never met her.

Everything must have a meaning and a reason.

Then what meaning would it have if he also died? If he never got to tell anyone what had happened or to see Amelia again? So he whispered, barely audible to himself:

"I'll meet you again, I promise. And little Dino, I promise you. You'll see your dad."

Then he felt he had promised too much, that such impudent words would bring bad luck, and he thought, at least I'll try my best. I might not be in control of anything. But I can promise I'll try my best. And God help me.

The sun was up and he realised he had managed to fall asleep. His tongue was dry in his mouth. The fern fronds were heavy with dew and his body was shivering, but he could already sense the warmth of a new day coming.

The Chetniks were dismantling the camp. Maka lay quiet. At one point, he perceived movement ten metres to his left in the ferns, when one of the soldiers waded into the forest to urinate. A bird sang in the beech trees, and the soldiers were talking while they undid the cords of the tarpaulins and pulled pegs out of the ground.

"Everybody, listen. We'll go to Milića Brdo," someone said.

"Fuck Milića Brdo. That's a three-hour march. When do we get relief?"

There was a muttering, collective agreement.

"Better there than up here. Sick of these boonies!" said another voice, and the troops cheered him on.

Maka thought the name sounded familiar. It was a hamlet near Milići where small roads converged. This unit maybe had orders to set up a checkpoint there. If that was three hours on foot from here, he believed he now had a rough idea of his location.

He'd been going the wrong way. He needed to go back, over that hill with the meadow.

And what if that other unit was up there? If they'd executed those people on the spot, they probably wouldn't have stayed behind. He hadn't heard the gunfire. Anyway, they'd probably marched them somewhere else to be murdered.

Maka waited among the ferns until all the voices had receded. When it was finally quiet, with only the sound of the lone bird singing, he started making his way back to the bottom of the valley and cautiously up the other side.

It must have been past noon when he reached the hilltop and the grassland. There was no one there. The sun was high and the day was growing hot. Maka did not notice any movement other than grasshoppers sailing through the air and the subtle swell of the ferns.

He got on his hands and knees and started crawling into the field.

Stumbling on a patch of flattened weeds, he spotted a familiar tin tobacco case lying in the grass. A name was punched into it – someone he had known from their weekend football gang. The case was empty. Maka set it back on the ground, delicately, as if it were a relic.

Nearby, he picked up an empty plastic bottle, realising it was his. It was in the same spot where he had dropped the flak jacket and backpack. Those were gone, but when he crawled further into the ferns and raked the weeds his fingers met the familiar metallic hardness of his assault rifle, the faithful old Yugo-Kalashnikov.

He couldn't believe they'd missed it. It was no match against the Chetniks, though. But the bottle was priceless, if only he could find a stream.

Continuing on all fours across the meadow, Maka came across someone's daypack. It bore a logo of the University of Sarajevo and had something heavy inside. He opened it to discover a maroon tracksuit. Under the garments was a big bottle of honey.

Back in the forest, he sat in the trees' shade and tipped the bottle. The honey flowed slowly into his dried-out mouth. It was syrupy and excellent, quite like a gift from heaven. Thank you for this, Maka said in his mind. He tried to remember if he knew anyone who had studied in Sarajevo. Whoever that was, the honey hadn't helped them. But it could give him just the strength he needed to get out of here. I mustn't take too much, though, he thought. Without water, he'd be sick. He took another long, sweet drink.

He donned his T-shirt, then the tracksuit jacket. The day was already hot, and the jacket embellished with sporty, colourful lines; still, he thought it was better than the bright white of the shirt. In the trousers' pocket he found crumpled deutsche mark bills worth fifty. He shoved them back and zipped the knapsack. He swung the pack on his back and attached the hand grenade by its spring lever to a loop in the shoulder strap. That was something. He gave it a yank to see that it hung firmly, then adjusted the straps so that the pack was tightly on his back, with the weight of the honey in it. He felt like a soldier again. Now, all he needed was water. He picked up the rifle and began to descend the steep hillside.

Maka went down all the way to the Chetnik logistics track. There was nothing on the trail and the forest was quiet. Thinking he had a bearing to the north, he crossed the trail and trekked deeper into the forest.

He spent the afternoon working through hills and valleys in what seemed like a green sea of trees. Maka was born in Srebrenica, but he had never waded this deep into the woods in his life, not even in the war. It was tough marching, even when slow for fear of the enemy. He had not spotted a hint of water and the dehydration was making him sick and weak.

The sun was setting again. The invisible dwellers of the woods started their evening concert; the strange sounds of the insects, rodents and birds were all around him, as if he were being welcomed amongst them. Then it was dusk and everything went quiet.

In a small hollow Maka found a thicket that made for a decent hideout. He began to build a shelter out of saplings and brushwood, tying them together with strips of willow bark. On the floor he put twigs that he cut from the trees. After finishing, he looked at what he had created and felt contented. The den blended well into its surroundings.

He figured the Chetniks had torched his house by now. He did not want to think of everything that had gone up in flames with it.

He did not want to think of the memories the house carried, or of his pride. The house had been burned, the orchard cut. Or maybe some Serb family had moved in and claimed the place was theirs. What did it matter when all he needed was to get out of here? Maka looked at the heap of brushwood he had put together.

It would do, for now.

He woke up to heavy rain in the night. Water was coming through the branches of the shelter and he was shivering in the cold. His abdomen was rumbling and cramping, and he crawled out and ran into the bushes and, holding on to a tree in the rain and the dark, emptied his bowels in a bout of diarrhoea.

Hugging the wet tree trunk, Maka felt dizzy. He feared he would pass out. It was becoming too much. Just way too much. For a moment he was sure he'd done something terribly wrong in life. Maybe there was God, after all, but he didn't want Maka to live.

He felt the raindrops. They ran down his face and onto his chapped lips. Licking them up, he made himself calm down. He was just an ordinary man. He could not imagine anything he'd done was so offensive that he should die for it.

The night glistened on the foliage around him in the dark like thousands of tiny, silvery eyes. He reached up and took hold of the branches, delicately, so that the drops would not shake off, and leaf by leaf he sucked water from their edges. After a while, he felt a little better.

Back at the hideout, Maka took out the empty bottle and placed it under a plant that was dripping rainwater. He sat back against a tree and waited. The sound of the rain was all around him, constant and soothing. He felt water dribble down his skin under his clothes. His bowel was cramping painfully and the shivers came in waves, but he knew he would be all right.

It was possible to survive like this, he thought. It was so painful, though. He just had to take it. He'd only have to endure this until dawn.

SIX

THE RAIN HAD stopped. There was a thin mist in the forest and Maka sat under the tree, watching it get bright. He was soaked and cold, felt sore in the gut and still had diarrhoea. All the same, he had taken more of the honey and drank another mouthful of water. He thought he was doing better.

He unravelled the shelter to leave no traces of himself. Then he threw the sack on his back and picked up the rifle, shook water off its cold metal, and started into the woods again.

The forest was deep green and wet in the dawning light. Sunrays penetrated the mist between the trees and shrill calls of sparrows echoed in the wood. Maka's feet made barely any sound in the moist, soft layer of the forest floor. In the end, the rain had been good in every way. He did not mind the wet clothes; they would dry. He knew it would be another hot day.

Coming across a small glade, fresh and bright in the sunshine, Maka paused to take in the sun. The ground was already dry. He sat in the grass and turned his face to the sun. It was getting warm.

An airplane was laying a white contrail in the sky. Maybe a NATO jet? Maka guessed it was enforcing the no-fly zone and returning to its base in Italy. It advanced soundlessly and steadily across the deep blue zenith.

He lay down on the ground and watched the plane. Just a tiny dot.

It must feel lonely up there for the pilot, he thought. It was like a different universe there, eight, ten kilometres in the sky.

There were such different worlds. Think of Bratunac. He'd met Amelia there, on a white New Year's Eve five years ago. That's where the small-town boys from Srebrenica went to meet girls. That was before the war. A New Year's disco in a hotel's ballroom. Two years later, the Serbs were rounding up civilians at the stadium and taking them to the nearby primary school to be executed. They shot them inside one of the classrooms. They dumped the bodies in mass graves in the surrounding woods and in the Drina, where some washed out to the Sava and as far downstream as Sremska Mitrovica and Šapac. One year on, the Bosniaks had armed themselves and Big Huse died in a trench on the city's outskirts.

Big Huse was afraid of nothing. He was a good squad leader, someone they all looked up to. He always said that those who'd never been in the first wave could never understand what it was like. In the reserve, just three hundred metres back in their own lines, they could never understand it. Three hundred metres made a world of difference.

That morning they were not in reserve. They had built small fires just behind their line to keep warm, and at first light they got the orders to attack. They cleared the no-man's-land and got into the Chetnik trenches, when the first shell landed right in front of Big Huse.

Maka remembered how the burly man begged him not to leave him. Big Huse was afraid of nothing. But that morning he was afraid of dying alone. A piece of shrapnel had gone through his aorta, and Maka remembered how his hands kept slipping when he tried to compress his abdomen and the enemy mortars were tearing the trench into pieces.

Then, in Srebrenica, somehow it felt as if you were never alone. You couldn't leave, after all, and the town had swelled with refugees from the nearby villages. Maka and Edin had taken in two families. Then there was the platoon, the army command pestering you, the village idiot asking for change by the town square. They called him Dajmarku – Gimmeabuck. He somehow found his daily *rakija* even during the siege, and they said that with his ignorance of the war he was the happiest man in Bosnia. Then the Chetniks with their artillery, trying to get you. That summer they got Dajmarku, too. An American preacher made it to Srebrenica, wanting to know what a war was like. Zlatar told him for some it was optional. He could leave. He did and he flew back to America. His universe, too, had been very different from theirs.

A faint sound of thunder carried from somewhere far away. Maka sat up and listened. It was a dull, crumbling rumble, but the sky was clear and it did not feel like there was a storm coming. He figured it was artillery, in the north.

There had to be an offensive underway on the Tuzla front. He wondered if it was the Serbs or the Second Army. Hardly the Serbs. They had their units tied up here. He listened to the fire intensify, then die down, then start again, rising and falling like storm gusts. After a while, there was again just the gentle wind in the trees.

Men are still dying, he thought. But no one knew about him anymore. Not even his own people.

Just then he became aware that he could hear flowing water. It came from a dell to the left of the glade. He quickly got up and descended into the dell. At the bottom he saw a hollow with a stream running through it. Trees arched over the stream and water cascaded between moss-covered rocks and sparkled in the sunlight coming through the foliage. Maka scrambled down and fell to his knees on the soft, moist bank and sunk his hands into the water. He drank from cupped hands until his stomach was full. He had drunk almost nothing for three days and he did not care if he would get sick from the water. It was cold and clear and wonderful.

When he was filling up the soda bottle, he noticed somebody staring at him, a few metres away. A man sat on the ground by the stream and looked at Maka silently. He was maybe in his late sixties and completely naked. A gunshot had deformed his knee. The patella seemed torn off and his lower leg looked as if it was out of joint.

Maka looked at the man but was not sure what to say.

"Are there any Chetniks here?"

"They were here about an hour ago," the naked old man replied, quietly. "They went downhill."

"Why didn't they kill you?"

"I asked them to... they wouldn't."

Maka realised he knew him. He did not remember his name, but the man had worked as a crane operator in the same construction company, before the war. Maka went over to him and offered water from the bottle. The man did not drink and his eyes stared into the distance. There was nothing in them to suggest he recognised Maka.

"Can you please shoot me?" he asked.

"No... I can't shoot you. But I can try to help you."

First, the man said nothing. Then he repeated his request.

"Look," Maka said, "I can't kill you, even if I wanted to. They'd hear the shot."

Again the man seemed to be thinking of something. There was that pallid emptiness in his gaze that settled in the eyes of a delirious person.

"Then give me that hand grenade and go," he said.

"The hell I will! Let's get out of here, together."

Maka put his rifle on the ground and took off the rucksack. He tried to pull the old man onto his back but the man screamed when his leg moved. Maka lowered him back to the ground. He understood he was too weak to carry him anyway. They were both catching their breath.

"Where are your clothes?" Maka asked.

"I don't know," he said. After that, Maka could not get anything more out of him, and the man sat motionless, staring into the distance again.

Maka rested on the ground, looking at the notches of the old man's spine that showed through the waxy skin of his hunched back. He would not be able to carry him. It was impossible. And he couldn't give him the grenade. With those Chetniks, it would be worse than a gunshot, and what if it didn't kill him? The man looked as if he was already numbed by blood loss and hunger.

He couldn't shoot him, either. He couldn't just shoot a man, like that.

He considered it a minute. If he'd do it from where he lay, behind his back, the man wouldn't know a thing. But he couldn't just shoot somebody in cold blood. Then there were the Chetniks.

Maka got up and lifted his backpack. The old man did not seem to notice. With a couple of strides Maka crossed the little stream, stepping on a stone in the middle that sent up tiny splashes of the rushing water. He turned, and the man was still there, unnoticing and staring ahead, his lips now moving as if he were having some silent conversation inside his head.

He was still like that when Maka left him.

It was sweltering hot. The summer sun of the Balkans was beating down on Maka as he climbed up a hillside, towards what he assumed was north. He was ascending higher and the deciduous forest had turned into fir trees and junipers. He was thinking of the old man. He hoped he wouldn't have to suffer for long. Maybe the temperature of the night would end it. He was starting to regret he hadn't given him the grenade. But he had to think of himself. He might need any little resource there was to extricate himself from this insanity.

He was good at leaving people behind, though. What else was there? Again, so little a man could do. Breathe and try to exist.

Near yet another crest he came across a path in the forest. Muddy and raw, it looked as if it had been beaten by thousands of feet. Maka figured it was the same trail he had trod in the column three nights ago. Here, it was quite high up. Looking through the trees, to the west, he could see valleys and mist in the lowlands far away and up ahead hilltops and more hilltops. There was no sign of life.

The trail would take him towards Tuzla. But, seeing that it had been the main escape route from Srebrenica, the Chetniks should have taken control of it by now. He might walk straight into another ambush. Still, he reckoned, he couldn't continue this brainless roaming.

He decided to take it.

The trail was waterlogged and slippery after the rain. Maka advanced slowly, holding the rifle so that he could fire it instantly. The forest was steaming and he sweated copiously. Little by little, the drinking water was gone. Right before the path opened into a large clearing on the mountain's face, he stopped to take rest under the shade of the trees.

He sat in the cover of some juniper shrubs, tired and sleepy. He took out the honey and ate some. His bowel was still growling, but to his relief, nothing was coming out anymore. With his eyes closed, he smelled the pleasant odour of the seed cones. All was quiet now.

Just a low, humming susurration floated over the windless silence, like distant engines idling.

Maka got up and sneaked his way to the edge of the forest. Peering past the trees he saw them: dozens of dead bodies covered the hillside down in the clearing. They had toppled in every direction and on top of each other, young, old, in civilian clothes, some in camouflage fatigues, all swarmed by a million blowflies.

A nausea of shock, suddenly rising in his stomach, pushed sweat to his face again. The blanket of corpses lay before him, the dead in unnatural poses, inanimate as rocks. Maka saw the ground at his feet was scattered with empty shell casings. The men had been gathered there, made to stand in the clearing, and the Chetniks had opened fire from higher ground. This was what would happen to those who got caught. Now the evidence was before his eyes, in all its paralyzing authenticity, yet he still could not believe it.

Maka looked around at the terrain. No sign of the killers. They had cleared out, for now, but they'd be back later to hide the corpses.

He went down to the bodies and started walking among them, turning over some that lay face down. His shadow stirred up clouds of flies, the buzzing convulsing into a wild drone. The faces of the dead were already swollen and discoloured like winter pumpkins, with the all-encompassing stench of rotting flesh.

Fighting his nausea, Maka returned to the trail and started working rapidly away from the clearing. What he'd seen felt unreal. If he left it behind swiftly, maybe it would stay so.

He kept on along the trail for many hours without seeing a living soul. Then it started to peter out, becoming just a faint path in the forest. When Maka mounted yet another rise, the sun had begun to set and across the distance he could see a flat valley and patches of fields and an asphalt road running through the valley. He stood there looking at the country. The fields were green and golden in the low sun and beyond them were more hills, as far as he could see, and somewhere beyond the prospect was Tuzla and the free government territories.

When he descended to the valley it was half-light. He waited in the forest until he could cross the highway. He was on high ground, on the skirt of the forest. He could see the road below through the trees. He sat on a log with the rifle on his knees, plucked a blade of grass and put it in his mouth, chewing it.

He sat and waited. Twice, a convoy of military trucks drove past. Between the noise and the olive-green movement of the cars, the road was deserted in the receding light. Maka knew he would have to cross it right after the sun went down. The moon would be up early.

When it was dark enough, he got up and descended from the forest on the road's tall bank.

He stood on the road. The hardness of the asphalt felt strange and comfortable underfoot after so many days in the woods.

Here, the road went north-west. Instead of crossing it, he thought, it might be better to take advantage of the night. He'd have to sink back into the forests anyway. The road might save him a few kilometres. The moon was coming up fast, but the sky had become overcast and he felt protected by the darkness.

Maka started up the road. There was now a shimmer of moonlight on the clouds' edges. The only sound was the water squelching in his boots, which were soaking wet from the forest. It was so quiet it was hard to believe there was a war going on.

He came to a small, gravelled lay-by with a stone water basin, the kind some people built to commemorate a relative who had died in a road accident. The tub stood under a ramada of thin wooden pillars and a wood-shingle roof. A metal pipe emerging from the hillside fed it with trickling water.

Maka stopped and drank from the tub, then pulled the empty bottle out of the rucksack and dunked it into the cold water, hearing it bubble. After placing it back, he bent over the basin to wash his head.

He stood under the roof, water dripping from his hair. The stubble on his cheeks felt coarse when he wiped his face.

If I ever make it out of this alive, he thought, the first thing I'll do is take a long, hot bath. That and shave. He'd have the meal of a lifetime. He'd find the money for a ćevapi and a beer, and if he couldn't have a ćevapi they'd give him canned liver pâté and a loaf of bread at some army barrack. A real feast.

He swung the sack onto his shoulders. He looked at the road and the sky. The moon was under and it was dark enough to continue.

In a while, he was passing a group of ravaged houses and a mosque. The base of the mosque's minaret had been blown up and the spire had keeled over against the neighbouring house, inclined now like a giant white rocket in the night. There was rubble of plaster and tiles by the roadside and a smell of soot in the chilly air.

Maka went on. Up the road he could see another broken building, its skeleton roof beams sticking out dark against the faintly moonlit sky. A scolding voice cut the silence:

"You bloody coward! There's no *Balija* around here!"

"Swear I could hear someone on the road," another voice protested.

"On the road... ghosts on the road!"

Like a flash, Maka slid into a ditch by the roadside. He pushed down the rifle's fire selector, holding it firm so that it would not click, then lay in the cold grass and waited.

The moon came out. Around him was the destroyed hamlet, the shot-through walls of the houses agleam and ugly in the eerie light. There was no movement ahead. No search party, either, and he could not hear the voices again.

It was the water in my shoes, he thought. *It saved my life, though.*

He took the boots off now, tied the laces together, then hung them on his neck and waited. When the moon went under a cloud, he got back on the road and sneaked back with his wet, bare socks.

Pausing opposite the destroyed mosque, he looked at it and the broken house next to it. Their empty doors and black windows seemed to stare back at him.

It was probably best to camp for the night. The mosque didn't feel safe, though. If anything, the Chetniks would use it as their lavatory, and it didn't have any upper floors left. But the walls of the two-storey house next to it seemed intact. Most of its roof tiles remained, too. He could hide in the attic.

Maka slunk into the building. The floor was covered with debris and there was a stale odour of dank soot. Fumbling his way into the darkness he found a concrete stairway. He climbed up and on the garret floor walked onto a thin foam rubber mattress. It was filthy and damp, but unburned.

He took off the backpack and the tracksuit jacket. He wrapped the jacket around the rucksack and put the bundle on the mattress for a pillow. The boots he placed next to the wall. Taking off his socks, he wrung them out and laid them on top of the boot collars. Holding the rifle close to his body, Maka lay down on the skirt of the mattress and pulled the other half over him like a blanket.

For a time, he lay silent, with his eyes open. It was so dark it made no difference. God, he was tired. He knew he'd never been this tired in his life. He felt the sleep coming. He thought of Amelia and his son in Germany, imagining them asleep, in their nocturnal bubbles. He knew they were safe. He closed his eyes and went to sleep.

SEVEN

THE NIGHT WAS quiet except for the occasional hoots of an owl and the whining wind in the roof tiles. Maka drifted in and out of sleep. When he slept he did not dream of anything, and when he lay awake in the darkness he thought he could still, at times, catch a whiff of the dead.

He knew he should have tried to flee Srebrenica much earlier. Things would look different now. But the authorities told him to stay and defend the town.

Maka was never sure why they fought or why the Serbs were assaulting them. They defended themselves because the enemy was attacking. But did the Chetniks attack because they were defending? He had never stopped to consider such things. In war, you did not think. You were only pulled into it, as into a giant whirlpool you could not swim out of. But with the image of that grassy hillside in his mind, the bodies strewn across and the clouds of blowflies, he knew he had done nothing wrong in defending himself.

When the sun was up, Maka did not feel well-rested and he was weak with hunger. He climbed to his knees and pulled himself to the empty window under which he had slept. Dazzled by the sunlight, he could feel the morning breeze on his unshaven cheeks. When his eyes adjusted to the brightness and he saw them, he went all cold inside and slumped back to the floor in shocked disbelief.

The enemy was right outside the house.

Maka jammed his back against the wall, holding his breath. *Okay. Now what?*

He looked around. He was in the attic of a bullet-riddled house, in an empty, partially burned-out room. Sunlight came from the gaps in the broken roof. His rifle lay on the foam mattress, next to his boots, as in the home of a soldier who had just returned from the front. In the wall near the corner was a jagged hole, punched in the bricks by a flak gun.

Maka turned on his knees and peered through it. The road he had been on cut across fields in a wide, shallow dale, with hills beyond the fields. Shadows were still long, but the morning looked warm. Chetniks stood guard on the road, one man every fifty metres, like posts in a fence. The nearest soldier was no more than twenty metres away. He was dressed in a Yugoslav field uniform. He had a Serbian šajkača cap perched on his head. The man held his rifle across his chest and scanned the surroundings lazily, whisking off flies that were already pestering him. He was so near that Maka thought he could smell his sweat in the wind.

He didn't see me, he thought. All the same, he was trapped. And if for any reason some of those Chetniks wandered in, he would die.

All right. Now what?

In the opposite wall was another bare window. Maka crawled to it and looked outside. The backyard was a field of overgrown, lofty weeds and beyond it were thick shrubs and trees and what looked like a small river behind the trees. On the other side of the stream rose a forested hill.

If he could make it there, he could vanish. If he crawled

through those weeds the house might cover him partly. But they could still spot him, he thought. And, looking down, tiny white flowers of tall cow parsley enveloped the side of the house and he was afraid to jump. He didn't want to get impaled by any junk or farming implements that might lie there. And think of the noise it would make.

He looked around: nothing one could use as a ladder. And that stairway gave out to the front and that Chetnik.

He wished he had a rope. And what if he had? They could still spot him.

Maka sat down on the mattress. He was out of ideas. This was it. He was done for. That was the net he was so sure he could swim through. It might have worked in the forest. But here, in the open? Impossible.

He sat there, in the emptiness of his hideout, trying to accept it. The refuge was a coffin. The temperature kept creeping up. He was already feeling giddy. He could not live on water alone. Besides, that and the honey would last him another day in this heat. Then what, young man? he asked himself. At some point, one of those Chetniks would take it into his head to search the house. That was how this would end. He rested his head on his folded arms and knees, his mind vague and empty.

It was early afternoon. New sounds broke his stupor. There was shouting going on outside, but it was playful and cheery.

Maka crawled to his spyhole: two elderly men were trudging up the road. One transported a thermal food container on his back. The other towed a large white sack over his shoulder. They went from soldier to soldier, dishing out ladlefuls of soup and chunks of bread. The Chetniks slung their rifles onto their backs. They dipped the bread in the soup in their canteen cups, eating and bantering with the caterers.

Potatoes and meat soup? Maka tried to fill his lungs with the scent.

Hey, neighbours, did you forget somebody? Give me some, too!

This is absurd, he thought. He couldn't even go out and beg. They'd shoot him like a rabid dog. But now, looking at the enemy, it came to him that they would probably guard the road only during daylight. It would make no sense to stand there in the dark.

Yes, he thought. He wasn't finished. He'd get out of here in the night.

Feeling an urge to urinate, Maka sneaked to the adjacent room. In a corner he found a crack in the concrete floor. At least my kidneys are working, he thought as he voided his bladder, careful to make it as quiet as he could. His head was almost touching the rafters. He felt the heat from the roof tiles.

Maka sat on the mattress. He put on his boots. They were damp, but the socks had dried out and his feet felt comfortable. He held the rifle on his lap, facing the staircase. He listened to the sounds from outside. The debris on the first floor would alert him to any intruder.

After sitting many hours in the same position, he felt hot and achy and he decided to take a nap. First, he was afraid he would snore. Finally he turned on his side and his tiredness took over, and he was asleep.

He dreamed of snow and his house. There were people in the house and Amelia was there, and all of a sudden the house was strange and the snow covered vast fields Maka had never seen before. There was something frightening in that cold, flat landscape. Yet, he felt happy.

When he awoke, it was morning and the Chetniks were back on the road.

Goddam fool, he chided himself. He was so tired he'd slept through the whole evening and night. But he should've known it. What an idiot!

Despite the sleep, Maka felt sapped. Where was he anyway? It was difficult to think. He took a sip of water. A mouthful of honey. A dash remained of both. His fingers were so weak he had trouble twisting open the caps. *Now, now…yes. What now?* Through the hole in the wall, he could see the road and the Chetniks.

It was too much. He was exhausted. The pain of the past years was stacked on his chest like stones, crushing his will. With this hunger and the thirst and the crawling like an animal and those cursed Chetniks, it all caved in.

This is it.

He would shoot some of them, then kill himself with the last one.

Maka counted his rounds. One in the chamber, four in the magazine. That was enough. And he had the grenade. He clipped off a cartridge and put it in his pocket. How many could he get? One? Two? More? He decided on three. A good number. He'd kill two on the road, then at least one more with the grenade when they stormed the house.

Three lives for his. It sounded like some sort of a deal.

He placed the muzzle of the automatic rifle into the rugged hole and took aim at the nearest soldier. He was about thirty metres away. Maka would drop him with a single slug. But when he looked at the man through the sights, over the blued metal of the gun, he felt bitter about dying this way. He knew the man outside was there to kill him and his kin, but what if he, too, was somebody's father? He was probably in his forties and distantly resembled a clerk who had worked in the post office in Srebrenica. This Chetnik also wore a šajkača, with its V-shaped top making his head look like a pig's hoof. He had a messy stubble and a moustache that seemed to hang from his long, thin nose, as he stood under the sun with weary eyes.

So, you're here to kill me?

It's you who's going to die now. But I don't do this because I like it.

If there were a way to leave this situation without killing anybody, let alone himself, Maka would do so. Just it was too late. It was far too much, and nothing could get it undone. He positioned the sights in the middle of the man's chest and calmed his breathing down. He took the slack out of the trigger, until he felt the tiny resistance of the firing mechanism in his fingertip.

So this was it? The last moment of his life, and that other man's life, and everything they'd ever known, one millimetre away? He tried to accept it. There was no anger or hatred. He was too drained for that. But it didn't feel right.

What was it Nermin said?

He remembered his brother now. That was a long time ago, before he went missing for good. There was that first time when he emerged from the no-man's-land near Bratunac, four days after a battle, when everybody was sure he'd been killed or captured. What was it he said, about killing himself?

They had gathered around him in a dugout, astounded and listening to his story. Nermin on the ground, drinking from the canteen Maka had handed him, dirty and tired but grinning, the medic examining the wounds of his hand. He was still carrying his rifle, even though two of his fingers were gone and he had spent all of his ammunition.

"I would've saved one for myself," an older fighter lectured him. "What would you have done if they'd caught you? Better take your own life than get tortured and executed!"

Maka remembered it now. Nermin had shut the man up. Something about hope and pain. That as long as you were alive there was hope. A lot of pain and agony. Then again, hope.

Maka lowered his weapon. It was true, he was tired and weak. But it was not too much. It was painful to wait, but he could take more pain. Another night would come. If the Chetniks searched the house, he would die fighting. But another night would come, and until then he'd try to keep his head clear and wait.

He dug the cartridge from his pocket. He pushed it back into the magazine. Maka reattached the clip, snapped the gun's safety back on, and rested the rifle against the wall. Then he sat there, trying to clear his head of all images and thoughts. After a while he could feel only his breathing, and leaning the back of his head against the wall he watched the white clouds move across the sky in an opening in the roof.

By late afternoon, something had changed. The wind was in the north, but it no longer carried the occasional shouts and laughter. Maka peered out and saw that the enemy was gone. The road was empty, with only shadows of clouds gliding over the fields.

They took shelter from the sun? But he couldn't see anything at the skirts of the forest, either. For whatever reason, that unit had been pulled.

All right, he thought. This was the chance. He put on his backpack and hung the rifle on his chest. Still afraid to take the stairs, he climbed out through the back window. Hanging onto the sill, he looked down. A damn long way. Only one way to find out.

He let go and fell, crashed through the cow parsley and hit the ground, tumbling into the weeds, his rifle spearing barrel-first into the field.

Maka got up, on his knee. He looked over the weeds, past the corners of the house. Not a soul. There was the destroyed mosque with its reclining minaret against the house. The stream was a distance behind him, he could hear it.

Maka picked a plug of clay and weeds out of the rifle's muzzle, started crawling and got to the stream. There were trees on both sides, like an alley through which the little river flowed. He stepped into the cold, knee-deep water.

Behind the trees were the hills. But now, seeing their dark outline through the foliage, Maka felt it would be a mistake to fall back. That was where he came from. This stream, though, was nicely screened by the bushes. And now he understood, the road he had taken wasn't the Vlasenica highway. That was probably still a distance ahead. Then the Jadar. Maybe this one ran into it.

The Jadar, he knew, was deep and rapid, even in the summer. It would be difficult to cross it carrying a gun. But he'd have to, eventually.

"Because you have to, it's nothing," he said aloud. He started wading downstream.

The water was achingly cold on his legs now. The stream bed was covered with stones in bright green, slippery river weed. Sunlight fell through the tree canopy and the clear, glittering water reflected it back into the undersides of the leaves. It was like a cool tunnel in the summer heat.

Maybe there's trout. It'd make a hell of a place for fishing. In his mind, Maka saw friends gathered at the grassy riverbank, having beers that had been chilled in the stream pools while roasting the catch on a campfire. He had not eaten for five days and he dreamed of the fish and how their flesh turned white over the embers. He imagined *Sarajevsko pivo*, and the dark, rich, cold Dalmatian wine.

Just then, Maka spotted the shadow of a bridge ahead. He stopped and listened. Through the sound of the river, he could hear somebody talking.

To hell with fishing, he scolded himself. He'd nearly walked straight into them.

Here the stream ran in a dell and was wider, with the banks two metres high and the view obscured by the trees. Maka got out of the water and climbed the left bank to observe the bridge. The approach came into view. It was a steel bridge and there were three soldiers standing by the rail. Maka and the Chetniks noticed each other at that same instant.

Scrambling back to the water, Maka could hear the men yell at him. He heard rifles being cocked and then shots were fired through the canopy. The slugs went into the riverbank to his left. Through his panic Maka knew he recognised that bridge. He had often taken it on his way to the construction sites in Zvornik. He ran back against the flow of the stream as fast as he could, splashing through the water. Orders were being yelled behind him. More random shots came through the foliage.

There was something in the riverbank. Something circular. The mouth of a culvert. Maka stopped and looked at it. He breathed like a steam engine and his legs trembled. It was a metre wide, covered in vegetation.

This was his best chance. Probably his *only* chance. He felt as if he were about to faint. He knew he was too weak to outrun them now.

The concrete duct was half-filled with clay and trash, a perfect lair for spiders and centipedes, but the fear of death made Maka crawl into it as if it were his home. Boots kicking, he cleared the way as he burrowed, feet first, deeper into the dark tunnel.

Then there was nothing left but to wait. He could feel his heart beat against the wet clay. Two metres ahead, behind the foliage that covered the entrance, was the semilunar brightness of daylight.

Maka waited. There came the sound of a truck's engine, a tailboard slamming, soldiers disembarking. He could hear them start to search for him.

By the sound of it, they combed the terrain in line. Every few minutes, someone would yell and try to trick him out of his lair: "We can see you! C'mon out!" Their bluff was bolstered by rifle shots. But the sounds went past him, then receded, and in a while Maka knew they had gone too far.

"He can't have gotten away," he heard someone instruct. "Look everywhere." The man spoke a Belgrade dialect. The voice was almost out of earshot.

More minutes passed.

"This is stupid. He's not here anymore," someone said barely audibly.

Excellent – let them believe I'm some commando, Maka thought. That he'd already bugged out, with the skills of an elite soldier. He knew he was just an ordinary townsman, but he thought, Let them think I'm more than I am.

The truck returned. Maka guessed it was collecting the search party. The engine noise mixed with jubilant singing: "We killed all the *Balija*, now we're heading home!"

Maka waited in the darkness, watching the luminous crescent at the culvert's mouth turn paler, then finally disappear. When he crept out, in the dark of the night and under a partially clouded moon, for a moment he felt like a moth emerging from its cocoon. His body was stiff and he stretched his arms like wings.

He stood in the quietly flowing water. He was alive. But he had made stupid mistakes. If it had not been for pure luck, he would have been murdered already. Now, he had to think. He knew where he was now. He knew which direction he needed to go. The Jadar wasn't far from here. From that bridge, it couldn't be more than two kilometres.

Maka ascended the bank and cut into the forest to the west of the stream. Looking back through the trees, he could see the road and the solitary houses on the other side. Their destroyed roofs seemed like gaping wounds in the moonlight. He was again surrounded by the blackness of the trees. He knew he had made a mistake wandering out of the woods. He might be just an ordinary townsman, but he'd grown up surrounded by the hills. He understood them intuitively. These Chetniks, they weren't the local Serbs. These were volunteer nationalists from Serbia. Maka had heard them talk in their city dialect. Thugs and weekend murderers.

Oh yes, he thought, they'd shoot him like a dog. Only they'd have to catch him first.

EIGHT

As HE STOOD still, listening to the darkness, there was a loud crack as if someone stepped on a branch. A whispering voice berated: "Shh… be quiet!"

Maka went on his knee and gripped the rifle. Now, all was silent but he knew he was not alone. Had they set a trap for him? He thought about it. It felt unlikely. These Chetniks would not prowl the woods after dark. They set up their lines in daylight, and they probably assumed he had cleared out of the area anyway. Then he remembered what he had thought about rabbits and the night. Who else would be scared of the dark, if not his fellow Bosniaks?

"Hey… hey, you," he whispered. "It's Maka Delić here…"

A silence enveloped the forest. It felt waiting, like a bodily, living being and made Maka hold his breath. He pressed the rifle's stock against his flank so that it would not jump if he fired. He aimed the muzzle into the darkness which now was one with the silence. It was too late to back off.

"Hey… can you hear me? I'm a Bosniak."

There was again only the silence. Then he thought he could

hear someone whispering. They were probably discussing their options now.

A man's voice said:

"It's Hamid and Salko here. Have you got a gun?"

"Yes. I'm a *borac* from the Second Brigade."

"We're Bosniaks, too."

"Good," Maka said. They said all this in whispers. He felt stupid talking this way, but he had no way of knowing who he was dealing with.

"We'll come over," the man said. "Be careful with that gun."

There was a rustling of leaves and two shadows emerged from the darkness.

"Are you alone? Where's your unit?" The man was short and thickset and carried a bolt-action hunting rifle. He must have been in his early fifties. Maka could not see his face well in the dark. Trailing him was a lean youngster. They both wore civilian clothes. Their T-shirts and trousers were so grimed they looked camouflaged in the night.

"Yes. I don't know," said Maka. "They're probably killed."

"We're from Zvornik," the man said, proudly. Maka knew he meant they had been refugees in Srebrenica, and now they were on the run again. He had short hair and wore a dark moustache and he looked very serious. His younger companion was in the shadows.

"Have you water?"

"Yes." Maka started taking the rucksack off his back. He had filled both bottles in the stream.

"No, we're good. We have it, too. I was offering."

"Thanks. How did you get here?"

"Through the hills. It was screwed up, I tell you."

"I'm sorry I don't have anything for you."

"It's okay. We've been chewing leaves. And the rain was good for mushrooms. Have you not eaten anything? We still have some."

61

He had a backpack, and digging into it he gave Maka a handful of mushrooms. They looked flattened and pale. Maka thought they were chanterelles.

"You know these are edible?"

"Yes. We've eaten them since yesterday, and we're not sick. It's not mushroom that's going to kill you here. I wish we had cigarettes, too."

"I'm a teacher by profession," the man went on, "elementary school, very good with children. My name is Hamid, but my nickname is Professor. You can call me Professor. I was the principal in Zvornik," he said, again as a matter of pride, as he talked of his hometown. "But I was a weekend hunter, too, so I know the forests around here, and I know what's comestible and what's not."

"This is mine." He tapped the rifle butt. "I used to hunt wild boar. Sold the meat, often gave some to my Serb neighbours. Now I would eat some, too, if only I'd come across any. The war has scared them from this area. Now the only swine in these woods are the Chetniks, and that would be worse than eating pork," he joked. He was chatty and Maka felt he was trying to keep spirits up because of his companion. The three of them sat on the ground. They were still talking in whispers. The young man, maybe in his late teens, had not spoken a word.

Maybe he was his son? Maka could not see either of them well. The moon was out but the trees were very dense. He put a mushroom in his mouth, chewing it. It tasted peppery and woody, like the forest. It was great to chew on something. His only sustenance had been the honey and that morsel of bread he'd shared with his brother and nephew. Was that four days ago? Or had a week passed already? So many sickening, unreal things had happened it was difficult to remember.

"It was pretty screwed up there," the Professor said. "We were in this large group, just off Koprivno. There was a lot of shooting during the night and we scattered like sparrows. Then us, and some other men, got near the Derventa road and there were Chetniks with Dutch armoured cars. Down there on the road. Goddam sons of whores. Blue helmets and all. They'd brought in some educated type, and that son of a bitch was summoning us in English. I said right away those are Chetniks. I said look at them, for God's sake! But none of the guys we were with listened to me. They'd swallowed all that 'protection force' garbage. Me and Salko here hid in the bush. Up in the hillside. But the guys bought it and that was that. We could see them start killing them. In the ditch by the roadside, just like that. That's when we beat it. What a fine business, I tell you. What a business this war is. Can you even call it a war? Here, have some more. Let's finish these."

The youngster had uttered nothing. Now, looking at Maka, he said, "We wanna go to Tuzla."

"I hope to get to there, too. Seems the Chetniks hold all the roads and hamlets in this valley. Won't be easy even to cross the Jadar. You know that the Jadar is right up ahead?"

"Yes," said the Professor. "It's about one and a half kilometres from here. And I know the country beyond the Jadar, too. We may be on the lam like scoundrels, but these lands are my home, and I have hunted these valleys. After the Jadar, the hamlets are all Serb. I assume they're all still inhabited. From here on, the only way to continue is to go over Udrič."

Maka was not sure about the terrain beyond the Jadar. He'd never had any business in that backcountry. But Udrič was the tallest hill of this region, its peak at a thousand metres. That was some climbing. He knew he was weak enough. He'd never climbed mountains. Maybe you couldn't call it a mountain. A kilometre of altitude, all the same. He wasn't sure what it meant when your body was sapped like this. The slope would be more, of course, two or three kilometres.

He thought about it.

"If you say it's the only way, then we should do it. But we need to cross the Jadar. The Chetniks have the bridges."

"I know a section not far from here where the water runs shallow."

"And there's no bridge?"

"No bridge. It's behind the highway, just farming lands. That's where we've been aiming for. It is three days since the rains. We should be able to ford."

It was getting cold, now that they had sat still. Maka's trousers and feet were wet from the river and he wanted to move on. Glancing at the sky through the branches he could not see the moon.

"Let's go, then," he said. "Looks like we've got clouds tonight."

"I hope it will rain again. Not before we cross. But it was good for the mushroom."

"Yes. Thank you."

"Oh, nothing. I just wish we had cigarettes. And I always told the kids how smoking's going to kill you. That's got to be the stupidest thing I ever said."

They got up and started into the forest. The Professor went first, Maka and the young man following him warily, feeling the ground and placing their feet carefully at each step to avoid snapping branches in the dark. It took them a good hour to close the fifteen hundred metres.

When the trees ended, Maka saw a paved road and, by the road, wrecked houses abutted by orchards. The moon was out now. After the darkness of the forest, the burned shells of the houses stood out harshly. The road looked open and disquieting. This was the Vlasenica–Zvornik highway, which the head of the main column had crossed five nights ago.

They waited under the trees for the clouds to come over the moon. Then, dashing across the road, they entered a stretch of fields behind the houses.

The field was fallow. There was a drainage ditch going into it. There was not much water in the dike and the weeds had not been cut for three summers. A sweet smell of flowering yarrow was in the air. They went into the ditch and crawled along it, pausing twice when the moon came out. The water in the channel was stagnant and gave a foul smell when Maka kneaded his hands and knees into the mud at the bottom.

The field ended in the Jadar. The Professor was right. The river was smooth and black and the other bank was covered in tall vegetation. Here, the stream ran about twenty metres wide and Maka saw boulders in the riverbed and the current rushing and swelling against the rocks; still, it looked shallow enough for fording.

Maka got into the water. It was cold and fast and waist-high. Underfoot it was gravel and it was not difficult to find footing. He waded on. The current tried to sweep him off his feet. He made it to the first rock and rested against it, the pressure of the water pushing against his hips. Ahead of him, the two others forded from boulder to boulder. Maka adjusted the rifle on his back, grasping the sling with one hand, and went after them.

The bank was slippery and muddy and covered in flattened grass, and they helped each other climb it.

The forest started right behind the river. Looking back, Maka saw the low field from where they had come: it loomed sinister across the river, with the smashed houses in the distance and the far-off, dark, undulating mass of the hills.

The Professor sat on the grassy bank, pouring water from his shoes. Salko squatted next to him and held the rifle. All this time, the youngster had not said anything except that he wanted to go to Tuzla.

"This continues all the way to Udrič," the teacher whispered, nodding towards the trees. "The forest here is dense and there are no trails. It'll take hours just to get to the foot of the mountain. *Inshallah*, we won't run into Chetniks tonight."

"*Pa jebo te Bog*," quipped the young man. Screw God. "Since when did you become such a good Muslim?"

"Since they told me I was one, and killed your mother," his father said, putting his shoes back on. Salko said nothing.

65

"Such foul language is like calling on bad luck." The Professor spoke to Maka, tying the shoelaces. "He wants to join the army in Tuzla. I try to tell they'll get him anyway. What's the age for conscription? Twenty? He's seventeen. You tell him what it's like. In three years the war might be over, but he wants to get killed on the front."

"I know what it's like," the boy said.

"You've no idea," his father rebutted.

"And do you? With your bad back?"

"Listen to him! Would rather see his dad killed. But kids went to school during the siege, too."

"If you have canteens, better fill them," Maka said.

With that, the two seemed to forget their quarrel. They got up and the Professor took back his rifle. Holding his son's hand, he helped the youngster to reach down to the water to fill a glass wine bottle he carried in the backpack. Salko screwed its aluminium cap on and put the bottle back into his father's rucksack.

"Gentlemen, ready for the hike?" the teacher said.

The bush of the riverbank was dense and they penetrated it in a file. The vegetation rustled as they vanished into it; the moon was high in the sky, and under its pale light the river moved smooth and silent as if the three had never disturbed its flow.

NINE

THEY STARTED ASCENDING the mountain in the early morning. It was still dark and the slope was steep and the jungle-like forest inhospitable and rotten. Maka held on to the vines and pulled himself up step by step. He had trekked the whole night. Thorns had scraped the backs of his hands and forehead, and sweat stung his skin.

The father and son worked the slope above him. He heard their heavy breathing and the hollow sound of rocks moving underfoot.

What if, he thought, this is another mistake? He'd made it through here on his own. Now he was again part of a group. It felt good to have company, though. But did this Professor know what he was doing? What would he have done differently, anyway? Not tramped up a damn mountain, for sure. He pressed on, working with legs that now were trembling. He was burning energy.

At dawn, when they were nearing the peak, Maka saw the sun rise from the eastern landmass of Serbia. He could see the meandering, imposing body of the Drina, still dark as ink in the shadows of the river canyons. Down south, on the Bosnian side of the river, the rolling green blanket of the hills that he had spent five days traversing was misty in the morning light.

One day he'd be back.

He knew it wasn't good to think of that now. Still, he could not help knowing that his father and brothers, and thousands of others, had been killed because of the land. He did not think of revenge. It wasn't bitterness, either. How could you even begin to feel bitter? he thought. There simply wasn't enough acrimony in a man for something of this scale. All he knew was the senselessness of it all as he struggled up the mountainside, with a scent of fir trees now on the morning wind. There would be a time when he wanted to start everything over. He wasn't sure if it would ever be possible. And what was the point of hating them? It wouldn't help him a bit. If he was going to hate them, he should hate them later. He'd made it this far. He should just keep going.

He knew, though, without food he'd soon collapse. The Professor and his son could not carry him. Just like he'd left everyone behind, they'd have to abandon him. That's how you became part of this land.

Bones in rotten clothes. In the end, that's all it made of you.

When they reached the crest the sun was already getting into the forest. Udrič's top was a large plateau, a kilometre across and covered in fir trees. There were men huddled under the trees, and for a moment Maka felt a panic thinking the Chetniks had made it there before them. Then he saw they looked just as bedraggled as he and his companions were. Many did not have uniforms, either. The trees were not very tall, still the forest was dense and it was hard to tell just how big the group was. At least two dozen, he reckoned.

A cluster of four sat in the shadows nearby. Maka started for them, but tripped on a root and fell. Trying to get up, he understood just how little strength he had left. His arms trembled as he propped himself up on an elbow, sweat burning his eyes and blurring his vision. He gave up and lay there, the rifle under his side, on a bed of moss scattered with brown fir needles.

The Professor and another man rushed over.

"No, let me stay," said Maka. "Can you get this off me?"

Someone grabbed the rucksack. Maka struggled to pull his arm free of the shoulder strap. He rubbed his eyes with the back of his hand. A tear ran down his cheek. He could not see well, but the man helping him was skinny and dark. He wore black jeans and a camouflage jacket and had a musette on his back. The coat looked baggy on his gaunt figure. Like the Professor, he held a bolt-action rifle across his shoulder. His weapon had a scope on it. Maka thought he'd seen him before.

He wiped his eyes again and recognised him.

"Zlatar? What do you do here?"

The man was searching through Maka's rucksack and found the water.

"Here, drink up," he said. "You look like a wreck."

"How did you make it here?"

"How did *you* make it? Thought you were dead. God's grace, I was wrong."

Maka lay on his side. It felt good just to lie there. He held his head up and drank, before handing the bottle back to the man who was a soldier from his platoon.

"The others?"

"Almost all dead in that ambush. May I?" The man took a long drink from the bottle. It was Zlatar, all right.

They had been together throughout the war. His real name was Šehić, but he had run the town's sole jewellery store and everyone had always simply called him the "goldsmith". He was a wiry young man with black, straight hair and eyes that were assertive and always seemed to move a little, as if scanning the world for small details. The last Maka had seen of him was on that trail, near Milačevići where they were hit. Zlatar had lost so

69

much weight Maka didn't recognise him at first. How was it even possible to slim down like that in a week?

"They fired from both flanks," Maka said. "They had that whole damn ravine covered. Adnan and I worked up the slope in the crossfire. He got shot in the head. But I suppose I got some of them, too."

"So Adnan's dead."

"Yes."

"God have mercy. Was no soldier like him. How did you make a way out?"

"Just scrambling. Firing at muzzle flashes. Burned all of my bullets. I swear, my barrel glowed red in the dark, that's all I could see. It was just too dark. Then I ran along that ridge in the forest, thinking the others had gone the same way."

"You fought like a *borac*. But, I don't know. We need a miracle to get to Tuzla."

"Any other *Petričani* here?" Maka was referring to their platoon, with its moniker. Many of the men had come from the same street in Srebrenica.

"Ten of us got away." Zlatar handed the bottle back to Maka. He sat down. His face was tired and he had dirt on the stubble of his cheeks.

"Three were civilians. The morning, we were near Derventa, and a shell slammed into this shepherd's hut we were sheltering in. Five killed, instantly. Two of those civilians. The others so badly hit none could walk. Couldn't carry any of them. It was like a death sentence. I'd gone down to fetch water when it happened." He paused, looking into the distance.

The Professor, who had been squatting next to them with his son, said he was very sorry for those comrades. "But we need to push on. Tuzla is that way about forty kilometres. We could make it in two days."

"Not possible," said Zlatar, shaking his head. "You haven't seen how it is. They're all over. You get down from this hill, you get killed." He nodded towards the others. "I met and joined these. Was a big group. We made it across the highway and Jadar. That's all the luck we had. Tried another crossing, almost thirty got gunned down. Had to fall back. By then those bastards were bloody everywhere. We've been looking for a passage. But they keep bushwhacking us, and now we're down to this handful. Got little water, no food. Almost no ammo."

He rubbed his head, brushing his hair.

"We thought we could hold it out here, in the high ground. Got here yesterday, saw there'd been a crowd here. There's a latrine area near the brow. Used bandages here and there, the shrubs all trampled. Must've been more than a thousand."

"That's got to be the head of the column," Maka said.

"Yeah, maybe. But the point is, they've headed north. The Chetniks have certainly noticed. That corridor is blocked off now."

Salko, the Professor's son, stood up. He looked at Zlatar fiercely.

"What are you saying? We can't stay here."

A man in army fatigues, sitting on a boulder behind them, gave a bitter laugh. He had a full beard and an old war wound diagonally across his forehead; it cut into a disfigured temple where the eye was missing. Maka saw him now. He was a soldier from another company. He'd lost that eye on the day when Big Huse died.

"Want to take chances with them?" The one-eyed fighter patted the worn-out double-barrel shotgun that rested on his lap. "With great weapons like this? They're all over the place. All over, *zcjebano!*"

Maka pulled the rifle's sling over his head. Sitting up, he looked at the men around him. Not much of a fighting unit, that was for sure. The drink had made him feel better, though. He had stopped sweating and his hands were calm. The sun had climbed higher and there was a little breeze swaying the crowns of the fir trees. The teacher's son was right. They couldn't stay here. They could maybe defend one slope for a time. Still, the plateau was too large and they only had a handful of men. They couldn't hold every side of it.

"Makes no difference if we were better armed," Maka said. "Staying here, the Chetniks can just bomb us to bits. They can't fly their planes. The Americans make sure of that. But they can bring in three-inch mountain guns, or heavy mortars, and blast us to hell." He looked at the others. "How high are we, eight hundred metres? They can reach us with mountain guns. Or they'll just wait us out. Maybe they haven't found us, but they'll figure it out. We need to clear out before they have us surrounded. So, what are you planning to do?"

As soon as he said it, he felt a fool. It was obvious no one had a plan. They were all too weak and tired of death that they hadn't been able to think of it. But there had to be a plan. Any plan was better than no plan. As long as they were alive, they should take the pain of their hunger and make a plan.

More men had gathered around. "It's forty kilometres to Tuzla," one said. "With the terrain, make it fifty. A lot of it is open ground. Farmlands and villages. It's all Serb territory. And, like your friend said, the enemy must have cut it off."

"No, the line is near Kalesija," said another, "about twenty kilometres from here. That's where those big guns fired three days ago. Wasn't that some sweet music?"

Maka remembered it. True, it must have been Bosnian artillery. The enemy wouldn't attack on the Tuzla front now. The column probably had made it there and tried to breach the lines, and the Second Corps must have fired their guns in support.

"It's still way the hell back," the one man insisted. "And it's all open land."

"We could veer towards Zukići. More woods that way," said the Professor.

Another proposed they all turn south towards Žepa. But

72

Žepa was another enclave, surrounded by the enemy and way back south, even past Srebrenica. Besides, they had no way of knowing if the town was still standing. Someone suggested they should wait here instead.

"Wait for what?" the Professor's son asked.

No one said a thing.

"And if," suggested the Professor, "we descend the north-west face? There's a river in a forest down in the valley. It's like where we came from. You saw there were no Chetniks," he said, speaking to Maka now. "I guess they stick to holding the roads and bridges only."

"Guess?" said Zlatar. "Wish, you mean? If it was that easy."

"Except that I know that forest. We could continue northward. We just head towards Zukići."

"I don't know."

"At least we have water if we go for the river," Maka said, holding the bottle. He had passed it around and it was empty. The morning was getting hot and the sky was high and clear. He knew he'd have to go down to that valley. There was something else about a river he wanted to think of, but he couldn't recall it now. At any rate he'd rather die by a river than up here. *In* the river, maybe, and let it carry him if nobody else could. He'd seen too many men die in the hills. It always looked vile how their bodies were dragged down.

Well, he was tired now. It was that what made imagining dying so frighteningly easy. He'd better think of water, or Amelia. Anything graceful.

"You do what you want, but choose well," he told the others. "I'm going down."

TEN

THE TREK WAS a mere two kilometres, but rough. The ground was soft and there were many unstable rocks. They had to hold on to the vegetation to keep from slipping and falling. The Professor went first, together with an old soldier who had a full magazine in his rifle and who looked very scared. Maka watched them descend. Above him, the Professor's son, Zlatar and a handful of men were coming down the mountain. Only the eleven of them had chosen to continue.

On ahead in the distance was the billowing mass of land that was now clear in the morning sun. It was all enemy territory they were heading to, and Maka could not see anything that looked like Tuzla. The city was too far to be observed. On the horizon stretched a faint pale line that was the Majevica mountain range. That was beyond Tuzla. He knew there had been heavy fighting there since the snow had melted, and that the Second and Third Armies had seen some successes. There had been fighting in the central region, too, and the Vlašić Mountain had been nicely captured from the Chetniks. That was as much as they'd heard from the command. In Sarajevo there had been a large offensive, but it was not successful and a lot of troops had been lost.

This is my fight, he thought, as he climbed down the forest. It was a fight he hadn't asked for and had nothing to do with. But now it was his fight all right, and it wasn't helpful to think of culpabilities. He was sweating more than he should and he knew it was because of his fatigue. He had still had episodes of diarrhoea. The clothes were sandpaper on his skin. The weight of the assault rifle had increased ominously.

Maybe I should ditch it, he thought. What was he carrying it for, the five rounds that he had?

Maybe he'd come across a deer. Or a hare. Or a Chetnik.

"So, do your best," he spoke aloud.

The Professor, also drenched in sweat, stopped and looked back at him.

"What is it?"

"Nothing. Nothing at all, this hillock."

It's nothing at all. So do your best.

And with what, may I ask? What do you have, other than your five bullets?

Legs, he thought. He had two legs and every step brought him closer to his family. Or perhaps closer to his grave. It wasn't up to him to decide. He had two legs, shaky but working, and that was all he'd got. All he could do was to keep moving, and fate would take care of the rest.

Then he felt angry at himself for thinking about fate. What if it didn't give a damn about you? He'd need to think for himself. What else did he have, other than his feet and his rifle?

A hand grenade? You couldn't eat that, either.

The metal cylinder hung from the strap of his backpack. A hideous contraption, like all the tools of war. But they would come down to another river. Maka remembered his idea now. By the looks of it, the valley was shrouded in woods. If there was no enemy down there, he could use the grenade. The only decent thing they were good for was blast fishing. He had enough men to stand downstream. If there were any fish in that river, he'd get some.

When they reached the floor of the valley Maka could see the river through the forest. It was narrow and beckoning in the sunlight. They approached it, cautious and slow, sending the men with assault rifles first. When Maka got closer, he saw trees bent over the stream and the water looked clear and there were deep, dark pools under the trees, and in the middle of the river was a shoal where the stream ran between rocks and dry, white gravel bars. It looked like a good river. Zlatar sent two pairs of scouts out along the stream. The others sat down under the trees and waited.

"Let's fill the canteens," Maka said. "Take a short rest."

"We should bathe, too," said Zlatar. "The way we stink the Chetniks can smell us from Banja Luka."

The Professor laughed. "What a great campsite. Anyone have a guitar?"

"No, you're right, it's a great river." Maka weighed the grenade in his hand. "Let's lob this into it."

"They could hear it," said the old soldier with the full magazine.

"Well, let's wait what the scouts say. We need to eat something. Got a lighter?"

"I've a flint," Zlatar offered.

"The smoke will give us away. You'll get us all killed!"

Maka looked up at the treetops. "With this wind, it'll clear. And we can eat them raw if it's bad."

The downriver scouts returned. It was all good. Lots of traces of people – probably the same group that had been up on Udrič. Nothing to suggest enemy presence. The couple gone upstream came back with similar news. One had taken off his shirt and was carrying something in it.

"Look at these beauties." He displayed a pile of bolete mushrooms.

"*Mashallah*, these are great," said the Professor. "It's best to roast them. Do you think you can find more?"

"We'll go and look."

The Professor and his son went off with the two men. Zlatar got the firestone out of his musette bag. He plucked dry grass and made a heap of it between the roots of a tall tree, then placed small twigs on top and started striking the flint with the back of a combat knife, kneeling and occasionally blowing into the grass. Watching him work, Maka knew they'd have a fire. This was the Zlatar he knew: quick-witted and resourceful, no matter how bad things got.

"You don't happen to carry any medicine?" he asked.

Zlatar looked at him. "No. What's wrong?"

"My bowel. It's strange. I haven't eaten anything for days. Maybe it's because of that."

"Then why don't you go blasting? I'll see if I can pick some herbs. Let's make tea. God willing, have fish, too."

Maka looked into the water, careful not to let his shadow fall on it. He had walked along the bank and observed the stream pools, but could not see any fish in them, probably because of their depth. He had selected what he believed was a good one, with the stream falling from behind large rocks on the other side and dark water going through it in a rapid, steady flow. Once he had made his choice, he asked the five others to go twenty metres downstream, where the river was shallow, to position themselves between the gravel bars along the width of the river.

They stood there in two lines now. Maka did not want them too far, otherwise they would miss the fish or the stunned ones might recover. It wasn't good to be too close, either. The grenade was a powerful fragmentation one. There was always the risk that it would land in shallow water. The pool he'd chosen looked probably a fathom deep, though.

"All right. Crouch down," he called out.

Twisting the pin off the grenade, Maka looked one more time

into the clear brown, rushing water. He lobbed the grenade in and quickly stepped back and lay on the ground behind the edge of the bank. Holy Peter and your nets, he thought. Give me a good one. He only had this one chance.

A shock wave went through the water. Maka could feel the thud in his chest, and a muffled blast lifted the surface of the river, spouting a white jet metres into the air. A fine glittering spray rained down on him. For a brief moment, a rainbow appeared over the river.

When the water settled back to its smooth flow, the fish started to surface. They were small and they floated down the stream like fallen leaves. His team, waist-deep in the river, was catching them wildly with T-shirts held as makeshift landing nets. Seeing the men, their bare torsos glistening wet and some cursing in good spirits as they missed a fish or two, Maka knew he had done well. They had something now. A few small fish, but he knew he'd made a good decision.

Back in the forest, they found Zlatar by a small campfire. Thin smoke rose into the trees. The goldsmith had used dry wood and it did not look so bad. There was a canteen cup in the flames, soot-blackened and boiling with a mixture of leaves. Zlatar was kneeling beside the fire, packing his musette. In his faded black T-shirt and black jeans Maka might have taken him for someone gone camping. He had hung his jacket up and his rifle, an old Mauser with a worn-out chestnut stock, leaned against the tree. The edges of the telescopic sight showed aluminium where the black coating had chipped away. Tucked under Zlatar's belt was an automatic pistol. He had a blue plastic bag with something bulky inside, and as he saw Maka and the men coming he quickly wrapped whatever was in it tighter and placed it back into the musette.

"See what your friend got," a man carrying the catch said. "I've thrown more bombs into the rivers than there ever was fish in them. Then he nails this. The chap should be promoted to general."

Zlatar stood up. "Delić," he said in a stagy solemn voice, "will you accept that weight on your shoulders? Lead us wisely."

"I'll make you a field marshal for that fire," said Maka.

"I'll give you the crown. Boy, would that make the Chetniks sore? Look, there comes Hamid."

The Professor and his son walked out from behind the trees.

"It was lucky to chance on those ceps," the teacher said. "There must've been plenty. The group before us picked them all. Well, we found something better. Lots of these by the river." He had several snails in his cupped hands, all withdrawn inside their round shells. "These are as good as meat. Need to boil them first, though."

"What a French table now," said Zlatar. "Let's cook them all. How do we do with the mushrooms?"

"Like the fish. Put them on sticks."

They gutted the fish and roasted them crispy over the flames on springy willow twigs. They had fifteen minnows and two small river trout. They ate them whole, heads and all, slowly, sitting around the fire. They cooked the snails and the ceps. One of the men had salt in a 20 mm shell casing that he had capped with a wine cork.

"That's pretty clever," said the Professor. "If everyone fought with cork bullets like that, nobody would be in this mess right now." His son sat beside the fire, staring at it.

It was Maka's first real food in over a week. It felt like a meal. He had drunk Zlatar's herbal concoction. Wild sage and birch leaves, apparently. Bitter as hell. But he thought it was making his insides feel calm already. Now this was the Zlatar he knew.

The goldsmith.

Before it all went up in flames, Maka had thought of him as another rich kid. Once he visited the store for the wedding ring. There, surrounded by expensive watches and necklaces and the ticking of clocks and the smell of old wood, he wanted to get twenty-four carats with some genuine stone, then settled for plain eighteen. That shop wasn't the kind of place a man like Maka would frequent, though Zlatar was the same age as him. He came from Zvornik. To Maka, that was a city, not a small town like Srebrenica. His family had run a jewellery store there. Zlatar had moved to Srebrenica to open a branch. He had a car, summer cabin, money. His world had seemed cold and walled off, and Zlatar himself distant and snooty. The next time that Maka had spoken to him it had been a year later, in the trenches in Bratunac.

If ever there's a force that unmasks you, it's war, Maka thought. He had seen his misconception. Zlatar was an unpretentious man. Quiet, with an air of sagacity. Slightly religious, too. Saying things like "God will help us" when all hell broke loose. Maka thought it was funny. He didn't need any divine assistance. In a way, Zlatar was lucky. He'd lost his fortune. But his wife and young son were safe in Tuzla. The men had stopped talking. That was some meal. Maka could feel it now. He leaned his head against a tree and shut his eyes. He could still perceive the glitter from the river. He heard the sound of the river. It was a great little river.

That poor bastard, Gostović.

He was dead, Maka was sure of it. But the grenade didn't kill him. Nor did it kill that naked old man. Mercy on his soul. Was there any difference? Yes, there was. It wasn't the grenade that killed him. A big difference. It didn't kill any of those Chetniks, either. Or himself, when he was hiding in that bush of ferns, scared and freezing. Yes, a good decision.

Maybe, all along, that weapon was meant to feed him.

Well, he shouldn't slip into the old fatalism, he thought. It was just luck, like when he found the honey. But what about his chances? He supposed he had some. Of course there was no dying by this river. Still, he'd never imagined things would get to this. Who'd be sick enough to picture something like this? He'd been busy trying to shape his future. Like any young man. A modest lot. Maybe with some money and women and success, nevertheless. Why had he envied someone like Zlatar? Had *he* ever thought one day he'd languish in the woods, eating snails and leaves, with someone like Maka? This insanity sucked in everything and everybody…

Maka woke up when somebody touched his shoulder. For a moment he was not sure where he was. Then he saw his friend's face and smiled.

"Need to keep moving," Zlatar said.

Maka saw the others preparing their gear. The fire had been doused. Their clothes were wet and dripping. They'd bathed in the river.

"Where will we head to?" he asked.

"No bloody idea. Hey, you," Zlatar called out to the Professor. "You know the country?"

The teacher looked up, a hint of embarrassment on his face. He had been discussing something in a quiet voice with his son.

"I never said that."

"Why, you told us the woods continue to Zukići."

"I know they do. But now I'm not sure how to get there. This valley looks somehow different from what I remember. I've hunted the forests south from here. That is for sure. But to the north…"

"Well, we don't have a map. Or a compass," Maka said.

"Okay. What the hell now?" Zlatar looked tired. "We don't know the way, but plenty of Chetniks out there to guide us."

"We should head back south!" insisted the one who had suggested Žepa. "At least the country is familiar!"

Maka saw the others were sick of it. Sick of it and silent. From their faces, though, he could tell they were considering.

What the hell?

"Well, that's it for Tuzla, then…" said the Professor.

That seemed to settle it. The men they all got up and started to prepare. Yet Maka wasn't sure. He really wasn't. Perhaps that was the only option. What else was there?

Zlatar pulled him to the side, then spoke to him quietly.

"You know – I can't make it anymore."

"I'm wiped out, too. But what else do we have?"

"I'm sorry. I can't make it to Žepa. Or to Tuzla. I just know I can't."

Maka looked at him. So, now he'd have to leave him behind, too? Okay. And what on earth would he tell his wife? He did not say this.

"Let's go to Serbia," said the goldsmith. He looked serious.

"How do you mean?"

"I mean, let's cross the Drina. There's a narrow section near Zvornik. Two or three kilometres from Vidikovac, that new hotel. Less than ten kilometres from here."

"But what do you mean, go to Serbia? Are you out of your head?"

"No, look, it makes sense. I know someone there. He's a Serb, but I trust him like an old friend."

"And if we're caught? Can this chap stop them from killing us?"

"Maybe he can. Maybe the Serbs in Serbia don't want to kill us."

"What's the difference?"

"You know there's a difference. Here, it's a civil war."

"And the good, decent Serbians just support the Chetniks."

"Some do. But they don't go to war."

"Some of them do, you know that."

"Technically, Serbia is not at war with us," Zlatar insisted. "Not the same. If we make it across, we can pose as two locals. We stay clear of checkpoints. We can steal from orchards. Make it to the town my friend used to live in. Maybe he's still there. He can hide us and help us on to Hungary. Imagine we apply for asylum."

"I'm not sure about this," Maka said. "Sounds crazy. At least here I know what the game is."

"Seriously, what better options do we have?"

Maka thought of it. True, they had no options. All their options were so dismal they didn't count as options at all. But he had those fifty marks. He remembered it now. In the forest it was just dirty paper. He hadn't wasted a thought on it. But in Serbia, where the deutsche mark passed as currency, it would be an asset. Maybe they could get bus tickets and food. He thought of it. It did make some sense. The Chetniks probably didn't expect someone to make their run towards Serbia. But with that money in his pocket he'd turn into a normal human being again – for as long as they didn't get caught, at least. Out of the blue, the idea of such relative normalcy was dizzying.

"All right. But this is the craziest thing I've done," he said.

"Maka, I'm tired of this hell. Let's try this one last time."

"All right. Let's do it."

"Let's do it. One last time."

"Okay. One last time."

"Good," said Zlatar. "But we have to go alone. The two of us. A group this size wouldn't stand a chance."

The others had already put on their shirts and rucksacks, and were starting into the forest. The Professor and Salko looked back at Maka and Zlatar.

"Are you coming?"

Maka looked at the father and the son. He'd do anything for people like them. He just wasn't sure if he'd ever get to see them again. All he said was, "Good luck, and thank you for everything. We'll try another direction."

ELEVEN

CRADLED BETWEEN THE mountains of eastern Bosnia, in a valley where the river Drina makes its way towards the Sava, was the twin-city of Zvornik. Sliced in two by the river, it was a typical frontier town. Zvornik — the historical name probably meaning bell tower — had risen on the western bank, while Mali Zvornik, or "Little Zvornik", sat on the eastern side in Serbia. To strangers' eyes, both towns appeared nearly identical, except for their size. Observing the forest-topped mountains that surrounded them one could not tell they now belonged to two different worlds.

Maka had worked a summer on buildings there. But what he knew the town from was the schoolbooks. Zvornik had seen more than its share of masters. Up on a hilltop on the Bosnian side, overlooking the settlement, Romans had built their fortifications over an Illyrian outpost's ruin. From there, they mined the hills and offered protection to merchants travelling north to Sirmium in the province of Pannonia. Huns, Avars and Slavs followed, and in the Middle Ages Byzantine lords came and built on top of the Roman ruins. The citadel that watched over the town and the eternal flow of the river was called Kula Grad – the tower city. Then came the Ottomans, conquering the valleys and establishing shipyards by the river shores.

The town prospered, but also suffered because of its strategic location. As an important intersection between Belgrade, Novi Sad and Sarajevo, Zvornik drew tragedy. The Kula Grad fortress was nearly destroyed when Austro-Hungarian troops forced the Ottomans out. Then there was another war, and another, and in the Forties the Croatian fascist Ustaše troops held the town until it was captured by Tito's partisans.

That was where Marshal Tito's suitably harmonised history books ended. Peace did not last for half a century. When the Serb paramilitaries attacked the city in 1992 and began killing the majority non-Serb population, the Bosniak survivors fled south, to Srebrenica, in thousands.

The crumbling walls of Kula Grad did not tell these stories. Weeds had rooted between the stones of the ancient towers and bastions. Looking down to the river from the citadel's embrasures, one could observe a modern anomaly, a hydroelectric power dam that packed the water. A wide loop of the river, engorged like a glutted snake's belly, caressed a peninsula that jutted into the emerald river like a ship's bow. The peninsula was invaded by small houses, their blanket of heavy, clay-tiled roofs making the sliver of land look like it were about to sink into the water.

If you walked past the peninsula, following the road by the waterfront, there was an overlook where a hotel had been built on a cliff. Further away, a stone quarry had been in operation since Roman times. Here the valley narrowed and the houses became fewer, and the mountains again took hold of the river as if it belonged to them. Shadows crept up the steep hillsides as the sun started to sink. People rarely wandered up to the crests of these cliffs, save perhaps for a scenic photo.

Late that afternoon, two men lay on the rocky surface, observing the river far below.

"Is this how you remember it?" Maka asked.

Zlatar watched the current. "It's fast as hell," he said. "The rains were four days ago. Why is it still swollen like that?"

"But you were right. It's narrower here. It must be less than two hundred metres."

Gazing at the river, Zlatar fell silent. Maka, using his friend's rifle, scanned the valley through the optical sight. Down below there was a road. About a kilometre downstream, towards Zvornik, he could spot what looked like remains of cabins in the vegetation between the road and the water. The river gleamed dirty-yellow in the afternoon sunlight, and on the Serbian side there was just a road skirting the curve of the river but no buildings.

"See anybody?" he asked.

"No."

"Me neither. Are those summer houses?"

"Yes."

"Looks like they've burned them."

"Yes. All of ours."

"You think they still use theirs?"

"Maybe."

"We better wait here." Maka passed the rifle back to Zlatar. "Let's climb down after dark and swim across."

The other one sighed heavily. He held the musette bag under his chin, resting his head on it. The sun was hot on their backs. "I'm not sure about this," he said. "To be honest, I'm not much of a swimmer."

"What's that? You yourself planned this."

"I'd no idea it was going to be this high."

"Can you swim at all?"

"Some," said Zlatar. "But that's two hundred metres. Look at the current. I'll never make it."

All right, Maka thought. Fair enough. He guessed it didn't make a difference now if it was the Chetniks or the river. But damn that Zlatar. They'd made it here. They couldn't stop, anyway. He observed the hills on the Serbian side. Down the slopes were scattered fields that looked well farmed and orderly. Farther upstream, just before the next curve, were small orchards and a vineyard. There was not a trace of destruction.

A country at peace.

They had worked across the terrain, avoiding dwellings and roads. Before leaving the river grove they bathed with their clothes on, and Maka's white shirt no more betrayed the fact that he had crawled in the woods for days on end. He now wore the tracksuit trousers. Had they not carried weapons, they could have passed for two local Serb men on a hilltop excursion.

"We'll swim together," Maka said. "We'll leave the rifles, and if you ditch that bag you can hang on to me. What's in it, anyway? Looks heavy."

"I'm not leaving it." Embarrassed, Zlatar tightened his grip on the musette.

So, that's what it was… Maka remembered now the plastic bag the goldsmith had hastily hidden in the musette.

"Think carefully," he said. "Is it worth the risk?"

"No way I'm leaving it! Besides, we'll need it."

Maka looked at his friend. Was he stupid or just plain greedy?

"Getting across is one thing," he said. "That stuff will get us murdered."

"I said I trust Branko," said Zlatar. "He's a good man and an old friend."

They lay in silence, side by side, staring at the river. It was a hot afternoon. A red van drove up the road towards Zvornik. They could hear it before it came into view, and Maka watched it disappear around the bend. Then there was again only the quiet chirring of insects and the heat of the day. Maybe Zlatar was right. Maybe old friendships were all they had. And the gold. Yes, the gold. That's what he had in the bag. All that was left of his life's work. It made sense. Yes, it made sense now. He'd grabbed his stash when the town fell.

Okay, I shouldn't think harshly, Maka thought. They'd need to travel to Hungary. They'd have to cross the border and source fake IDs and bribe a bunch of officials. Okay, they could use that gold. That was all right. But they couldn't swim the river with such a damn sinker. He looked down to the road. It was already in shadows, and soon the evening would take the river and the hills, too.

"What if," he said, "you wait here? I'll go and scout for something we can cross with."

"How would you find a boat? They wouldn't leave them unchained."

"Not a boat. Anything that floats will do. A jerrycan or something. There's got to be cabins there that haven't been torched. Just I better go alone. Somebody might know you."

Maka had given away one of his bottles when they split from the group. That would have come in handy now. Well, it was gone. He scanned the surroundings. The hilltop was bare, but nearby was a waist-deep indentation, flanked by a small rock face. Not the best hideout. But no one should have any business venturing up this cliff.

"Why don't you stay there?" he said. "I'll be back before it gets dark."

"And if you meet someone?"

"I don't know. I'll just pretend I'm local."

"Better leave your *ciganka*. Want my pistol?"

"No, you keep it. It wouldn't do any good."

He went to the depression and put his pack on the ground, laying his rifle across it. He got back to the cliff's brow. "If I don't return before nightfall," he said, "you know what it means. Then you find your own way across."

He took one final look at the road. It was more than a hundred metres down. There was no movement on it. He went over the edge and started climbing.

Zlatar followed his progress from above. "You sure about this?"

"No," said Maka, climbing. "Anyway, what can we do? Just go back and wait."

The rock face was precipitous, but holding on to the scrub pines and sliding on the bare surfaces Maka was able to descend. It was hard work and he thought it was taking him too long. He climbed on and, when finally down, staggered thankfully over the scree rocks at the base.

He stood by the roadside sweaty, dusting off his trousers. The road was paved and there were no buildings in sight. No people either. Tall summer weeds grew by the roadside. Down the riverbank, now seeing it up close, the water was frighteningly fast. It was smooth and swirly and made no sound. On the other side of the river, two hundred metres away, were the hills of Serbia.

Maka knew this road. It followed the river going up to Zvornik and on to Bijeljina. Behind the bend, he remembered, was a cosy riverside restaurant. He used to take girls for dates there. Between the restaurant and the Divič peninsula were clusters of summer huts in the waterfront, and that's where he might find something. Maybe some of them were standing.

Well, I'm just a local guy, he reassured himself. He started along the road.

He walked on the right shoulder so that he could see the water's edge. The sun was still bright on the river. He went on casually, trying not to show his fear, or that he was scanning the waterside.

After a bend the restaurant came into view. All that remained were charred stone walls and weeds reaching towards the sky inside the carcass of the building.

Of course – the owner was a Bosniak.

Maka went on. Up ahead he saw two old women coming down the road, leading a cow. They wore rubber work shoes and had headscarves around their wrinkled faces, tied under the chin, and faded flower-patterned aprons covering their aging, large waists, like any grandmother in the Balkans. As they met, Maka gave a nonchalant "*dobro veče*". The women eyed him askance and passed without saying a word. The animal clip-clopped on, whisking flies with its filthy tail.

Down by the water, the summer cabins had been torched. The debris and cracked basement stones were visible in the tall fireweed.

Surely they could've saved those. If nothing but for their own enjoyment, he thought. What had they ever done to become so despicable? Even on the frontline, Maka had never recognised how frightening a person he was to some. In war, men killed men, so the killing seemed to serve some sort of morbid purpose. But here, seeing the degree of vandalism, the madness of it all was becoming apparent. You couldn't go back, he thought. Who cared about cabins? But so much was lost, and you couldn't go back. Then how would you ever get forward?

And nothing that looked like it'd float.

The road went over a concrete bridge, across a mouth of a tributary coming from the hills. Carved into the hillside of the tributary valley was a vast stone quarry. It seemed to stretch a kilometre inland, its pale, rugged moonscape glowing in the setting sun. There was no one in sight and it was frighteningly quiet.

Crossing the bridge, Maka kept an eye on the quarry. An entrance road went into the valley. Nearby were hangars and carcasses of large trucks that lay in a grass-grown gravel yard. The place looked like it had been out of operation since the war.

Maybe there's something there, he thought. An inner tube from one of those earthmovers? That'd be more than he could hope for.

The yard was bestrewn with rusty metal scrap. Maka went around, checking the trucks, opening doors and looking into the cabs. The seats were littered with glass shards and faded papers of drivers' logbooks. Did they even keep inner tubes with them? The wheels were so big that in case of a puncture they'd probably have to change the whole tyre. Of course. What was he thinking? You never changed tubes on cars, either.

Without any warning, a gruff voice spoke behind him:

"What are you looking for?"

An old man had walked up to Maka. A faint wind was whispering between the trucks and he had not heard the sound of the gravel. The Serb was a head shorter than him and his face was toughened by the sun, with deep creases around his eyes and a grey stubble that framed his thin mouth. A threadbare wool sweater made him look out of place in the evening heat. Maka felt his bones go cold. Of course they'd have someone guarding the depot, even during the war. He noticed the black handle of a pistol poking from under the man's leather belt.

"A tyre," he replied. "I had a puncture."

The old man did not say anything. He was assessing the trespasser with unwelcoming eyes.

"Was carrying livestock from Srebrenica," Maka continued, thinking: *If he goes for that gun, I have to kill him.* "Now, stuck with those damn sheep. The truck's down the road." He said this instinctively. He hadn't thought of it, but when the town fell the Serbs must have looted everything, including the animals.

"No spares here," said the man. "You'll need to go to Zvornik."

Maybe imagining the troubles Maka must have with the flock of animals, the old Serb's coldness seemed to dissipate. "Zvornik's three kilometres up the road," he said. He advised about a repair shop in the outskirts. He thought the owner lived in the same building. Maka would just need to knock on the door to find someone for help.

Maka thanked him and went back to the road. *Goddam geezer.* He looked over his shoulder and waved his hand. He started out along the road, walking towards Zvornik. Backtracking now would look conspicuous. And he still hadn't found anything for Zlatar.

On ahead the road ran through a tunnel in a cliff. Before the tunnel by the river was a group of buildings. The houses were in shape. As Maka saw them, he remembered it was a motel. It looked as though it was still in business. The parking lot was vacant, but over the main building hung the tricolour flag of the Republika Srpska. By the parking was a barbecue shelter with a huge redbrick oven for roasting sheep, or suckling pigs nowadays, maybe.

It was strange and unnerving walking under the enemy flag. Just after he had passed the barbecue area, a new voice intervened:

"Hey, you. Where you going?"

A young soldier stood in the shadow of the tall oven. Maka could not have spotted him until after rounding its corner. The youth had an assault rifle on his back. He looked at Maka.

Now it's over.

No. It can't be.

"Sorry, what do you want?"

"Where you going?" said the soldier. "Lemme see your papers." He had no menace in his eyes, but he was doing his duty. Maka knew he was in trouble. He'd just walked into a trap.

"Oh? Sure. I've my licence in the truck. Lost a tyre. It's around the bend."

"Wait, you don't have your ID?"

"It's in the truck. I'll go get it."

"Why, you should have it on you. Why did you leave it?"

"I can fetch it… if you don't believe me, why don't you come with me?"

The sentinel was smaller than him. Maka knew he'd have to fight him. He was very weak now. But he'd take him by surprise. He'd slug him in the back of his neck. Just one punch. He'd put all his force into it. But, in this world of thieves, who'd leave anything in a broken truck?

"Can't leave my post," the soldier said. He slid the gun off his back. Behind him, in the main building, another man appeared

92

in the doorway. He also carried a rifle. His military shirt hung open and he had a small transistor radio in hand. A Serbian pop song was on. Maka saw a third soldier inside the building.

"What's it now?" the one with the radio asked.

"He's got no papers. Says they're in his truck, down there."

The man came out. He switched the radio off and measured Maka from head to toe.

"Let's call the cops," he said. "He can sort it out with them." Then, shouting over his shoulder, "Časlav, get the sheriffs! Something for 'em!"

He scanned Maka again, his eyes narrowing. "I don't know you. But you wait here. The cops will take you to that truck."

Maka knew he was in a jam. A cold lump had formed in the pit of his stomach, growing larger and heavier. The jam of his life. Please, God, don't let it end like this, he thought.

The old man from the quarry walked up. He must have seen Maka get stopped.

"This young man is in trouble," he informed the soldiers. "He's got livestock stuck in his car." Years ago, he said, he'd also kept sheep. He understood their distress when they were left without water.

"Where are you from, son?" he asked.

"Vlasenica," he said. It was the first Serb town he could think of. He'd once built a house there.

The old man's eyes widened with delight. "Oh? Me, too."

Go to hell, Maka thought. "Well, from a village nearby..."

"Oh, me, too!" said the old man. "What's your name?"

Oh go to hell! "Petrović," Maka said, giving the commonest Serb name.

"Petrović... Petrović..." The man was digging through his memory but could not seem to remember Maka. They waited in silence. The sun had gone behind the hills. Maka was sweating. He had three armed Serbs surrounding him and he knew he could not beat them. All he could do was wait and hope that something would save him. So far, somehow, all his moves had turned out to be right. But he'd run out of luck. Work this out? He had no idea how to, anymore. He saw a car come through the tunnel. It was a standard blue Yugoslav police car, a beat-up little Zastava. It turned to the motel yard and parked.

Two policemen stared at Maka through the windscreen. Then the driver's door opened and a bare-headed, middle-aged, sturdy officer stepped out. He was in a blue-grey and black camouflage uniform. He looked big coming out of that tiny Fiat copy. He had sergeant's stripes on his rank slides. The hair on top of his head was thinning and it made him look older. He looked at Maka with hard eyes. Maka saw the holstered pistol on his belt and something sank to his stomach.

"All right, where's that truck of yours?" The cop spoke with the cold authority of a man who can do what he wants, in a world where the only laws are his.

So, this is how it ends, Maka thought. There was no point in spinning another lie.

"There's no truck." The words sounded strange, as if the voice were not his. Maka put his hands up. "I'm a Bosniak from Srebrenica. I'm unarmed."

The cop's eyes narrowed. An odd expression of shock lit on his face.

"Fuck! Shit!" he cursed. "Goddam fucking shit! You have a gun? No? Any money?"

"I've got fifty deutsche marks."

"You've got to be shitting me? *Jebem ti mater!*" he swore, deploying the strongest profanity in the Serbo-Croatian vocabulary. "Why does this shit happen to me?"

In his fear Maka tried to think. Wasn't it he that should be doing the cursing? The policeman wiped the side of his chin and glanced at his colleague. The other officer, a junior sergeant, was sitting in the car. He held an assault rifle between his legs and watched the flow of the river, looking bored and uninterested in Maka.

"You guys can piss off now," the sergeant said to the two soldiers and the old man, who now were staring Maka coldly. "I'll handle this."

The cop told Maka to keep his hands up and step behind the car. He shoved Maka against the hatchback and frisked him, before swinging him around. He had the bunch of German marks in his fist.

"This is really all you have? No ID? No passport? Nothing?"

"No. I came over the hills."

"What do you mean? How did you get here?"

"I walked through the hills."

The cop stared at him, incredulous.

"If you let me go, I can pay you," Maka tried. "I'll give you thirty thousand marks."

He had no clue where to get such money. He'd never seen such money in his life. But there had to be thirty thousand somewhere. That sounded like a good sum. You could buy a car for a couple of thousand, or a farmhouse for twenty, but what's that? Thirty thousand sounded like just the right price for a man's life.

The shadows had now climbed up the hills on the Serbian side, too, and the light was gone from the hilltops. The night was coming on. The policeman stared at Maka and shook his head, looking disgusted. Maybe Maka had been wrong. He'd never had to bargain for life before. He didn't know if there was any going rate for human life. Maybe there was, and thirty thousand wasn't enough.

"Get your ass in," the cop said.

They put him in the back seat of the old Fića. The junior sergeant sat close next to him with his rifle. They did not bother handcuffing him. The sergeant got behind the wheel and started the car. He veered tightly onto the road and Maka was pressed between the frame and the other cop, who still had shown no interest in the catch whatsoever. Maka glimpsed the old man and the two soldiers still against the motel, watching after them.

Inside it smelled of cigarette smoke and gun oil. A withered air freshener hung from the rearview mirror and swung in the windscreen. The sergeant's faded service cap was on the dashboard. The officers were quiet. They went through the ancient road tunnel, then passed the hotel on the lookout and turned around a bend and past the Divič peninsula, and the river went behind the houses. Then it came into view again and there was the dam across and it was already getting dark. Maka watched the river, wide and smooth and dirty-yellow as jade. They rode into the shadow of the Kula Grad fortress hill. They were on the outskirts of Zvornik and there were more houses and buildings and they were driving towards the centre now. It was only a three-minute drive, but Maka felt every second like a grain of sand slipping through an hourglass. His mouth was dry. The cold weakness inside him had gone into his legs.

When the car stopped, they were in front of a police station, still at the edge of the town. The building was without lights except for a solitary window on the first floor.

"Get out," said the sergeant.

He pushed Maka up the front stairs and into an entryway and switched on the light, tossing his cap on the reception desk. There were papers and notebooks and an empty ashtray on the table. The other cop walked behind them, holding the rifle. They went through a dark corridor and exited into a windowless, brightly illuminated hallway, lined with cell doors.

A third officer came into the hall. He carried a bundle of keys and he was young and sleepy. He went through the keys, yawning. He found the right one and opened one of the doors. It was a small concrete room with no window and nothing inside, just the bare concrete floor. No one said a word.

Maka stepped into the cell. His legs felt hollow. He heard the door shut behind him and then it was pitch-black and the lock clanked twice in the darkness.

TWELVE

THE NIGHT HAD come. Maka could not see outside but he could feel the silence in the cell. It was very hot, around 30 degrees as nearly as he could say. The concrete had baked in the sun. He sat on the floor, resting his head against the wall. Under the door was a narrow gap with light outside. After a while he could see the walls of the cell. The hollow coldness was gone from inside him. He felt just numb. It was finished.

He'd let them take him so easily. Why? He did not know. It didn't matter anymore, just how it would end. With a knife? A bullet would be easier for everybody. It'd probably be a bullet. He hoped it would be a bullet. Maybe he'd get a beating first. He'd never been beaten before. Never had he fought anyone in his life, not even in school. He guessed it didn't matter, either.

So, it was his turn.

Three years earlier, the killing had started in Zvornik. The war had come full circle. He would die here, too. He sat in the darkness, his heart beating. He wondered if the Professor and his son had made it. No one ever made it. It was the rational people who always got caught up.

They had refused to believe the news. No, there won't be a war, they thought. There can't be, they said, even as they watched the smoke rise from the valleys. Then the refugees arriving in the freezing rain, first in hundreds then in thousands, carrying what little they'd been able to salvage, the children's wailing and the horror in their eyes, the stories of torture, rape, pillage and killing; the first shells slamming into town, roaring and sending smoke and plaster and rubble on the streets, and the baker's daughter lying outside the čaršija, like a wax doll, her blood along the curbstone, a narrow, bright-red streak that ran into a storm drain down by the Dom Kulture.

They believed it now. It was real with the artillery. It was true with the explosions that shook the dust off the bare trees in the schoolyard and the kids studying in the basement. Then, one day, his youngest brother came running to the house. Come quickly, Nermin said, out of breath. There was a bus leaving. He worked at the station and he knew it would be the last one. That morning Maka's mother was visiting her sister. But Amelia would make it. She had no time to pack. They took her to the station. It was a cold April day and it had been sleeting. Maka had grabbed *burek* and cheese and a can of juice, and he handed them to her through the bus window. In the scramble, they did not have time to say goodbyes. He watched the bus drive up Maršala Tita, and when it was gone there were just the tyre tracks in the slush and the steam of his breath, and the Križevica that flowed as always in the cold mist.

Then, for three years, only weapons to hold and soldiers to talk to.

If there were any meaning to this life, maybe it was to pass it on. If that were so, he'd done his share. It just felt wrong that he never got to hold his son. Maka knew the kid had been born via an emergency C-section in Croatia. He'd had his umbilical cord wrapped twice around his neck. Strangled at birth already. It took a lot to survive here, and the world always seemed to have some obscure reason for knocking you off.

And why should he, Maka, be killed? Because of his name? He buried his face in his folded arms. Remembering Edin and Hassan in that forest again, he felt as though something was choking him. They were dead now. Dead, dead, dead. Everyone dead. And where was his mother? He hoped she'd at least made it. He felt like crying, but it didn't come. I'm sorry, mother, he thought. *I'm sorry that I left you. I'm sorry, Amelia. I'm sorry, everyone. Dino, I'm so sorry.*

I didn't make it.

The lock rattled again, and a bright gap opened into the cell. It was the sergeant. "Get up," he whispered.

He took Maka into the hallway. A door was open to a duty office and Maka saw the young policeman asleep behind a desk. The sergeant took him to a lavatory in the back of the hallway: he pushed him in, then stepped in and closed the door.

It was dim inside. There was a barred window by the sink with pale light from a streetlamp. There were two toilet booths. A mop stood in a bucket in the corner. The cop looked at Maka.

"You have any family?" he asked quietly.

"Yes. I'm married," Maka said.

"Where's your wife?"

"In Germany, with her family." Germany sounded good. Germany always sounded like money.

"Anyone else?"

"No. I heard she's given birth, so I've got a son, too."

"Got her number?"

Maka had it. Amelia had put it in a Red Cross letter, hoping the telephone lines would get restored one day. It was the only concrete thing he had of her, and he had memorised the number.

The cop scribbled it in a small notebook. He slipped the book and the pen back into his breast pocket. He looked at Maka.

"I'll call your wife. It's imperative that none of my colleagues or anyone else know about this. Do you understand? If you're taken away from this station, you will die. You understand what I say?"

Maka understood.

"It's midnight," the cop said. "We don't have much time. They'll come for you in the morning. Do you need to use the toilet?"

"No. I haven't drunk much today."

"I'll bring you water. That tap doesn't work."

With that, the policeman banged his fist on one of the booths.

"All right, finish it up, for fuck's sake!" he said in a loud voice.

He brought Maka back to the cell. The night watch was asleep. The sergeant locked the cell door and Maka was again alone in the darkness.

He sat on the floor. He was sweating again. The temperature did not seem to go down even though it was past midnight. Things seemed a tad less catastrophic. But he knew there was no thirty thousand marks. Amelia or her family didn't have such money. He'd only bought time with his lie.

Then how about Zlatar and his gold?

He'd probably left the cliffs already. Headed for Žepa. Good for him. Maka knew he could never betray his friend. He'd only get both killed. But it was best for Zlatar if he was gone.

Maybe he'd tried to swim across. Maybe he had drowned. Over the centuries, just how many men might've ended in the bottom of that river with a bag full of gold?

He sat in the darkness and waited.

The policeman came back. He stepped inside the cell, leaving the door slightly ajar. He handed Maka a pack of biscuits and placed a glass of water on the floor. He was again talking in whispers:

"Eat them now. I need to take everything back."

Maka tore the pack open. They were the same, tasteless protein crackers that the Americans had once airdropped in Srebrenica. They stood in the darkness, Maka eating, the policeman watching him.

"I spoke with your wife," the cop said.

"Was there any problem regarding the money?"

"Look, let's just leave money out of this. I'm not doing this for money. I know you've got a small kid. I know what the situation is. And frankly, your situation is very difficult right now. Everyone knows that you're here. We need to think how to get you out."

For a moment, Maka thought it was a jest. Get him out? But the cop's face looked serious.

"I'm okay with anything you say," he said. "I'm the one locked up."

"I can only think of three ways. You have any friends or relatives in the Bosnian army? Anyone in a high position, I mean."

"I don't suppose I have."

"You're sure? No one in Tuzla? Sarajevo? Maybe someone who knows a unit commander or an official? If they could arrange a prisoner exchange. I've a relative jailed in Tuzla."

"Sorry to say," Maka told him, "I don't know of any such connection. I'm just from an ordinary family. Same with my wife."

"How about other relatives? Anyone in Serbia? Maybe they could help?"

"No one there, either…"

Most of his relatives were dead, as far as he could tell. But in the back of his mind Maka was thinking of Zlatar and that Serb friend. All he had was his name, Branko. That wasn't going to help him. He took a long drink from the glass.

"That leaves us with the last option," the cop said. "I'll try to set you free. But you'll need to hide somewhere for a few days until things blow over. I'll organise some trusted men in Serbia to help you across. From there, on to Macedonia. The problem is, there aren't good hiding places here, around Zvornik. But you already survived for a week in the bush. Maybe you'll manage a few more days."

Maka thought it over.

"If that's the only option… it sounds like a good plan."

"Let's do it then. But we need to be very careful. Just two days ago, seven men that had crossed into Serbia were returned here. And I know, those are dead already."

"Wouldn't the same happen with me?"

"Not if I get my friends to help you. But we have very little time. It'll be morning soon."

"What a rotten business. Have you lost anyone?"

"Give me that glass. The wrapper, too. I'll go make the calls."

Maka was again alone in the cell. He lay on the floor. The concrete felt cooler; still he could not sleep. And he couldn't figure out why the cop wanted to help him. Maybe he was a man of law after all. Talk about a *ray of hope*. But he couldn't imagine how the officer could release him. It would land the cop in trouble, for sure. He realised he didn't even know his name. The biscuits had been marvellous. It didn't feel like the last meal. The cop had spoken to Amelia. She was awake now. She was with Maka now. They were thinking of each other, right now, knowing they were both alive. Her and the boy in Germany. No one could take that away. Then he thought of those seven men.

They'd nearly made it. Now their bodies lay mangled in some pit in the woods.

After two or three hours the cell door opened again. This time it was the junior sergeant. He told Maka to step out, then handcuffed him. The young duty officer was with him. His eyes seemed to avoid Maka. The police sergeant with whom Maka had talked was there, but the cop stayed silent.

They took Maka outside and put him in the car. A half-moon was high, and there was the lonely streetlight opposite the station house that had shone into the lavatory. The town was dark. They started along the through street and turned onto the riverfront highway, driving towards the centre. The junior sergeant was again next to Maka in the back seat, the assault rifle between his thighs. The older sergeant was driving slowly, with only the daytime lights on, and Maka saw the apartment blocks by the waterfront and the road empty in the moonlight. It was over three years since he had been here and the city looked the same, except now, without lights, it was like a ghost town. They went past the old steel bridge that connects the town with Mali Zvornik. The dark water was high against the bridge's massive stone pedestal in the middle of the river. They were driving north, towards Bijeljina, and Maka understood that this somehow wasn't part of the plan. There would be fewer dwellings and farmlands south from Zvornik, around the area where he'd been arrested, better places to hide. Why were they taking him north?

Everyone was silent. The sergeant was driving slowly. The road ahead was dark. They had already exited the town and were riding into the flat farmlands of the Sapna tributary.

"What if we release him?" said the sergeant abruptly.

His colleague said nothing. He seemed just as indifferent as he had been in the daylight, smoking a cigarette and blowing smoke out the half-lowered window, lazily watching the moonlit fields.

"Say, what if we let him go?" the sergeant said again.

The colleague said nothing.

So, there you have it. There was an order. They're not out to free me, Maka thought. They were delivering him to the Chetniks. He figured the Serbs had brought in special units to carry out the executions. If they were to kill all the men, they'd have to shoot and bury fifteen thousand. They were probably doing that in the hills north of Zvornik as they'd done in 1992. The order must have come abruptly. The sergeant didn't have time to place those calls. And it made sense. In the night, everything made sense. Murdering people, in the thousands. Yes, a business for the dark of the night.

So, now this is finally over, he thought. They were going through the wide, low fields, the Drina far on their right. They had just passed the town of Kozluk and they would probably soon turn west, towards Jasenica. Maka could see the air freshener

103

dangling in the cold moonlight. He guessed they were taking him to the woodlands beyond Jasenica.

"What if *I* let him go?" the sergeant said. He looked straight ahead and his voice was tense.

"Do what you like," the other one snapped. He flicked the cigarette butt out, sending a cloud of sparks into the night. "Whatever it is, I'm not part of it."

"You are already part of it, *pičku ti mater*! Why would you let them kill this man? He's never even seen his kid. Fuck this war! Fuck Karadžić and fuck his whore of a mother! You know as well as I do, they'll kill him as soon as we get there."

The colleague said nothing.

Yes, Maka thought, why would you let them kill me, you son of a bitch? Because you'd both get yourselves into shit if you released me. But he had to do something. He needed to get this rotten bastard on his side. Maka had been trying to accept his own death, and he'd been running away from it, and when he resigned himself to it he knew he had nothing to lose and everything to win. He turned to the junior sergeant and said, "If you're human, and if you'll let me go, I'll be grateful to both of you for the rest of my life."

The officers were both silent.

"I don't have much to give. But that's the one thing I can say," he continued.

The sergeant cursed profusely. He stopped the car by the roadside and cut the engine. He kept his hands on the steering wheel and said nothing. They were surrounded by the fields. There was the silence and the cool smell of the farmlands. Somewhere far away Maka could hear a cock crowing. The cop next to him lit another cigarette, his mug illuminating in the darkness like the face of a wax sculpture.

"Fuck the war, huh?" the cop said, scornfully. "Go fuck it, then."

The sergeant began swearing again. He put the car in gear and made a U-turn. They drove back, through the fields and past the dark houses of Kozluk. When the few lights of Zvornik came into view again, he followed the highway by the river, instead of going through the centre. In a moment the town was behind them and they were again passing the Divič point. They went through the tunnel. On the other side, the lights were out in the motel. Maka could not see if there was a sentry in the yard. He felt like holding his breath; these cops were now deciding whether he'd live or die.

They went over the bridge and past the stone quarry. When they were at the burned-down restaurant, the policeman pulled the car into the old parking area by the ruin.

"Give me that gun," he said, leaning over to the back seat. He took the rifle from his colleague. He got out and opened the door on the other side and folded the front seat forward, looking in at Maka.

"You, get out."

It was chilly outside. The river was below, near, flowing silently in the moonlight. To the right were the cliffs. This was not far from where Maka had left his weapon and Zlatar. He could see the dark silhouette of that same hilltop against the sky.

"Put your hands here." The cop pointed at a headlight. In its beam he unlocked the handcuffs and took them off. Opening the bonnet, he took something from the trunk. The junior sergeant had stayed in the car. There was a glowing dot that moved up, glowed more brightly, then moved down. The man was smoking again. That's got to be the most jaded person I've seen in this bloody war, Maka thought. The son of a bitch almost got him killed.

The sergeant came back, holding the rifle. He had something under his arm.

"Go down to the river," he said. "Don't be afraid."

They walked down the bank. Maka stood facing the river. It was smooth and fast. He could see driftwood floating by. Behind him, the policeman cocked the rifle. He shot twice in the water, then three more rapid shots, the sound of the blasts crashing over the river. Then there was just the acrid smell of gunpowder in the still night.

"You're free to go," said the cop. "Take these." He handed Maka a plastic bag.

Maka looked into it; from what he could see in the dark, there were two loaves of bread and a can of corned beef.

"Have you got any cigarettes?" he asked.

"*Jebemu ja tebe*... no, I don't," said the cop. Then he felt his breast pocket and dug out a flattened, half-empty pack and gave it to Maka.

"I must thank you, really. But do you have a light, too?"

"Fuck you, man! Take that." He handed Maka a box of matches. "Remember, you're a dead man now. If you're caught again, then do me a favour. You've never been to Zvornik, or at the police station."

"I understand that. Can I ask, what's your name? Just so that I know who saved my life."

"It doesn't matter who I am," the cop said. "I'm just doing this for your son. I hope you'll get to see him."

He turned around and started up the riverbank. His shoulders looked hunched in the moonlight. He did not look back. Maka heard the engine start, then the sound of the car pulling away.

It was quiet again. Maka walked up. He stood on the road. That was it. That simple? He was free. But it wasn't that simple.

The air was chilly. He looked around. The cliff where he had left Zlatar wasn't far. He would have to climb up in the moonlight. That rock's surface had been precipitous, and he wasn't sure how it would go. Here the slope looked better. He didn't want to spend any more time on the road than necessary, anyway.

He cut into the weeds by the roadside and started ascending.

Climbing up turned out a little easier. Once he slipped and fell back but could hold on to the shrubs and stop his fall, squeezing the plastic bag in his armpit. A couple of times his feet sent rocks tumbling down the cliff. They made a nasty dull sound in the night. The half-moon was high above him. It shone well enough for him to find handholds. As he scaled higher, Maka could again see the width of the river, silvery in the moonlight, and the square ruin of the restaurant that was far below him.

When he reached the top he was still about half a kilometre from the hideout. He started circling the hilltop. Near the location, he whispered out to Zlatar, but got no answer. He walked onto the cliff and looked down at the indentation. The backpack was there and his rifle lying across the pack. Zlatar was gone. He searched around the indentation and went to the other side of the rock mound next to it but found no trace of his friend.

Maka checked the backpack for a message. There was none, of course. Zlatar had nothing to write with, and it could as well be the Chetniks reading the note.

He stored the bread and the can in the rucksack. The tracksuit jacket and the water bottle were there. Donning the jacket and looking out over the valley, it came to him that the cop hadn't given back his fifty marks. Maybe he'd forgotten about it. Either way, I got a plenty good deal, he thought. To the east, across the Drina, a blue-orange glow was already rising from behind the hills. Many stars were still visible in the high, dark sky.

He stood there for a while, watching the dawn. There was already dew on the crispy lichen that covered the cliff. He figured there'd probably be a search party. Maka put the rucksack on his back and picked up the rifle. He was on his own again.

THIRTEEN

THERE WAS A park in Munich that Amelia knew where, if you came early in the morning before the groundskeepers arrived, you could sit in the shade of a large mulberry tree and enjoy a scenery as still as a painting. The gravel paths were clean and moist, the parterres crimson under a clear, blue sky. It was, in fact, a forecourt of a cemetery; you could see the old, white-granite tomb monuments behind the hedges, fanning out into a sea of trees. The basilica and the arcades that cordoned the gravel courtyard made the place seem like an old Spanish plaza rather than an entrance to a burial ground.

It was Monday and she was by herself on the bench under the old tree. She was trying to gather her thoughts. It was difficult to feel anything except dread when tired like this. Last night, she hadn't managed to sleep after that miserable phone call. Today she'd return to work. But what to think of it? She only knew she needed this quiet moment to try and calm her nerves.

Amelia watched the canopy. The early sun blotted the lawn between the trees. She liked that there were so many trees in Munich. It reminded her of Bosnia. Only it was all flat. She missed the mountains. But it was pleasant in that park. She liked the mornings and sunshine. It was the nights that were difficult. They'd been bad for three years. Now she was scared of the nights to come.

The war delivered one horror after another. Now she was safe, yet the worst had come in the form of these past two weeks. In Bosnia she'd been so focused on mere survival that she had not noticed, or had not allowed herself to notice, the sickening fear that builds up inside a person. Now, being this far away, especially since the attack, she felt utterly powerless and scared. The poorly slept nights, she figured, plus the influenza she'd just recovered from, didn't make things any easier. She had no way of knowing what had happened to Maka: where he was, or what was being done to him. She had no way of helping him. It was the helplessness that was the worst of it all.

Now the stories started coming through.

She used to call Maka's cousin in Tuzla. The girl, whose name was Sabina, had married and moved there before the war. As her house had a phone, they would console each other, exchanging rumours and information. But the news was so terribly mixed now. Maka's mother had made it to Tuzla, together with women the Chetniks loaded on buses in Potočari. Sabina had not seen her for three years. Munira, Amelia's mother-in-law, was so shocked and exhausted she could barely speak.

First, there was the heavy shelling. Munira saw some die in the blasts as they evacuated towards the UN base. There, the Dutch were not able to protect them. When the Chetniks arrived they started separating men from that crowd of thousands of women. Maka's mother was crammed into some factory building with hundreds of others. In the night the Serbs continued taking men out, some young as boys, and she heard the screams and the rifle shots outside, and in the darkness of the factory hall a man had hung himself from the steel trusses. None of those who were taken came back, but the Chetniks did, looking for more males and taunting the Bosniaks, shouting things like, "Where's your Alija now? Is he going to help you?" They bayoneted an old man who tried to speak against them, in front of everyone, and they took out young women, the pretty ones, the girls' screams echoing in the night as they were being dragged away. Sabina sobbed and cried as she retold this. "After two days of that terror," she said, "when the buses came, only boys and the old ones remained. Still the Chetniks pulled some out of the cars. They took my father's uncle. An old man who never hurt anyone. Why? Why?"

Bringing herself to calm down, she said she'd heard the first groups from the columns had breached the enemy lines in Kalesija. Her two brothers had made it. She hadn't had a chance to see them yet.

"Things are still very chaotic. And I'm so sorry. Nothing about Maka."

So, there it was. There it was. The dread was there and it was as sick-making, as discouraging as ever. It was one thing to fear for the worst, another to actually find out. She felt she was caught in a bad dream. Two weeks as if on autopilot, she thought. The other two families knew she had relatives and a husband in Srebrenica. She hated their unspoken pity. But what could they say? She herself didn't know what to say. Then, that evening, came that wretched phone call.

Two weeks of horror, capped by this. She just wanted it to stop.

But it would not.

The first people came into the park over the courtyard. It was a young couple with two young kids and they had a bouquet they were taking to someone's grave. Amelia watched them walk by, all in neat clothes, as if it were Sunday, and became aware that it was time for her to go to work.

Well, I guess you just have to take it, she thought.

I guess you just take everything.

She got up and walked out of the little park, past the courtyard and into the street through a gate in the stone arcade. Behind the cemetery was a residential area of cosy-looking apartment houses that had been built in the Fifties, after the Allied bombers reduced the city to ashes. There were cars parked under the linden trees along the cobblestone streets, many of them expensive. Their owners were still waking up. The lawns between the pavement and the buildings were tidy and fresh, and she walked towards the avenue thinking, They rebuilt everything from scratch… fifty years without war, and they're rich, clean and civil… just like we were. Except we never made laundry of our past.

On Dachauer Straße she got on a streetcar and went to Moosach, where she changed to a bus. It was eight o'clock and outside the station the baker was opening his business, putting out the chairs. There was already a trace of heat in the morning air. On a summer Monday like this, it would have been easy to feel as if it were the start of something new and exciting, not another week of labour.

Amelia sat on the bus feeling nothing. She rode into the suburb, watching the green, forested areas and the highway interchanges pass by, empty-hearted, and got off the bus outside the sprawling civil–military industrial complex. The factory hangars where the jet engines for the German air force were built spread out behind expansive, still vacant parking lots. She passed the car park and crossed the plaza where a hulking Tornado jet fighter stood on display, then went into the massive office building that she had been cleaning for the past three years.

She was in her work clothes, sitting in the fourth-floor break room. The other cleaners watched her guardedly. There were five of them, all immigrants. They all liked Amelia. She knew she was a diligent and approachable worker. Today they were quieter than usual. The Iraqi Kurdish girl, with whom she was the closest, was trying to console her:

"Isn't it good he's found someone to help him?"

Feeling the need to share her situation, Amelia had told them about the phone call.

"Good?" she said. "Is it good if you're caught? I don't know what they've done to him."

"Maybe it's just some sort of scam?"

"Hey, they're slaughtering people. Have you not seen the news?"

The girl went silent. She dropped her gaze to the floor, sitting cross-legged and holding her knee. "He'll be all right, I'm sure."

"Still better than if they'd killed him right away," said the middle-aged Lebanese man who did the first-floor offices. Then, realising his slip, he set down his coffee mug. "Well, I need to get started."

They listen but they don't understand. How could they? It was good they didn't understand. They didn't have to anymore. They'd put their battles behind, now they were forgetting. But whatever happened, she would not forget.

Was that all she could do? There had to be *something* she could do.

This was what she was thinking, later, as she pushed her trolley from one office to another and when she stood in the service elevator between the floors. When she wiped the surfaces and the door handles in the engineers' workspace she was telling herself, I can't stay put. And when the office workers were being cleverly funny to start the day, Amelia smiled back at them, knowing that the only thing she could do was wait. And that was the worst. Waiting without knowing. Her muscles were still sore from the flu and, with the lack of sleep, she found it difficult to be amicable.

At eleven she took a pause and called the apartment. Leaning on the bristly, felt-covered wall of the telephone closet and sucking on a carton of orange juice, she dialled her home number. Her mother answered.

"Anything yet?"

112

"No, nothing… I've been waiting by the phone the whole morning."

"Mom, you don't need to sit there."

"I rang Sabina. But I made it very short!"

"How is she?"

"Better. The brothers just arrived in Tuzla. Munira is still very weak; I couldn't talk with her yet."

"We need to tell her about that phone call. Oh, God. How can I tell her?"

"Let's let her rest for a day or two."

"Are the brothers well?"

"Oh, yes, but they marched for seven days!"

"Did they hear anything about Maka?"

"No… listen, darling. It sounds it's been very tough. But they think Edin and the boy were in one of those columns. Many of your dad's relatives, too."

"Thank God," Amelia said. "Look, Mom. I can't just wait here. So I'm thinking, I'll go and buy clothes for them, for when they get to Tuzla. Imagine how they look after three years! And they won't be able to get anything there. Let's send Sabina jeans and T-shirts and sneakers. Some money, too. We must get them something nice. And for Munira. Do you know when there's the next convoy?" She meant the system of bus routes and go-betweens they used for sending goods to Bosnia. Now that the fighting had ceased on the Adriatic coast, they could again reach Zenica and Tuzla via Mostar.

"I think there's one going this week."

"Good," said Amelia. "Let's get them all something. How is Dino?"

"Oh, the boy sleeps like an angel!"

Back on the office floor, Amelia continued her round. One of the engineers, a young man with a tight shirt and bossy eyes behind horn-rimmed spectacles, rolled back in his chair to let her mop under the desk. He looked at her teasingly.

"What is that, a Monday face? C'mon, cheer up!"

He tossed a ball of crumpled paper to the cleaning trolley's waste bin, missing it.

"Bungo!"

Amelia picked the paper up and binned it. She was thinking of her son. She had tried to talk to Dino about Maka. He was now three and began to understand things. In the playground the older kids would ask him why he didn't have a dad. "*I have!*" he'd respond proudly, almost indignantly, then go silent, perplexed by his own words. He was still unable to comprehend why Maka didn't come home. And Amelia would tell him, "*Daddy needs to stay in that faraway country a little longer.*" He was doing something important for that country. But how could she say it was, in fact, their home? For the kid, Munich was home. The only thing the boy had perhaps known of the Balkans were the shock waves from the artillery blasts while he was still inside his mother in Bosnia. Then the eye-hurting brightness of the hospital lights in Croatia, and the rocking and jolting of the autobus as he slept, tucked inside a blanket, in her arms, through Slovenia. He already spoke more German than Bosnian. And he had that little yellow toy telephone, his favourite, which he'd use to call his father, saying "*Tata? Tata?*" and then listening, silent, for a long time, and Amelia would feel her heart break every time she saw it, not knowing if at the other end Dino could hear his father answer or not. Maybe, in his mind, Maka talked to him. And now it seemed his father's voice would always sound to him any way he'd imagined it.

He was a lovely boy. She hoped he'd become like his father, strong and kind. Those two qualities came together so rarely. But Maka had them. Always considering others and being so optimistic. Like when she met him. Stuck in her friend's dinky Yugo, the car stuck in the snow, the blower not working, their breath steaming in the cold and the windows frosted over, then Maka and some other boys from Srebrenica appeared and tried

114

to push the car, rocking it back and forth, digging in the snow with their bare hands, freezing in their T-shirts, laughing and telling the girls it was not the car, the car was great, it was just that the snow wasn't cooperating and the wheels had dug in too deep. But there was a party at the hotel; it was warm there and it would go on all night, and in the morning they'd get a tractor to pull the car free or some real men. And he'd turned out to be just as funny and diligent and reliable as a husband. He worked in construction, but he rarely drank, or, if he did, he'd only become more gentle and considerate.

I was so lucky to find him, she thought, as she mopped the floor. She used to think it was sad many people never enjoyed such love. It took a lot of circumstances, the right timing and place, for two souls to find each other. So many never did. It didn't mean they didn't have love out there. Maybe they just turned a corner too early. Decided to take the trash out first. Maybe they heard some noise and turned to look the other way. It was so banal. And they'd been so lucky to have each other. Even if it was only for a couple of years. But why did it have to be taken away in such a cruel manner?

I guess I should feel guilty, she figured, about thinking of myself when thousands are dying. But she could not help thinking it was so cruel. They had such a beautiful life, and what was left of it? All these things had come to mean so much to her. How would she continue if they all vanished into thin air?

And how do you explain this to a child so that the kid doesn't grow up to hate people? What do you say when you can't tell how his father met his end? When you don't have a grave and nothing to show? She didn't even have a single photo of him. She didn't have any souvenirs. A *burek* and a can of juice, that's what he gave her. Maybe she should have saved that can. She hadn't, of course, thought of it. Better that way. A rusty old juice can on the bookshelf? Just too dismal.

If I were better at drawing, she thought, pushing the trolley, I'd sketch a picture of him. She should do it when she still remembered his face. She wondered how many years would pass before she'd forget what he looked like. Her Maka, ever so handsome! But she couldn't draw. And where was he now? What were they doing to him? Had they beaten him? Or given him food? She wondered if he was in pain. Oh, her Maka! She wished she could do something. She wished he could hear her speak. She knew it was crazy. But she wished he could hear her, wherever he was. She'd tell him that she would be all right. Now there was talk of air raids. She hoped they'd bomb them! They had talked for too long. Maybe some of the engines from this factory would fly there and blast those dirty Chetniks! But what would happen to Maka if NATO started it?

Scared of even the prospect of European military intervention, Amelia had her lunch in the tearoom. Then, with fifteen minutes left of her break, she went back to the phone closet.

Again, the phone rang just once. Her mother had still been waiting next to it.

"Still nothing?"

"Still nothing, honey. Your father took Dino to the playground."

"Good. Will you stay home and watch the phone?"

"Yes, of course. Don't worry about that."

"I'll be home late. I'll go straight to buying those clothes and things."

"Get some boxes, too."

Amelia hung up. She went to get the floor buffer for waxing the human resources hallway. She felt a little better. As she was operating it, fighting the heavy pull and push of the rotating machine, she was contemplating practicalities. She needed to pay the phone bill. She'd get groceries and a flower for her mom and pick up those cardboard boxes. There was a clothing section in that same supermarket. Nothing fancy, but they had sports suits and jeans of decent quality that were not very expensive. She would not buy anything second-hand. After three years of war and that terrible hike through the hills, Amelia wanted the men to be welcomed by new, unworn clothes. A new summer dress for her mother-in-law. She could fit all she wanted into two or three boxes. She wasn't sure if she still had packing tape. Better buy that, too.

She was thinking of this, in the constant loud droning noise of the floor buffer in the long, shiny office hallway, gyrating her way over the shadows and sunlight.

FOURTEEN

T HAT MORNING THE sun rose into a clear sky and the half-
moon stayed up with her, pale and lonely across the
blue. Maka had trekked south over the cliffs, away from the
Drina and into a ridgeline in a forest from where he could
see another valley and a stream along a road and two broken
houses down in the valley. It was already warm and light wind
wafted in the trees. When he sat on the slope watching the
morning, the ground dry and soft, he saw two military trucks
drive down the road and stop in front of the houses. A half-
platoon disembarked, spread out along the road and started
advancing uphill towards him. He could hear the Chetniks talk
and the shouted commands of the squad leaders. Maka knew
they were on the hunt for him, the skinny Bosniak in a tracksuit
who'd escaped the lockup. He stood up and went rapidly up the
slope and over the brow, then came down the other side in an
alder forest with the sun and the little warm wind and the birds'
singing, knowing he needed to find another hideout quickly or
he'd end up dead. The trees were young and sparse, and it was
not a good forest for hiding.

Just how many times had he died? He'd lost count. He knew he couldn't go too far, as he had seen a hamlet ahead in the lowland. If he followed the side of the hill, the road would cut him off as it curved north-west towards Kamenica. He didn't know if there was another line coming from the west. But a few hundred metres into the slope Maka sighted a little creek with a cluster of large boulders at the bottom. He climbed down, looking at the rocks. There was a space between them, large enough for a man to hide.

He crawled into the cool, mossy crevice and sat there, watching the sky. He kept his weapon ready and waited.

Maka knew the Chetniks' line would stretch out as they advanced deeper into the forest. With a bit of luck, they'd miss the gulley. If they didn't, they might not bother to come down and search the rocks. There was probably another group advancing westwards from the Drina and one coming rapidly down from the north. Soldiers were always like that, in a hurry to get out of any rotten forest. They'd meet up somewhere near that hamlet to establish that the quarry had, no doubt, slipped from them.

They were doing their dumb sham again. Shouts and occasional rifle shots echoed in the slant of the hill. Maka sat and listened, resting his feet against the rock. The worn-out army boots looked out of place, sticking out from the maroon-coloured sports trousers. He heard the Chetniks veer too much to the north. The tail of the line must have passed close to the gulley, for at one point he could smell a whiff of tobacco smoke.

He needed to give them a little more time. He wanted them more downhill. But where could he then go? He had no plan. The forest was again silent. The scent of tobacco had made him remember the cigarettes in his rucksack, and he fished out the pack of Morava. There were eight cigarettes.

It was probably safe to smoke. The matchbox had five matches in it. Leaning low to shield the flame, Maka struck one, then sat up, smoking.

He felt dizzy and good as the nicotine hit him. The day was warm, and it was very quiet.

It was personal now.

Those troopers were going after one man. Usually, the war was just chaos. Everything swirled around, people getting sucked into the meat grinder without any special discrimination. Just lads shooting at each other. Mere close-combat necessity, he thought. Nothing personal. Apart from the artillery, maybe. The field gun crews sat in the rear, firing when it suited, and when the shells screamed down on you and smashed everything to pieces it always felt as if they were out to get *you*, specifically. But that was different, too. Now it was these guys trying to root him out. Nothing to be bitter about, though. They missed him again.

He heard the wings of a bird swish above him. When he took a drag, the tobacco made a small crackling sound as it burned. He wished he could have a coffee, too. A fine copper *džezva* of strong Bosnian coffee. No, to hell with it. Any pot would do. He took out the bread and ate some. He wondered what the cop had told his superiors. That Maka had jumped out of a moving car? That he'd needed to piss, then started running? That the cop had shot him into the Drina? But why had they been south of Zvornik and not on the way to Jasenica, where the cops were supposed to deliver him? Maybe the sarge hadn't thought it all the way through.

That other cop probably snitched on him, he thought. But he saved Maka's life, all right. He was in a jam now. Well, he'd get over it. He was fifty marks richer. I got a discount, all right, he thought. Thank God he didn't take Zlatar's pistol. A weapon made an enemy. He wouldn't be here, smoking and talking. And he needed a plan.

Serbia?

How on earth would he cross the country, looking like a tramp? He had no money now. He knew no one. Got no papers. It was one thing to dream of Hungary or Macedonia, and another to actually get there.

Maybe he should also go for Žepa.

The policeman hadn't mentioned anything about it. Maka didn't know if the enclave was still standing. He wished he had asked about it. Forty kilometres, was it? At least he had some food. But brother, wouldn't it be *killing* if he made it, just to find the Chetniks were in town.

It had been quiet for a while. Maka drew open the rifle's bolt carrier to make sure he had a round in the chamber. He did, one of five. He put the gun back on safety. Then he crawled out, emerging slowly from between the boulders and glanced around. The forest was all peaceful.

He went walking up the long hill and came to the crest of ridge again. The valley was quiet, and in the distance the road was empty. The trucks were gone. Just like he'd imagined it. They'd pick up the half-platoon in that village.

Looking through the forest, about a kilometre to the east, beyond the valley's mouth, Maka could see a section of the Drina. Down below, where the trucks had stopped, were the two shelled-out houses.

I've a history with such shacks, he thought. The same fiasco shouldn't repeat itself here, though. He'd seen the Chetniks search the buildings already. The cop had said it would take a couple of days for the dust to settle. Maybe it was best to hide there. The nights were cold and he needed to sleep anyway. It would be easier to think clearly.

Maka sneaked down the slant of the hill. Through the trees, he saw the houses. They were swell houses, made of brick and robust in the sunlight. The walls were heavily pockmarked by gunfire and the roof tiles all blown away. There was plaster and rubble in the yard. A rusty little white Yugo 45 was decaying in the weeds between the two buildings, equally riddled with bullets and the window glasses and tyres gone. Maka could hear the stream behind the houses.

He entered one of the buildings. The front door was missing

and rotting pieces of smashed furniture littered the floor. Coming from the sunshine it was very dark inside. As soon as he walked into what had once probably been a living room, there was a loud metallic crash from the adjacent space, as if someone had accidentally kicked a kettle. Maka swung around, bringing the rifle to his hip. "Who's there?" he shouted.

A man stood in the shadow of the hallway, pointing a pistol at him. Maka pulled the trigger, but the rifle would not fire.

The goddam safety!

His finger found the fire selector and snapped it down, just as the man in the hallway called out:

"Maka? Is that you?"

He froze, staring at the man.

"Where the hell were you?" the other one said. It was Zlatar.

Maka lowered the rifle. Zlatar put his pistol up, uncocking the hammer. There was something, mud or soot, grimed on his face and forearms. Standing there in his black jeans and T-shirt, with his rifle slung on his back and the musette strap across the chest, he looked like death itself.

"How did you know I was here?" he asked.

"I didn't." Maka felt his legs start to shake. He'd been a millisecond away from blasting a slug through his friend.

"Then how did you find me? Where the hell you been?"

"Listen, I almost shot you," Maka said.

"Me, too. God, you gave me a scare."

"How come those Chetniks didn't find you?"

"How you know about the Chetniks?" Zlatar stood there, looking at Maka coldly. He had the pistol in his hand.

"I saw them."

"How did they know I was here?"

"They didn't. It's me they're after. I'd no idea about you."

"Been here since last night. I waited until midnight. Where were you?"

"Let's talk about that later." Maka glanced around. "Can we hide here? How come they didn't find you?"

"I still don't get it. Where the hell were you?"

"I was captured. Overnight in the can. Sorry, I couldn't put out a communiqué."

"You must be crazy," said Zlatar. He tucked the pistol under his belt. "Hit your head on the way down or something?"

"I'll tell you. Can we hide here?"

"Not really. It's all trashed."

He pointed to the back of the room where there was a heap of broken particleboard and rotting curtains. It was very dark in that corner. He said he crawled under the debris when he heard the trucks stop right outside the building. The trash had covered him only partially, so he quickly rubbed mud off the floor and smeared it on his face and arms.

"Two came in, searched the house. Stopped right there but didn't see me."

"They got in from the sun," said Maka.

"I lay under that rubbish. Wasn't even breathing."

"Thank God you've a black outfit."

"Those bastards stood there, two metres away, making fun of me. Said, even that *Balija* wouldn't be dumb enough to hide here."

"They were talking about me," Maka said.

They went into the adjacent room and sat down on the floor. They were in somebody's kitchen. There were broken pans and plate fragments littered in the corners.

"So, what happened?"

Maka gave him the short version. The capture and the phone call. He said the cops took him back to the river and released him.

"You're not well in the head," said Zlatar. "You're hallucinating, aren't you?"

"Well, believe me or don't. This is the situation. What are we going to do? You still want to go to Serbia?"

Maka told him what the policeman had said about the seven Bosniaks. Even if they made it across the Drina, they could be murdered if the Serbian police or military caught them. And he'd lost his fifty marks. Try buying bus tickets with a bar of gold. Besides, Zlatar needed some sort of a raft. Having seen the river now, Maka understood how fast it was. Who knew how many days it would take for it to settle? If it rained again, it would get even higher.

Zlatar thought it over. He said he believed Serbia was still the best option. "I've got some money, too," he said.

"How much?"

"Enough for a ride."

"How much?"

"Five thousand."

"Holy shit, Zlatar. They'll kill us for that. How much gold?"

"Just some necklaces and rings and such."

"How much gold?"

"About three kilos."

"Three kilos, for heaven's sake. Listen, Zlatar. It won't take a Chetnik to kill us. Any good citizen would murder for that, Serb or Bosniak."

"Well, as long as we don't get caught... Not gonna be cheap to sort out the things we'll need. Transport and clothes, documents and all. Grease the cops at the Hungarian border. Branko can handle all that. But it's going to cost."

It was true. They needed money. And that was a hell of a lot of money.

"It's more than enough," Zlatar said.

"How much is the gold worth?"

"Was about hundred and twelve thousand marks when the war started, or seventy thousand American dollars. Don't know how much it is now. But imagine we get a bath and a shave, new sets of clothes. Hell, we'll dress up like dandies. Where you wanna eat? Let's go to Tri Šešira in Belgrade and have *pljeskavica* and *sremski* cheese, and smoked beef and beers. French cognac for dessert. We'll go to Skadarlija. Dinner at Dva Jelena. Boy, is that something." He sat there with his eyes closed, imagining the food and his new life in Serbia.

Remembering the can of beef, Maka dug into his bag.

"Let me have your knife."

Zlatar straightened up, his eyes widening. "Where'd you get that? That for real?"

"No, I'm just hallucinating. Hand me that knife."

Maka opened the can with the battle knife, then took the bread and cut it into slices. He laid the pieces on top of the rucksack, then cut chunks of the canned meat and put them on the bread. He wiped the blade against the bread and gave the knife back to Zlatar.

"Podravka. Good old Croatian." Zlatar was holding the empty can and studying the label. "Haven't seen this for years."

"Commerce still works," Maka said.

"It's the only thing that works."

They ate slowly, savouring the taste. The water bottle stood on the floor between them, clear and moist. There was a small window in the back of the kitchen. Right outside was an overgrown willow. It moved gently in the breeze and blocked the view, with some branches growing into the kitchen. Next to them was a bathroom with a broken toilet seat in the middle of a green tile floor. They could hear the stream outside. The day was already hot, but it felt cool in the building. Maka got the cigarettes out.

"Good God, you're loaded!" Zlatar exclaimed.

"You have a bag full of gold."

"Right. How much for one? A kilo?"

"Oh, shut up," said Maka.

They lit their cigarettes with the same match, then sat there, on the floor in a ruined kitchen, leaning back and smoking. Neither said anything.

"Boy, this is good," Zlatar broke the silence.

"We've three matches left," Maka said.

"When we get to Serbia, let's look for a lighter. People often throw them away when there's still gas. Hell, we can buy one."

"That's the thing. First, we need to get across."

Maka scanned around the room. It was all trashed. The cupboard doors had been ripped off and the shelves were empty. The toilet door was gone. Maybe they could have used a door as a raft. But everything in the building had been ransacked. Only a wrecked chest freezer stood under the concrete stairs to the second floor, with shrapnel holes across its side.

Maka looked at the freezer.

"Say, is that our ferry boat?"

Zlatar glanced at it. "Too heavy to carry," he said. "We're a kilometre from the river. And look at those holes."

Maka thought about something. He had seen a chest freezer like that float in a river, in news footage years back, when there were bad floods in Croatia. The thing had sailed past the camera, filled with water, yet floating.

"Listen," he said. "We won't use it like a dinghy. We'll take just the lid. Those things float. There's something inside of them makes them buoyant."

They went over and looked at the freezer. The lid was the size of a large coffee table. Zlatar opened it. There was a musty smell and nothing inside. They tried to take the top off, but it was bolted into the shell. Maka tried the rivets with the knife. They would not break. The hinges were strong, too.

Zlatar pushed a finger into one of the shrapnel holes. "There's some sort of insulation. Feels like Styrofoam."

Maka started enlarging the holes, cutting the aluminium skin with the knife. It was a rugged build. "Let me try with this," said Zlatar. He had gone to look for something and came back with a rusty garden mattock. He started chopping the freezer, peeling the metal sheet open from the side.

Maka went into the kitchen window to keep watch. He could see the empty road through the willow. It was sunny outside. Behind him, Zlatar was working on the freezer, sweating and hacking and cursing. Finally the goldsmith pulled free a large slab of white Styrofoam and held it out, inspecting it and wiping his forehead. The mud on his face had started to wash away.

"Could be our raft all right," he said.

"So we're going to Serbia?"

Zlatar looked at the Styrofoam, turning it over and measuring its thickness. He rapped it with his fingers. It made a solid sound.

"Should be good for two hundred metres."

"Remember that guy Papillon?" Maka said. "The one that escaped that island on a sack of coconuts."

"That's some reassurance. Hell, I remember reading that."

He set the Styrofoam aside and sat down.

"I was a kid when I read it. Thought it's sickening what people have to go through. But I remember thinking, that's fifty years ago."

"I know," said Maka.

"I don't often understand this world."

"I know. Who would?"

"Well, how you wanna go about it?"

"Let's wait until the sun goes down."

They walked to the Drina in the dark. The night had turned cold and misty and the moon was partly clouded. The road was empty. They skulked slowly through the valley, ready to run off into the forest any second. Zlatar had wrapped the brightly white Styrofoam in his army jacket. They could hear the stream alongside the road, flowing to meet the river. On the way, they passed other destroyed houses in the mist and came out where the road joined the highway along the Drina. The river was before them, cold and menacing and dauntingly wide.

"The narrow section is that way," Zlatar whispered, gazing up the road that faded away into the fog.

"How far?"

"Two kilometres, or more."

"It's risky," Maka whispered. "It's too near Zvornik. Are you okay to do it here?"

Zlatar looked at the river, shuddering.

"I suppose I am…"

They crossed the highway and slunk between two ruined buildings by the roadside, clambering over rubble in the weeds, then down the bank. Near the water, Maka shoved his weapon into the shrubs until he could not see it. Letting it go, he did not feel anything. It wasn't part of him. But he knew he couldn't shake the war off that simply. Coming down from the house he had felt like hell. He tried to ignore it. It was necessary to stay focused. There was the night, the river, the cold water, and there were the procedures once they reached the other shore. He rolled up the camouflage trousers and hid them, too. It was only then that he understood how worn-out and thin the patched fabric was.

Zlatar wrapped his jacket around his rifle and tossed the weapon into the bush.

"So long, baby. There goes my three years of shit."

"Let's keep your bag," Maka whispered and dropped his backpack. He didn't want to go around in Serbia with anything that had a logo of a Bosnian university on it. He had nothing to carry, anyway. Just the bottle. He drank it empty and screwed the cap back on, then gave it to Zlatar. "Chuck that in, for buoyancy."

Zlatar pulled the pistol from his belt.

"I'll keep this," he whispered. "For the gold."

"What you think you gonna do with it? Whip it out like John Wayne?"

"Never know."

"I say it's dumb to take it."

"Let's hide it on the other side, then. At least we got a gun stashed."

"All right. But ditch the knife."

They stripped to their underwear and stuffed their clothes into the musette bag. Maka stacked the four boots on the Styrofoam slab and laid the musette on top so that the shoulder strap passed under the slab. He shortened the strap until it held the bundle together firmly.

It was a cold night. The river looked silvery in the partial moonlight, with fine mist over the water. They stood on the wet rocks by the water, shivering.

"Drina is a cold river," Zlatar whispered.

"Just hold on to the raft and use your legs," Maka said.

"It's always so cold. Now it's cold and high."

"Just don't let go of it," Maka said. "I'll swim next to you."

"You know… to survive for three years…"

"It's going to be fine."

"Hope so. If not… please tell my wife that I tried."

"What the hell," Maka said, looking at his friend. "It's nothing, I tell you. We'll have coffee in Serbia. Let's go?"

They stepped into the water and it was freezing. It got deep very steeply and they launched into it, Zlatar pushing the raft in front.

The water was very cold and black in the night. First, they swam lightly. After a few dozen metres the current started getting stronger and Maka felt it start swirling his legs. It was taking the men downstream where the river curved and threatened to push them back to the shore. They began to swim diagonally against it. Maka saw his friend kick the water. Zlatar was struggling to keep his chin on the raft, gurgling and spitting water. Gripping the Styrofoam, his hands looked almost just as white. There were leafy tree branches floating along and the current was swift and icy and they kept swimming against it. Maka could see the opposite shore, but it was nearing painfully slowly. When in mid-river, he heard a distant droning in the night. It sounded like a two-stroke engine and it was coming closer.

"We need to go faster," he said, swimming. Zlatar was kicking frantically, spitting water and gagging.

They got past the midway. The sound of the engine was growing. Maka tried to push Zlatar with one hand. "You've got to swim faster," he said. They swam, and the bank was coming nearer, the bushes and the hills rising dark against the night sky.

They were about twenty metres from the shore. They heard the engine loud now. It was definitely a boat. "I can't make it," Zlatar croaked. "Can't feel my hands. Can't hold on." His arms were shaking, fists clutching the sides of the raft. He was becoming hypothermic, and his kicks were losing power.

"Ten metres. Come on. You can do it. Grab me." Maka pulled his friend's arm around his neck and caught the raft. He started thrashing with his feet, kicking as fast as he could.

He felt his toes touch the bottom. The engine was coming closer. They waded through the water, Maka holding Zlatar up and dragging the raft, and they scrambled out of the river and over rocks, stumbling through the reeds at the shore. Down the river, a searchlight beam swept the water and the riverbank. It was a Serbian border patrol and it was coming up fast. They got to the vegetation. It was all thick, tangled, razor wire–like thorn vine, but they dived into it and seconds later the searchlight made a pass over them.

They lay motionless inside the vines on the stony ground. Holy heaven, Maka thought. Holy, sweet heaven. His wet skin was so cold he could not feel the thorns. He was sick in the chest and his whole body was shaking. Next to him, Zlatar shivered and breathed heavily. Maka felt his cold, wet legs against his. *Oh sweet, holy heaven.* The light swept the foliage again, sending shadows through the vines, then the vessel went chugging past them. Maka heard its wake wash into the rocks.

They stayed still until the sound had receded up the river. It was freezing cold. When they got up and started penetrating into the thick cover of the bush, boots and the musette in hand, Maka was all numb and shivering. Up the bank, they found a small clearing and started dressing. The clothes had stayed almost dry. The boots, in contrast, were soaked, but it was torture walking on the thorn-vines and Maka was glad to put them on.

The mud was gone from the goldsmith's face. He sat there, hugging himself and shuddering. Maka could hear his teeth clatter. There was plastic drift garbage clinging onto the tall bushes around.

"My God, I'm cold," Zlatar whispered. "I'll never go near water again."

"We better stay here until morning."

"God, I'm freezing."

Maka felt something warm trickle down his spine. He had dived into the bushes back-first. He guessed the thorns had cut him well. He hugged Zlatar, rubbing his arms.

"Think of that coffee. We'll get breakfast someplace."

"God, I'm cold. Can't we start walking?"

"People don't walk at night. And no ruins on this side. But think of that. Hot coffee, no fighting."

"Shit, why did I leave the jacket?" Zlatar's teeth were chattering. "You think the cigs are dry? Let's have a smoke. Fuck that river."

"Now you're talking."

They sat in the cover of the bushes, smoking. It must have been only midnight. Anyway, it was a midnight in Serbia.

FIFTEEN

A T DAWN THERE was mist over the river, and the river moved coldly and broadly in the new morning. The dark, spiny bushes that concealed the two men were heavy with dew and the wet, brittle shreds of plastic bags. They lay side by side, in cold torpor that had never rendered Maka fully unaware of his discomfort.

Sitting up, shivering, he saw the Bosnian hills on the other side, mist clouding their flanks and the sky grey and soggy. His clothes were clammy and when he bent forward to rub his shins he felt the stinging on his back. Next to him, Zlatar was stretched out and breathing deeply, as if sleeping. When Maka sat up, his friend also moved.

"What's the time?" Zlatar whispered. His voice was hoarse from the cold.

"The sun must be up soon."

"Hell, what a night," he said, rolling to his side. "Three and a half years... and coming back like *this*."

Maka strained his neck to see over the bushes towards the higher ground. The road was there, behind the vegetation. He had observed it from the top of the cliffs the other day. He could not see it now, but all was quiet.

"It'll get sunny. Where will we go from here?" He wanted to get out of the riverbank before people started going about their business but realised they had not discussed any details.

"Branko's house is in Šulovača," Zlatar said, rubbing his cheeks. He had a short, dark beard and the swim had not taken away the ingrained dirt from the creases around his eyes. His face was tired. It had been fifteen days since the Chetniks had attacked Srebrenica.

"How do we get there?"

"I guess we must walk. It's thirty or forty kilometres, though."

"How do you know if he still lives there? The war has changed things here, too."

"Let's go there and see. If he's not there, we can ask around. We'll do it discreetly. Be his old classmates or something. I am, actually. We'll figure it out. Let's go to Mali Zvornik first, catch a bus from there."

"We better avoid that area now," Maka said. They were both tidying up, combing their hair back with fingers and brushing bits of dead leaves off their clothes. A lone car passed up the road. Through the vegetation, they could see the white of its body zip by.

"Then let's go up the road, cut inland before Mali Zvornik."

"You mean, into the hills?"

"No, no more woods," Zlatar said. "Tired of the woods. And if we're seen walking some headlands it'll look bloody suspicious. We can take the roads, the smaller ones." He was inspecting the pistol, cleaning it with the hem of his shirt. "There's a Muslim village nearby. I've still got my Yugoslav identity card. I guess if we get stopped, a Bosniak name shouldn't be anything unusual here."

"How about me?"

"Say you left it home. I'll vouch for you. Would you not trust a chap like this?" He made a silly face, and Maka remembered why he'd survived three years side by side with this man. Being careless was stupid. In war, too much levity was bound to kill you, but you needed some to detach yourself from the fact that every day was like a roll of the dice with your life.

They worked up a plan: they were two local men, on their way to help with someone's vegetable garden. The punctured tyre scenario that Maka had employed in Zvornik had ended in a disaster, but there were always orchards and fields, one after another. Should someone stop them, they would not, of course, be working on these, but always on the ones a bit further. They had not managed to get a ride and, as buses did not drive on the small back roads, it was only normal for them to walk. It was early in the morning. The pale greyness of the sky was already subsiding: the day was set to be sunny and hot.

"You shouldn't bring the musette," said Maka. It looked military. Zlatar could just carry his hoard in the plastic bag. A hundred thousand marks in a worn-out shopping bag. Somehow, he thought, it made it feel unlikely that someone should bother you.

"I guess it makes sense. How about the gun?"

"No. Aren't we done with guns?"

"I suppose so…" Zlatar was weighing the pistol in his hand. "It's a good gun, though. Maybe I'll come for it when the war's over."

"You won't need it when it's over."

"Well, with neighbours like ours…"

He took the plastic bag with the money and the gold out, then went to hide the musette, with the pistol inside, under the vines. He did it on the higher ground of the clearing, so that if the river flooded the water might not take the bag or damage the gun. Maka saw him place a large, flat rock on top of the musette. No one could find it by chance. They'd have to know what to look for.

"Let's go get that coffee," Maka said, holding the soda bottle. He had gone to the water, but the river was murky. Come to think of it, he now had nothing left of his life. Nothing but the boots and this bottle. Well, he thought, he'd refill it in that village…

They sneaked up the bank through the vegetation. After making sure there was no traffic, they stepped out and started walking along the road.

The scenery looked almost identical to the Bosnian side. The asphalt road skirted the shore at the foot of the hills, going now and then over little streams that ran into the Drina. But here, the land was not steep, and soon they saw farmhouses with small fields between the elevations in the grey daylight. Thin smoke came from some of the chimneys. Behind the houses the green hilltops were lighting up with the rising sun.

"People are making breakfast," Zlatar noted. They strolled on the shoulder of the road, with the wide yellowish-green of the Drina to their left. The houses looked peaceful and quaint in the mist that now was thinning rapidly. The walk was warming Maka up and there was a smell of smoke. In his mind he saw how a family was sitting around a kitchen table, spreading jam on thick chunks of home-baked bread; the bubbling of a pot of coffee on the stove, them all wearing clean clothes that smelled of softener, with the man reading yesterday's paper, wondering if the war across the river would one day come and give him trouble in any form.

"You reckon someone would give us food over there?"

"Better not push your luck!" Zlatar said. "Let's find a restaurant."

"I wonder if those operate."

"The commerce, Maka. Remember?"

"Any store in that Muslim village, then?"

"Don't know," Zlatar said. "Don't remember ever being there."

"I bet no one's living there anymore. They destroyed all of ours. Why would they leave any standing here?"

"They're not the same, I tell you…"

Somehow Maka wanted to believe so, too. It was nice to think that the war's lunacy hadn't spread across the border and that the Serbs on this side were different. Still, it was difficult, after all that had passed. Now that they were out in the open again, this gnawing doubt had started to build up inside him. He'd managed well in the forests. Every time he'd left the woods, things had gone downhill. And they now had plenty of roadsides to trample on. Forty kilometres to Šulovača, and what if this Branko had moved out, or died, or changed in the heart?

He wasn't worried about Zlatar. Zlatar could walk. They were both weak, but they could walk and maybe they could find a bus. A bus was better. Certainly, more people to stare at them, but two tramps riding a taxi would be worse. He didn't know anything about this Branko. But he trusted Zlatar and, if Zlatar trusted the man, that was all he needed to know. Not much else he could do about it. Things only got complicated when you had too many choices and began to doubt one or the other and started to compare the options, without really understanding them. The hardest part, he thought, was knowing how close they were to making it. How close he was to Amelia and Dino, to shedding the remains of this senseless war. He shouldn't think of the possibility of capture, nor of what he knew would happen if they were handed over to the Chetniks. It didn't help a bit. They were two local men, simple as that. They didn't mean harm to anyone. With Zlatar's money, they wouldn't even have to steal. But it was finding this Branko that was the main thing, and avoiding the authorities or anyone who might get suspicious about two skinny, bedraggled bums tramping away under the hot sun.

God, when they got to his house, he would call Amelia. She'd pick up the phone, and he would say, *Honey, it's me.* Nothing more. Just, *It's me. I'm back.*

He knew it wasn't that simple. But, by God, the first thing he'd do was call her. Maka wanted to hear her voice. He wanted to hear the boy. The kid was soon three. He wanted to hear himself say,

Hello, it's your daddy here. How have you been? I've missed you. I've missed you so, and I'll be with you soon. But he knew it wasn't all that simple.

It was getting warm already. The mist over the river was gone and the country was clear, too. There were small butterflies in the roadside hay. The weeds were moist from dew. They were passing many fields and orchards now. In some of the fields, Maka could see solitary people, bent over and working the vegetable beds. The farmers did not seem to pay any attention to them. A lone tortoiseshell cat jogged by on the other side of the road, equally uninterested in the two men. A small truck drove up and barrelled past them, making the weeds by the shoulder sway. It was carrying lumber on its open bed, and it went up the road without raising any dust.

Far ahead was the large loop of the river where it curved around the Divič point. They had passed some small farm trails, but no proper road going inland. So they kept on along the river and there were more fields. Here, it seemed no one was out yet. The valley was wide and bright in the sun, and they were going towards the village Zlatar said was majority Muslim.

They saw the first houses near the road. In the distance, more buildings studded the face of the valley.

"No minaret?" Maka said. "Have they blown up the mosque?"

"I don't think they ever had one…" Zlatar said.

They walked on. Maka tried to spot some signs of habitation. He couldn't see any farm animals. There seemed to be no cars parked between the houses and no smoke from the chimneys.

"Look, there's a restaurant."

On their right was a two-storey house with a sign announcing a *ćevapnica*. There was no patio. The door was closed and the windows were blocked with curtains. It looked as if it was out of business, or perhaps it was just too early. They walked past it and by the roadside there was a little three-sided, green-painted wooden shack.

"Is that a guard post?" asked Maka.

"Nonsense. There's never been military around here." Zlatar's voice was tense and he was looking nervously at the buildings ahead.

"That was before the war, don't you reckon?"

"Why would they have them now?"

They went past the open-sided shack. Inside was a wooden chair and it looked an awful lot like a guard booth for a daytime checkpoint.

"For men like us, I suppose." They were walking into the village, but Maka didn't want to have anything to do with this hamlet. He liked the woods. The woods were good.

"What should we do?" Zlatar asked. They were pacing on, automatically, trying to look casual. Maka could feel the familiar hollow tingling in the pit of his stomach again.

"I don't like this a damn bit. Turn back?"

"That'd be conspicuous as hell. Suppose someone's already seen us? Those people in the fields."

Just then, someone yelled: "The two of you! Stop!"

That someone was running after them. It was a soldier in an olive-drab uniform, holding an assault rifle. He had exited from the restaurant building; he must have seen Maka and Zlatar pass by. He was a young man with a smooth face that did not need shaving, and his uniform looked clean and oversize, like that of a conscript.

"Good morning," Maka greeted, cursing in his mind.

"Good morning!" said Zlatar.

"Yeah," replied the soldier. "What is your business?"

"Oh, just to help with the harvest…"

The soldier looked at them, puzzled. He had a palatal, southern Montenegrin way of speaking. He must have been no older than eighteen.

"Where is that?"

"Just beyond the town," Maka said. His throat felt tight.

"Don't you know this road is closed?"

"Closed?"

"Where are you coming from?"

"Down near Amajić," Zlatar said. "Why, what's the matter?"

"Let me see your IDs."

"Pardon me, I forgot mine…" It was as if Maka had seen this scene before. Not so much in real life as in some living nightmare. "I've got it," said Zlatar, amicably, digging into his jeans pocket. "How you doing today, mister?"

The young conscript didn't answer. He was holding the rifle by the grip and with the other hand took the card. The paper was yellowed, inside a yellowed plastic pocket. He turned it in his fingers and studied it. Then his eyes widened in shock and he threw the card down as if it were on fire.

"You're from Srebrenica!"

Hell, no! That damn card had the address on it. Maka had completely forgotten! The soldier staggered a step back, levelled his *ciganka* and snapped down the fire selector, eyes blazing with fear. "Don't shoot man," Maka shouted, "don't shoot!" He and Zlatar both stuck their hands up, the empty bottle and the plastic bag high in the air.

"What you have? Throw those away!" the soldier yelled, looking like he had shrunk a size more inside his uniform. Zlatar tossed the bag onto the roadside. It landed in the weeds with a thud, and Maka's bottle bounced down the asphalt.

The soldier stared at them. He glanced over his shoulder towards the restaurant house. He stared at them again, the gun pointed at them.

"Just take it easy," Maka told him. His head began to work. Every word and gesture would count now. Now look at this conscript. Just as scared as himself. He'd never felt so ill. It was history repeating itself and, by God, he did not want to die. No one needed to die. He was sick of dying.

"Petko! Petko!" the soldier yelled towards the building.

The door was wide open and another conscript, young and

tall, came out, looking at them.

"Go get the sarge! I caught two *Balija*!" the smooth-faced one shouted. Holding Maka and Zlatar at gunpoint, he stepped aside and pointed towards the building with his chin.

Inside, it looked more like a deserted bar than a *ćevapi* restaurant. Maka stood in the entry, keeping his hands up. The counter, the tables by the walls and the wall panels were dark wood, giving the place the air of a saloon. The shelves behind the counter were empty. No cash register. Years of tobacco smoke had left its odour in the room. Yellowed lace curtains were drawn over the windows, with daylight filtering through warmly, and in the dim back of the hall was the tall soldier called Petko and two other young men. One of them was also armed with a standard *ciganka* rifle, while the third, a scrawny punk in a sleeveless white shirt, hung a submachine gun over his groin. They all stared at Maka and Zlatar.

"I caught these outside," the first conscript boasted. "Where's the sarge?"

He drove the Bosniaks behind a table in a corner, keeping the rifle pointed at them, now with more excitement than fear. Maka backed up and sat on the worn-out pinewood bench lining the wall. So, this was it? It was cool inside the building. He felt the sweat come on his temples. This was it. There would be no miracles this time.

They watched a man descend from upstairs, drowsy and taking the stairs bow-legged, tightening his belt and tugging up his uniform trousers. This one was rotund and looked a couple of years older than Maka. His head was round and shaved bald and he had small, sleepy eyes that examined the two men doubtfully.

"What's this?" he said.

"*Balija*, from Srebrenica," the first soldier declared. "It was I caught them!"

The sergeant looked at them, loosened his belt, then found a comfortable length under his potbelly and fixed it, all the while looking at the Bosniaks with squinted eyes.

"Have papers?"

"I do," Zlatar said.

"Well?"

Zlatar nodded at the first soldier. "I gave it to him. He threw it away."

The sergeant looked at the conscript.

"Why'd you do that?"

The soldier shrugged his shoulders.

"What else you have? No packs?"

"I had," Zlatar said. "Your man told me to throw that away, too."

The sergeant again looked at the conscript. The young soldier stood there, uneasy.

"I thought maybe it was a bomb," he said.

Maka heard the punk with the submachine gun sneer in the back of the room. This was possibly the most amusing affair since they were posted in this hamlet. He figured they were border guards.

"Why would I have a bomb?" said Zlatar.

"Shut up. What was in it?"

"Gold. I'm a goldsmith."

Goddam, Zlatar, Maka thought. Did he just say that without thinking? The sergeant looked as if someone had slapped him in the face. The somnolence all gone, his small eyes got wide and he told the young one, "Go get that thing, for fuck's sake!"

In a minute the soldier rushed back, carrying the plastic bag and Zlatar's ID card. The sergeant went straight for the bag. He emptied it on a table: a bundle of gold chains and bracelets slumped out, with gem-studded rings rolling and spiralling on the coffee-stained wood. A thick wad of banknotes, fixed with a rubber band, lay on top of the glittering heap.

"Wow," said the sergeant.

He ran his fingers through the jewellery, staring at it.

"Wow."

The man picked up the money roll. He snapped off the elastic and started counting the bills. Everyone in the room stayed silent, watching him count. Maka could feel the fear inside him grow with every little slip of a banknote. They'd kill for that amount. That was a fortune to make anybody rich. They'd steal it. They would not leave witnesses.

"Well, I'll be damned," said the sergeant at last. "Four thousand five hundred ninety." Then, coldly: "Where'd you get all this? You looted this from the Serbs? How many did you kill for this?" His voice had turned low and menacing.

"I've never killed a soul," Zlatar said. "I'm a goldsmith. Fourth generation."

"You're a goddam liar."

"No, sir, listen. That's what I had left of my business in Srebrenica. What should I have done? I can prove it. Are you from around here? You know Columba, the jewellery store in Zvornik?"

"Well, that shop's but a memory, I can tell you," the man said. In the corner the punk with the submachine gun snickered again.

"I'm sure… but that was my family's shop, too."

The sergeant kept staring at the gold and the money, his mind working. Maka knew he was thinking of it now. The thug was making his calculations. Then, straightening up and the coldness gone, he asked, "Are you boys hungry?"

"Yes, we are, sir," Maka and Zlatar both said.

"We only have pork. Are you okay with that?"

"Yes, sir, we are."

Maka's first thought was that the bald Serb was mocking them. But the sergeant ordered one of the men to fetch the food. It was a can of liver pâté and a loaf of bread, which, ironically, as he remembered, was what he'd dreamed of when he first walked out from those hills. Maka did not remember if he'd ever eaten pork, though. He wasn't a practising Muslim. It was merely for culture. He had his God, perhaps, but it was a God who did not give a damn whether you prayed for him or not, whether you observed the Ramadan or not. The sort of God who didn't care if you ate pig – or if a pig ate you, for that matter. His home, his family, his life had been destroyed. Did anyone give a damn? And, well… was he going to die? He might as well do so with a full belly.

They sat in the corner and ate. The young soldiers kept guard with their weapons ready, staring at them as if they were some wild animals. The sergeant questioned them. Were they in the army? How did they get here? Where did they cross the river at? That sort of stuff. His questions were all rather meaningless and it was done unprofessionally, without first separating the two. They answered truthfully, trying to sound inconsequential. There was no need to hide any facts. The sergeant did not ask anything about the massacres. Maybe he wasn't aware. It was hard to believe so. How could you not know, Maka thought, if across your border thousands were being slaughtered? Anyhow he did not touch on the subject. Maybe the man was trying to make them feel at ease.

"Did you have anything else with you?" He had some form in front of him and he was writing these things down.

The goldsmith said he'd left his musette on the riverbank.

What the hell, Zlatar? Being open and being offered food had made him lower his guard. But that damned pistol was in that bag. Yes, the pistol. A pistol that would make them an armed enemy, with intentions to kill. Already there was the gold and the money. But it was too late. The sergeant asked Zlatar to describe the location, then ordered Petko the tall conscript to go after it.

Zlatar glanced at Maka. Yes, Maka thought. Now you remember. All valid reasons to kill a man. And the dead never came back to claim a thing.

If he could wrench the submachine gun from that simpering little brat, he could clear the room in three seconds. Then what?

They were in Serbia. If they killed anyone, they'd be hunted down like beasts. Besides, they'd been given food. Why feed a dying man? Maybe it was better to talk. Maka was tired of killing, tired of dying. Surely, it was better to talk. Something common. Like men to men, he thought. No politics. No religion. Nothing about the war. Then what was left? Talk of what?

No, there was plenty left.

Like what?

Like football. Like ćevapis and those southern wines. The girls. The trout in the rivers. All that was still left, and more. But now there was the damned pistol.

The sergeant had gone to the room in the back. They heard him speaking on the phone. Then it seemed the talking was done. They sat in the corner, quiet and waiting, while the young conscripts stood guard. Maka kept thinking of the gun. He was sweating and thinking of it. The goddam pistol.

After an hour, Petko the conscript returned.

"Found it." The tall young man displayed the musette. He was in good spirits, though sweating, his grey military shirt wet at the armpits. It was still early, but the day was going to be brutally hot.

The sergeant took the bag and opened it. "Nothing in here?"

The conscript said nothing.

But of course, Maka thought. It was a new model Zastava gun, worth a thousand deutsche marks at the black market. *Good on you, Petko. Have fun with it. A gift from Bosnia.*

The sergeant looked at Zlatar.

"I didn't say I had anything," Zlatar said. The sweaty conscript stood silent in the back, a knowing glint in the corner of his eye. "But you see, we're not lying. That's where we crossed the river."

Seeming satisfied with this answer, the sergeant made them sign the paper he had been filling out. His report, or maybe their confession. They were not given a chance to read it. Maka did not care about reading it. He'd sign anything. The more forms, the better. Evidence that they'd been here, alive. Then again, what was a piece of paper when hundreds, probably thousands, had been murdered? Still, he supposed, any trace of their existence might make their disappearance less likely.

They were taken to the basement. They stood in the corner of the bare concrete hollow, in half-dark, with the scrawny youngster sitting guard up on the stairs. He was pointing his submachine gun at them. Their hands were free, the Serbs had not bothered tying their wrists. The door behind the conscript stayed open. They could hear the others talk, up in the bar. There was an empty storage rack by the wall. Clearly the restaurant was not in operation. The Serbs had relocated, probably forcefully, the whole village. Nothing had been burned. But they'd relocated the Muslims.

By the stairs, in a corner next to the soldier, stood a rusty shovel against the wall. Maka could see it in the light from the open door. He sensed that Zlatar had noticed it, too.

The conscript looked at them.

"You know what I saw two days ago?"

They kept quiet. They knew they were supposed to.

"Saw two of you *Balija* get burned alive."

They said nothing.

"Don't ya wanna know how?" He was making a point of pointing the gun at them. He seemed barely twenty and had a skinny, acned face and spiteful eyes. In his white tank top and baggy army trousers he looked like one hell of a brat for a soldier.

"How?" said Zlatar.

"See Vidikovac there?" He meant the hotel on the lookout across the Drina. "They set 'em on fire and dumped 'em in the river. Doused 'em with gasoline and whoooshh! Like living torches. Kicked 'em over the cliff. I saw it."

Maka and Zlatar said nothing. They were both thinking of the shovel in the corner.

"Man, they screamed like dogs. All the way down. I could hear 'em so loud across. Terrible, unbelievable screaming." The brat had a nasty, excited gleam in his eyes as he said this. Maybe he's faking it, Maka thought. *Trying to scare us. Oh, that little punk. With his shiny new German gun.* Maka knew how to shoot that weapon. One of their snipers had carried one. The police had been issued those just before the war broke out. Thirty rounds in the clip, 9 mm. Fire selector on both sides. He saw the young man had it on full auto. The spade stood in the far corner, next to the soldier. There was no way to reach it. Then he remembered what he'd just thought about talking. How to talk to a punk like this? He hoped Zlatar wouldn't try anything. It was better to let everything come. If they managed to stay on this side of the river, they might make it. If these Serbs handed them back across, it would be curtains. They had no way of knowing. But if they went for that brat's gun, they'd die all the same.

They stood in the half-dark, waiting.

SIXTEEN

I~T WAS TWO~ in the afternoon when the policeman came. He was
alone, and he handcuffed Zlatar's and Maka's wrists behind
their backs and loaded them in the back seat of the patrol car. He
was fat and poorly shaved and moved with careful difficulty, as
if his trousers were about to burst at the seams. After squeezing
himself in and sitting down behind the wheel, breathing heavily,
he turned sideways looking back over the seat and grinned, sweat
glistening on his temples.

"I hear you had money and gold. How much?"

Zlatar told him.

"Fuck! Why wasn't it me caught you!" The cop made it sound
like a joke, but Maka sensed something more in it. Had it been
this gentleman arrest them, who knows if they might've ended
up in the Drina, with a bullet in their neck… He started the car
and grunted, as if to himself, "Always out of luck. No luck in this
damn country."

They rode along the wide curve of the river, seeing the Divič
peninsula. Behind it was the line of the power dam. They left the
little village behind and were going towards Mali Zvornik, which

was beyond the point where the dam joined the hillside. The river was swollen and brownish yellow, with the sunlight glimmering on the water and between the bulrushes near the shore. The cop had his window down and the fan blowing at maximum. They could smell the river and the dead reeds. The road and the country ahead shimmered in the heat.

In Mali Zvornik they sat in the police station. They had been left by themselves, on a bench, leaning awkwardly forward with hands cuffed behind their backs, in what looked like a break room. The room, with its worn-out vinyl tile flooring and a cigarette-burned plastic table, was on the first floor. The window next to them was ajar. There was nothing they could do about it. Like petty criminals, Maka thought. Sitting there, knowing the game was played, waiting for the penalty, and here it was death for any crime. The room was getting hot, with a little dusty smell of the afternoon and exhaust gas. Outside they saw the parking lot and other houses and the main street behind. It was a small station in a small town, with perhaps a dozen personnel. The door was open to a corridor. People would pass by, glancing in with subdued curiosity. The heat had made everyone languid.

An officer walked into the room, a tea mug in his hand. He went over to the cupboard where there was an electric kettle and a box of teabags, noticed the two men that occupied the bench by the wall and froze. He stood there, the mug in his hand. He looked at Zlatar.

"What are *you* doing here?"

Zlatar pointed out the window with his chin.

"Got arrested. For crossing over."

"Srebrenica?"

"Yeah."

"*Jebemu pičku...*" the cop started, his face visibly upset. He set the mug on the table and looked at them. He was a tawny man with an athletic bearing, about the same age as they were. He looked very irked.

"Anyone get hurt? Did you have weapons?"

"No," said Zlatar. "Of course not."

The cop was contemplating something. There were people walking in the corridor. He turned and started making himself a cup of tea.

"Is it possible to see Branko?" Zlatar asked.

"No, not now."

"Can you let him know I'm here?"

The officer was stirring his tea, thinking. Looking vexed and without saying anything, he walked out of the room.

"What was that?" Maka whispered.

"My old schoolmate."

"A good one?"

"Sort of."

"Suppose he'll get Branko?"

"I don't know. Five or six years since I've seen him."

Five or six years. People change, Maka thought. They changed in normal times. They changed when you didn't see them. But war changed them in strange ways and much faster. The weak it changed in days or months, and everyone else along the way. Maka hoped this was one of the strong ones, though. Maybe he would talk to his boss. Maybe he'd get a word out to Branko.

After a quarter of an hour, the man returned. He was with the fat, sweaty colleague and had two plates of *burek*. He set them on the table, uncuffed the two Bosniaks, then reattached the handcuffs in their front. The fat one filled two glasses from a tap.

"See, I give you drink. I get nothing. The draftees get everything."

"Cut it out," the other one said.

Yes, Maka said to himself, the gold stayed with that border unit. Confiscated by the military. That sergeant would concoct some excuse. There'd be a hell of a wrangle, for sure. Maybe they'd claim there never was any gold, nor money. It was up to that sarge to split the booty. They stole Zlatar's fortune, all right.

It didn't matter. What did was what these cops were up to: what their orders were, where they received them from. Maybe they could call some of the shots themselves? Maka knew he and Zlatar needed to stay on this side of the river at any cost. The fat cop made another coarse joke, but he did not hear him. He was eating the *burek*, his mind working. This was his first warm meal for two weeks, not counting the fish by the river. That was a good sign. Or maybe it didn't mean a thing. Zlatar sat next to him, eating. The cop that had brought the food had left again. It seemed he didn't want to speak with Zlatar. Suppose, Maka thought, he already knows we'll be executed?

Two other policemen walked in. They were both old corporals and they both looked hostile. Staring coldheartedly, one said to Maka, "You first."

They took him to a room on the second floor. It was a worn-out bureau, impregnated by thousands of hours of cigarette smoke. The lieutenant, a tall, tired-looking man in about his late forties, sat behind a desk. He looked at Maka dryly. There was another desk where an expressionless woman clerk was waiting behind a typewriter. The two corporals had Maka sit on a chair facing the lieutenant, then left the room.

"So your name is Maka Delić?" the officer started. "Where and when were you born?"

Maka told him. The typewriter began clacking.

"Any family? Kids?"

Maka told him.

"You were in the army. Which unit? What was your position? Tell me everything from the day the war started until today."

He told him. He spoke for a long while, with the lieutenant frequently interrupting with additional questions. The cop wanted to know the dates and places of the operations. This was likely to back the Serb claims that the Bosniaks were but a bunch of terrorists, busy annihilating the Serb population around the enclave. It made no difference to Maka. Dates he did not know, places he was not sure of. He imparted to the cop whatever he could remember, recounting the events as they had unfolded: a dishevelled platoon, underfed and often sharing the rifles, fighting with no greater ideology than to defend their homes and to survive. In the end, it was a very straightforward philosophy.

The officer asked him about Naser Orić, the Bosnian commander in Srebrenica. Did Maka know him? Was he related in any way? But Maka had never even spoken to the man. There was a pecking order and he'd been just a regular trooper. As far as he knew, the top command had fled Srebrenica before the enclave fell. Was Maka religious? No, not particularly, if he meant going to a mosque and all that. How about his friend? He wasn't sure. It was better to ask him directly. The questioning went on like this for a good hour, and finally Maka detailed how he made it across the hills and swam the Drina with Zlatar. He did not say anything about his arrest in Zvornik. The officer listened pensively, taking notes.

Maka wasn't sure what he'd expected, maybe a beating, a lot of screaming, yelling and pain, but there hadn't been any of that. It was all very civil, even making it feel grotesque, knowing what was happening elsewhere, that they were nearly within earshot of the firing squads.

"Have you killed anyone?" the cop asked. The woman behind the typewriter paused. Maka could feel her watching him.

"I don't know," he said. "I've been shot at, and I've shot back, like everybody. I don't know if I ever hit anyone."

Just then someone knocked on the door. A young woman came in with a coffee tray. Maka had seen her when they brought him and Zlatar into the building, a sullen Serb girl with plump cheeks, one of the secretaries at the station. When she placed the tray on the desk she glanced at Maka warily. Her face was hot and ruddy.

The coffee was Turkish style in a small copper pot. The cop poured it into two little porcelain cups. He set one in front of Maka.

"I believe you. You did the right thing."

Maka wasn't sure what he meant: answering the questions honestly, not killing anyone or escaping to Serbia. Either way, the interrogation was over. Again, he received a paper for signing. He felt it was better not to start reading it, and really, it still didn't matter. Just another document proving his existence. When he leaned over to sign it, his eyes caught the words "Married. Father of one. No importance."

All this time, he had tried to figure out the officer: what kind of a man was he dealing with, where along the battle lines did the cop stand in this pretty little mess. Now the coffee had made him feel like wanting to smoke, and an idea came to his mind.

He'd finished the pack of Morava by the river. He was glad not to have it. It was Serbian tobacco. This cop might allege he'd taken it from a dead Serb. But maybe Maka could test him by asking for a cigarette. Was he a good guy or not? And maybe you didn't waste fags on a dying man.

The cop gave Maka one, lit one himself, then walked to the open window and sat smoking on the sill. It must have been four in the afternoon. The trees outside stood heavy in the still heat. What bliss it was to sip coffee. Maka held the cup and the cigarette wrists crossed because of the handcuffs. What bliss, and to have a smoke with it, even if it were right before the pit in the woods. But if only he could say something to Amelia and the boy. Nothing compared to that. One or two words before the gun fired. No coffee, no smoke. No meal, no bath. No gold. His feet were sore, the skin had sloughed off from the soles. His whole body was aching, as if the muscles had shrivelled on the bones. In his mind, he saw Edin again. He was sitting under the beech tree, his breathing crackling with blood. He remembered Nermin and Šemso, his other two fallen brothers. He saw the nephew, smiling, on Jovanovića, with his buddies, the sun high and the boys' reflections in a flower shop's window. Women selling vegetables and cured meat in the čaršija and the cars going by. People walking up the through street, smiling. The white walls of the *džamija*, the water in the Križevica cool and glittering in the sun, the town with its terracotta roofs shaded by old plane trees, picturesque and hot in the valley in the afternoon. Himself walking with Amelia, her laughing and her hair brilliant in the sunshine as she looked to him. Oh, she was so beautiful. He was still breathing. No, not only breathing. He was thinking. *I'm still a man.* And if they delivered him back across that river, he would die like a man. And there wasn't any damn thing *they* could do about it.

He took a puff from the cigarette and watched the cop sitting in the window against the brightness of the day.

"Now that you've asked me maybe a hundred questions, can I ask you one?"

The cop gave a short, dry laugh. "I know what you want to ask. You're going to make it. You'll see your son, all right. About your friend, I'm not sure. He had so much gold and money, and we don't know how or where he got it from."

Here we go again.

"Well, that's his property. He's a goldsmith, don't you know?"

The cop put his hand out the window, tapping off the ash and Maka thought, You don't know how to get your hands on it. That's what he meant to say. So, he was going to make it? But he couldn't let them take Zlatar.

"He never hurt anyone," Maka continued. "His family had two jewellery shops. One over there in Zvornik, one in Srebrenica. That's where it's from. What he should have done, left it behind?"

"I'm a policeman," said the cop. "I need to get the facts straight."

"Well, those border guards took it. Because they took it, it's theirs? Okay, it's theirs. I don't think he cares about it. You know, he has a son and a wife, too. How about them? They never wanted to have any part in this. But don't you believe the son has a right to have a father? One weird country, I tell you.

You take something; it's yours. You take everything away from a man – it's nothing. Child's got nothing but his parents, you take them away, and it's nothing. I haven't seen much of other countries," Maka said. "But I'll be damned to hell if this is the way things work."

The cop dropped the cigarette outside. He was smiling his dry, self-conscious smile. The typewriting woman had already left; they were alone in the room. It was hot inside. Maka could feel beads of sweat run down the small of his back. He crushed the cigarette to the bottom of the coffee cup. It made a little hiss as it went out. There was a rage inside of him. No more of the cold hollow, but a growing, burning rage that he knew he could not show. These people were so cocksure and conceited. The looting, destruction, murders, it all got played down so easily by some convenient comment. A policeman. The facts. But they'd killed his family. They'd taken his home. How was one supposed to feel about that? They took the whole enclave and killed everyone, for God's sake. What was one supposed to feel? Maka did not know. There was just a fire inside of him. It had been there for three years. He knew he'd have to suppress it. Now, and for how many years to come?

"You talk like you're hateful," the cop said.

"I'm not. Though, don't you think losing everything you've ever had might make you? But you know, about Šehić. You got the gold. You got the country. Now let a man keep the one thing he has left."

"Well, if he stole any of those valuables in the Republika Srpska, he'll have to answer to the police in Republika Srpska."

There you have it. The man knew the two things, that Zlatar had stolen nothing and what would happen to him if they handed him over. What this cop wanted was to make it a police affair, so he could grab the gold from the border guards. There was nothing Maka could do about it. The officer called the two corporals. They came and took him back to the tearoom.

Zlatar sat where he had been, talking to a man in a checkered dress shirt. The man sat on the bench, leaning with his hands on it, legs straight, listening. When Maka entered the room, they both looked up.

"This here's Branko," Zlatar said.

The man nodded, his face serious.

"Thank you for coming," Maka said. "Sorry for the trouble."

Branko just shook his head. You could read from his face that he knew what was at stake. He looked like a decent man, as Maka had imagined him. Decent and unremarkable in his capacity to possibly save their lives. And what am I saying? Maka thought. Thank you for coming? He wanted to go and embrace this man he'd never even seen before. So, this was Branko. *The* Branko, the one they'd bet their lives on. Thank God he came. Thank God or Lady Fortune or whoever had brought him.

They were just the three of them in the room.

"I drove down as soon as I got the call," Branko said.

"Mladen alerted him," said Zlatar.

"Who's that?"

"The one brought us the *bureks*."

"I've been giving Zlatar the situation," said Branko.

"How is the situation?"

"How can I say…" he started, "We hear terrible things. Many things may have happened that shouldn't have happened."

"What about us?"

"Take a look," said Zlatar. There was a newspaper on the table. Zlatar turned it over to the front page. News in Cyrillic – Serb offensive in Bihać. Situation stable in Sarajevo. Srebrenica liberated. Someone strong in Tour de France; something else. Then, at the bottom, *Eight hundred Bosnians cross the Drina.*

"That's men from Žepa," Zlatar said.

"Almost a thousand of them," said Branko. "They wanted to surrender on this side. I guess they figured they've better chances here. Now that it's in the news, they can't be returned that easy."

"Why not?"

"Just too much uncertainty around this. The things we hear from Srebrenica aren't very pretty. All sorts of rumours coming in. There's a foreign ministers' meeting in London. Saw it on TV just now. They're threatening airstrikes against us. The stuff we hear is not good. Apparently, quite a lot of people have died."

"Yes. They slaughtered everyone."

"The women got away," Zlatar said. "Seems they put them all on buses."

Thank God, Maka thought. That had to mean the Chetniks expelled them to Tuzla. His mother must have made it. If she cleared the shelling and reached Potočari, they must have put her on those cars. But what a horror, he thought. The women had been through hell, and thousands of them had lost husbands or fathers or sons. His old lady didn't know about Edin and Hassan yet. Three of her sons gone now, plus her grandchild.

"What do you think they'll do with those men?" he asked Branko.

"Apparently, they plan to intern them here."

"What's that, intern?"

"Put them in a prison camp," Zlatar said.

"All right. How about us? We're not eight hundred, and we're not in the news."

"They'll send you into that same camp." Branko looked at Maka with his solemn, businesslike face. "I talked to the chief already."

"You mean that jack upstairs? Sounds like he wants to croak Zlatar."

"No, not him. His boss, in Šabac."

"Why would he want to kill me?" Zlatar asked.

"Doesn't want you coming back making any claims."

"I'll tell him they can keep the gold."

"I told him already."

"Thanks, you're one friend," Zlatar said, trying a joke. "But you see, there's no need to kill anyone, is there?" He looked nervously at them. "Imagine a prison here in Serbia. Imagine we'll make it? We'll be all right!"

Branko got up and walked over to the kettle.

"You'll be all right. But I don't know this cop. He's the local police lieutenant. I'll ask Mladen to talk to him. It should be okay. Tea, anyone?"

Just then the two cops with corporal's stripes reappeared at the door. They looked at Zlatar.

"Okay, golden boy. Your turn."

"Go easy on him. Just go easy" said Branko, brandishing a teaspoon at them. "You know, this is a very good man. A *very* good man."

They glanced at Branko disdainfully but didn't say a thing. Zlatar got up and went to the door, then stopped and looked back, looking resigned and forlorn with his handcuffed wrists and his sad smile, and said, "I go now." Then he was gone.

Maka stood at the window, looking outside. Between the opposite houses he saw a section of the Drina, and on the other shore of the river the first buildings of Zvornik and the hills of Bosnia that rose in the hazy afternoon, green and deadly. He knew the Kula Grad fortifications were on top of the tallest peak, but he could not discern them in that harsh sunlight. The heavy clay-tiled roofs across the street looked dilapidated and the houses ramshackle and unkempt. All this in three years. There had been no fighting on this side of the river, but the war had destroyed something here all the same. And there wasn't a thing he could do for Zlatar.

"When did you see him the last time?" Maka was still looking out. Behind him was the sound of Branko doing something with the teacups.

"Four years ago. You understand, people started withdrawing into their corners already when it started in Croatia. I didn't want to, but my parents begged me to move out of Zvornik."

No one wanted, Maka said in his mind, gazing at the river.

"Things went to pot very quickly once the fear settled in," Branko continued. "But you know, this can't last for long. Not like this. Something's got to give in. I don't know how much you know, but this summer has been very tough in Bosnia. There's been heavy combat around Sarajevo for a month, and it continues in Treskavica. They say your troops lost a thousand men there alone, three times more in wounded. Our side hasn't fared any better, it seems. I mean, the Republika Srpska troops. There's fighting in Bihać and Majevica, in Doboj, too. And it's starting in Croatia again."

Yes, something's got to give in. Something's got to break. What's there left to break?

"And these cops are okay with your telling me all this?" Maka asked.

"Absolutely. It's all in the news. But I'm sorry that I can't help you and Zlatar."

"You've already helped us greatly."

The sun made his eyes ache, yet he could not take his gaze off the hills across the river. When had he slept last time? He felt impossibly tired, and suddenly that was all he felt. From the open window came a warm waft of air and with it the hollow, monotonous sound of someone chopping firewood on the slope under the station house. Behind him, the kettle came to a boil, the water's sputtering hiss ascending rapidly.

Things come, things go, he said in his mind. But it will always be my home.

PART TWO

THE GOOD CITIZENS

SEVENTEEN

I T WAS HOT and completely dark inside the van. They knew they had ridden out of the town, but had lost count of the turns and had no way of saying whether they were being taken north or south. It was a windowless police van, and they sat, sweating, in the gasoline-smelling, engine-noise-reverberating darkness, on a low bench, with their hands cuffed to a steel pipe that ran under the seat. In his head Maka was counting minutes.

"Five already?" Zlatar spoke over the noise.

"No, not yet."

"Suppose there's a UN checkpoint on the bridge?"

Maka was concentrating, counting sixty seconds at a time. He was at four minutes. The old steel bridge at Zvornik was the only crossing in this area. They estimated it was no more than five minutes' drive from the police station where they were loaded on. The prison camp talk was perhaps simply a sham to calm them down. They knew that if they were taken across that bridge, back to Bosnia, they would die.

"They'd search the vehicle, wouldn't they?"

What the hell? The UN had let the whole enclave get

massacred, yet Zlatar was pinning his hopes on them?

Maybe it was better than nothing. If the blue helmets stopped the van, they could at least plead for their lives. And get some fresh air. Four minutes, and already it felt as if Maka was running out of oxygen.

"Five now." The sweat was burning his eyes.

"They're not slowing down," Zlatar said. "You think we're past it?"

The car was doing a steady speed and Maka sensed the road was free and straight. He felt the van make headway.

"We must be past it," said Zlatar after a while. "I swear we're past it."

Maka knew it, too. He was at his eighth minute. They were not going for the bridge. Whatever place they were being taken to, it was not the bridge and Zvornik. Perhaps there were more execution sites north of there, towards Bijeljina. But wouldn't it make sense to get rid of the goods as swiftly as possible?

Sitting back, he felt the tension leave his body. They'd make it. By God, they'd make it. Again, a move closer to Amelia. But why had he not given her number to Branko? He had a perfect opportunity, except he'd not thought of it until it was too late. They gave him *burek* and coffee and cigarettes, yet he didn't keep his mind sharp and he screwed it all up. This was no place for screwing anything up. There was no room for even minor errors, and he'd screwed it up big time. He wanted to rub the burning from his eyes, but his hands were chained to the bench.

"I think we're going to make it," Zlatar called out. "You old fox, we're going to make it! Just looks like we'll have to skip those drinks in Belgrade. Oh, what the hell, we'll have 'em. We'll have 'em all right. Make the money somehow and have 'em. But why is it so damned hot in here?"

"They've cut off the ventilation," Maka said.

"Maybe they think we enjoy hammam? They call us Turks, after all."

But it wasn't funny. They sat in the darkness, sweating and rocking with the movements of the car. The temperature was climbing, and it did begin to feel like sitting in a sauna. It was getting difficult to breathe.

It was the two hostile corporals that had handled them at the station. They had loaded Maka and Zlatar into the van, knowing they could not deliver them to the Chetniks. They still had a chance to finish them off, their way. An unfortunate accident. Perhaps they'd call it an experiment. Rotten bastards, he thought. Maybe they'd done this before with some common criminals. Maka figured the back of the van was hermetically sealed; against tear gas, he assumed. The heat and the lack of air were starting to make him feel nauseous.

More minutes passed, and Zlatar was also feeling it. "I can't breathe," he moaned. "I think I'm going to black out."

Maka started banging the metal floor with his foot. Rotten bastards! But he wasn't going to go away silently. They were chained near the back doors, too far from the cabin, but he kept stomping and very quickly the car slowed down and pulled over.

The double doors slung open and fresh air rushed in with the brightness of the sunlight. It must have been above thirty degrees outside, but the air felt cool and wonderful.

"What is it?" the cop asked. Maka saw the other one stand behind him, watching amusedly.

"I can't hold it," he said, gasping in the new air.

The cop cursed and called him a name.

"What do I look like, a nanny? Get out, then."

He unlocked something under the bench, grabbed Maka by the shirt and pulled him out. It was late afternoon and the sun had set low in a cloudless sky. Maka stood on the road, his head dizzy and legs weak. Around them was a forest of coniferous trees. Not far from where they had parked he could see a diverging road going into the forest and a sign for "Hotel Omorika".

Tara National Park? He knew that hotel by name. It was the one Marshal Tito and the oligarchy of the *savez komunista* had frequented, famous for its Brutalist concrete architecture. It was named, as he remembered, after the Serbian spruce found only in that park. So they were probably at a thousand metres' altitude?

"You wanna pee, you fucking *Balija*?" The other cop pointed to the forest and cocked his service pistol. "Go on, run then. Go take your leak." The look of amusement was gone from his eyes. He watched Maka with the steady cold stare of a murderer.

"I don't think I can go now..." Maka wiped the sweat from his eyebrows with the back of his hand, the handcuffs' chain hitting against his nose. The first cop cursed again.

"You're just garbage to us. Why do I even bother? Get in!"

Delivering another slur and a kick on Maka's ass, he made him climb back and reattached Maka's hands to the bench. But the manoeuvre had worked: their mobile coffin was loaded with air, and about twenty minutes later, when Maka and Zlatar again were starting to feel sick, the car stopped and they were both ordered to disembark.

They stood, legs shaky and the clothes glued to their skins, in a yard of what looked like a dilapidated, long-abandoned boot camp. There were three single-storey barracks, long and identical. One had its roof partly caved in. Further away stood two houses of equally neglected appearance. The place was in a valley surrounded by fallow fields and clear hillocks, and across the plain of the valley loomed the ubiquitous green hills of Old Herzegovina. Down by the fields were clusters of farmhouses. A broken chain-link fence ran along the camp's perimeter. On the other side of the fence stood two yellow, rusted-out cement silos of a forsaken batching plant. Maka saw workers making repairs on the fence. A single electric wire ran across the yard, suspended in mid-air by a timber pole that had been freshly dug in and that cast its long shadow on the hard, sun-parched ground.

164

The two police were by the barracks, talking to men in camouflage uniforms. Maka peered at them, wondering if these were military. They wore black berets. On their jackets they had patches that said *milicija* in Cyrillic. They had that unmistakable, casual air of veteran soldiers, and they glanced at their new internees with unappreciative contempt.

"I bet this used to be a camp for construction workers," Zlatar whispered. "In the Seventies, when they built the Užice–Podgorica line."

"Look," Maka said. "Those are MUP police."

Zlatar's face turned ashen.

"Fuck. You're right."

These were the militia of the Serbian Ministartsvo Unutrašnjih Poslova, the interior ministry, infamous from Croatia's Slavonia to eastern Bosnia. Officially not at war, yet seen wherever the villages and cities had burned, these so-called special police units had carried out executions and expulsion of the non-Serb population in all of the ex-Yugoslavian fronts. With part of their ranks made up of criminals and convicts, these were Chetniks par excellence. So, these thugs were running this place? What was this about? Maka scanned the yard in quiet desperation; apart from the fence-builders and the cops, the camp seemed eerily deserted. Weren't those eight hundred from Žepa supposed to be here?

"Fuck. This ain't right," whispered Zlatar. "If those hear we're soldiers, they'll kill us."

"Quiet now. They're coming."

The MUP police grabbed them by their necks and started dragging them over to the building. They were manhandled, like packages. Maka was shoved into a small room, pushed roughly against the wall and frisk-searched by three special police. They all looked well-fed and robust. They had pistols and nightsticks on their belts. One of them, a tall, dark man with a flat nose and two missing front teeth, held a metre-long steel pipe in his fist. The room was stuffy and hot under the corrugated iron roof.

"Where ya sonovabitch from?" the flat-nosed one asked.

It came to Maka that the transport cops might not have handed over his information. Maybe it was in the paperwork that might arrive later. Perhaps it never would. They'd all had their run-ins with the Tito-era bureaucracy. Now it was the post-Yugoslav chaos. If he got lucky, his file would never arrive. These cops might know his name; maybe that was all. He realised all this in a moment, his heart racing. He sensed that being from Srebrenica wasn't good. It wasn't good to have escaped the killing. He could say "Žepa", all right. He *should* say "Žepa". Except that these bastards might know it already, or they'd find out, one way or the other.

"Srebrenica," he mumbled, his cheek pressed against the wall.

The cop seemed taken aback by this. "I was there," he said, resting the steel pipe on his shoulder. He had dull eyes and no emotion in his words. "I fought in Croatia in 1991. In Osijek and Vukovar. Then in Srebrenica, in 1993. I had a great time there. In April 1993. What front line were ya sonovabitch at?"

Maka felt his heart beating against the wall. "I didn't go to the front. I was a cook."

The cop gave a scornful snort.

"Fuck, how come y'all were cooks?"

Another one grabbed him. "Get in there, chef. Get your hair nicely."

They pushed him into the next room, where a middle-aged woman in a white lab coat took charge of the prisoner. In the background stood three men with a television camera, documenting the medical check-up. The woman listened hastily to Maka's lungs, then grabbed his chin, aggressively, turning his head from side to side as if to inspect his features under the electric light bulb that had been rigged on the wall.

"See, that is a foreign news crew," she said. A man behind thick, oversize eyeglasses directed a microphone towards him and asked something in English. A second fellow interpreted:

166

"What is your name and where do you come from?"

He told them. The third man, crouched with the large camcorder on his shoulder, brought the apparatus closer. Maka could see his own reflection in the lens: a bearded, skinny man sitting on a stool with the tracksuit jacket on his lap and the chest bones showing on his naked torso. It didn't look like the man he'd known.

"How have the Serbs treated you? Has there been any maltreatment?"

"No, nothing of the sort." He'd been given food and water. There'd been no violence or such, he added. The second man interpreted this, but his sentences were oddly short and impassive. There were a few more questions. The microphone-man spoke English with a strangely Balkan accent. They're faking it, Maka thought. The presumed doctor or nurse pocketed her stethoscope and said she was done.

Maka was taken out and across the yard into one of the long barracks. In the shadow of the broken roof he found people, as many as several hundred, crammed in the cavernous space, like cattle in a barn. From what he could see, they were all in civilian clothes, emaciated and defeated. They stood and sat there, crowded closely against each other. Some turned to look at the newcomer. What he saw were the familiar Bosnian war faces: hollow-cheeked, unshaven and scared.

So, they were here after all. Maka scanned the silent crowd, hoping to recognise someone. He had not had acquaintances in Žepa, and with the evening sun in the broken roof contrasting the darkness, and the mass of people blocking the view, it was difficult to see. The windows were nailed shut with plywood. There was a sickly-sweet smell of unwashed bodies and urine in the hot air. Next to him sat a man on the concrete floor whose eyes were swollen shut and half of his face was in red bruises, the fresh kind that had not turned black yet. Maka could feel people watching him. He wanted to go and find a place for himself, but it seemed too packed even to stand. Taking unsure steps he worked his way into the crowd of men. He wanted to be as far from that door as he could.

Someone called out his name. Maka turned to see a teenage boy push through the wall of men. Then the boy stood there, in the same jeans and the holey T-shirt he had worn in the forest eight days ago. He stared at Maka, his uncle, eyes wide.

"Is that you?" he whispered.

"*Hassan?* For heaven's sake!" Maka looked at the boy who was there, alive.

"What happened? Where's your father?"

"I don't think he made it," Hassan said. "I had to leave him there." The boy hung his head low, staring at the floor.

"Look, Hassan. I thought—" Maka started, then knew it wasn't right to say it. They hadn't killed the boy. The bastards got Edin, but they hadn't killed the boy.

"How did you get here?"

"I don't know what happened. It was so bad. We got separated, and I hid in the bushes. Please forgive me, Maka… I didn't mean to leave him."

"Nonsense. Don't say it."

"I thought you were dead, too. Please forgive me." Hassan stood there, his gaze on the floor.

"Don't say it. There's nothing to forgive. How did you make it here?"

"I hid in the bushes. A lot of people got killed. I think they killed at least a hundred on that slope. I heard them do it. Some with knives. I just couldn't move."

"That was a full Chetnik platoon."

"First I couldn't move, but I knew I had to get away before the sun came up. I didn't know where Dad was or where you'd gone. So I just ran. I ran, and I kept running. I think I went right through them. I must have run two or three kilometres. My hands and face were all cut."

Maka could see the crusted abrasions from the trees on his face. He took the boy and held him. Thank God, he thought. Thank God.

"Dad stayed there. They got him. He was so badly wounded, then he got hit again in that detonation." The boy wept against Maka's chest. "I'm so sorry. I'm sorry for everything that happened."

"You mustn't say that, Hassan. Listen, *sinko*. We all ran. It was the right thing to do. He wouldn't have made it anyway. Just how did you end up here?"

Around them, the men had been listening and some of them started to make space. "You two, sit here," said the man with the beat-up face.

They sat down on a concrete step. The legs of the others were all around like trees in a dense forest. The floor was filthy and above them the roof was broken and they could see the darkening sky and all around them the men in dirty clothes.

"I came across another group," Hassan whispered. "Many were from our street. Do you remember Dennis?"

"Zekira's nephew?"

"Yes. He said his father was killed a day earlier. In Kravica. His mom was there as well. They'd lost her and he didn't know if she was alive."

Maka remembered the kid, Hassan's friend from school. His aunt was Maka's old gymnasium teacher and one of the lucky ones who'd gotten out in time. She now worked for the Red Cross in Tuzla, they said. But why had the kid's mother gone for the hills? Why didn't she flee to Potočari, like the other women? Maybe she didn't want to leave her husband and son. Suddenly, Maka was utterly grateful that Amelia was safe. He felt sick at the idea of her in those forests.

"So, what happened?" he asked.

"Some of us wanted to go for Žepa. I felt that was the best. So I asked Dennis to come with me. But there was this tall man, I forget his name now, but he was also from Petriča. You remember? The one that kept bees."

"Babić, I guess."

"Yes, Babić. He wanted us to try for Tuzla, and he talked Dennis into going with him. He said, 'Stay with me. I've protected you until here.' So there we split up."

"That's how you got here?"

"Yes, but it took four days to reach Žepa, and two of us got killed in a landmine. I don't know how we slipped through the lines, but later, when we got into the town, we learned that the Chetniks were preparing for an offensive. The next day, they attacked. So we had to decide again what to do, where to go. There were hundreds or maybe thousands of people, but no food and no weapons."

"Yes, it was the same there. The UN had taken their guns."

"So it seemed. So, this commander, he told us to try and cross into Serbia. The last of the *Armija* units went northward. They said they'd try to break through the Chetnik lines, to make it look like everybody was heading for Tuzla."

So, they created a diversion, Maka thought. To help the others gain time... He imagined the hell such commandos must have endured. Maybe none of those men were alive now.

"God bless them," he whispered. "I hope they got through."

"They had radios, they said they could listen to the Chetniks. There was fire all along the line when we started."

"I hope they made it. Where did you cross the Drina? In Bajina Bašta?"

"No," said Hassan, "that was too far. We built rafts and went across the lake. The Perućac. We had many rafts and we crossed in the night. All the men that were left, many hundred, and we had to make many runs," the boy explained.

"Eight hundred, it seems."

"Something like that. We all got across. On the Serbian side it seemed no one had seen us, so we started hiking up a road in this very steep mountain. There was this really big canyon. We got all the way up. Then it was morning and the Serb army was there and three got gunned down, the first ones they saw. When they understood how big a crowd we were, they stopped firing. But those three, they got killed. I just heard the shots. Was told about it afterward."

"So when did you arrive here?"

"Two days ago. It's really bad here. Those guards beat us. On the first day, they beat up almost anyone, and they took anyone who was *Armija* and put them in a building that's back there. We could hear it all night. It made me sick. I couldn't listen to it. They just wouldn't stop."

"They're what they call the special police. It's normal to be scared of them. But you were not in the army, and as long as you do as they say you should be all right."

"Just don't tell them you're in the *Armija*, will you?" He looked up at Maka. His eyes did not look like the eyes of a fourteen-year-old.

"Of course not. We'll be all right."

"I can't stand it when they do it. I don't understand why they can do that to someone."

"Try to ignore it, sonny. There's nothing we can do about it."

And what's going on with Zlatar? he thought. Maybe it was his turn in the mock medical check-up. Maka hoped he'd be through soon.

The bruised-up man sitting next to them snorted.

"We heard that those blue-helmet clowns radioed their command," the man said. "They knew we were going across, and said they'll call the *Crveni Krst*. They'd tell them we'd crossed. Then the *Crveni Krst* would come and help us."

"It's true," another man whispered. "But where's the bloody Red Cross? And where's the UN? They beat us up like animals, no one shows up!"

"Have you gotten anything to eat?" asked Maka.

"No, nothing!" the bruised-faced one said.

"How did *you* get here?" Hassan asked. He was looking better, now that he could speak to Maka. The light was gone from the rafters and it was almost completely dark. Maka could feel it getting cooler. Up here in the mountains, the heat went out with the sun.

"A long story. I'll tell you later."

"What do you think they'll do to us?"

"Don't worry about us," Maka whispered. "We'll be all right."

He thought of the electric cable and that fence perimeter. Those looked like the first efforts to build this place into a camp. If just holding men for execution, why bother fixing it? It was the fence that gave him confidence. But where the hell was Zlatar?

Someone whispered in the dark:

"Hey… you're Maka Delić? From Petriča Street in Srebrenica? There's someone here says he knows you."

Maka saw the shapes of three men squeeze through.

"*Es-selam alejkum,*" they greeted, whispering.

"*Alejkum selam…*" Maka returned.

"You are here? I cannot believe it." The man who said this, Foric, was the husband of Maka's cousin. The other two had lived along Petriča, a couple of houses down.

"Hassan told us about Edin," Foric said. "My sincere condolences. I was in that forest when he got killed. The whole thing makes me feel awful. Then it was I who persuaded Hassan to aim for Žepa…" He sighed, shaking his head. "As far as I can tell, we're the only ones here from Srebrenica."

They looked like some wild beasts, crouching in the dark. The last Maka had met any of them must have been days or weeks before the onslaught. It was strange to see them now, like this.

"My wife went to Potočari," Foric went on. "I've no way of telling what's happened to her. It's a cursed thing. There was so much bloodshed!" He sounded very angry and bitter.

Maka told him what he'd heard from Branko about the women. She was probably safe in Tuzla by now. Foric kept silent.

One of the other two recounted, quietly, how his girlfriend had fled to the hills with him. They didn't want to get separated, so they made it through the forests, surviving two ambushes. They eventually reached Žepa, then ended here. Now the Serbs had taken the girl. The man did not know where she was, or what they were doing to her. He held his head in his hands as he spoke.

"There's only men left," said Foric. "All civilians. The ones they identified as soldiers they took away for torture. What the hell is this all coming to?"

Maka looked around. It was too dark to see. He could not tell if Zlatar had been brought in.

"It's a murder," Foric spat out. "A massacre! They never had any intention of taking us alive. Anyone they caught they slaughtered!" He listed off names Maka also knew and said those men were now rotting in the woods. And he'd heard rumours, stories about busloads of people taken to places like Branjevo and Orahovac, who were crammed into factory hangars and gunned down, or marched to the fields and executed. "Hundreds, hundreds, if not thousands!"

Yes, it was a massacre. Maka understood it now. A systematic eradication. It was almost as if the Chetniks were, in their sick minds, paying back for Kragujevac, for what the Nazis had done fifty years ago. He'd known it, but he hadn't believed it. It was becoming clear and impossible to deny. The entire enclave had been exterminated. Here, the few lucky survivors. Could you even call this luck? And what about those Serb sons of bitches? What were they planning?

"Yes, it's a cursed thing," he whispered. "Still, we need to figure out how to beat it from here."

A door opened in the back of the hall and a flashlight beam swept the sea of men. Maka heard a thud and a cry of pain, then a raging voice that yelled, "Silence! Everyone quiet, goddammit! So quiet I can hear a fly!"

At dawn, five buses rolled into the camp through the newly fixed entrance. The guards started loading men onto them. The cops had lists of names and they called them one by one, cramming eighty into each car.

Watching through a hole in the crumbled fibre-cement wall, Maka could see the buses. It was early in the morning, with the sun already up and the valley clear. He heard the guards' shouts in the yard. The buses were dusty and battered. They stood there parked, and men were loaded onto them one by one. There were about a dozen special police for the freighting. They formed a corridor leading to the cars, smacking the men with their batons and rifle butts as they boarded.

Maka and Hassan had sat the night on the floor, leaning on each other. They were high up in the Tara Mountains and they did not sleep from the cold. Through the night they heard the distant sounds of beating and the muffled screams, and Maka held his nephew tightly, hoping the boy could fall asleep. But it was difficult and in the morning, when the roll call started, they were both tired, hungry and in despair.

Maka kept counting the names. Somewhere after three hundred he was surprised to hear Zlatar's. At the other end of the barrack he saw his friend stand up and walk to the door. So, he'd been there, after all. There was that other entrance in the back, he figured. Maka watched him walk out into the yard, taking fast steps, then jogging to avoid the cops' ire and disappear into one of the cars.

Hassan's name got called. The boy stood up, awkwardly, and looked at Maka.

Maka nodded to him, and the nephew walked out, his legs reluctant. Foric was called, as were the two men from Petriča. Maka watched them all get on the buses, then the cars drive out of the camp and down the road and away across the plain, with the morning sun catching on their windows far across the valley.

He held on, leaning across the wall and looking out. They took four hundred men. Probably another four hundred left. It was still too much, though the barrack now appeared more spacious than before. Why didn't they take him? They called all the others from Srebrenica, so why not him? And where were they taking them? He felt sick and hollow in his chest thinking about it. But the cops hadn't tied their hands behind their backs with wire like the Chetniks would have. None of the men got their hands tied. This made him feel a little better, and he sat against the wall, looking at the blue sky through the broken roof. Maybe they were taken to another camp. That had to be the explanation. Eight hundred was clearly too much for these shanties. Maybe that's why they were halved. But all the men from Srebrenica were put on those buses.

Why didn't they take him?

EIGHTEEN

IT WAS LATE July, and Maka and the four hundred men were locked up in the cell barracks. These buildings had rooms along a central passage, with fluorescent lamps fixed to timber rafters in the corridor. They were about dozen in each small cell. It was very hot in the daytime, but at night the temperature dropped rapidly. They had been given one old army blanket for every two or three men, and for six nights they had slept crammed on the gritty concrete the best they could.

The lights in the corridor came on late in the evening. There were no roll calls and they were always kept inside, except at noon when the cops marched them out to the yard, in a long file under the sun, making a loop by a thermal soup container, where they were handed a slice of bread and a scoop of greasy hot water that they had to swallow on the spot, with one of the guards counting the men; then, back into the barrack and their cells. That one hundred grams of bread per day and a dash of soup, practically a spoonful, was all they were given.

In Maka's room they had a shared bottle that they could fill at a tap outside. Behind the barracks was a makeshift latrine area.

There were guards assigned purposely for the toilet watch. The prisoners did not get beaten in the group, but when they ran to the shack they got lashed with nightsticks or whatever the cops had. For the guards, it was a game; the inmates would hold back until their bladders ballooned. But you have to go eventually, and when they returned they had welts on their arms and faces and their fingers hurt from trying to block the strikes.

The group of isolated Bosnian army soldiers was still kept in the little building at the back of the camp. There were about two dozen of them, mostly those that had been identified as squad leaders or platoon commanders from the Žepa division. They were still being tortured. Maka could hear them, though at night their voices grew faint and inconstant. You could become so tired of anything, even pain, that it could simply overwhelm you.

The cops, too, grew bored with brutalising the same men. They would go around the barracks, bursting in the rooms and taking men at random, or look for the ones that had complained about the first day's bashings to the "foreign" camera crew. The inmates were made to kneel and hang their heads low in the cops' presence. If one looked up he got bludgeoned across his head. The cops called out names and took the prisoners, one at a time, to the dilapidated, empty barrack of the first night where they got trashed with belts and broken stool legs and had their faces kicked in as they crouched on the floor, taking the blows. They were interrogated, yelled at, accused of war crimes, made to write false statements. The guards made them stand in attention in the yard and had them stare at the sun until it felt like their retinas were melting. They would assign them Serb names and force them to sing Chetnik war songs. The ones that could not do it in tune got the nightstick in their kidneys. All this must have given the cops a sense of justification and great entertainment.

There was one that everyone was especially scared of. This was the tall, flat-nosed guard that had spoken to Maka. The inmates knew him as Slavko, though it was not clear if this was his real name. The metal pipe was the beast's signature tool. This nightmare of a man, though he spoke and looked like an oaf, had a way of getting creative when it came to cruelty. He would use that steel cane on the inmates' shins where it hurt the most, or force them to take turns beating each other. If one did not do it savagely enough to Slavko's liking, the prisoner would get a vicious pelting himself. This was the kind of life and game Slavko seemed to enjoy.

Maka, for some reason, had never been dragged out. Perhaps it was because of his little trick. Then again, there were lots of "cooks" in that group of four hundred emaciated, scared men.

His cell was a cramped space, with fibre-cement walls and flaking-off paint. It had a large glassless window the Serbs had nailed shut with wooden boards. Out of the gaps you could see the weed field behind the barrack and the patched-up fence, and far beyond the hayfields the hills and occasionally the guards patrolling the perimeter. In the middle of the room stood an old table left by the railroad builders, nailed together from splintery timber. They kept their five blankets folded on it, and during the day they sat against the walls, hoping the door would stay shut.

Maka shared the room with ten others. There was a young man who was called Bielo because of his straw-coloured hair, and who had destroyed a Chetnik tank with a rocket-propelled grenade during the battles of autumn 1992. He had managed to hide his army background and, so far, none of his mates that were being tortured in the isolation seemed to have snitched on him. There was a photographer from Sarajevo who had been vising relatives in Žepa when the war broke out and had gotten stuck in the enclave. There was a farmer they called Juka. Juka had been shot in the leg crossing the lines and his wound was infected and he was running a fever. Another man, Hukanović, had been diagnosed with colon cancer a year earlier in Žepa. Hukanović, in his fifties, was slowly getting weaker with it. The starvation seemed to have a bigger impact on the lanky man:

his skin looked transparent and his eyes sat deep in his head. None of them talked much. There were four other townsmen whose backgrounds sounded similar, and Maka had difficulty remembering their names. The camp's youngest and the oldest inmate were in his room, a boy and his grandfather who had escaped to Žepa from a hamlet east of Višegrad that the Serb paramilitaries had burned. The boy was fifteen and his father had been shot in a cornfield at the edge of the village. Maka took a liking to them, maybe because the boy was about the same age as Hassan. The old man and the grandson were his blanket-buddies.

They all called the man simply Dedo, which was slang for grandpa. Dedo was seventy-two and his heart was giving him problems. The grandson, Amir, was a quiet and easily frightened boy. Dedo was giving half of his bread slice to him. "Eat," he would say. "You've got to get out of here, for your dad's sake. Never mind about me," he'd say. "I'm just an old man without a country. But you, you still have a future." Dedo was wiry and dark and he looked older than his age. He had been working on the lines, repairing the entrenchments until his chest started getting worse. His hair was thin and faded by the sun.

"What makes you so sure?" Bielo asked him.

It was morning, and they all sat on the floor. Dedo had just told them he knew their location exactly.

"No other place in Tara but Šljivovica, where those tracks come near," Dedo said.

"That line's crooked like a snake," said Bielo. "We could damn well be anywhere. You saw the mountains yourself, old man."

Twice a day, around noon and a few hours after the sunset, they could hear the distant clatter of the electric train. Dedo had explained how, in 1974, he had worked clearing timber from the course where the rails would be constructed. That was twenty-one years ago. They slept in tent camps and washed in the river canyons. He'd never been on that train. At any rate, back then, when the line was finished, it took eight hours from Belgrade to the seaside in Montenegro, running through hundreds of tunnels and crossing hundreds of more bridges in the rugged Serbian terrain.

"I've seen the mountains, all right," he said. "I was fifty-one, and I worked better than you young folks today."

"That don't mean a thing. You ain't got no map in your head."

"Well, I say we're near Šljivovica. West of Užice," the old man told them.

"But which one is the southbound?" Maka asked.

"There used to be two or three services, both directions. Now, with the war, I don't know. I guess it is the evening one."

"And what will you do then?" Bielo was sitting next to the door, keeping guard and listening to any sounds from the hallway.

"When?" asked Dedo.

"If you get to Podgorica. They're all Chetniks these days."

The men seemed comfortable talking about escape in Maka's presence now. The first days they had suspected him as a spy, someone the cops had planted in the camp. They had not said it, of course, but he had sensed their wariness and it was natural to think so. What had happened over the past three years, and finally, gave plenty of reasons for paranoia. None of these men from Žepa knew him. He had not gotten beaten up like the rest. But he was just as scared as anyone else and being starved like everyone.

"There's no need to go all that way," Dedo said.

"No? You're out of your mind. Where do you jump off?"

"The line passes via Štrpci. You don't disagree?"

"And you'll end up dead," said Bielo, "like the ones in 1993. Who the hell would want to go back to Bosnia? We've just escaped from there!"

It was true, the rail made a loop on the Bosnian side. But that was Republika Srpska now. It was in Štrpci where the Chetniks had pulled nineteen non-Serb passengers off the Belgrade–Podgorica train and tortured, robbed and murdered them.

"A hell of an escape," Maka said. "Here they'll kill us slowly, that's all."

"Then how about Montenegro?" Amir joined in. The boy had been listening and wanted to defend his grandfather.

"Look," Bielo said. "The border is over a hundred kilometres from here. Then it must be another hundred to Podgorica. What do you do if you get there? They turn refugees over to Bosnia and the Chetniks kill them."

"And if you go towards Belgrade?" the photographer whispered. His name was Čerkić and he was the quietest of them all. He had been badly beaten the first day and he now looked like a raccoon with his two black eyes.

"Listen, it's nonsense," Bielo told them. "You'd only get the rest in trouble. What to do is to wait. The Red Cross will come. I'm sure they will."

Maka hoped he was right. It wasn't a thing to go through the window. The chain-link fence also still had gaps in it, and the Serbs had not laid any razor wire yet. In the daytime, the MUP cops were there. They ran that perimeter in the night, too, but to escape in the dark wouldn't be such a thing. The train must run slow in the mountain passes. Getting on it might not be impossible either. Still, Bielo was right. There was nowhere to go. It was just mountains, and in both directions the railway took you to the Chetniks. There would be a manhunt. Certainly the trains would get searched, too. Then those left behind would get it again. It was nice to know they were near Šljivovica, or whatever that town was called. But it was no use. Every day, with the hunger increasing, it was becoming more difficult to think clearly. You didn't consider the past or the future anymore. The only energy you had, all you did, was sit and wait for that next morsel of bread.

So, you can't escape… but you're dying slowly, he thought.

If only the Red Cross would come. If the fighting across the border had cooled off, they'd eventually come. There was a Red Cross office in Tuzla and the inmates' names might get listed there.

"I wonder how the war's going," Maka said.

"How'd you suppose?" Bielo spat out. "Fucked up, how else?"

Just then the door swung open. It hit Bielo on his feet and the men startled and drew in their legs and the photographer, closest to the door, rolled over and crawled under the table.

Three guards were at the door. Slavko stood there, foremost, looking flat-nosed, dark-skinned, portentous-eyed and holding his steel pipe like a cane. He was staring at the Bosniaks.

"Well… who's fucked up here?"

They all sat quiet, hugging their knees.

"You – what d'ya know about fuckin' anyway?" he said to Bielo, poking him with the pipe.

Bielo sat there. He shrugged his shoulders.

"Hey, look at that ass," one of the cops laughed, pointing at the man under the table. Čerkić had only managed to fit in there partially, with his behind sticking out.

Slavko looked at it, then again at Bielo.

"So, ya know much about fuckin'?"

Bielo said nothing. They all stared at the floor.

"Look at that big ass there. I say that's a woman's ass, isn't it?"

No one said anything. Stepping inside, Slavko kicked Čerkić's bottom. It was not a light kick and Maka heard him yelp under the table.

"I say that's a woman's ass!" Slavko shouted. Then, to Čerkić: "Say it!"

"That's a woman's ass," replied the photographer's voice weakly.

Turning to Bielo again, the cop glared at the Bosniak.

"You've got a lady there. What ya waiting for?"

Bielo's gaze was on the floor. He shrugged his shoulders again.

Maka stole a glance at them: Slavko, all worked up, standing with the steel pipe raised, his bad teeth showing through a grimace and Bielo sitting at his feet, quiet like a statue. Maka saw the cop grab the blonde Bosniak by the collar and drag him up. That flat-faced son of a bitch was a tall man, and suddenly Bielo seemed to be standing on tiptoes.

"You! You've got a lady there!" Slavko yelled at Bielo's face. "What ya waiting for? Fuck 'er!"

"That's not a woman," said the Bosniak quietly.

Slavko socked him with his fist that was holding the pipe. It landed on Bielo's cheek, making his head swing to the side. "What? Shut up, ya crazy bastard!" Then, to the man under the table: "Aren't you a woman?"

"Yes," said Čerkić feebly.

Slavko glared at Bielo. He was holding the Bosniak by the collar and breathing heavily through the nostrils, his Adam's apple going up and down.

"Ya heard her. Now fuck 'er. Get down and fuck ya' woman."

The two guards in the corridor behind Slavko were tittering. They held their bellies and laughed that soundless, unstoppable bystander laugh. Bielo looked at the man's bottom that was protruding from under the table.

He shook his head slowly and swallowed.

"I can't do it."

Slavko hit him again, this time so hard he fell back to the floor.

"I say get ya' pants down and fuck that ass!"

"I can't do it. I can't do it to a man," Bielo said, lying on the floor. He looked away from the cops, blood in the corner of his mouth. "Do what you want. But I'm not going to do it."

Maka could see a rage rise on Slavko's face. It seemed to inflate his eyes, and he whacked Bielo twice with the pipe. It made a high-pitched sound, hitting him on the head, then a dull thud as it landed against his raised forearms.

"You goddam arrogant filthy *Balija!*" Slavko grabbed Bielo by the hair and dragged him out of the room. The other cops stepped back as if their colleague was hauling something contagious, shaking their heads and laughing as if saying: Oh, good old Slavko! What a crazy bastard!

The door slammed shut. There was a sound of beating from the corridor. Maka could hear Bielo being dragged down the hallway and the batons landing, then the yelling recede away and out to the yard.

He sat, feeling shaky and empty-chested and gazing at the floor. He could hear the others' breathing around him. No one moved or said a thing. In the corner, the boy started to sob. The old man took the grandson under his arm. He looked as if he, too, was about to cry. He held the boy and they all sat there, everyone quiet, in that new Serbian morning.

They brought Bielo back two hours later. He could not walk, and they tossed him in like a sack of potatoes. His face was swollen, he had cuts on his scalp and his hair was caked with blood. One of his front teeth was missing. He was in plenty of pain, but you'd never believe, somehow in good spirits. He was in pain all right, but trying to grin through it.

They had nothing to nurse his wounds with. Maka had him sit under the window where the air was the freshest and where you were the farthest from the door. Dedo tipped him a drink from the bottle.

"How's your head?" Maka asked.

"How does it look like?" the tank-killer said. Then, grimacing, "The fuckers hurt my legs."

"Do you know where we are?"

"Oh, cut that doctor-thing." He was trying to laugh. "Oh, fuck it hurts. Maybe it would have been easier to just do it." He spat a bloody gob out between the window planks.

Dedo grinned. "With that cracked tooth, you and Slavko look like brothers."

"Oh, that son of a whore. I'll kill him."

"You've got to wait some. He worked you pretty well."

"That's all right. I still feel better this way than— *Uh, jebemu...*" Bielo grimaced, the pain shooting as he tried to move his legs.

Čerkić, the photographer, had been sitting in the opposite corner, watching them shyly with his bruised eyes. He was a middle-aged man who had never been interested in politics or matters of nationalism. When Maka had asked him what sort of photography he did, he told him he took pictures of food, mostly. "Food?" was Maka's reaction. "You know," Čerkić clarified, "for restaurant menus and advertisements." He knew a good deal about how to make broccoli look shiny and ćevapi less greasy in the right lighting. Not many people considered it, but food photography was a specialty of its own. He knew about other things, too, such as cycling and jazz records. But this war business was something he'd never wanted to have anything to do with. He had a wife and two kids in Sarajevo, and a small studio where he'd done passport photos as well, and birthday shoots and such. The building was just on the Bosnian side in Grbavica. He'd gotten the word that it had been shot to rubble.

"You're a good man, Bielo," he said. "You're much braver than I am. Thank you for not doing it."

"Well, I gotta tell you..." Bielo groaned. "You have the unsexiest ass I've ever seen." He started to laugh, but it ended in a bout of painful coughs.

"These Chetniks seem to get kicks from it," one of the men said.

"It's their thing," another one added.

"Maybe they should get them gay-porn magazines."

"You suppose such things exist?"

"Hey. How would I know?"

Maka just shook his head. It was supposed to be funny, okay. It certainly hadn't been funny and it would not be funny, years later, when they'd think about it and when so many other things would. But it was droll and stupid just then, for that short moment. Then it was gone.

That noon they were again led out for their morsel of bread and the soup, but now the cops ordered the inmates to stay and assemble in the yard. They stood there, all four hundred, except for Juka, who was too weak to move with his rotting bullet wound, in a square formation facing the unused barrack. It had been raining and the sky was overcast. The yard was muddy and the air humid and fresh with a scent of pine needles. Maka and Amir were supporting Bielo. His shins were swollen and he was breathing painfully, with broken ribs, it seemed.

The camp commander strode out from the guards' house. Maka had not seen him until now, but he knew who he was: a little man in a plain, brown infantry uniform who walked with a slight limp. He had a thin, blusterous face and when he talked his lips seemed to barely move.

"Muslims," he started. "You are here guests of Serbia. You will respect our hospitality. You now have nowhere to go. Today, I can tell you – the war is going well in Bosnia. Today, the Serb army has taken Sarajevo. The city of Tuzla has fallen, too, and mopping-up operations are underway. In Croatia, the Serbs are winning. Dubrovnik has been liberated and the Vojska Republike Srpske is advancing north."

The man had resentful eyes. A humid, warm breath of wind came from across the hay fields behind him. Maka held Bielo with his arm across his back, feeling him breathe shallowly. So, the war was lost? There was a hollow, nauseous aching in his chest, the dispiriting feeling of anguish that comes with the knowledge of a catastrophe. If what that little fucker was saying was true, Maka's country had been wiped off, if not the whole nation. There'd be unimaginable chaos and agony. And the Red Cross would be late. They might never even come. They might never come, and Amelia might never get to learn about him. If they'd take him down some ravine in these endless mountains and pump a bullet in his head, no one would ever know.

The commander slid his hands loftily in the chest pockets of his field coat. The guards stood behind him with their assault rifles ready, glooming at the inmates. One of them was chewing on something and spat a long, brown streak on the ground.

It might take months, Maka thought. *But to kill us, only a few more weeks.*

"The course of the war is sealed," the little man concluded. "You *Balija* have lost everything."

NINETEEN

IT WAS TEN days later that the Serbs finally sent for a medic. Juka, the shot-up farmer, had been persisting in the corner of the cell, having night sweats then chills in the daytime when it got hot; every noon, when the men came back from the food scraps distribution, they could smell the pus mixed with the imbued stink of their squalidness before their noses again got used to the room. They would bring Juka his piece of bread and the dab of grease-water in an old sardine can. The lack of calories and the infection had already made the man delirious. Only after the guards thought he would die did they send for help.

He was lying against the wall in the sun. His face looked waxen and his eyes pale and absent. Maka and three others had carried him outside and propped him sitting up against the barrack. It was another hot August day. The men cast their shadows underfoot on the dry ground. The medic was a young nurse assistant, a snotty fellow who looked like a butcher in his coat. You called it white, except it had been sat yellowish-grey on the backside and groped dirty around the breast pocket where the man kept his fags. He had brought with him a plastic first-aid box that he set down at his feet.

"What you waiting for?" he said, sucking on a cigarette. "Take the rags off."

They started unwinding the bandage. The medic looked at the wound and grimaced. Juka moaned and tried to move. Maka, squeezing the leg in his armpit, turned his face away. It was the smell that got him, the smell and his weakness. The sun hurt his eyes. There were four guards behind him, leaning to their assault rifles and watching.

"You don't like it?" one of them said. "You ought to. That's what a *Balija* smells like." The cop had uncut, curly hair that protruded from under his beret, making him look like some greasy violinist who had by a mistake been supplied with a militia uniform and a gun. This one was a good friend of Slavko. Not as sadistic, but trying hard to catch up. You put a man like Slavko in a group and they'd all get the bloodlust. The cops changed shifts once a week. While things had been better under the other team, now the nightmare crew was back.

Juka groaned and moved.

"Come on, hold him tight," said the inmate who was unrolling the bandage, thin-lipped and sweating. The medic squatted down and dug through the contents of the box.

"Hey, you! Come on over here," the curly-haired cop shouted at someone.

A man, beanpole-like, in a frayed red sweater, was coming from the toilets. He had possibly sensed an opportunity to go without being beaten and now tried to sneak back to his barrack.

He shuffled over, looking warily at the cops.

"Do you know 'Deca su ukras sveta'?"

The sweater-man, dumb, glanced from one cop to another. One of them started chuckling:

"Hey, Čupo, I think he knows it."

"Of course he knows it."

The fourth cop said nothing; this was the gloomy one that always seemed to keep aloof from the others. Čupo the curly-head grabbed the beanpole by the sweater and started marching him over to the guards' building.

"You stand here and sing it," he said. He positioned the man in front of a window. It was partly open and the curtains were drawn. Maka knew it was the night watches' sleeping quarters. Since his first day at the camp he had been taking down times and the cops' movements and trying to figure out the layout of the buildings. There were the two cell barracks, plus the third, the broken one. Between those and the guards' house was the toilet shack, where they also had the water tap. In the camp's south-east corner stood the building where the special-treatment group was still being tortured. The guards ran two perimeters: one near the barracks and the outer one over by the fence, where you were more likely to get beaten up as there you were almost out of earshot. Every seven days these swine rotated. There was the battered civilian van, twice a week, bringing the guards provisions. There were the two trains in the distance. But it was getting challenging to make sense of any of this as the weakness took hold, eating Maka up from the inside.

"Go ahead, sing it," he heard Čupo the cop tell the beanpole. "Sing it strongly, so that your fellow *Balija* will get better."

Maka watched the Bosniak stand facing the window and hesitate. Slowly, the man started finding the words of the old children's song:

"*Nema sveta ni planete...*" he commenced shyly. "There's no world or a planet... that a child can't reach..."

"Why can't you do this inside?" said the gloomy cop to the medic. The aid man was assembling a needle and a syringe he had fished from his toolbox.

"Smells like shit in there. Go do it yourself. It's too dark, anyway. Like a bloody skunks' lair."

"*Jer sve dečje staze vode...* because every child's path leads... from play to freedom..." Across the yard, the Bosniak was crooning in a barely discernible voice. Maka saw the cop poke him in the ribs with the muzzle of his *ciganka*. The beanpole winced and raised his voice a notch:

"From play to freedom… from play to freedom."

"Sing it, you bloody git!" the cop spat out.

The man got intoning a little louder but haltingly. The cop stepped back, cocked his rifle and levelled the gun on the Bosniak.

"Sing it, goddammit! Sing like a man!"

"Flowers are garden's decoration!" the Bosniak shrieked. He stood there, shoulders hunched, looking haggard and sang. The rhyme of the old kids' tune now sounded oddly like a military marching song:

"And a butterfly – is a decoration – of a flower!"

The medic jabbed the needle into Juka's thigh. The fever had made the farmer nearly unconscious; still, it was enough to make him react.

"What? Does it hurt?" The medic had the fag in the corner of his mouth and was exhaling puffs of smoke as he mocked Juka, injecting the antibiotic. The out-of-tune singing merged with Juka's moaning. Maka noticed "*Opšta Bolnica Užice*" stamped over his breast pocket. So, the old man was right, he thought.

The door of the police barrack flew open and Slavko burst into the yard. He had been trying to sleep after the night watch and was tired and irate. Wearing slippers, an undershirt and unbuttoned fatigue trousers that hung on suspenders, he took two long strides to the hollering beanpole and smacked him right in the face. The beanpole had just been in the part that tells you how children are full of imagination and how they're the world's decoration, when the song came to a halt with a loud thwack, like two buck goats in a head-on crash.

"Fuck you, ya fuckin' assholes!" Slavko yelled at his comrades, flipping a finger at them. Looking sleepy and pissed off, he marched straight back in and slammed the door shut.

The three cops were having a time. The Bosniak who was knocked down sat on the ground, his skinny legs fanned out straight, face buried in hands and his hair all dusty. Čupo the cop was shaking with laughter. He walked over to the man and poked him with the gun.

"Alija, you're useless because you're *Balija*," he warbled, imitating the song with a childish lilt.

The other two had difficulty getting serious. Then, harshly, one said, "You're so useless, all of you."

"What the hell. We'll give y'all to Luka. Lukić will come and sort you."

"There's one who knows how to sort *Balija*."

Maka was still holding Juka's leg. He supposed they meant a certain notorious Chetnik, said to have murdered scores of Bosnians in and around Višegrad. He'd locked them up in houses and burned them alive. Tortured them to death by the riverbanks. Some rumoured it was this Lukić who'd killed those passengers on the Podgorica train. Maka wiped sweat off his forehead with the back of his free hand. Another sham? And Jesus, it was so hot. The medic had finished the injection. They had washed the wound and were putting on a new bandage.

"Let go of that paw now," he told Maka.

All this time, the gloomy cop had stood aside and said nothing. He seemed about the same age as Maka and had serious, grey eyes and an angular boxer's chin. The others had had their fun, but Juka's case still kept them occupied. An opportunity, if there ever was one.

"Sir, citizen Simo requesting permission to visit the toilet," Maka said to the gloomy one, using the Serb name the guards had assigned to him. He stood in attention and made the sign of the cross like they were told to.

The cop said nothing, just pointed towards the latrines and nodded.

Maka started for the shithouse. A light breeze blew between

the buildings, cool on his damp face. His legs were weak, but it felt good to move them. He walked carefully, his boots raising small puffs of dust that blew away with the wind. The ground was dry and hard. Under the eaves of the guard barrack grew tall, spiny knapweed. The building had a faded clapboard siding and a corrugated tile roof that grew lichen, with a television antenna rigged on it. One of the windows was ajar. The breeze made the blue fabric curtain inside move idly. When Maka went past it, he heard what sounded like a television. The set was on loud, and he could listen to a newsreader talk about aerial bombings. Multiple targets in Pale had been taken out, the male voice stated solemnly.

That's odd, he thought. Pale was the Chetnik stronghold near Sarajevo. That's where the Republika Srpska headquartered. Hadn't they taken Sarajevo already?

"The air defence shot down one French fighter-bomber," the presenter continued. "The NATO planes attacked Serb forces also in the Igman Mountain and the vicinity of Sarajevo. The Serbian foreign minister officially protested—"

"Hey, switch that TV off, for fuck's sake!"

The cop on the toilet watch had noticed Maka coming. He kept on walking. The guard ran to the window, barking through the curtains: "Switch that fucking thing off! Turn the volume down! You running some *Balija* news service here or what?" The cop's neck was bulging and glossy with sweat.

Inside the crapper, the sun doubled the effect of the steamy rankness, and Maka wanted to finish his business as swiftly as he could. It was a grimy, foul-smelling pit latrine with plywood partitions. A cloud of aggressive flies surged from the depths of the pit. So, he thought, what the commander had told them was all gaslighting? By the sound of it, the Serbs were anything but winning. NATO bombing the Chetniks? That was something. That was unbelievable. Maka had waited, hoped, prayed for something like this to happen, and now it was unbelievable. But he'd heard it. Heard it clearly.

Back in the room, the others had laid Juka in the corner. The farmer had fallen asleep with a rolled-up felt behind his neck. The men all looked at Maka as if he'd lost his mind.

He told them again: "That's what it said."

"I don't believe it," Bielo said. "Why now? They never did a damn thing." He spoke in whispers in the half-dark, knowing that Slavko would soon get up for duty.

"Because of Srebrenica?"

"The hell you say. The world doesn't care," Bielo said. His legs were recovering, but with the broken ribs he still had trouble employing his cynical snort.

"I know what I heard. And if it's true?"

"Then I suppose we'll get out of here. When the war's over, they'll have to free us."

"Some Frenchmen bombing doesn't mean it's over," said Dedo. "It can go on forever in these mountains."

Čerkić crossed his arms and watched Maka curiously. Ever since Bielo's beating, he had been talking about escape. "They'll take it out on us" he said. "And if that thing about Lukić is true, we're in a jam."

"Yeah? I thought we're in a jam already," someone said.

Dedo smiled dryly and poked Amir in the shoulder with his fist. The boy had been silent and withdrawn the past days, staring at the floor mostly.

"That's just gaslighting," Maka said. "Same as with Chetniks taking Sarajevo and Dubrovnik."

"Aren't you worried?" Čerkić asked Bielo.

"Hell, I ain't worried about a thing. We've got full board here, life's good."

"If they find out about you they'll put you in the *rezerva*."

"Or they'll dress *you* in pink and call you Tamara," the blonde Bosniak said. "Why you have to get so damned gloomy?"

They had nicknamed the building where the soldiers were locked up. The men in the *rezerva*, "the storage," did not exist to the world anymore. They could even be killed, and no one would find out. It was good, in a way, that Zlatar and Foric and the others from Srebrenica were gone. But when Maka thought about it, he couldn't help wondering where they were and what was being done to them. Maybe they'd eventually crack and rat on him.

Or maybe they'd already been murdered.

"True or not, we need to prepare," Maka whispered. "If they start taking men out of the camp, especially if in small groups, so that they don't return, we'll have to make a run."

He wasn't sure how it would work out practically. They couldn't all go, not all eleven of them. And many had friends and relatives in the camp. It would be a tough choice to make when it boiled down. But he'd make a plan. Any plan was better than no plan.

Well, that mantra had worked out only until Serbia. But for Dino's and Amelia's sake: when it got to existence, and when the stakes were not just your life but everything you'd ever lived for, every man would think for himself. Every man would place himself first. You had to.

"Why don't you guys keep it shut?" said someone sharply in the half-dark. "Slavko will be on shift soon."

TWENTY

B UT SLAVKO WAS back on shift the next day. He was on the
outer perimeter and he had put a chair in the far end of the
camp where the ground sloped gently up to a copse of hazel trees,
and from where you could see over the faded roofs of the camp
the fields that looked sunbaked and the green hills hazy in the
afternoon heat. The flat-nosed cop had placed the metal folding
chair in the shadow of the leaf canopy, where it was pleasant.
There were shrubs around that bore tiny white flowers and the
grass was fresh after the dew. That morning Slavko was idle and
sluggish, but a quarter of an hour into his shift, when he had
observed an inmate walk back from the toilet shack, he called the
man up to his post on the hillock and beat him up.

This Bosniak happened to be from Maka's cell. Slavko had
sent him back with his face smashed, with instructions to send
him another "*Balija*" to mess up. His shift was two hours and two
hours made him bored. He was listless because of the day's early
heat and wrathful because of NATO's bombing. The boredom
and ire were a toxic combination; so far, he had thrashed three
men.

The third inmate now returned to the cell. He had his palms pressed to his loins in pain.

"He wants the next one," he groaned from the door.

No one said a thing.

"He wants me to send another one. Otherwise, I'll have to go back for more."

They all sat quietly and no one moved. The man ran his eyes over them, looking at them one by one. There were not many candidates left, with Hukanović enfeebled by his cancer and Bielo and Juka still recovering.

"Looks like we'll all have to go. You?"

"Don't you dare," Dedo growled, shielding Amir under his arm when the man's eyes fell on his grandson. "I'll show that scumbag..." The old man started getting to his feet, unsteadily, leaning to the wall, his thin white hair falling over his eyes. He had still been giving half of his bread to Amir and got dizzy whenever he tried to walk.

"No..." pleaded the grandson, clinging to Dedo's wrist.

Maka grabbed the old man by the sleeve and pulled him back down.

"No, not you. Not with that heart. I'll go."

He stood up, feeling numb on the inside. So far, he had managed to avoid the violence. In his mind he had prepared for it, and he knew it was merely a matter of time when he would get it, too. He stepped out of the room. In the dim corridor, seeing the rows of cell doors and the dirt on the floor and the fluorescent tubes above that would come on after the sunset, and at the end of the corridor the narrow, rectangular, bright gap of the doorframe, he wasn't thinking of it. It didn't help to.

Outside, with the small breeze, it did not feel hot. But the sudden sunlight was dazzling and the sky above dizzyingly high. Maka walked across the dusty, open yard and past the guard at the inner perimeter, who watched him knowingly as he wobbled by, then slowly up the grassy slope to the hazel grove.

Slavko was reclining on the metal chair, legs stretched out.

"Oh, it's the chef... what we cookin' today?" the cop said, indolently. He had picked hazelnuts from the branches above and was eating them, spitting out shell bits. His assault rifle, with the metal stock folded in, lay against the chair. Under the chair, in the grass, was an opened bottle of beer and across his lap he had a long, stripped hazel tree bough that he had chopped from the thicket behind him. Its tip was frayed and broken.

Maka stood before him and could say nothing. What could you say?

"Come 'ere, chef. I'm feelin' too lazy today even to get up. Take off ya' shirt and get on all fours." The grass at his feet was flattened. Maka guessed that's where the rotter had thrashed the previous three.

What could you say or do? Nothing. He stripped off his shirt and did as he was told.

Slavko looked at the scars on his back.

"Where'd ya get those?"

Maka told him how the thorns had cut him by the Drina. For a moment Slavko remained quiet. He was digesting the information. Then his intrinsic lividity rose inside him, and he slashed Maka with the hazel cane as hard as he could across the back.

The blow felt oddly cold and hot, and Maka did not receive it as pain. It was pain all right and it shot through him, but it felt like something different.

"You filthy *Balija*!" the flat-faced cop yelled. "Ya pigs come over to my country! We give ya food and shelter! And ya bring the Americans to bomb us!"

He hit him again. The cane swooshed in the air then made a sharp splash as it landed. This time it was genuine pain.

"They bomb us, and ya pigs revel here like kings!"

He started landing the lashes like a madman. It was real pain now. Holy God it was pain, white-hot, all-piercing, searing pain.

"If you'd stayed where ya belong, we would've dealt with ya!" Maka's tormentor shouted. "Where d'ya even belong? Turkey? Fuckin' Saudi Arabia?" He was yelling his twisted monologue and landing more blows. Maka could feel the skin rip on his back. Holy God and His Prophets it was pain, but it wouldn't kill him. He gritted his teeth and thought, I'm not going to show it to this bastard, and for the love of holy God, it wasn't going to kill him, then, what if it *will* kill me? Slavko was gasping furiously and hitting him, sitting on that chair, and Maka saw the chair rock from the force of the blows and the assault rifle keel over into the grass. The white-hot pain flashed in synch with the strikes and the rifle was within his arm's reach, and he knew it would all end if he grabbed it. It would all end, for the love of sweet heaven the pain would end, but so would everything else.

"Assigned to this fuckin' *Balija*-nursing unit," Slavko spat out, gasping and raising the cane for another strike. "If I'd been in Srebrenica…"

Maka pressed his forehead against the ground, clenching tufts of grass in his fists, gritting his teeth. He would not show it. He would not give him the pleasure.

The blow did not come. All he heard was Slavko's heavy panting, and there was the searing pain, and from somewhere far away came the sound of engines. Maka turned his head in the grass. The cop, now standing and shielding his eyes from the sun, was gazing over towards the camp. From where Maka lay, he could see the compound entrance. Two white Land Cruisers had been let in through the gate and were parking by the police barrack. There were guards walking towards the vehicles, and he saw two people disembark from each car. Maka could not discern their faces, but the Toyotas had those large, circular, French-worded emblems painted on their doors, with that fat, blood-red cross in them. He knew, instantly, who they were. They'd sometimes driven to Srebrenica in the early days of the war. When it became increasingly difficult for anyone to get through the Serb blockage, their visits waned, but when you'd seen them once you remembered.

Slavko, still breathing heavily, was squinting his eyes at the white cars. He must have seen the emblems, too.

"You," he said, "put ya' shirt on. Get back to ya' cell." He sniffled his nose and wiped his mouth with the back of his hand. Picking up the rifle from the grass, he folded out the stock and hung the weapon from the sling across his chest. He stared poisonously at the cars and the people that had gathered around them.

"Get back into ya' cell. I'll finish ya later."

Maka picked up his shirt and got up. He started down the slope as well as he could. The ground felt like a ship's deck under his feet and he could feel drops of blood trickle down his back. For the love of sweet heaven, they'd come. He didn't feel the pain now. It was there, but he didn't care. He'd always thought of them as utterly useless, something akin to war tourists and empty career bureaucrats. He'd feared they'd never come but they had; now he felt like the arrival of that handful of men in two four-wheel drives was about the best thing that had happened to him in these years of insanity. He walked through the tall summer grass and far behind him Slavko's voice boomed: "Put that shirt on, *Bog te jebo!*"

This time, the men in his cell believed him. This development, though not entirely unanticipated, came so suddenly that an unvoiced excitement now gripped them as they all sat still, waiting and hoping for the door to open.

When it did, a middle-aged man, accompanied by several guards, peered in. He had short, dark hair and a short beard and his forehead was wrinkled with solemn, authoritative creases. He was dressed in a linen shirt and a khaki multipocket vest. It had the Red Cross emblem on the breast. On his side hung a satchel bag with plastic folders protruding out and he carried a clipboard with a bunch of papers pinned to it. Behind him were the guards and another man in civilian clothes. The pocket-vest man looked taut and nervous. He ran his finger towards each of the inmates, his lips counting, without a sound. He turned to the guards and said something in English. When he did not get a response, he spoke to the other civilian, in what sounded like French.

"Where's the twelfth?" the other asked the guards.

"Only eleven in this one," one of the cops said. The man interpreted this to the pocket-vest man. The foreigner looked at the inmates again. Then, speaking in French, he said something to the cop.

"There's one looks like a child," the interpreter said. "What's his age?"

"How would I know?" the cop grunted.

Looking at Amir, the foreigner asked him in English: "How old are you?"

Amir told him. He also said it in English and it made him look proud and bright. The foreigner, turning again to face the cops, shook his head sulkily. Maka could see the sweat glisten in the back of his neck. He spoke in his tense-toned French again.

"The boy says he's fifteen," the interpreter said.

"How would I know?" said the cop. "Look how tall he is. They're all liars anyway."

The foreigner in the pocket-vest shook his head silently and handed the clipboard to the interpreter.

"Listen, everybody," the interpreter told the room. "I'll give you a form each. I've got only five pens. Share them, but please fill out the forms promptly. We're a bit short on time. But please fill them as accurately as you can. It is important. Oh, we are from the International Committee of the Red Cross. The ICRC. You can see our badges. Please, fill the forms correctly."

The Bosnians passed the papers among them and Maka started to examine his. It was some sort of a registration form. There were sections for personal information: name and place of birth, last known address, details of family members, and so forth.

"Don't waste too much time on them," the interpreter urged. "We'll be back later for a more detailed interview."

The foreigner tugged on the interpreter's sleeve and they commenced what sounded like some argument with the cops. Maka noticed now a third civilian, a short and wide-shouldered man in a lumberjack shirt, in the corridor beside them. He was standing there, his eyes dumb and hands deep in his trouser pockets, looking a lot like an outsider.

"Where's this information go?" Maka asked him.

"Their office in Tuzla." The lumberjack man nodded his head towards a direction where the city presumably was, a hundred kilometres across the mountains.

"Hadn't you Serbs taken Tuzla already?"

He looked at Maka, puzzled, and pulled his hands out of the pockets.

"Hey, get the driver out of here," one of the guards said.

The inmates were scribbling their information down, some with the papers against the wall, some doing it over the coarse wooden table, while the others waited for their turn with the pens. The pocket-vest man was done with his disagreement with the cops, and was looking as nervous as ever. He spoke again to the interpreter.

"You all done? Everybody remembered to mark down their wife's maiden name, those who are married? Yes? Good. Return the forms, please."

"When will we get food?" Dedo asked. Next to him, another man, one Slavko had just whipped, turned his back and looked as if he were about to strip off his shirt. A guard made a grim face behind the visitors and drew a finger across the throat. That was it.

"Look, we've very limited time. We have other rooms to see," said the interpreter. "But you shouldn't worry. We will be back."

Maka had finished with his form filling. He handed it and the pen back to the interpreter. The door closed. It was very strange.

That kind of piece of paper and a ballpoint pen. They could change everything. He felt the burning on his back again. For God's sake, it was sore. But it didn't matter now.

"That was the Red Cross?" Čerkić whispered.

"They counted us?" said Amir.

Dedo smiled at him. "Yes, they know us now."

"Tuzla is still ours," someone noted.

"I guess we won't stay hidden much longer, then…" said Hukanović.

Bielo sat against the wall with his hands behind his neck and stared at the ceiling. Maka looked at him. The tank-killer seemed sombre and low-spirited.

"What's the matter? You all right?"

"They didn't give us cards," Bielo said.

"What do you do with a card?"

"If the Red Cross registers you, you get a card."

"Maybe we'll get them… when they come back," said Juka. His fever had gone down in the morning, and he sat holding the water bottle on his lap, watching them clear-eyed, high cheekboned, stubble-bearded and pale.

"Who knows if or when they'll be back," said Bielo.

"Listen to him," Dedo said. "You're the one was so sure they'd come. They came. What more do you want?"

"A meal, like yourself?" somebody wised off.

"You believe they're real?" Bielo said it to no one in particular, staring at the ceiling.

"I suppose they are," Maka said. "I saw them coming. The cars and everything."

"How are you?" he asked, looking at Maka. His eyes were tired and Maka noticed the dark rings underneath and the cuts and the bruising on his scalp.

"I'm all right."

"Good. Welcome to the club," the tank-killer said.

TWENTY-ONE

W HAT IS HOPE? Somewhere along the agony of August Maka
asked himself this, just to realise that such abstraction could
only exist with freedom, or, at least, with prospects of freedom.
Then what was hunger? He had seen it in Srebrenica, except
never like this. You never truly recognised it before it reached a
certain level and when there was simply, absolutely, no possibility
of making it go away. This was the ultimate way of controlling
a man. Like strangling off his oxygen, as had happened on the
transport van. Only now it happened slower.

It was not constructive to think of the past, but he could not
help remembering the woods. He had been hungry in the woods,
too, but free, and he'd had the potential of finding something to
eat, or of hunting himself a meal. Here, he had nothing. No hope
of even stealing. And as the days crept by his head was turning
increasingly cloudy.

They were still getting the same scrapings. A slice of wheat
bread per day. Maka imagined it was less than what the prisoners
ate in Auschwitz. Here, they were not forced to carry out heavy
labour. Still, even sitting down is a lot of work when you're in the
final stages of starvation.

Days went by. There was no sign of the Red Cross returning. No sign of anybody taking an interest in the four hundred incarcerated refugees. The visit had done nothing to suppress their tormentors' malignity. The military men were still in the *rezerva*. Maka could still, occasionally, when the wind was in the east, hear them. They themselves would still get walloped on their toilet trips; men got singled out for the guards' amusement.

Like that one two cells down the corridor. The one with constant diarrhoea. Outside in the yard, one of the pigs had thought forcing him to eat *vezankas*, those intensely pungent peppers, was a masterly form of torture. Unbeknownst to the cop, this Bosniak was a lover of hot spice. When the first chili didn't seem to hit him, the stinker gave him another, which the man eagerly gobbled down, sweating under the sun, then another, and another, until his colleague angrily intervened:

"Hey, what you doing? Can't you see he's eating them? Why the hell you give him food?"

You've got to be an exceptional kind of sadist to be aggrieved by something like that. Still, this pepper-loving inmate, also a big smoker who couldn't take it without cigarettes anymore, approached him and declared, "I don't care about food. I don't even care if you beat me. But give me a smoke!"

The cop knocked him down, of course. "Good you don't care," he said and walked away, lighting himself one.

Maka witnessed these sorts of spectacles, as he washed the guards' plates outside by the water tap. He cared about very little now, and the violence meant nothing. Had the guards not been around, he would have forgotten his dignity and licked those greasy aluminium plates. But the only yield from the dishwashing duty was these bizarre visions of abuse through the water sprays and mist that sparkled in the strong sunlight. Returning to his cell, sweaty and dizzy, boots and trousers wet, they only made for little grim storytelling. This, nevertheless, still generated some cynical chuckling in the room. Absurdity was the one conception they had any energy left for.

The cat was playing – the mouse fought for his life.

The days went by. Between the various chores which the cops assigned to the inmates, Maka would sit in his cell, one abysmal hour after another, carouselling in and out of wakefulness. For a week after his caning his back had been too raw to sit against the wall, but he would lean on his knees, skinny arms as a pillow, and dream. He thought very little, but visions appeared behind his closed eyelids. He was not sleeping anymore. Something happens to your sleep as malnutrition advances. It disappears and is replaced by daydreaming. He would dream of running in the hills, dream of the forests again. Through the mountains pounded the electric train. Dark and serpentine, it was like some beast from hell. Maka saw himself running alongside it on the crushed stone of the ballast shoulder and grabbing the rungs of a freight car with both hands, as the train slowed to take a curve before a tunnel, the mass of the car yanking him up. With his arms still strong, he wrenched himself onto the gondola in these dreams, again and again. He felt the wind and the tremors of the railcar, and he saw himself riding to the seaside in Montenegro, then the floating and rocking with the waves as he swam out to the bay. Always floating, on his back, in the warm saltiness, with the aquatic sunshine on his face and chest, and grabbing an anchor chain of a cargo ship and scaling it like a knot ladder. Then the sleep on the soft, warm, dry-smelling sacks of grain and feeling the waves hit the bow and the shivering of the hull and the ship rolling as she slowly headed out to the Adriatic.

Stirred up by the sound of a sudden assault and screams next door, he was instantly transported back into his cell in the prison camp. Here, it was the real world, and in the real world there were no fantastic escapades. You only stood to lose and be killed.

It was September. The autumn days fluttered on, tucked deep in the Serbian countryside. Hidden, forgotten and lost. What had happened to them, the past three and a half years, was incomprehensible. Yet, the memories of normal life seemed swept away and gone. There was only the war, and somehow the war and their imprisonment now felt like the natural state of affairs.

Two weeks from the first visit, the ICRC returned. They came with the two white Toyotas, and a truck loaded with provisions. Amir, the boy, had been outside in the dishwashing, and he told his room how he'd seen the cops proceed to unload cartons of soy milk and what had looked like military rations.

Just the thought of food was enough to make Maka crazy. This time, it was different personnel, five volunteers in white canvas vests with Red Cross logos, and a staffer who spoke with a northern Serbian accent. They brought in a spring scale. The men were all skeletal and Maka, who had always been on the slim side, recorded forty-nine kilograms. He had lost whatever there had been left to lose after three years in the siege.

Food and hope: the ICRC staffer confirmed that their names had indeed been sent to Tuzla. "You boys are going to be fine!" Yet Maka could only stare back, not fully understanding the meaning of such a word. The Serbs took the scale and left. The men sat in the cell, quiet, waiting. They heard the engines in the yard start and the cars roll out of the camp. It was another hot afternoon and Maka could taste the dust coming in through the window boards.

They waited. By late afternoon it was evident that they would never see any of that food. The cops had kept it all.

It was the motherfuckers' best joke. Here, the quality of a jest wasn't measured by how it made you laugh but by the state of stupefaction it left you in. That afternoon they all sat silent in their cell, everyone dumbstruck. No one was trying to wise off on this one.

By the time the ICRC returned, a week later, Maka understood he had nothing to lose. Death by starvation or by rifle butts, it made no difference.

"When will they feed us?" he spoke up. "Look at us. They didn't give us any of what you brought. How can they treat a human like this? You see, they'll kill us."

The delegate's face turned sour. This was not the pocket-vest one but a younger Swede in steel-rimmed eyeglasses. He stood at the door with his men, looking at the inmates.

"What do they give you?"

"Nothing," Bielo joined in. "A slice of bread, that's all! Look at us!"

Some lifted their shirts. The Swede stared at their cadaverous rib bones. He turned and, via his interpreter, said to the staffers:

"Go get the boxes. We'll distribute them directly."

You cannot imagine the happiness of receiving an American field ration. With an animal zeal, the same second they laid their hands on them, the men tore open the pale brown plastic packs. Maka knew the guards would snatch the food as soon as the visitors left.

They were comparing the items now, trading some, their mouths stuffed. There was Bolognaise spaghetti, chicken with rice and beef stew in a pouch, peanut butter and marmalade, vacuum-packed pound cakes and bags of M&Ms and Mars bars – both of which Maka remembered from advertisements but had never had a chance to taste – potato mash powder, instant coffee and hot chocolate in sachets, tea bags and sugar and pepper. There were crackers and matches, plastic spoons, chewing gums, packs of tissues and suchlike. The rations even had some chemical reagent pouch to heat the main course without a fire. It all made his head spin.

The men were joking:

"Cheese burrito? *Caramba*! Never tasted Mexican in my life. What a place to start. But it's beautiful. I love Mexico already."

"It's American. It just reads Mexican, but it's *A-me-ri-can.*" The man who said this was a big fan of the USA. When the war was over, he'd immigrate to Texas, where everything was good and plentiful and where no one cared about your name.

"Then, what do you have? Pork chow mein? Sounds Chinese," Bielo said. "Hey, guys, check this out. Captain America here eats Chinese. Chinese *pork!*"

The man paused and stared at the thick, brown noodles dangling from his spoon, then went on stuffing his mouth and mumbled, "It's American. An oaf like you would not understand."

"Give me the Tabasco, you don't need it," Maka said to the burrito man.

"What's *tabaško?*" asked Juka.

"It's famous American chili sauce," the noodle man explained.

"I'll give it to Mustafa." Maka meant the man in the other cell who had eaten the *vezankas.*

"Don't try," someone warned. "Take it on an empty stomach, it'll kill you."

"Not Mustafa. Nothing will kill Mustafa."

"Hey, Čerkić, why don't you take a photo of this?"

There was a unanimous agreement that Čerkić should take a photo, so he positioned himself, leaning back in the corner and holding an invisible camera, and took a picture of the posing, laughing men as they displayed their meal packs.

One by one, they were called to an interview. When it was Maka's turn, he had finished his meal and felt like a boa constrictor that had devoured a prey too big for his size. He supposed it wasn't all safe to gorge like that after being starved. They'd been given multivitamins and minerals, though. Somehow that was supposed to help. He had stored wheat crackers and a candy bar into his trouser pocket. Other than that, there was no place to hide any of the food.

The jailers took him to the empty, open-halled barrack where he had spent the first night with Hassan, and that the cops now used as an impromptu torture quarter. The ICRC had set up a table and three chairs in the windowless anteroom. The foreigner was young and very matter-of-fact. The Serb interpreter who accompanied him was a big, well-built man with big hands and a serious countenance. The guards stayed outside. Through the door Maka could hear them talk and smell their tobacco smoke. The light bulb that had hung on the wall was gone and it was dim inside. The Swede had set a battery-operated lantern on the table. He dug a paper folder out from a canvas messenger bag.

"You are Maka Delić?" he started. "From Srebrenica? How did you end up in this camp?"

Maka told him. Then, reading what looked like a photocopy of the form Maka had filled a week earlier, the man asked about Amelia and Dino. Did Maka know their whereabouts? He spoke in English, with the Serb interpreting.

"No," said Maka. But they'd been in Germany, and he gave the ICRC delegate the telephone number and the street address he had memorised. The Swede wrote them down. In the quiet of the room, under the timid light of the lantern, Maka could hear the pen write and his own breathing. He felt the translator watching him interestedly.

"You have three brothers?"

"Yes. Two of them are dead, as is my father. The third one was wounded in Kostraća and again near Kravica. That's where I saw him the last time. I don't know if he is alive."

"Which one of these is he?" The Swede was arranging his eyeglasses and studying the paper.

"Edin Delić," Maka said. "Can I ask you, what's the name of this place?"

"I'm sorry," said the Swede, "according to our rules, I'm not allowed to disclose it."

"Then, do you know what happened to the others? The ones that were here in late July? Four hundred men. Where did they take them?"

"Unfortunately, I'm not allowed to discuss such details. But you don't need to worry about them," the delegate hinted. "Here's something important."

He handed Maka another form, a letter-size notepaper.

"According to the rules of conflict that the Serbian government has agreed with, you have the right to send a letter, a Red Cross message. I encourage you to exercise this right. You can address it to an individual, such as a family member, or a relative. You were in the army, were you?"

"No," Maka said, suddenly uncomfortable. The Serb translator kept looking at him curiously. Outside the door he could hear the guards speaking and joking in their coarse southern accent. "I mean, yes. But I was just a *kuhar*."

"Nevertheless, you can't send this to your army unit or anyone currently in the Bosnian military. But you can write your relatives and inform them about your circumstances. I strongly encourage you to do so. Only, you should be aware, this is an open letter. It will be read by the camp command or passed via censorship in Belgrade."

"How long will it take to deliver?"

"It's difficult to say. There's a war going on. My guess is, from one to two months."

Maka took the pen. For a moment, he paused. He didn't need to think twice about whom to address it to. But what to say? He had that one page of dotted lines to write on. He'd have to keep it short. He'd need to be cautious, too, if the guards were going to read it. He shouldn't make them sound like the animals they were, and she didn't need any more anxiety than what she probably already had. How about the location? Maka had seen the sign to the Omorika Hotel, and the old man knew the names of the nearby towns. Perhaps it was best not to reveal this to the cops. Maybe she couldn't use such information, anyway.

He began to write:

Amelia,

You must be worried, but I guess you'll feel better when you get this. I'm in a reception centre somewhere in eastern Serbia. We've got food and they are treating us well, like refugees. So please don't worry about me at all, just take care of yourself and our son. Save up some money, because we will need it.

Have you got any news about my mother? I trust she made it to Tuzla and is with the relatives. I don't remember Sabina's address, but please tell them about me. Is there any news about Edin? He was in a forest somewhere near Kravica and badly wounded. I'd like to hope he made it, but I do not believe so. Hassan is here in Serbia.

I hope to see you soon. Please write and let me know how you and Dino have been, how your family is doing, Vedrena, Jasko and Nirzo. Give my greetings to everyone there, especially to Sefija. I wait for your reply!

Love you, endlessly,
Maka

"You're done?" the Swede asked. "If you've finished, I'll take this back. We'll send it to—" He looked over at the cover of the letter, holding it under the lantern. "Your wife in Munich. Are you sure of the address?"

Maka was. He had a bolus-like tightness in his throat, and he felt a choking emotion coming up inside in his chest. He could not say it, but he nodded, and he was sure of it. He was sure. In his mind, he'd spoken to Amelia when he was lying in the woods and when he'd waited for execution in that police cell. He was sure now, just as he was sure then. He was speaking to Amelia, now in reality, in that little paper form. Yes, how strange. A little paper like that. It was possible to change anything. Yes, it was possible. He knew Amelia would hear him. She'd always hear him.

The food Maka had ingested was now starting to take effect. He was feeling increasingly somnolent. Then he remembered the men in the *rezerva*.

Who would hear them? If it was possible to change things, he didn't want to care about that interpreter.

"Listen, there's something I need tell you," he said to the Swede, leaning over to him.

TWENTY-TWO

THE OLD MAN they called Dedo died in September after a two-day storm. The wind blew from the south, bringing sea clouds, grey and ragged like used steel wool, that poured down on the valley and the gusts drove rain against the window planks, making them wet and dripping, with pooling water on the floor of the cell. Outside the camp the trees bent in the heavy wind and the hayfields were flat in the rain. It was a summer storm but it wasn't warm: the police stayed holed up in their house and grey smoke puffed from the stovepipe and was ripped away flatly in the wind. The cops had reduced their perimeter to a few that huddled in the far corners. In their olive-green ponchos the guards looked like some strange, dark-glistening mushrooms behind the rain. Then, after the storm broke, the drizzle continued for a day and the hills were deep green and misty, and the rusty old silos of the batching factory stood out brightly in their crumbling yellow paint. There were pools of water on the paths between the barracks and tree branches blown across the yard and everything was washed out, fresh and silent.

That afternoon they were corralled into the third barrack. The hundreds of inmates stood waiting, packed in the hall now, happily surprised by the announcement of an additional tea portion. The previous police crew had repurposed the building as a prison canteen. On the low counter the inmates had built, a gas stove was alight. On its grate sat a fifty-litre, boiling aluminium kettle. Maka stood behind the cauldron with another inmate, a ladle in hand, feeling the heat from the little blue flames that flickered underneath. This other man, a short and wiry commander of a recon unit in the Žepa division, had been in camouflage fatigues when the Serbs caught him, but he, too, had successfully claimed to have served as a *logističar* in a soup kitchen. The others jokingly called him Glumac – an actor – for his performance. They were both assigned to a task, under the eyes of Čupo, Slavko and seven other guards with assault rifles. The air in the hall was humid after the storm.

"All right, get in line!" Čupo, the curly-haired cop, announced. "One by one! Come and get it – mountain herbs!"

Slavko, stationed by the pot, watched as the Bosniaks began forming a queue from the back of the hall. He had finally broken his beloved metal pipe and was leaning on a long, thick, wooden bat.

"Give 'em a full cup," he said.

"Yes, sir," said Glumac. He was stirring the big kettle, where green bits of grass swirled in the boiling water. Maka, too, was happy playing his role. Things were tolerable. Lately, there had been many small improvements. The inmates had removed the plywood from the new canteen barrack's windows and patched the roof with tin sheets. They did not have enough materials for tables or chairs, but they'd cleaned the building out, and twice a day sat on the floor for their meals. At midday they got bread, now more of it, and a scoop of pea soup that they ate from empty sardine cans that everyone carried. The evening meal was a pouch of something from the American rations. It was not enough for sustenance, yet an improvement from the starvation regime of August. The inmates now had lice, though. The guards, probably afraid of catching them, had allowed them to build a shower head near the latrine. The water was cold and they had two bars of ordinary soap for the four hundred men and had, until now, had a single opportunity for a quick shower. So the lice infestation was far from being overcome. But it was tolerable. Even the men in the *rezerva* had been released. Maka was not the only one to have tipped off the Red Cross and, although they were in such shocking condition that the arrival of these tortured, walking skeletons had horrified the others, the inmates began to feel that things might turn for the better; that they had finally achieved at least something. These things had all taken place last week, during the better police crew's rotation. Perhaps the camp commander had started to sense something – that after the war, one day, certain things might come back to haunt him.

The first inmate, a skinny gazehound of a man, stood before them, holding his tin can.

"Go ahead, fill it up," said Čupo, smiling.

Maka sank the long-handled ladle into the boiling concoction, the hot breath of the stove stroking his forearm. The cops called it "herbal tea" but it was just ordinary grass he and Glumac were told to pick inside the perimeter that morning. He poured a ladleful into the prisoner's tin. Immediately the lanky man's face distorted as the water burned him through the metal.

"Drink it," Slavko told him.

The man danced his fingers on the tin, bringing it to his lips. But the liquid burned him and the can fell on the concrete with a metallic clink, spreading its steaming contents. It was at that same second that Slavko's club landed in his midriff. The cop had swung it sideways, like a baseball batter, jack-knifing the man.

"Get outta here, ya bloody swine!" yelled the tall, flat-faced jailer. The prisoner was crouched on the floor, gasping for air.

Slavko sunk his boot into his side for effect, making him twist in pain. "Get lost before I fuckin' hurt ya!"

Two of the cops dragged the man aside, leaving him panting on the floor.

"Next one," said Čupo, grinning. "Be careful not to spill."

The prisoner next in the queue looked at the cops. He looked at the boiling kettle, then at Maka and Glumac. The happy surprise was gone from his face.

"Show us that goddam can," said Slavko.

But of course, Maka thought. The bastard now had his grudges. NATO must have given the Chetniks a proper hiding. Then there were the improvements. *Of course. All right. Get your payback, son of a bitch.* He dipped another scoopful. First, this inmate could hold the tin, shifting it delicately and rapidly from hand to hand, but he cried out as the water burned his mouth, and he also let the can drop. As it fell, so did the Bosniak; Slavko kicked his feet from under him, then together with another cop flailed him with batons.

The next prisoner tried his luck. It was impossible. One of Slavko's cronies hooked him in the jaw and the man collapsed to his knees. The Bosniaks in the back of the hall all looked scared now and Maka saw some of his roommates in the reluctantly advancing queue. There was Hukanović, who had just enough strength from his cancer to stand up and walk. A distance behind him were Bielo and Dedo. The sun had broken out and the old man was in the bright light of the window, hunched forward and supported by his grandson. He had his fist pressed to his chest, his old face sickly ashen and glossy with sweat.

One by one, the Bosniaks had to step forward to get burned and beaten. Finally it was Hukanović's turn. He stood facing the counter now, his long arms down by his sides, a sardine tin in one hand.

"Let's see that teacup," said Slavko.

"Just do your thing, but cut this tea nonsense," Hukanović told him.

The cop kicked him in the abdomen, putting his whole weight into it, as if trying to break in a door. Hukanović was thrown against the two Bosniaks behind him, all three falling back and onto the floor. Oh, you bastard… Maka thought. Oh, you're so dead, you son of the great whore… Seeing them hurt a dying man, the old fire inside of him flared up. One day, he swore, we'll get that piece of garbage. He could say nothing, of course.

"Is this how you show appreciation?" Čupo called to the inmates. "We prepare you a fine thing and you don't want it?" He motioned to Maka to distribute the next scoopful.

Right then Amir, the boy, cried in his teen voice, "Help him! Please, someone help him!"

The boy was on his knees, looking over his grandfather, who lay on his back on the floor, eyes flat and mouth agape, drawing short, agonal gasps. "*Deda?* Can you hear me?" Amir shook Dedo's head, making the thin, white hair quiver. There was blood on the floor and Maka knew that in going down the old man had hit his head.

The Bosniaks around stared at them. "He ain't breathing," someone said. Another inmate put his fingers on Dedo's neck, searching for a pulse:

"Nothing. I think he has a heart attack."

Bielo shoved the man aside and knelt beside Dedo, pushing Amir also out of the way. He placed his hands on the old man's chest and started compressing it, leaning over Dedo, his arms straight and pumping the frail chest, the old man's head nodding with each compression.

"Get back in the queue!" yelled Slavko.

Amir, crying and kneeling, looked at the cop.

"Can you please help him?"

"Get out of my face! Back in the line!" The cop kicked the boy and gave him a good one with the baton. Bielo, still doing the compressions, got Slavko's boot to the side of his head, knocking him out. The inmates behind him quickly dragged him off and someone grabbed the boy, too, pulling him away.

"Back in the line, all of ya!"

The cops stood over Dedo, who lay motionless on the concrete. He was not gasping anymore. His eyes were open. They looked glazed and his mouth was agape with a grey tongue and the sparse teeth showing. It was very quiet.

What do you do for a heart attack? Maka wanted to go over and help, but he could not move. What do you do anyway? That thing Bielo had been giving looked right; he'd seen that in a movie, maybe it was just a movie thing, maybe it was better than nothing. But what else could you do out here in the mountains?

"Think he's dead?" asked Čupo.

"Looks dead to me."

The old man lay at the cops' feet, mouth open. In the back with all the inmates, Amir wrestled himself free from the arms of the man who held him.

"Can you get him to a doctor?" Now he wasn't crying but looking fiercely at Slavko.

"You, ya better shut ya' goddam trap," the flat-nosed cop growled.

"Should we get him to Užice?" asked a guard.

"What the fuck they gonna do with a dead *Balija?*"

It was silent in the hall, with only the bubbling of the kettle and the quiet hiss of the gas stove. Maka, still behind the cauldron, watched Dedo. The old man's face was pale and moist with sweat. Maka knew what a dead man looked like. He'd seen them in the trenches and in the makeshift morgue behind the mosque in Srebrenica, with their half-open, lacklustre eyes and all life gone from their bodies. Now Dedo looked like any of them, just lacking the wounds from the shrapnel.

"What the hell's going on?" someone called out.

The gloomy cop stood in the open door, the sunlight behind him. He was looking unappreciatively at Slavko with his grey wolf-eyes.

"What in the hell are you doing?"

Slavko and the other guards all stared back at him but said nothing.

The gloomy one walked over to Dedo. He looked at the old man, then stooped and put two fingers on Dedo's neck while holding his assault rifle slung on his back. Shaking his head, he straightened up.

"Well, you got your first one."

"What's that to ya?" said his flat-nosed colleague.

The gloomy one looked around at the big, boiling kettle and saw the water and the bits of soggy grass that had been spilled on the floor.

"A dead prisoner, that's what it is to me."

"Fuck him. What ya gonna do about it?"

"I'm not going to do anything about it," said the gloomy one. "*You* are. Get him over to the hospital."

"And what the fuck they gonna do with a stiff?"

"Well, put him in the morgue? Or you want him to rot in here?"

"Oh, screw him. Screw you, too."

"He's my grandfather!" shouted Amir angrily.

"Dammit, brat! I told ya to shut it!"

"*You* shut up and get to it," said the wolf-eyed cop. He tossed a set of keys underhand at Slavko. "Take the car. Take him away."

He turned over to the Bosniaks. "This circus is over. Everyone back to their cells! If anyone needs to go to the toilet, go now. No one's going to beat you."

"Know what, Rado?" said Slavko. "Sometimes I think you're a goddam *Balija*."

The other gave a scornful laugh.

"No need to get that sour, con-boy. It's your first kill, isn't it?" he said. Then, speaking to Maka and Glumac, "Cut the gas and get rid of that muck."

After the inmates were gone and the guards that had loaded Dedo's body into a matt-brown utility car had driven out from the camp, with the corpse wrapped in a blanket and slumped in the back, Maka and Glumac returned, carrying the big aluminium vat. They had emptied it by the fence. It was sunny and hot, with water standing in pools between the buildings.

The cop whom Slavko had called Rado, which usually was short for Radovan, was out on the yard watch.

"I want you to clean my room," he said to Maka as they passed. "Not now. Do it after my shift."

In the cell, Maka found the others talking with Amir. The boy sat with the shared water bottle on his lap, bereft and quiet. It was as if they were holding a wake, just without the body.

"Did you know Dedo was an old *borac*?" Bielo said to Maka.

"How do you mean?"

"Fought the Chetniks in the big war."

"All the way through," said Amir.

"Really? Is that so? How come he never told us?"

"The old man wasn't dumb," said Bielo. "He knew the cops would give him hell."

"He told me not to tell anyone," the boy said. "But he was in Novi Pazar and Sutjeska and such places. I know *Deda* was wounded. Twice, too. I found the decorations in the house. He never talked about it. But everyone in our village knew he was a *borac*."

"So, he knew the mountains!" said Maka. That's what he'd meant, the shrewd old jack... Well, they got him anyway, he thought. What a story. He fought them in the World War, went through those horrors. Then fifty years later they got him. What an awful place. Everyone each other's keeper and captive. Just like that fat one put it. No luck in this damn country. Any other where every generation had known war like this? Afghanistan? Well, we come finely in second, he thought. We got the silver, all right. Silver for the silver town boys.

They all stood up as one of the men started the *janazah*, the funeral prayer. Maka held his hands palms upward, looking through them into infinity while trying to remember and recite the words. What a shrewd old jack, he thought. He ran his hands softly down over his face to finish the prayer, wishing the old man well.

When Maka walked over to the police barrack to muck out Radovan the cop's room, the sun was already drying up the yard. The cop had come to fetch him and they went together into the maroon clapboard house and entered the cop's chamber. It was a small room, with a bunk bed and a little oilcloth-covered table. The cop stowed his rifle in the corner behind the bed, then took off his pistol belt and set the heavy leather holster on the table. He sat on a chair by the table.

"Sit there," he said, unsmiling, pointing at a stool in the corner.

"How do you want me to clean?" Maka asked.

"No need to clean anything."

He took a plastic container that was on the table and handed it over.

"Go on, open it."

Inside were three boiled eggs and a couple of bread slices.

"Eat them here," the cop said.

"Thank you," said Maka. "Why are you doing this?"

"Because you look so thin."

The cop had a box for himself. They peeled their eggs in silence and ate, Radovan the cop staring out the window at the valley beyond.

"I'm sorry for the old man," he said after a while. "I feel bad for the boy. But he'll be released among the first, when the time comes."

When will it come? Maka wanted to ask, but didn't dare to.

"Is it true you're from Srebrenica?" the cop asked.

"Yes. There were others, too. They were all taken away."

"They're in another camp. In Mitrovo Polje, if you want to know. A hundred and fifty kilometres from here, near Alexandrovac. It's a former youth centre for the Pioneers. The conditions are better there. You're the only one here."

"Do you know why was I left?"

"I think it was just an admin mistake. You know how it is. How it's always been."

"Slapdash?"

"That's how it goes."

"What's your roommate going to say?"

"Nothing. He's on shift."

He gave Maka two more eggs. For a moment he looked as though something was holding him back, then asked, "Is it true that they killed five thousand over there?"

"I don't know," Maka said. "I saw many bodies. I saw Chetniks kill people. I don't know how many." He was thinking about the eggs. It was too late for the old man, but he wanted to bring the boy one. It was enormously risky to cross this cop. But he felt like pocketing one.

"You sure it was the Serbs that killed them?"

"Quite sure," Maka said. "I didn't recognise anybody, though," he added swiftly. He couldn't tell what this cop was up to. He sensed that he was sincere, but in this country with no luck he'd learned to watch what you say.

"It's disgusting," the cop said, wiping eggshells from the table into the plastic container. "You sure it was the Serbs that did this? I don't agree with what's happening. I don't agree with a lot of things. War's war, but the rest is unnecessary. This is not how we Serbs are. They don't represent us. A nice fellow like you, how can they beat you?"

"Some of your colleagues view things differently."

"Mean that flat-nosed, tall one?"

"For example. Is it true what they say, that he got his face flattened in combat?"

The cop snorted. "He's never been in combat. Who said so?"

"He told me he'd been to all these places, Osijek and Vukovar. In Srebrenica, too."

"That's a load of balls. He's never been in the troops. He's just a petty criminal. They hired him straight from the prison in Kragujevac. That's where he got that snout smashed." He looked at Maka. "*I* was in Slavonia from the start. In the Krajina Republic's Special Forces. Then in Jajce, then Bihać. Got shot through the chest. That's why I got transferred here. This is a reserve unit. The men have never been to the front. But you're a fighter, aren't you?"

"No, sir, I wouldn't know about fighting."

"I know you are. I know one when I see one."

"Why are you doing this?" Maka said, trying to change the subject. As the cop turned around to place the food box back on the shelf, he quickly slid the remaining egg into his trouser pocket.

"I told you," the cop said, turning back to Maka. He looked at him with his grey, flat eyes. "You're a decent fellow, but you look so awfully skinny. It's not natural."

"Many here are worse than me."

"It'll get better."

"I hope so."

"All right. Get back now. Don't tell your mates about this."

"I will not," Maka said. "What's your name? You're a good man. When this is over, I want to let people know what you did for us."

"Look, it's not a good idea," the cop said, opening the door. "I've got no name here. And you don't need to thank me."

TWENTY-THREE

IT WAS TOWARDS the end of the month when the unpredictable summer weather reached Munich. Between the rainy days, the heat would make people gather in parks and in the Stachus fountain kids played in the water and the ice cream kiosks were doing well. For a week, Amelia had lunched inside, in the air-conditioned tearoom of the office building. The windows faced north and sitting there it was cool and you could see over the roofs of the suburb to the green farming fields beyond.

"You haven't taken any time off," Johann told her. He was her shift manager, the only native German on the cleaning team.

She smiled back, holding her sandwich. "It's all right. I don't think it would help. But thanks."

"I didn't mean it that way," the man said. He looked flustered. "You haven't skipped a day in three years."

"I just had a week off in July."

"Doesn't count when you're sick. But you know, you've got a lot of paid days. It's so sultry now. Why don't you go to the mountains? You'd like it there. Your kid would love it."

"Thanks, really. You're so sweet. I'm still coaching Khadra."

"Gizem can finish it. I can do it, too."

"I'll think about it."

"What's today?" Johann glanced at her meal.

"Salmon and eggs."

"You're lucky he takes such good care of you."

"Aren't I?"

There was a 24-hour supermarket at the station and each morning, on the way from his night shift, Amelia's father would buy the past evening's discounted sandwiches and salads. They kept them in the cooler and you didn't really notice a difference, except for the money saved on every meal and the time on cooking. Yes, she was lucky to have such a great father. Johann was nice, too. He didn't mean any harm. But the unused holidays would convert into a small bonus at the end of the year, and she'd need every penny. She was now the breadwinner.

That wasn't accurate, though. Her brother and father both worked. But she was alone with Dino, and she'd need to move out of that den at some stage. No, they'd all need to. But free-market rental was costly, and the Germans didn't want refugees. That's the way it went.

She'd get Khadra up to speed. Gizem, the Turkish girl, was no good and she didn't care about Somalis. She didn't care teaching how important it was to learn the German ways, to get on top of it before it brought you down. Their boss was nice, but Johann understood it the least. The Kurdish girl had quit. She was good, but she'd quit, and now it was up to Amelia.

Since her friend had left, Amelia was having fewer conversations with her coworkers and more time to think. She was sick of thinking. Yes, she missed the mountains. She was sure Dino would enjoy there, too, but she'd only end up brooding more and it wouldn't do her any good.

She wiped the breadcrumbs from the table, slapped them off her palms into the empty lunch box. She took a sip of coffee. The clock on the wall showed half past twelve. She had too much time lately.

She remembered reading somewhere that in a grieving process you have three stages. First came the denial, then the anger, and finally, months or years later, acceptance. Maybe there was a fourth stage, too; she forgot. She knew she was left with only the one. It was ten weeks since Srebrenica had fallen, and she was angry. She was angry at the Serbs. Angry at Maka for putting her on that bus. Mad at herself for leaving. Maybe something would have gone differently if she'd stayed, and Maka would be safe.

But what could she have done, five months gone, in the siege?

There was just the anger and no denial. Anyone who hadn't come clear of those hills by now was dead. Anyone who hadn't made it to Tuzla had not survived. She understood it crystal clear. If you didn't make it in two and a half months, you never would.

She still called Sabina. Her apartment was two kilometres from the Red Cross office, and the girl went there with Maka's mother, who'd stand outside with a photo of her sons that Sabina had found in an album. There were hundreds of people flocked to the street, wanting to read the ever-growing lists of the missing, and no one had seen or heard about Maka and Edin Delić, another two young men from Srebrenica.

Some of the rumours were starting to be confirmed: vile, unthinkable reports, but they corroborated and a picture began to form. Apparently, they shot most of them in locations like the aluminium factory in Karakaj or the cultural centre in Pilica. From the air, the Americans had photographed bodies lying in the fields. There were signs of large ditches that had been emptied and the corpses relocated somewhere, probably to secondary, better-hidden mass graves.

There was one story about a group that was executed by the river Jadar. The Chetniks had shot them in the water. From there, his body might have washed out to the Drina and surfaced someplace. But it had been nine weeks since that phone call. Nine weeks since Maka was captured. If in that time a corpse hadn't emerged, it was not in the river.

Maybe they weighed him down, she thought, like the fishermen weigh their traps. She felt nauseous thinking about it. She hoped he hadn't suffered. She hoped he hadn't had time to think of anything like she now had. God, she was so stupid. If only she'd believed it when there still was time to pack up and leave. When it all started in Slovenia, there were already clashes in Croatia. It should have been obvious that Bosnia would burn, too. Looking back, it was plain to see. Why hadn't she understood it?

Because it wasn't real, she thought.

When the war broke out in Slovenia, they had been on the Croatian coast for a honeymoon. She'd always wanted to see Venice. The piazzas and the cathedrals from the novels. Still, Italy was expensive and they would have travelled through the part of Croatia where people were already being assassinated and JNA, the Serb-controlled Yugoslav National Army, was setting up roadblocks. It wasn't so much about the money as about safety, Maka had insisted. But his boss said he had a relative who ran a small hotel in Primošten. A charming medieval town; why would they not stay there? The old man would let a room half-price, and there were no tourists anyway, because of the troubles in the north.

It was a lovely trip. Amelia did not want to think there would ever be any other honeymoon, but it was a lovely two weeks, the best there'd ever be. In her mind, Maka came to life now, as clear as if it were yesterday: Maka, in his white linen shirt and the sun behind him, smiling, like someone out of a Godard movie.

"What do you think? Is she a little wobbly?" he asked her. "If you want, we can borrow life vests from the fishermen."

They stood on the old wharf by the esplanade where the sea lapped against the stonework and looked down at the dory. It was small and quayed next to flat-bottomed skiffs and painted light blue on the outside. It bobbed gently in the water and they could hear the water lap between the boats. The turquoise bay glimmered in the late June sun. Behind them, the cafés in the limestone buildings along the promenade had put out their chairs, though there were only a few customers. It was ten in the morning, and it was already very hot.

"No, I trust it," Amelia said. "It's a lovely little boat. Do you think it has a name?"

"Rowboats don't get named, do they?"

"Maybe we should name her. How about *Bounty*? The old man was very generous to lend it."

"He's a good old fellow."

"We should get him something in return."

"We'll get him many big *komarča* and lobsters," Maka said.

The Croatian whitebeard running the hotel had asked them to check his fish trap on the way in. He'd pointed it out from the terrace of the hotel, holding up two fingers of his outstretched hand to show Maka how near the float marker was to the jagged, black scar, by the point where the sea opened.

"Oh, I hope it'll be full," said Amelia. "But he'd only serve them to us for dinner. He's such a nice old man and there's just that other couple staying."

"Well, we'll get supper for them, too. Sure you don't want the life jacket?"

"The old man wouldn't lend us a sinker, would he? And we'll be swimming anyway."

"That's a positive angle." Maka went down the narrow stone steps to the waterline, balancing with the basket in one hand, and pulled the boat closer by the painter rope. He placed the basket with the towels and the sunscreen on the bow thwart. There were pale barnacles on the stonework of the quay where the water receded after each wave and a strong, salty smell of algae.

"It's an awfully old boat, though," Amelia said.

"Yes. Can you see how the gunwale is smoothed out like that? I guess that's where he used to pull in gillnets when he was younger."

"Poor *Bounty*. I didn't know she was that old."

"Well, she's time-tested. Do you want to have anything before we go?"

"I couldn't think of eating. All I imagine are those beaches."

"Let's pop into Admirala first. Get some water. God, it's hot already. What's it going to be like in the afternoon? I want to get the paper, too."

"Maka. Couldn't you not think about it today?"

"It's not that I can't. It just bothers me. Scares me, in a way."

"But there's nothing we can do about it. Why do you have to spoil such a lovely day?"

He was back up on the wharf and he put his arm around her waist, held her close and kissed her. His arm felt strong on the small of her back and his leg solid and firm against hers. He'd worked the full construction season from March, when the snow melted, until last week, taking almost no days off, spending nearly nothing.

"I'd never spoil anything for you, hon," he said, smiling.

"Do you really need it?"

"Newspapers are useful on boats. You'll see."

They walked up to the plaza where narrow streets led from the ancient town gate towards the centre of the promontory and the Saint George's church and its cemetery gardens that overlooked the old fishing town. Most of the shops lining the plaza were shuttered. Turning up towards the rectory, they came to the café bar. A young, lean man in a dress shirt and round eyeglasses was sitting by the window with an espresso and listening to the radio that the waiter had placed on the counter. A newscast was on and a woman newsreader was talking in rapid, tense sentences about something.

"Good morning," said the waiter. "Lovers up so early?" He was an acquaintance of the hotel owner, a smooth-mannered boy who came from the lavender country in Istria. The old man had recommended the place for their shop-roasted coffee.

"Good morning," Maka said. Amelia dismissed the innuendo with a little laugh. "How are you?"

"I'm good as always."

Maka, leaning to the counter and taking off his sun hat, looked at the radio. "What's the news?"

"Their Teritorijalna Odbrana got the orders to start a counteroffensive."

"No," Amelia said, looking at the grave-faced waiter.

"When was that?" Maka asked.

"Last night. There's armoured columns advancing towards Ljubljana. Six JNA brigades."

"It's happening too fast. They declared independence only three days ago."

"Well, it's happening, all right," the waiter said. "Yesterday they shot down two helicopters. Now there's fighting on the Italian border. The Slovenians have bogged the tanks down and are busting them."

"But it's insane," Amelia said. "Everybody's lost their mind."

"The generals seem to think it makes perfect sense," said the bespectacled man by the window. He lit a cigarette and blew smoke towards the ceiling, his head leaning back, then stared out to the street, where a group of loud young men was passing, waving Croatian flags.

"It's not the generals, Dragan. It's the politicians," the waiter said.

"Generals, politicians, mayors... they'll blame it on the Serbs anyway," the man reckoned.

"His family is in Vukovar," said the waiter.

"I'm sure they'll be fine," Maka said. "The common people will keep their cool, and things will settle down."

"Coffee?"

"No, thanks. We're going out to the bay."

"Lady? It's on the house today. You're not in a hurry on a day like this, are you?"

He made two espressos, and Maka bought a pack of Yorks and lit himself one, all of them listening to the newscast on the radio. A stocky man with short-cropped, grey hair and a walrus moustache came into the café, sweaty and out of breath.

"Did you hear about it, Karlo?" he said. "God of mine, what's this coming to?"

"The columns?" offered the waiter.

"That's old news. Now the bloody Serbs are deploying the air force. They've just bombed Ljubljana."

"No!" Amelia said. How could they bomb a city? It sounded like some monstrosity from the past, from the World War, and she looked at the man, unconvinced.

"Not the city, the airport. But still, bloody jet bombers. Goddam crazy bastards. This thing's getting ugly."

"I'd rather you didn't say *Serbs*," said the man called Dragan. "It's the JNA."

"Well, there's only Serbs left," the moustached man said. "With all of our guns." Then, to the waiter, "Give me a *konjak*."

"Where did you hear this?" asked Maka.

"It was on TV. God of mine, it's getting ugly."

"Where are you from?" the man by the window asked Maka and Amelia. He sounded very polite.

"Srebrenica," she told him. "I'm from Bratunac."

"Holiday?"

"Honeymoon," Maka said, smiling.

"Congratulations. You're a lucky couple."

"How do you mean?"

"Your home's in the countryside."

The stocky man turned around, leaning back against the counter with the glass of liquor in his hand. He looked at the Serb by the window and snorted.

"Lucky? Surrounded by Chetniks? It's going to be worse in the sticks."

The Serb's face went sour, and he stubbed his cigarette in the espresso cup.

"Give me the bill, Karlo," he said.

"It's on the house. Why don't you come back for supper?"

"I need to figure things out."

He stood up and went out to the street.

They looked at the stocky man reprovingly.

"What? What did I do?" He looked around at them. "The JNA's all Serbs now. It's no secret. Only Serbs left. And it's the rednecks that's going to ruin this for us. Always been the rednecks!"

"Why doesn't he travel back to his family?" Amelia asked.

"Says someone's attacked their business in Vukovar," said the waiter. "He's waiting for them to come over. He's got a holiday house up in the bayside. But now they're afraid to travel."

"Let's go, Maka," she said. "Let's start rowing."

"You have today's paper?" Maka asked the waiter.

They got the paper and two bottles of water, and went to the port, where Maka unhitched the boat and they started rowing across the bay towards the point. The sea was calm and Amelia watched him row, bending forward taking the oars far back in a long smooth motion, then pulling against the water and feathering the oars and bending forward again. She liked watching him row and listening to the steady groan of the oarlocks. There was a warm breeze over the water and a smell of seaweed, and the boat rocked gently in the swell. Amelia looked back towards the town, where the ancient houses now looked small and white, the lines of their stonework indiscernible, the maroon roofs rising towards the hilltop and the church's tower that rose from the trees. To the east of the old town the line of the long gravel beach came into view, with the row of houses along the seaside promenade, then the inlet in the cul-de-sac of the bay where many white fishing boats were moored.

This is the way I want it, she thought, watching her husband.

"It's good, the paper, isn't it?" Maka said, pulling on the oars.

"It's terrific. Just don't start reading it."

He had laid the *Slobodna Dalmacija* on the stern thwart, which was dotted with gull droppings, and Amelia was sitting on it. She was wearing dark Bermudas that wouldn't show ink stains and a wide-brimmed beach hat. She felt better now, going into the breeze.

"Aren't you getting tired?" she asked.

"This is nothing, hon. It's less than a kilometre across."

"You've got to veer more to the right."

"Yours or mine?"

"Mine. To the starboard."

"Where did you learn such nautical language?"

"*The Sea-Wolf.* Jack London. Actually, I'm not sure if it's port or starboard," she laughed. "Anyway, you need to aim more to the right." She pointed with her arm towards the black rocks that were jutting from the sea and getting bigger.

"You brought a book with you, did you?"

Amelia pulled one out from the canvas bag that she had laid on a coil of rope on the bottom and, showing it to Maka, put it back into the bag. A small amount of bilge sloshed on the multiple layers of old paint of the hull.

"We'll find a nice cove where you can read," Maka said. "God, it's hot. I can't wait to go for a dip."

"If you're tired, let me take the oars."

"No, it's fine. Are we there soon?"

"Maybe a hundred metres. Just keep this course. Maka."

"Yes?"

"Let's not think about it today. It's so lovely out here."

"I'm not thinking of it."

"No, I mean it. I felt so miserable in that café."

"I'm sorry."

"It's not you. I just didn't want to hear the news."

"Let's not hear any more news today."

"We can't do anything about it, anyway. Look, there it is! Just to the left. To your right, I mean."

Maka stalled the boat by the buoy, a plastic motor oil container that had a red dot painted on it. It floated in the waves.

The rocky hillside of the bay was right in front of them. They could see groves of olive trees extending up towards the top. To their starboard were the rocks that the old man had pointed out. The boat bobbed in the surge and Maka caught the marker's rope with an oar, pulling the container closer, then took hold of the wet cord and hoisted up the fish trap. It was empty. Maka let it sink back into the water. Amelia watched it go down and the pattern of the wire mesh become distorted in the prisms of light before it disappeared into the green, dark depth.

"Let's check it on the way back. Maybe there'll be some," she said.

"I'm sure there will."

"Look at that hill. Isn't that strange?"

In the distance was a small island that rose from the sea like a giant turtle's back. One side of the island was yellow with flowering gorse and the other covered in something red.

"Are those poppies?" Maka asked.

"Can't be. They don't flower with gorse."

"Isn't gorse the kind that flowers whenever it wants?"

"Yes, but this is not the time for poppies. They bloom in the spring."

Maka began to row the boat around the point where they knew good, secluded beaches were, and doing so they came closer to the little island.

"Looks like poppies," he said.

"It's strange, don't you think?"

"Well, these are strange days."

"Oh, what the heck. Let's find that beach."

They found it and it was a deserted, lovely little pebbly beach backed by tall cliffs, bordered on both ends by boulders that extended into the water. They beached the boat and laid towels in the shade of the pine trees that grew in the cliffs. The water was warm, but cooled where it got deeper, and they swam in the turquoise sea, playing in the waves. In between the dips they lay in the shade, Maka watching the electric blue sky and the sea, smoking, Amelia reading her book in moist bikinis. She was doing *Quo Vadis*, by Sienkiewicz. She loved history, fictive or real. When she was younger, everything romanticised about the New World and the American Indians had fascinated her, and she had read all the tomes of Karl May's Winnetou novels and all she could find from Laura Ingalls, then moved on to the medieval times of the Balkans, and now it was the Romans she wanted to spend time with. She knew she'd always been a bookworm. By coincidence, their neighbour in Srebrenica was a very old woman who also read – an endearing, fun old lady with her unconventional ways. They had developed a sort of a private book club, exchanging novels. This one was from her.

When the sun moved, Amelia placed her towel on the boulders to the west of the beach. But the rocks were already burning hot, so she went down to the shallow water, walking in between the rocks, looking for blue crabs. There was a bucket in the boat and she called out to Maka, "We'll get the old man something!" But there were no crabs nor any other sea creatures.

They decided to move further south, down the headland, to try another beach. Rowing along the rugged bluff towards the Kremik bay and the marina, they passed many little clear-watered rocky inlets. In some of these bays they spotted the ends of wooden piles riddled with dark-blue mussels jutting from the water.

"Are those oyster farms?" Amelia was sitting in the bow, with a page from the newspaper covering her legs. It was baking hot and they had run out of sunscreen.

"I think so. They attach the nets into poles like that."

"I didn't know they farmed oysters here. Think we could try some?"

They scanned the hillside and noticed a little road that followed the shoreline, fenced by a low drystone wall. Amelia saw olive tree farms and vineyards covering the slope, and some distance ahead there was a small bay with a wooden pier. Behind the pier was a wide, shed-like structure under the pine trees that looked like a restaurant.

Maka took the boat alongside the pier and Amelia made the bowline fast to a pylon. There were two dinghies with outboard motors and a wooden skiff moored at the pier. They stepped off the rowboat, feeling the dry, sunbaked planks under their bare feet, and went up to the restaurant.

It was a wooden terrace, covered by a roof and facing the sea, and there were only two other customers. The men sat at a table, eating. By the counter in the back, a man was fixing a beer tap with a set of tools.

"Good day," he said. He was a tall, weedy man with a rough, tanned face. "Coming from Primošten?"

"Yes," Amelia said. "Glad we found you. It's an awfully hot day."

"I saw you rowing."

"Yes, we've been cruising a little."

"It's a lot of work, rowing. Pardon me. This damn thing ain't working yet."

"It's all right," said Maka. "We saw that oyster farm. Got any on the menu?"

He had. He was the proprietor and he brought Maka and Amelia the menu. They sat at the other end of the terrace from the two men. The owner sent a boy, maybe fifteen, on one of the dinghies out to the bay. Amelia watched the little boat and the youth disappear behind the bluff where they'd seen the poles.

"Coming from the big city?" The proprietor watched Amelia and Maka with solemn, inspecting eyes. It seemed like he had trouble placing their accent on the map.

"No, from Bratunac." Amelia wasn't sure if he'd know Srebrenica.

"A different world, huh?"

"It is."

"You've got *mladica*." This was the big, freshwater salmon of the Drina.

"Nothing like over here," said Maka.

"We didn't know you could farm oysters here," Amelia said.

"It's not common, and you need a licence. But in this part of the bay there are underwater springs that keep the salinity low. It's good for oysters. You'll like them. Anything to drink?"

"You wouldn't have any beer in bottles?" Maka asked him.

"No, I'm sorry. But I've good wine. Local white."

"It sounds lovely," said Amelia. "Does wine go well with oysters?"

"Nothing goes better with oysters."

"Good. Let's have one, shall we?" she asked Maka.

"Yes, let's celebrate well."

The man looked at them strangely but didn't say anything. He brought the wine in an ice bucket. The boy had returned with the oysters and opened them with a clam knife, and they ate them from an oval metal plate, sprinkled with lemon juice and salt. The wine was very cold and fruity and Amelia, who usually never drank, thought the man had been spot-on; she could imagine nothing that would go better with the oysters and the sun and the waves lapping in the pylons, the little wind in the pine trees and her husband sitting with her, without any hurry to go anywhere.

The proprietor came and brought Maka an ashtray.

"I'm not sure about this secession business, though," he said.

It was three days ago when Croatia had declared independence, together with Slovenia, and there had been big jubilations in Primošten with people driving their cars along the waterfront, waving the Croatian checkered flags and honking horns. And up in the north, fifteen kilometres across the bay of Šibenik where the city was, Amelia had seen tiny flashes she thought were fireworks.

"Why not?" Maka asked.

"There are many Serbs living in this area, Bosnians, too. We've always lived peacefully together and always minded our own businesses. I don't like this going forward thing. All of a sudden everyone says they're moving forward. What I see is something else."

"Are you concerned about what's going on up there?"

"Here, on the coast, I'm only concerned about the oysters. The tourists are gone, though."

He looked out to the sea, thinking of something. The other two customers had left and it was very lonely now on the terrace.

"I took my radio to the kitchen so that nobody would ask me to switch it on. But now there's no customers."

"You're very kind," Amelia said.

"Thank you. You should come again."

It was afternoon when they rowed back. The sea was calm and Maka worked the boat lightly. They had wrapped the wine bottle in newspaper and while crossing they had another drink from paper cups the owner of the oyster shed gave them. That was one of the last fond memories she kept. The fish trap had still been empty, and it was ten weeks later that the JNA attacked the area surrounding Primošten. By that time, battles were raging in Vukovar and a month later in Dubrovnik; half a year from there, the war started in Bosnia.

Why did I fail to see what was coming? she thought, packing away her lunch box. You can't make things undone, but if she'd reacted differently, thought differently, Maka would be alive. Now she was left with what? With this anger? She didn't want to accept it. She didn't want to think of him being murdered in those rotten woods. She wanted to remember him like he was, in that linen shirt, smiling, with the wind in his hair and the sunshine. But it was difficult to stop the images of death from creeping into her head like some obnoxious weeds slowly taking over a house that has been abandoned.

Well, she had to go and do those offices. And at some point

she needed to ask Sabina to make a copy of that photo. At least she'd have a picture of him.

Amelia got up to leave. It was one o'clock and her lunch break was over.

TWENTY-FOUR

S HE LOOKED UP; someone was in the doorway of the lunchroom. It was Sefija, her sister-in-law, and the girl stood there, hands spread on the doorframe as if holding the building from collapsing. She was out of breath and the front of her blouse was wet. She looked at Amelia, panting and trying to say something.

Your mind can go through so many ideas in an instant, imagine so many terrifying things you never want to hear. She's supposed to come in at three, flashed in Amelia's head. Without any warning, the old, nauseating hollowness was inside of her.

She's supposed to come in at three.

She felt like she did not have legs anymore and she slumped back onto the chair. "What is it?" she shouted. "Say it! What's happened?"

Sefija swallowed. "Wait. Everything is all right. Maka—" she tried, choking. "Maka is alive."

Amelia heard her. But it was some kind of a mistake.

"Why— what did you just say?"

"Maka, he's alive. He's alive! Listen. I ran—" she started, trying to hold back laughter. "I missed the bloody bus, so I just ran the whole way."

She was from the same cleaning company. There were many part-timers like her working the factory, doing certain tasks or areas such as the staircases or toilets. Sefija did the vacuuming. But she was two hours early. Amelia did not understand.

"What are you talking about? Come here, sit down. You don't make any sense."

She came in and took a chair. Her arms were trembling.

"Sabina called. She's saying Maka is alive." She was laughing now.

Amelia said nothing. Then, slowly, "What do you mean, he's alive?" If this were some kind of a joke, she'd strangle that lass.

"Alive. Alive! What do I mean? Alive!"

Amelia, still quiet, looked at the girl.

"Has he come to Tuzla?"

"No, but his name's on some list. Some list of prisoners. Sabina saw it today at the Red Cross."

She was looking at her. A *list* of prisoners?

"Is it not some captives that have been killed?"

"No. I don't know. She says he's alive. Go home and call her, for chrissake!"

Amelia changed; she had never changed as fast, and she sprinted down the staircase without waiting for the elevator. In the yard she ran through the vast parking lots, thinking, what if it's not true? What if it was some other Delić? Surely, it was some mistake. Someone was playing a cruel joke on her.

At the bus stop she told herself to calm down. The next one would come in four or five minutes. Minutes meant nothing when she'd lived with this pain for many weeks. But now she had new fear inside. Maka, alive? Sabina wouldn't say so unless it were certain, would she?

Slowly, her lungs calmed down. Her mind was calming down. She saw dark clouds gathering in the south and there were many small birds flying away over the forest across the road. It looked like it was going to rain.

Good, she thought, enough of the heat. But she'd never say so, unless it were true?

She stood there and waited. She saw the bus coming down the street.

In the apartment Amelia sat on the floor, next to the television, holding the receiver. Dino was playing, stacking colourful wooden bricks on a wooden lorry. Amelia stroked his head as she spoke. The phone's speaker was on and her parents sat on the sofa, watching and listening. It was still bright outside, with the first raindrops plinking against the window.

"Then it was almost an hour before I got hold of someone," Sabina's voice came through the speaker. "I said, are you sure about this? It's not a mistake? Not some other Maka Delić? And they told me it's not and they had your name and the address in Srebrenica too, so it can't be."

Amelia needed to grab the television table again, though she was sitting. She remembered the other phone call and her head spinning then, too, just for a very different reason. He was alive. Maka was alive, they hadn't killed him, and yes he was alive, he wasn't dead. Just this morning he'd been dead, but now he was alive and the emotion made her dizzy. And how on earth did he end up in that camp in Serbia? That other call came over a month ago. If he'd been captured then, how had he ended in Serbia, with all those men from Žepa?

Maybe that call was a hoax. The man had said he didn't want money. But maybe he was good, and the money talk would come later. She'd heard of such blackmail happening to others, even when the "prisoner" was already dead. Maybe Maka hadn't been captured at all, first, but had somehow made it to Žepa.

"Did they say anything else?" she asked. "Can I call him or write him?"

"All they told me was wait for more information. Things are still very mixed up here."

"Can we send him anything?" asked Amelia's father from the sofa.

"I want to write him a letter!" Amelia said. "If I send it to you, and money and clothes, would you be able to get those to him?"

"I don't know. I'll go back and ask."

"Would you do that?"

"I'll go there."

"It's less crowded in the mornings, isn't it?"

"I can go in the morning, too," the girl said. "I go there every day. Still nothing about Edin. Nothing about the old lady, either."

She meant Amelia's neighbour, the book lady, who had not been seen in Potočari with the thousands of other women. She had not been on the buses. A frail old woman like that wouldn't have crossed the hills, either, so… Amelia couldn't imagine anyone, not even the Chetniks, could do something to a sweet old grandma like her. Except that now her name was on the lists of the missing persons, together with six thousand other names, lists that kept creeping longer. Amelia couldn't even call such horror gut-wrenching. She didn't have words anymore. Just names of the dead. That's what Srebrenica had been reduced to. Lists of the dead and the missing.

But the man who had rowed her across that bay in Primošten and whom she loved, the father of her child, was alive. It started to sink in.

An hour later, the rain was heavy and walking up in their building's stairwell she could hear it on the roof. Another woman, about her age, was coming down the stairs. She was short and chubby and dressed in a blue raincoat.

"Is Mladen home?" Amelia asked her. "I want to talk to him. Is it a good time?"

"Looks like it's always a good time, lately," the woman said. "He says he still can't go to work. Is that a chocolate cake?"

"Sachertorte. I baked it yesterday."

"You're too good to us. Don't let him eat it. I'm telling him to exercise, but he's using the hand as an excuse."

In the upstairs apartment Amelia sat in the kitchen. The cake was on the table and the short woman's husband was making coffee, while two young boys, barely as tall as the table, eyed the treat attentively.

"I believe it's better to do nothing," the man said. He had been reading the papers and smoking when Amelia rang the doorbell. He wore a sleeveless shirt and had a plaster cast on his left forearm. He had slipped in the shower a month ago and broken his wrist. His wife was not happy. Mladen had been drinking and when he drank he drank too much. Amelia often heard them upstairs, quarrelling. He and his wife were Serbs from eastern Croatia. They had lived in Munich since 1991 and they said it was not safe for them to return to Slavonia. Mladen's uncle was an officer in the Serbian army.

"What makes you think so?" Amelia said.

"It's always better not to do anything. At least you know where he is."

"I don't actually know where that camp is. And I've no idea how they're being treated there."

"But it comes with risks."

She had asked him if there was anything the uncle could do to help Maka. Maybe send an enquiry through army channels, or even visit the camp?

"It might make somebody think your husband is important," Mladen said. "It's always better to be nobody in a situation like this. You don't want to attract attention. *Mrsh!* Boys!" He shooed the kids away from the cake and began to cut it. "Who knows what could happen if he's transferred somewhere else?"

"I guess you're right…" Perhaps Amelia had gotten too excited. When she thought of it, Mladen was right. At least she knew Maka was in that camp.

"It's just so difficult," she said, "to sit here doing nothing, now that I know."

"Of course it's very important that he's alive. That's the main thing. But it's best not to take action. They'll all get out of that camp, eventually."

Later in the afternoon the rain stopped and the sun came out, shining through cracks in the clouds. Amelia went for a walk with her father and son. It was fresh and the sidewalks were wet. Dino played in the pools that had formed on the asphalt, splashing the water with his tiny rubber boots.

I can't tell him quite yet, Amelia thought. She didn't know how long it would take. She didn't know what calamities could happen. There was still, always, a chance that something would go wrong. God forbid anything would happen! She still wasn't in sync with the idea that Maka existed in this world with her. But she was getting used to it, and now she knew why she hadn't accepted anything. Her anger was still there, she could feel it, and she knew it might never dissipate completely.

That evening, when they were back, they prepared a meal in celebration, and all three refugee families gathered in the living room. The idea of Maka being alive was starting to become real in Amelia's mind.

She felt so happy she could hardly sleep.

When she woke up to go to work, it was sunny and warm. She put on makeup and her nicest summer dress and let her long, black hair stay loose.

At the factory offices, upon seeing her bright and smiling and dressed up, many of her work friends congratulated her for her birthday. Amelia was no princess-type and they were all used to seeing her with her hair tied and without makeup, in her faded Diesel jeans and a simple T-shirt. But today she was shiny and happy and she laughed, telling her colleagues, "Oh, no, it's not my birthday. Not at all. My husband is alive!"

TWENTY-FIVE

THE MORNINGS WERE cold now and the blanket of fog that stretched over the hayfields across the plain of the valley only lifted after the sun was well above the hills.

"Are you Maka Delić?" the man asked. "I want to speak with you."

It was the same French-speaking, solemn-faced Red Cross delegate from the first camp visit in August. His short-bearded head peeked in from the doorway. Behind him were two of the jailers and that same robust, big-handed Serb who had earlier interpreted for the Swede.

They took Maka to the usual interview room in the canteen barrack.

"My name is Jean Klauser," the man said. "I'm from Switzerland. I work as a detention delegate for the International Committee of the Red Cross. Our office is in Belgrade. I'm not sure if you remember me. I was here briefly in August."

Maka remembered. You remember many details, many minutes, most of the days. He remembered the form he'd scribbled his information on.

"Yes," the Swiss said, "your name has been listed in our Tuzla office. That's actually why I'm here today. Do you know a certain Zekira Kovač?"

"Maybe." Maka was suspicious of anybody who was not a fellow prisoner. Even among the inmates there were some he did not trust.

"Mrs Kovač works for us in Tuzla. She sends you her warmest regards. She said you were one of her pupils."

"That's right. That was in the Eighties."

"When she saw your name, she asked if I could talk to you. It's about her nephew, Dennis Salihović. I wonder if you could help me. I understood that the boy had lived on your street?"

"Yes, that's right," Maka said. There were only two chairs and the big Serb interpreter stood in the back. Maka again felt that the man was watching him. He was starting to wonder if he should get worried about it.

"Was Dennis not here?" asked the Swiss.

"No. I thought he was heading for Tuzla."

Maka told the man what Hassan had told him, about the group in the forest that had split up and Dennis going northwards. It sounded like the boy never got there.

"No. Only this man, Babić, did. What happened was they'd aimed for the Jadar. Somehow they knew an old grist mill by the river that hadn't been destroyed. They wanted to spend the night there."

"We think harming a mill brings bad luck," Maka said. "That's maybe why the Chetniks hadn't burned it. It's a kind of local superstition. And everybody needs bread, anyway."

"That's true, yes. Mr Babić said he thinks a Serb unit had tracked them. They attacked in the first light. From the group of twenty-two Bosnians, fifteen got killed at that mill. Babić, Dennis and five others managed to escape. Seeing the heavy Serb presence in the area, most wanted to turn around and head for Žepa. Only Mr Babić continued northwards. He arrived in Tuzla on the nineteenth of July."

Listening to this, Maka remembered the woods. The aimless, scared roaming, with death at your heels. By the sound of it, that boy had not made it. Not in time, anyway.

"If Dennis ever reached Žepa," he told the Swiss, "it must have been after the town was already in Chetnik hands."

"It's tragic," said the Swiss. "His father died in an ambush. His mother was in the hills, too, one of the few women in the columns. She survived. She's in Tuzla, but not in very good shape. Zekira is helping out, trying to find clues about Dennis. She'd hoped the boy was safe."

"I wish to God I could tell you he was. But everyone I know is in a similar situation. My brother is probably dead. I don't know if my mother has survived."

"I understand," Jean Klauser said. "I *try* to understand. Of course, my home hasn't been burned and none of my family murdered."

"It's all right. Do you know, is it true what they say, that five thousand were killed?"

"Look, I... we don't know how many. In the ICRC, we focus on the living. Did you already give us your relatives' names? Please, tell them again, in case."

The Swiss wrote them down and also took Sabina's name.

"I'll see if there's anything I can do," he said. "If I talked to your cousin, though, I'd be in breach of my mandate. The Red Cross messages are the only form of communication we're allowed to relay. But I'll see if there's anything."

"Thank you. Would you call my wife in Munich?"

A look of small disquietude took over the delegate's face.

"That's something I'm not able to do, unfortunately."

"Unable, or reluctant?" asked Maka.

"Mr Delić, it's very clear in our rules."

"You're talking to Mrs Kovač, though," Maka said. He knew these people were here to help him; still, it rankled him. Zekira Kovač was in the club. He was not. The Swiss, still uncomfortable, arranged the memo pad back into his satchel bag.

"I wish you could see it from my side," he said. "It goes against our rules and, like you said, everyone is in a similar situation."

"I just wanted to let her know that I'm all right. That's all."

"Believe me, I know. But pardon me."

"Well, I understand. Then again, I don't. But it's all right."

Okay, so this was a professional, Maka thought. He would not do it. When all he wanted was that one phone call. Two months in the making. The one in Zvornik didn't even count. But all right. This one was a professional.

What could he say, anyway?

Well, he guessed the letter was on its way. He figured things would get easier from now on. Zekira Kovač didn't know him well. He'd been just one of her pupils. She probably didn't even know he'd gotten married or had a cousin in Tuzla. But if Zekira had noticed his name on those lists, then Sabina had probably seen it too and, if Sabina had seen it, she would have called Amelia in Germany. If only Sabina was safe and if Amelia was safe. And why would they not be? The Chetniks shelled Tuzla, but Sabina was probably okay and nobody had shelled Munich. But it was going to be tough. It was going to be a long road and he needed to keep himself sane and not lose any more weight and try to get rid of these lice. The others were all dead but his mother might have made it, and even though the others were dead and there were five thousand of them at least, since what Radovan the cop had heard from his people was probably an underestimation, he couldn't let the bitterness and anger seep in. Because it wouldn't help him, just as looking back had never helped anyone unless it was to learn from their mistakes.

And what mistakes did we make? Well, he thought, we made plenty of them. But they were not our mistakes, and we're going to come out of this without guilt or shame and that's how I want to see them when I'll see them. This war had been a bitch and there had been many whores and bastards running it, but life was not a bitch when Amelia and Dino were in it and he was in it with them.

He wished he could tell this man about Dennis, though. But the boy was probably dead, too. It was eerie, not knowing if a person existed anymore or not. He should ask the Swiss about the neighbour as well, that old lady Amelia used to swap books with. On the last day, when the Chetniks had broken through, Maka had sent someone running to her house to get her. But she was a proud old woman and she'd refused to leave. Anyway, he should ask about her, but then there were so many others. He knew he shouldn't overburden this Red Cross delegate. He'd need to pick just one. Who?

"One last thing, if you don't mind," Maka said. "Do you know about my nephew? The one who met Dennis in the woods? I was told he's in another camp, in Mitrovo Polje. There are others I know from Srebrenica, too."

"What are their names again?"

Jean Klauser went through papers that he took out from a manila envelope.

"Yes. They're in Mitrovo Polje. I'll go there later today. Our delegation has visited the camp twice. They have somewhat better conditions there. But how are you? I imagine it must be like a living nightmare, this situation. How are you being treated?"

Maka told him about the beatings. The guards were still doing it, just less visibly now. Batons to the soles of the feet and the kidneys, and so on. He told him how Dedo had died. Hukanović, the man with colon cancer, whom Slavko had kicked in the abdomen, was bleeding rectally and could barely walk. He'd asked to be taken to the hospital in Užice but had thus far been denied all medical attention. The scrawny inmates had pressure ulcers from having slept two months on the concrete. They still got less food than what was required to sustain a man. The lice were having a feast, though. They were allowed to take a cold shower once a week, in groups of ten, but had no lice soap. It was bearable, compared to being killed. But why were the Serbs doing this to them? What were they incarcerated for? Were they criminals? Prisoners of war? Refugees? Animals?

"This is not acceptable," Jean Klauser said. "Your conditions and treatment can't continue like this. I will engage in dialogue with the Serb authorities and see what can be done."

"Do you know what our status is? What are we to these authorities?"

"Well, it's complicated. The Serbs decline to acknowledge that you're prisoners of war. They say Serbia is not at war with Bosnia, but they don't recognise the Sarajevo government either. They imply that you're refugees or internally displaced people. They haven't spelled that out in writing. We've asked Belgrade to clarify, but we have no authority in the matter."

"Come to think of it," Maka said, "if Serbia hasn't recognised Bosnia, if we're such good citizens in Yugoslavia, why treat us this way?"

"I understand your frustration. Everything is very complicated in a war."

Maka guessed that was one way to put it. Frustration, complication… that was one hell of a way to put it. But that's the way it went, like Radovan the cop had said.

The two Red Cross men got up to leave.

"Thank you for your time," said Jean Klauser.

"You were lucky I found a slot in my schedule," Maka said. Jean Klauser laughed and went out.

From the door, the big Serb who until now had not said anything except for his interpreting, looked back and said, "Hang in there."

Maka thought he winked, too, but he couldn't tell if it was just a tic.

TWENTY-SIX

A MELIA WAS PUTTING on her shoes when the telephone rang. She had been baking with her mom and remembered they had nothing for the men, so she had taken off her apron to go out to a store that was open on Sundays and where you could buy liquor. A girl she knew from Bratunac was coming to visit with her husband and her grandfather. The old man got along well with Amelia's dad and she knew they'd be talking about the bad days and the good days, and whichever days the men talked about, they liked to remember them over a glass of something.

"Mom, can you get it? I'm going!" she called out to the kitchen.

"No! I've got dough all over!"

She kicked off her shoes and went to the phone.

"Good day, is this Amelia Delić?" a male voice said. He had a Serbian accent.

"Yes." Amelia's mind flashed back to the call two and a half months ago. She sat down on the television table.

"My name is Jokić. I'm an interpreter for the Red Cross in Belgrade. Is this a good time for you to talk?"

"Yes, of course," she said. *Belgrade?* She was trying to recall how the other caller had sounded. All she remembered was that he'd talked in that disconcerting, hushed voice. This one was pleasant and businesslike.

"Good. It's to convey greetings from your husband. I couldn't actually talk to him myself. I've been interpreting when our delegates have visited the camp where he is, and we've quite strict rules. But I'm sure if I had, he'd have sent you his best wishes."

Amelia held the receiver to her ear, staring straight ahead, as if the phantom of the caller were standing in that cluttered living room. She inhaled deeply. She exhaled.

"Where is he?"

"The camp is in Serbia, near a town called Šljivovica. I've visited there twice, both times interpreting for him. I wanted to call to tell you that he seems to be in good health, mentally and physically. The conditions there have been quite harsh and he's lost weight. Other than that, talking to him he seems very strong."

Amelia was quiet for a moment.

"Why do you tell me this?" she said.

"First of all, you should know that I'm not allowed to contact anyone directly like this. So, I hope you'll keep this a secret."

"I will, of course. I appreciate you doing this. But why do you call me to tell me these things if it puts you at risk?"

"The men in that camp have been through a lot. I thought I'd help your husband a bit, or at least let you know that things will be—" He sounded like he wanted to say *fine*, but paused and said, "At least things will be *better*."

Amelia sat on the low table. In the kitchen she saw her mother moving. It was a sunny day and the other two families had all gone out. Her father had taken Dino to the backyard, where the playground was. She could hear the children play, their screaming and shouting coming from the half-open kitchen window and, on the other side of the building, on Dachauer Straße, the screeching and clonking of the streetcar.

"But why Maka?"

The Serb gave a pleasant laugh.

"I don't know why, exactly, but there's something about your husband that makes him a quite likable person. He seems the most inoffensive man, yet he's got a lot of dignity, given the circumstances. Then there's the fact he's never met his child. Dino, is he?"

"Yes."

"My apologies, I feel like an intruder. But I know these details from the interviews."

"You're not intruding at all! Look, mister... sorry, what was your name again?"

He said it again.

"Look, Mr Jokić. I really do appreciate you've called me. This is mildly put."

"It's nothing. It is easy for me to do. I only wish this conversation remains between your family and me."

"It will. But tell me, how did Maka end up in that place, Šljivovica?"

"If I remember, he'd crossed the Drina near Zvornik. He got arrested on the other side."

"Do you know when that was? Before or after the eighteenth of July?"

"Oh, I wouldn't remember such detail now. Why so?"

"You haven't called me before, have you?"

"No, this is the first time," the man said, adding that Maka had written Amelia a Red Cross message. He had seen Maka write it. The letter would probably arrive later this month. Amelia could then write him back. He told her there was censorship, but if she'd write directly to him, Jokić, he would smuggle the letter to Maka. This way they could communicate freely. The ICRC aimed to visit the camp weekly, and he'd alternate with another interpreter. So, he'd be going to Šljivovica fortnightly. She could send him money, too, and he would deliver it. He said he couldn't take in anything big, like parcels, for he had to pass an inspection at the gate. But money and letters would be fine.

"Can they spend anything in there?" Amelia didn't want to sound distrustful, but she couldn't help it.

"Not yet," Jokić told her. "But it's always good to have some money in the pocket. Eventually their conditions will improve and they might be allowed to make purchases. He'll need a lot of basic supplies. We, the ICRC, will, of course, try to provide some. For example, they have a shower but it's cold and they don't have any lice shampoo."

"Oh my God! Is it that bad there? Does he have *lice*?"

"Well, I don't know about him. But that's the risk in a camp like that. Anyway, please take my number down. You can call me anytime if there's anything. I might not always be able to help, but I can always try to."

After the call, Amelia sat by the phone for a long time, looking at it. In the kitchen her mother was taking something out of the oven.

"Not gone yet? Who was it?"

"I will, Mom. I will."

"Who was it?"

"A friend."

Amelia looked at the phone, thinking, I'll tell her later tonight. I will tell Dad, too. But how on earth did people get by before there were telephones? If this was a lonely and frightening world she lived in, how much lonelier and scarier had it been back then? Unexpectedly, her world felt like it was opening. It was like coming out of the woods to a bright, sunny meadow.

Maybe not quite, she thought. Maybe that was a bit too pompous. But she knew it was an open place that felt like a meadow. If the world was a forest, there were meadows in it.

Right. Brandy and beer. Right, so. Things would maybe never be fine again. But they could always get better. Then they'd get a little better again.

TWENTY-SEVEN

A ROUND THE SECOND week of October, the inmates saw
cars with government plates drive into the camp. A cranky-
looking old fellow in an ill-fitting polyester suit and sunglasses got
out from one of the Mercedes and, surrounded by his security
details, started touring the facilities.

Maka heard the man question the occupants of an adjacent
room, the discontentment in his voice increasing. "What's
happening here? What do you mean you don't know? How come
you look like a zombie? Speak up!" Then, speaking to the guards:
"What do they get for meals? How do they shower? Look at them,
filthy as hell. Not your responsibility? Do you want me to show
you responsibility? Then don't talk to me about responsibility.
Where's the commandant? How do you mean, Kraljevo? Isn't
this his camp? If you're not happy, let me know and I'll show you
responsibility."

Then, coming to the door of Maka's cell and looking
disgustedly into the room where the cluster of scraggy prisoners
languished, he asked, "How are you being treated? Say it, now."

Nobody said anything.

"Who's the room chief?"

Maka put up his hand. There were still no daily musters, but each room had been assigned one inmate whose responsibility it was to report that everyone was present.

"You all look mangy like dogs. How come? Speak up."

"We're not getting enough food," Maka said. Then, lifting the shirt of one of the inmates who had been beaten the day earlier and showing the long, purple and black welts from the rubber hose across his back, "This is what they do to us."

He exposed his own scrawny midriff, the ribcage visible and his skin scabby from flea bites and the constant scratching.

The man seemed to get very angry behind his amber-coloured shades.

"From now on, nobody will touch you!" he announced, his finger in the air to make a point.

Maka never found out who the bigshot was. Some rumoured he was the deputy from the Serbian foreign ministry, others the head of a major political party. Nevertheless, from that day on the beatings stopped. A week later, the MUP cops were replaced by a team of regular civilian police. These looked rather sore to have landed this unconventional job for a copper, but they were benign jailers compared to the MUP bastards.

The inmates started getting three meals per day, and the canteen hall was refurbished with camp tables and chairs. They had spoons and ate pea soup and bread from plastic plates. They got to take a shower twice a week. By now the water was ice-cold, but they were given lice shampoo and a chance to wash their clothes.

Another humanitarian group, the International Organization for Migration, visited the camp in the middle of October. Not long after, a large quantity of lumber and other materials was hauled in. Under the direction of the two detainee carpenters, the men built bunk beds in the cells and covered the windows with plastic sheeting. The nights were very cold and sometimes, in the morning, going to the latrines, the air was crisp and there was frost on the weeds by the path. They had clean blankets, however, and the room now resembled more a human dwelling than the animal pen it had been a month earlier. In Maka's cell they had nine inmates left. The old man was dead and Hukanović admitted to the hospital in Užice.

These were all small ameliorations in the context of human existence. To Maka, they felt like giant leaps in terms of decency and morale.

Then there was the letter.

It was from Amelia. The robust Serb interpreter handed it to him in the dimness of the interview room, together with an envelope containing five hundred deutsche marks. "Should you need anything else," the man said, "you can always talk to me, and I'll pass the message on to your wife." Maka was not sure why this man, Jokić, was helping him. He did not ask anything for his favours, just advised Maka to keep tight-lipped about the arrangement.

Holding the paper, Maka felt as if he were holding on to life itself. It was too early for letters to arrive through regular channels, so he first read it secretly in the latrine, then again lying in his bunk, facing the wall and under a blanket, hearing out each word and sentence that Amelia had written in her beautiful longhand.

Now everything is all right here in Munich, she said. *We have no problems and my family they're all doing fine. Dino is growing up fast and missing you. I miss you awfully, too, but I know we'll be reunited before long.*

We haven't heard anything about your brother, she said. Maka knew she was implying that Edin might not have survived. This was something he already had accepted, like you accept that a tree has fallen when you see it ripped from its roots after a storm. And there were so many others. *Your cousin Senad didn't make it*, Amelia said. *Your other cousins Izet and Amra arrived in Tuzla. Your mother is there, too, she's staying with Sabina's family and I speak with them daily. She is a strong woman and she sends you her love! I'm sending you all of my love!* She said she was enclosing five hundred marks, and, although Maka knew what she thought about smoking, she'd wanted to send him cigarettes as well. But the man whose name she shouldn't mention here had said it can't be done yet, so she was asking Maka to please hang on there, and be a good boy without smokes, for now. *I love you, always – Your Amelia.*

Maka lay in the bunk, the upper one, hearing the other men in the room talk. Their voices sounded strange as if coming from a great distance. He held on to the letter. Then he read it again. Everything was all right in Munich. A lot of love. Good boy without smokes. It was Amelia, talking to him. That Serb, Jokić, he was a strange and good man. Just like the policeman in Zvornik. Jean Klauser was helping, too. The two were in cahoots, no doubt.

For the first time he felt an inkling that he had ridden out the war.

Nothing bittersweet about it, he thought. His life had been shattered, blown to bits so that you couldn't even tell by the foundations that anything had ever stood there. But he'd outlasted. He had two strong arms to start building his life again. Only he didn't know where and how. There were rumours the war was winding down in Bosnia. He guessed everything burned out at the end.

Three and a half years. Not much left for the flames to eat.

Then it was November and the trees outside had begun to turn. Cast iron stoves were installed in the rooms in preparation for the winter. The amount of firewood they got was scant, and they burned it in the morning when it was bitingly cold and dark outside. It was a ritual: lighting the stove up, waking up hearing the fire crackle and seeing the glow of the flames on the wall. They welcomed the new day not just with the warmth, but with the little dignity that came from the act of being in control of something.

By the month's end Jokić could inform Amelia that the inmates had hot water. The Serbs had sent an electrician and they had built an indoor shower area with a boiler. Jokić, that incredible wizard, also brought Maka news from Mitrovo Polje. The Red Cross would always visit the two camps running, and the interpreter had smuggled in a letter from Zlatar.

By the sound of it, the goldsmith was in good spirits. The first two months had been very difficult in their camp, he wrote, but things had improved and he knew they'd eventually have those beers and *pljeskavica* together. Maybe not in Belgrade, though. Zlatar had written something that looked like "screw Belgrade" in brackets then struck it out. But Maka, the old fox, could be sure they'd have them. Hassan was doing well and the fine young man had been interviewed by the IOM about asylum in the United States. Maka should not be a stranger and he should write back and let them know how things were keeping. Zlatar thought they were on the right track. With comradely wishes from his friend, Sakib Šehić.

That all sounded swell, Maka thought. But on the right track to where?

The crisp winter weather was definitely there. Sitting outside the barrack and watching the distant hills, the sun didn't warm you anymore and the hazel trees at the back of the camp, where Maka had been beaten, were barren of leaves.

One afternoon the inmates were all mustered into the yard. A headcount was first taken, which made it feel as if something important was at hand. Then they waited, in a formation of haphazardly made rows under the cold sun, shivering in their worn-out summer clothes. Maka had screwdrivers and a hammer weighing down in his tracksuit's pockets. He had been in the canteen, together with Glumac and a couple of other pretenders that still made up the catering team, installing the newly delivered cooktops. Now they stood surrounded by the policemen with their guns and the torpid old German shepherd dogs that these new cops had brought with them. The silence and the waiting made Maka notice traces of the old hollowness in his stomach. He was still naturally afraid of any guards and announcements.

The new camp commander came and mounted a wooden grate to address them. Much like his predecessor, he was a tired-looking, small man and Maka wondered if they made small, jaded men like that prison bosses on purpose. This one also never referred to them as prisoners.

"Gentlemen!" he called out. "You may have already heard. Yes, I know you talk and gossip like old women. You may have heard about the ceasefire in Bosnia and Croatia. So far, it has held." He scanned the formation with an imperious gaze. "Now, two days ago, a peace agreement has been reached in the United States. This was done in a place called Dayton, Ohio. Hence, I will call it the Dayton agreement."

The man sounded very smug to have this geographical knowledge. "This peace deal is a very special deal," he went on. "It will be, later on, signed by the Serbian, Bosnian and Croatian leaders. Practically, it has already been implemented. Gentlemen, it means that the war is over. Finished!"

He held a long pause, maybe expecting some sort of a response from his haggard audience. There was only the distant chirping of sparrows in the trees.

"You should know," he continued, looking irritated, "that this agreement recognises the borders of the Republika Srpska in Bosnia. This means the Serb Republic has now been established. Established! And it includes the former areas of Žepa and Srebrenica." After having stared the crowd down for another pause, he said, "Gentlemen. You fought for nothing."

"For nothing, huh?" whispered Maka. "Tell us something new, you goony little son of a dwarf." He heard the men around him snigger. What did you ever fight a war for, if nothing? He doubted if there ever was a greater exercise in dumbness than adult men running in the woods, trying to croak each other with automatic weapons.

"Hey, we're Serbians now," someone else whispered. "Maybe Milosević will give us all a pension." This one also generated chuckles, and the camp boss shouted, "Silence! Silence in the formation! Listen. To celebrate this historical event, tonight at supper everyone will get an apple. Now, dismissed!"

Going back to the canteen to continue the kitchen installation, Maka tried to identify his feeling about the war ending. What was he supposed to think about it? In his mind there were no victory parades, no confetti raining, no crowds cheering. He'd known it would end and now it had ended. At some point, all wars ended. In the trenches, at least. The wars ended in the trenches. That was the problem. They ended only in the trenches. But was it finished?

Well, his hometown was. That's as much as he knew. He'd install those stoves today and think about that later.

TWENTY-EIGHT

"LET ME TELL you. Know why Germany refused us?"
Juka was concentrating as he spoke, studying the cards in his hand. The farmer pulled one out and slapped it on the table. He was angry about Germany.

"Because they're effective. That's why! Who wants a bunch of shot-up, over-the-hill cretins? When you've got an excess of the buggers already."

The men around the table were playing switch for cigarettes. Maka, lying down on his bunk, watched the game from above. He had just finished his morning shift in the kitchen when the bad news came.

He was not angry but he felt pretty downhearted. There was a fire in the stove and it smelled like pine resin burning. Clothing hung on the bunks' ends and they had crude shelving on the walls where they kept their things and pictures of half-naked girls from magazines were taped on the door. It was warm inside and he was tired. They say you get used to disappointments, but it's not true. They just add up.

"They used to come to Sarajevo for holidays," Čerkić said.

"They swarmed the coast, too. Every autumn. When they bought film, it was always the best quality slide."

"Well, they're not swarming anymore, I tell you. They've had enough of us *Mujos* and *Suljos*," said the farmer.

He told the old joke about a Brit, a Frenchman and a Bosnian arguing whose language was the most beautiful by comparing the word *butterfly*: how you could see the little *papillon* or the *leptir* flit gracefully in the air, before they all turned their attention to the German (who usually was an outsider in this joke and was building something like a rocket engine out of sheet metal) and the German saying: "Jawohl. In Deutsch it is *der Schmetterling*."

"Get it? Derr. Schhmet. Terr. Ling." Juka rolled the Rs exaggeratedly, like a robot. "Now, these types don't fuck around. Why would they take us? What are we good for? Can you engineer? Do you know mathematics?"

He slammed down another card. It was not a good one, and Bielo collected the cigarettes for the round. The blonde Bosniak tossed one at each man in the room, pocketing the rest. Maka caught his and lit it.

Yes, what am I good for? he thought.

"He knows how to shoot an RPG," someone said. "Tell us how you got the tank."

"Oh, tired of that story," said Bielo. "I don't even think I scored it. Think it was Selimović that hit it. Who cares, anymore?"

It was the middle of December and the Dayton peace agreement had just been signed, officially ending the war in Bosnia. To Maka and the others, it brought no reprieve. They now had the Red Cross cards, but the Serbs had refused to stamp them. They still did not know what their status was. Perhaps one day they would be classified as something, as refugees, or maybe illegal immigrants. Practically, they were captives. They had no idea where they were heading to or how they would get there.

They had interviews with various refugee agencies. Different options and countries were dangled before them: Sweden, Denmark, Austria.

"These have already taken in their share during the war," a woman from the United Nations Refugee Agency explained. "They might each admit only a couple more from this camp." Her face was thin and reluctant as she examined Maka over a pile of documents.

A handful of them had already been released. These were all men with special circumstances, such as Hukanović, who had been flown to Ireland for cancer treatment, or Amir, an orphan whose whole family had been killed. The boy got to Australia – another country with a stringent immigration policy and not a realistic option for Maka, she said.

"Look," he told her. "I don't care about other countries. What I want, what most here wish for, is simply to return home. Bosnia is my land. That's where I belong."

"That is understandable," the woman said. "But it's complicated. You crossed over to Serbia. What if some now consider you as a traitor? Naturally, I am concerned for your security."

Maka's reaction was incredulous laughter. What the bloody hell?

"Look, we fought for our country. We crossed that river only to save our lives. No one will accuse us of anything, let alone treason."

"True, very true, that. You made an excellent point. However, travelling on land through the Serb Republic can be dangerous."

"So, you still can't protect one bus convoy?" All right, he got that. Yes, he got that. "Can't we just fly from Belgrade?"

"This, unfortunately, is not an option. Because, you see, Sarajevo Airport is considered risky. The aviation infrastructure has been damaged by war. The agency puts your safety first." She was reciting these catchphrases from a UN playbook, and it all sounded like bullshit. Their personnel did fly in and out daily.

266

There was something cooking behind the scenes that Maka had no way of understanding.

Then, talking to Jean Klauser, the Swiss suspected that the difficulty of repatriation simply stemmed from infighting between the UN offices in Sarajevo and Belgrade. Also, Croatia was refusing to allow convoys through their territory, and Hungary wouldn't give them transit visas. And it was perfectly possible that the Serbs were using them as bargaining chips in some diplomatic game. Why give anything for free when you could trade it?

Anyway, it sounded like Bosnia was not on the cards for now.

A few days later it was announced that the United States would take them all. It was a confirmed deal the UN had negotiated.

Maka tried to imagine himself living in America. He was adaptable. He might find work in construction or farming. Maybe even as a cook, just to continue an old joke. The more he thought of it, the better it sounded. But would Amelia and Dino be able to join him? What if their visas took years to process? He was tired of waiting and of the separation. He was sure Amelia would like it there, though. Hell, she probably knew the names of the places already from all those western novels.

The days dragged on, with no further news about the USA.

Next, they were told everybody could go to Germany. This was also a done deal, and anyone who wanted to leave the camp could fly there after the New Year.

A jackpot, he thought. Germany was reasonably close. Amelia was there. New Year's was a good month away. His wife and son just a month away. It would not close this chapter. Nothing could ever close this. But it would be the new beginning he'd dreamed of.

Only two of Maka's roommates declined the offer. The pork-noodle man was fixated on the USA and was prepared to dig his heels in for as long as it would take. The other, Čerkić, just wanted to return to Sarajevo to his wife and kids. "Do not believe them," the photographer had advised Maka. "They can't stop you from going home if you want to."

But there he lay, forgotten in a cage. That morning, when the word abruptly came that the Germany deal had been suspended, it was not so much the rejection that had exhausted him but the realisation of being merely a pawn, a number in someone's file. These foreigners had screwed them up during the war and they still kept screwing them. Bielo joked that the UN had probably set up a whole new agency solely for the purpose.

The tank-killer was dealing the cards now. "All right," he called. "No goddam alliances. And knock when you have to. Čerkić?"

Watching the game and smoking, Maka tapped ash into the sardine can that he still kept on the shelf. Well, he thought, at least the barracks now resembled a proper camp. The ICRC letters were reaching them officially. Some of the inmates had received money from their relatives, and the Serbs had organised a weekly canteen van for cigarettes, biscuits, toiletries and such. With no explanation, though, the van stopped coming. But the cops picked up the service, dealing goods on demand. This black market activity benefitted both the captives and the jailers. The cops' salaries were shit, and for the right price the inmates could now source whatever they could afford, including *rakia*.

One of the aid agencies brought in a mountain of clothes. They were in good condition, albeit used, and Maka had finally departed with his bedraggled tracksuit. He had two shirts, a pullover, trousers, a change of underwear, a winter jacket. They were given a pair of scissors and he got a haircut. They had razors, too, that were so dull it hurt to shave, but he took off his beard, save for a moustache. Talk about a new man. He had turned thirty-two and the only thing he kept from his old life was his army boots. The leather was sort of mummified, but they still fitted his feet like a second skin. Soldiers always had some superstition. These were the boots in which Maka had survived three years of bloodshed. So, when they got donated new sneakers, he swapped his for a bottle of Croatian brandy. It now stood on the shelf translucent amber, long-necked and tempting, waiting for some special occasion. Maka did not know what or when. He assumed there would eventually be one.

It was just the uncertainty that frayed him.

The new round of cards had just started when the door opened and a prisoner with a metal bucket peered in. This was the inmate tasked with clearing ashes from the stoves.

"Delić here?" the man asked. "There's a foreign TV crew. They want to talk to someone from Srebrenica."

"Tell them I'm not interested." Maka remembered the fake news crew from July. Nothing good had come to anyone from that.

"Sounds like you need to tell it yourself. They know you're the only one." Looking at the stove where little flames flickered in the fire box, he added, "You folks cosy here, huh?"

"Just leave the bucket," said Maka. "We'll take care of it."

"Nah. Already lost one, got into enough trouble. You coming?"

"All right." He snubbed out the cigarette.

The news crew was outside, talking with the camp commander. They were three men from Switzerland and a Serb girl who interpreted. It was windy and very cold in front of the barrack. They huddled inside their down jackets like fluffed-up birds. The man carrying the large Betacam had a leather jacket but no gloves and he looked like he wanted to go inside.

"These people are making a programme about Srebrenica," said the camp commander. "They want to interview you. If you choose to talk, be assured that you can talk freely about anything."

"I'm not too keen to talk about anything," Maka said.

"That's a pity," said one of the reporters, a thin man with a grey ponytail. "They say you're the only one from Srebrenica. Are you sure you don't want to?"

"Quite sure."

"Look," said the man with the camera. "We'll visit Srebrenica, too. If you give us your address, we can go to your house and film it."

Maka thought over it for a minute. In his mind he had bid farewell to the house. Still, he couldn't help thinking of it daily, wondering if it had been torched or not.

"How about," he asked, "could you send a copy of the programme to my wife?"

"Hmm. We can't promise that," said the ponytailed man. "We'd need permission from the producer."

"In that case, I'm not sure."

"What the hell. We'll send it," said the cameraman. His fingers were red from the cold.

They shot the interview in Maka's cell. They had first filmed the premises outside, then the inmates having their lunch in the canteen. Maka understood now why that morning they had been told to scrub the canteen hall spotless. Today they got an extra portion of bread and, for the first time, an orange per man. It was for the show, for the camera.

He sat by the table, smoking. His roomies were perched on their bunks in the background, waiting to hear him. The camera lens was pointed at him but he didn't feel like talking. It wouldn't bring back anything. He didn't trust the camp commander. He knew he'd still have to watch his mouth.

"How did you get here, to Serbia?" the ponytailed man started.

"I swam across the Drina," Maka said.

"Why did you decide to come here?"

"Didn't have a choice."

"How come?"

"My options were either surrender to the Serbs in Bosnia or give myself up here. My chances of survival were better here."

"What made you think that?"

"What do you mean? If one country says they're not at war, I don't see any reason why they'd kill me."

"So you're saying you thought Serbia was a country at peace?"

"Yes, it's a country at peace," Maka said. "People have migrated here before, and they haven't been killed." He was placing his words carefully and thinking, where's this going?

"Why did you not try to go to Tuzla?"

He looked at the ponytailed man. This was a good one.

"I did try to get there… but how do you do it when they're waiting for you with guns and you've got nothing, just your bare hands?"

"Did you see any dead people?"

In the background the men were talking quietly and someone said, "Tell them how many you saw being murdered."

Maka took a puff on the cigarette and looked away from the camera. *What the hell? Tell them yourself.*

"The Chetniks know it," he said. "What do I know?"

He was quiet for a long moment.

"I saw a lot of bodies. How could I tell how many? I didn't count them."

"Did you see people suffer? How was it? Did you see people die?" The Serb girl was talking over the ponytail man.

"Yes, I saw… they were shooting. People were falling and they were shooting. You couldn't even surrender."

"Where did they shoot from?"

"From every direction. They shot from every direction, and around you people were just falling."

"Was it just men? Males only?"

"It was everybody. Women, children, men." Maka looked past the camera, took another puff. He glanced at the ceiling. What was he thinking? This wasn't going anywhere. He wasn't in the woods anymore. He was here now.

"You don't want to talk about it?"

"No."

"Is it difficult to talk about it?"

Maka looked at the interpreter. She was a young girl with almond eyes and short, braided pigtails. The door was closed and there were no cops in the room. The seven other Bosniaks sat in their bunks, watching him. He could feel their eyes on him.

"What makes you think it might not be?" he asked the girl. "I lost three of my brothers and my father. You think I want to talk about it?"

"Did you see them?"

"I was with my brother when he got killed. The others, no."

"All right. I see," said the ponytailed man. "Thank you. That's all."

The man in the leather jacket, who had been holding the heavy Betacam steady on his shoulder, rigid like a mannequin, put the camera down and sighed.

TWENTY-NINE

AMELIA HAD BEEN at work when the phone rang again, and her brother had answered. It was someone who introduced himself as a producer or such for a television channel. The man – Nirzo forgot his name – said they'd interviewed Maka in Serbia and filmed his house in Srebrenica. He had promised to courier the tape, so he'd called for the address. It would probably have to wait until the programme aired, though.

"In Switzerland it was, I think," Nirzo told Amelia.

"No! How could you? Never crossed your mind to take these down, did it?"

"He sounded like he's going to do it."

"Could have still asked for *his* number?"

She set down the heavy grocery bags in the vestibule to take off her sneakers. The floor was taken over by what looked like a hundred pairs of shoes of all sizes and colours, with the walls above covered by a hundred suspended jackets and umbrellas. Every time she entered the apartment she felt like diving into a tunnel in some goddam anthill.

Nirzo shrugged his shoulders and offered a penitent smile.

What a lamebrain, she thought. Outside it was cold but she had sweat on her brow from hauling the shopping. Her nerves were racked by all these anonymous calls. More helpless waiting now? She knew she'd always had this, her tendency to worry and panic. Just couldn't help it. Sweating about trifling matters, then ignoring the big things... well, she couldn't do much about those anyway. And it was good news, after all.

Dino charged at her from the kitchen.

"Mommy!" He clung to Amelia's legs, ignoring the groceries.

"Oh you little devil. *Baba* been indulging you again? How many times have I told you?"

"I want to see Daddy! I want to see Daddy!"

Amelia gave Nirzo a homicidal glance. She'd very much like to stay behind the wheel of these things! Interview in a bloody concentration camp? She remembered those terrible pictures from Bosnia, with emaciated, scared men behind razor wire, like cattle.

"We're gonna have dinner now," she said, detaching the little human burdock from her thigh. "Uncle Nirzo will cook!"

Two weeks later the man called again. He told Nirzo – again – that they could watch the programme directly. It had been sold to a German network and it would air in the third week of January. He said he would send the tape anyway.

Nirzo took his name and number down. It was Max Günzel from *3Plus Schweiz*.

He met Maka, Amelia thought. She was excited about the idea. Mr Max had filmed Maka, and all of Germany would see him. Such exposure would protect him. Surely it would? It was one thing to be registered by the Red Cross, but now the whole world would see him. *She* would see him. Surely such exposure was a good thing.

Another thirteen days went past. On January 20, they were all packed in the living room. It was hot inside. The windows were ajar and they were drinking tea. It was late in the evening.

The show would start after midnight. Amelia had never felt so nervous; she sat on the sofa, squeezed between her parents, and neighbours and people from the other families had filled the room, some sitting on the floor, some crowding the hallway. Nirzo and Sefija were there, too. Only Dino was missing. All day the boy had been excited and playing outside, telling the other kids how his daddy would be on the telly. But he had worn himself out and, to Amelia's relief, was asleep now. A pitiful denial, she thought. But it was better this way. If it turned out to be fine, he'd get to see Maka when they got the tape.

The programme came on. It was a German news magazine show and it opened with an impeccable-looking couple, a man and a woman, each behind their desk, in a studio, talking about Bosnia, how the war had started and how it had ended, taking the viewers through the developments of the past months, the Dayton peace agreement and the alleged mass killings in Srebrenica.

"Come on, cut it out," Amelia thought out loud.

"Look, that's Selmanagića!" her mother whooped when the camera left the studio and cut into the main street in Srebrenica. The sky was grey and bleak with the clouds hanging low. The thoroughfare with its empty storefronts looked deserted and the houses more damaged than Amelia had remembered. But she recognised it immediately.

"*Jebo majku*, they've shelled it worse than I thought," said one of the Bosniaks who lived downstairs.

"It's just the lack of maintenance," someone said.

"Shh. Let me hear what they're saying," said Amelia's father.

Amelia was quiet; a strange merging of hope and apprehension was gripping her head and she could not say anything. Yes, let me hear it, she thought. Come on now. Let me see him.

A reporter in a black down jacket, with his hair tied in a small ponytail, stood in the middle of the empty through street and spoke about Srebrenica.

"There is no life in this town anymore," the man said. "Although the residents have changed, this is a dead city."

The camera cut to a residential area. There were detached houses and dark, leafless trees along the wet street going up.

"As you can see, behind me, somebody is painting a house. The new occupants want to erase all traces of the people who once lived here."

The reporter, holding his microphone and the camera following him, crossed the street to the three-storey building, where a stocky man was applying a coat of white plaster to the cinder block wall. The man had on a wool sweater that would have been too thin for the December weather had he not been working. Beside him was a large bucket, and he had white specks of plaster on his trousers and boots. Wooden ladders were propped against the front of the house.

"The previous owner – or, should I say, the current owner, since he hasn't sold the house – is a Bosnian Muslim who escaped into Serbia from the killing and who is now incarcerated in a prison camp. Now, there seems to be a Serb family living in his house. Let's hear what the new occupants have to say."

"They got the wrong house," Amelia's brother huffed. "*Pičku mater*, it's the wrong house."

"Hey, watch your language," his mother said.

Oh, no, Amelia thought. They went to the wrong house! She knew this one, though, and she remembered the people who'd lived there. But it was the wrong house, a hundred metres before theirs on the Petriča.

The man doing the plasterwork was not shy about the camera. Holding the hawk and the trowel, he laughed and said proudly, "Yes, the Serb army drove them away. Finished, gone! All gone!"

"Don't you feel wrong occupying somebody else's home?" asked the reporter.

"Not at all." The man looked boastful about taking care of the house. "If the army hadn't kicked the Muslims out, they

276

would have left voluntarily, anyway. Like fleas jumping off a dog."
He laughed again.

The reporter asked if they could film inside the house. The
man's cordiality left him. He was not smiling anymore. "You
upadač better get out of here, too," he told the reporter.

"Fucking Chetni—" Nirzo started, then remembered the
Serb couple from upstairs was watching the show with them.

"Isn't that Nanić's house?" someone asked. "At least they
haven't torched that."

"They probably didn't burn any downtown."

"It's an expensive area there, Petriča."

"Hey, boys. Be quiet now," Amelia's father said.

The camera shifted to what looked like a half-ruined
construction hutment. Amelia felt her heart rush as she realised this
must be the prison camp: long, single-storey barracks with stove
pipes protruding from the roofs and the yard muddy and bleak.
There was a tall, ugly chain-link fence around, and it was all in a
flat valley of rotten hayfields. In the yard, nobody except a couple
of soldiers in dark-blue uniforms with assault rifles huddled in the
wind. The camera cut inside to a dank, makeshift shower area.
Another nondescript low building was shown from the outside.

"He must be somewhere behind a curtain," Nirzo joked.

"Yes, they're still putting on the makeup."

"Shh!"

"Don't worry, dear," Amelia's mother said, rubbing her
shoulder. "He'll be there in a moment."

Then he was. He was sitting in the middle of a small room,
sideways to the camera, as if reluctant to deal with it. There
were other men stooped on the bunk beds behind him, but what
Amelia saw was Maka: his hair with an aspect of grey now, yet
full as it had always been, his eyes looking past the camera, the
same strong, kind eyes she'd always known. He looked thin and
somehow nervous, but it was the same Maka, her Maka from
their life before.

"Look, there he is!" one of the neighbours shouted. "That's him!"

"Oh no," Amelia cried out. "He's got a moustache! I hate moustaches!" She was laughing and wiping tears from her eyes. Why did he have to have a moustache?

"They're interviewing him," someone said.

"Shh! Never mind the moustache," Amelia's father said. "Let's just watch."

They all watched.

Maka looked at the camera. Someone was speaking to him.

"I didn't have a choice," he said. He looked away again, sucking nervously on a cigarette.

"How come?" asked a female voice outside the camera.

"My options were either surrender to the Serbs in Bosnia, or give myself up here," said Maka. "I had better chances here. Didn't see any reason why they'd kill me."

"Boy, how he talks carefully," Nirzo said.

"You would, too," one of the downstairs men said. "Are you recording this?"

Amelia had completely forgotten! She dashed to the television and started going through the pile of VHS cassettes under the table next to a recorder, looking for an empty one or something that she could erase.

"Let's just watch it," her father said. "We'll get the recording later."

Right, she thought. What was she panicking for? She went back and sat down. She watched Maka speak. She was so happy she could hardly breathe. Oh, he looked so uneasy and skinny! With salt and pepper hair! But he looked all right. Oh, he was so handsome. And he was all right.

Then he was gone, and the camera was inside a long and open canteen hall. There were tables and many men, and they were all in mismatched, clean-looking clothes and eating soup from white plates and breaking up pieces of bread and mixing them into the soup. They had oranges, too. One of the prisoners walked past a table and stole one, jokingly, from another inmate. He pocketed the fruit, then gave it back, bantering. Most of the men looked serious, though, and Amelia thought she saw fear in the eyes of some of them. The whole place was pretty bleak, resembling one of those camps she had seen in old movies about the other war.

The Srebrenica segment ended, and the impeccable couple in the studio went on talking about something else.

Amelia was left speechless. She sat on the couch with her parents.

"It doesn't look that bad there," her mother said.

"Well, there you see," said the man who lived downstairs. "Your hubby's doing good. He looks like a fighter. Like Che Guevara with that tache."

That got her laughing. So true, he did! Heck, what was she panicking for? She was just so thankful and happy. She hadn't seen the house, though. They hadn't shown it. But who cared about a house now?

THIRTY

THE CAMP IN Mitrovo Polje was closed on February 9. Of the
four hundred men imprisoned there, half had been granted
asylum and sent to the United States, Ireland and Australia. The
other half the Serbs relocated to Šljivovica.

Standing at the door of his barrack, Maka watched the
headlights emerge from the quietly falling snow in the valley. In
the failing light, with the country and sky all white, the yard and
the roofs of the barracks covered in snow and smoke drifting from
the stovepipes, the camp looked as if it was trapped inside some
giant ping-pong sphere. The buses came, skidding and struggling
to clear the little icy slope of the gate. They stopped in the yard,
and Maka saw them begin to disgorge their passengers. These
were the same men he'd watched taken violently away half a
year ago.

Like sudden apparitions, before him stood Zlatar and Foric.
They looked plenty down at heel but their eyes smiled. They both
had new cotton jerseys and carried what looked like a bundle of
spare clothes. Snowflakes were piling up on their black hair and
they stood there, shivering in the dying winter day.

"Great to see you, old fox," said Zlatar. "Would you put up a couple of tired travellers?"

They took up vacant bunks in Maka's room.

"It *is* very basic here," Foric said.

"You had it better in your camp?" Maka asked, though he already knew it from Jean Klauser and from Zlatar's letters. He was very happy to see them.

"Yes, except the first two months were terrible. I don't want to talk about it."

They sat around the table with blankets wrapped around their shoulders. Zlatar was pouring brandy into two enamelled cups. They had water and juice for mixers, and smoked meat and cheese that Maka had sourced from the police. There was a small fire in the stove and two candles lit on a shelf. The fluorescent light was on in the corridor, but they kept the door shut to preserve the warmth. It was dim but cosy inside.

"Let's not talk about it," said Čerkić. "It was pretty rough here, too."

The photographer was sitting on his bunk. Juka, the stoic farmer, was there, and a third man lay on the berth above, with his back towards them. The room felt spacious; they were the ones left from the original eleven cellmates. From their camp, too, almost two hundred had been shipped out.

"I suppose you couldn't say it in the letters?"

"No," Maka said. "But it was bad, all right."

"Tonight we're fine." Zlatar screwed the cap on and put the bottle back on the floor. It was the Croatian brandy Maka had bought with the sneakers.

"I heard you came here wounded. How's your leg?"

"It's healed up okay," Juka said from his bed. "It just gives me cramps."

"If they'd sent you to hospital, it'd be better," Foric said. He was slicing the meat with a jackknife.

"I guess it's always better if they operate," said Zlatar.

"Not always," said the farmer. "It just gives me the cramps, that's all."

"The scumbags should have sent you. Here, have some of this."

The *suho meso* was deep wine-red and chewy, with a fine taste of smoke, the kind of cured delicacy that had been expensive even before the war. They passed the two brandy cups around. It *was* a very special occasion, Maka thought. It tasted like the real world, the normal world. But there was a heaviness, a sort of sadness in his chest, like the feeling of something coming to an end that you can't quite put your finger on.

"What do you think you'll end up doing in Austria?" Čerkić asked.

"Anything they'll let me," said Foric. "I'll clean, cook, drive. Pick up trash. Anything. Hell, they shot my brain up, but my body still works." He took a swig of the brandy.

"One thing I know," he continued, "I'll never leave the asphalt."

"How do you know they'll put you in a city?"

"I'm not joking. I promised Amra. When I get there, I'll never set my foot off the concrete again. Ever."

In Srebrenica Foric had been in a reconnaissance unit, and only two others from his squad had survived. He was waiting for his paperwork to be finalised for the asylum. His wife – Maka's cousin – had made it to Tuzla on the bus convoys in July. Foric was dead serious: she would join him in Vienna, and together they'd never venture into any woods in their lives again.

"The mountains might look like back home, though," Zlatar noted, squatting by the stove. He chucked a piece of cordwood into the firebox and started blowing into the cinders. "The UN wanted me to go to Austria, too. I told them, just take me to Tuzla. I'll manage... all I need is a set of goldsmith tools. And, God willing, I will... get by."

He spoke slowly, with the glow of the embers in his eyes, as if he were performing some sort of incantation on the stove. The wood ignited, illuminating his face. Maka watched his profile. He wondered if Zlatar ever thought about the gold and the money. Probably not. He wasn't the type that looked back. They'd all learned not to, anyway. But he felt bad for him.

"Have *you* heard anything?" Zlatar asked him.

"No. I don't know what the logic is."

"There isn't any," they heard the man lying on the top bunk say. He had been silent all this time and was still facing the wall. Now, when he spoke, there was no emotion in his voice. It was the same man whom Bielo had called Captain America and who, like Maka, had been waiting for news about the United States.

"No?"

"No. Not any," said the man, facing the wall.

He and Maka had not been given any explanation for why they were not considered or interviewed for America. They had been told already, back in November, that the US would take them all. It was the UN representative who said this. A hundred men from the Mitrovo Polje camp had gone there and another seventy from theirs. Maka's nephew Hassan was among the first. So was Bielo.

Captain America – Hilmo was his name – was devastated. Maka was not exactly in high spirits, either. Afterwards, ninety men from their camp were finally accepted to Germany. Maka was not in that lot either, even though he had family there.

He reached for the bottle and poured into the cups again. Maybe Hilmo was right. Maybe there was no logic. All these fine organisations and agencies, and people with fancy titles, gave you the impression that somewhere, someone was in charge of things. What if it was just a smokescreen? What if nobody was in control of anything?

Well, he was working his brain way too much. Life was easier when you didn't think and you stopped caring.

That wasn't a solution, though. Suppose you became a hard man when you ignored even death? He didn't want to, and he'd never looked up to the callous ones like Bielo just because of their toughness. But he knew he wasn't afraid of dying; it was something we all faced anyway, eventually, and he knew not being afraid of it was something the ones that hadn't seen the trenches could not feel the way he now felt it. What he was scared of was it coming prematurely, so that he wouldn't have the chance to do the things he'd want to.

And what was it he wanted?

One was easy. He'd get there and he'd see them and hold them. But after it was done, and the war done, what was it that he wanted?

Should he tell people about the trenches? About the young and old he'd known by name, the ones that had been dragged through the mud by their ankles, their equipment trailing as the fire kept coming? Or did he want to talk about men like Hukanović, who died a month after he got to Ireland? About Dedo or the three others that succumbed in this camp because they were starved and denied medical care? Or all those missing that he didn't know?

Seven thousand, and counting, they said. It wasn't a small incident. Articles, studies and books would be written about them, he supposed. Yet those thousands would remain numbers. Always just numbers.

No, he wasn't afraid of dying. He was afraid of bureaucrats, and not having enough time to figure out the things he wanted, and then to go for them.

But the one was easy.

Right. He could feel the drink now. It was a very long time since he'd had liquor. He thought of it. He couldn't remember when. And he should stop thinking about his family as it didn't bring them any closer. He heard Čerkić talking about Sarajevo. His wife, he said, had found a new flat for them and he would start photography again. The trouble was the apartment had belonged to some Serb. What if that family returned?

But Čerkić had a plan. So had Zlatar. Foric, too, with his intention of staying forever on the asphalt. Juka had given up hopes about Germany, but he had relatives near Zenica, and he'd take up farming there. Only he, Maka, had no idea, outside of not dying yet. Well, Hilmo was stuck, too, he thought. He'd been banking on America. Poor bugger. He never talked about his family. Maka hadn't dared to ask if he had one or what had happened to them.

"Can we get another one?" Zlatar asked. He had poured the last of the brandy and mixed in some water.

"One of the cops has," Čerkić said.

"How much you think it is?"

"Forty."

"What a sly profiteer. Let's let him exploit us some more."

He found the money. Čerkić took it and slipped out.

"What will you do if both Germany and America refuse?"

"I don't know," Maka said. He was a little drunk. He could feel the heat from the stove. Outside, in the dark, the snow was falling behind the double plastic sheets of the window. "I guess I'll go to Bosnia."

"What will you do there?"

"I don't know. I'll figure something out."

Yes, what if he couldn't get asylum? Suppose he could scrape through in Bosnia, but how would he find a place to live? He was lucky he didn't have a mortgage. Many of the people he knew who'd lost their houses owed money to the banks, and, though their homes were lost, he guessed the banks and the debts were not going anywhere. Still, how would he finance a new place? It was unrealistic to expect support from the government either.

"How's Amelia doing?" Zlatar asked.

"She's fine."

"Maybe you can get to Germany later," Foric said.

"Maybe. I don't want her back in Bosnia."

"Not a good idea, now that she's got work."

"No," Maka agreed.

"Is she writing to you?"

"Yes."

"That Jokić is a great fellow," Zlatar said.

"He is."

The three of them were still drinking when the lights were supposed to go out. They had the candles burning and it was warm in the room. Čerkić had found the booze-dealing cop, then excused himself and gone to bed. Juka and Hilmo were asleep, too.

"Watch out, I think a cop's coming," said Foric. He had his ear to the door.

"Oh, fuck the police," said Zlatar.

The door opened and a guard looked in.

"Who said that?" the cop demanded.

They all stayed quiet.

"Who said it? Fuck what?"

Nobody confessed.

"Okay," the cop said. "Tomorrow the three of you will be on the work shift."

In the morning the sky was blue and high. Everything was covered in new snow. The plain of the valley spread achingly bright under the sun and the hills were white and sharp against the sky. The air was dry and cold. Maka worked with his breath steaming, the sleeves of his pullover tucked up. They had been handed snow shovels and they were clearing the yard and the paths between the barracks.

"Now, this starts to feel like a proper Pioneer camp," Zlatar said. "We only need red scarves."

Foric gave a laugh. He was shovelling frantically, with a cigarette in the corner of his mouth.

"Today, as I enjoy salubrious mountain air with my comrades," he pronounced solemnly, "I give my idiot's word of honour to never again trust a politician, or the seniors who screwed us up." The cigarette wobbled up and down as he spoke.

He seemed to give it some thought.

"But I shall be a loyal and honest friend of the immigration office."

"You forgot the one about spreading brotherhood and unity." Zlatar was taking a break, leaning on his shovel and wiping his forehead. He looked quite hungover.

"Screw that. It's the 'valuing people who respect peace and freedom' that's the tough one. Ain't many around."

Maka was also resting. He had made good headway and the area between the two accommodation barracks was clear of snow. He was starting to feel good about it. He had a slight headache, but he had been eating the clean, soft snow and his arms were starting to feel their old strength again. There were fellow inmates loitering outside the barracks, taking in the winter sun and smoking, and making jokes about the "chain gang". He thought they were funny. It felt good to do something physical.

"Say, I got an idea," shouted Foric. He was hurling snow over his shoulder in a rhythm, working his way towards the camp's gate. "I'll start a snow removal business in Vienna. Digging out their cars in the morning. What you say?"

"Sounds like you're all set," Maka called back to him. "What will you do in the summer?"

"Haven't thought it out that far. Ain't nothing a Pioneer can't tackle."

Maka rubbed his arms; he could feel them begin to function the way he remembered. He'd managed to gain back some weight and it was good to put these hands to work. The sun was bright on the snow. He felt warm from the shovelling. Nights were nights, he thought. It was always easier to feel better about things in the morning.

THIRTY-ONE

THE PRISON POPULATION kept shrinking. Maka was now alone in his room with Hilmo. Zlatar had spent only a week in the camp, then left for Bosnia, with a large group, together with Juka and Čerkić. Foric had been assigned to the kitchen team and had worked the morning shift with Maka. Then his paperwork for Austria was ready and he, too, was taken out of the camp.

Time passed slowly, now that the conditions were tolerable, and Maka's only chum was not of the talkative kind. When things had been bad, mere survival had mattered and you didn't waste energy on rumination. Now there was nothing except waiting.

Germany had announced they had taken their share from the camps, and so that door had slammed shut before his nose. There was no decision or news regarding the USA.

Now what? Wait longer, or return to Bosnia?

It was the fence-sitting that was maddening. He had watched the buses depart for Tuzla, his friends waving at him through the dusty windows. He knew he could have gone on those cars, had he chosen to.

The days were clear and cold now, and the snow in the yard had crusted over. Jean Klauser visited the camp again. He came with the other interpreter, a poker-faced, bespectacled woman from Skopje.

"I've thought about it," Maka told him. "I better go back to Bosnia."

"Life's tough there now," Jean Klauser said. His breath was steaming. The three of them sat in the interview room, nestled inside their jackets. "Lots of internal refugees, no jobs, lack of housing and government support. Where would you stay?"

"I guess I'm still enlisted," Maka said. "They might house me at some barracks."

"I wouldn't count on that. There's a demobilisation underway."

He considered it again. He guessed it figured. The peace agreement limited the number of troops and instead of incorporating more soldiers they would have to kick out at least a hundred and fifty thousand burned-out fighters. The Dayton deal divided Bosnia into two de facto countries, the shaky Croat-Bosnian Federation and the Serb Republic. His house, assuming it hadn't been burned, was left on the wrong side. He had no job and most of his relatives were dead.

"I know it's your country," Jean Klauser said. "But would you want your wife and son to come back into such a dismal landscape?"

"No. That's one thing I know."

He lit a cigarette.

"I guess I'll just wait for a place in America."

"We don't know when or if they'll accept you," the Swiss said. "But I've spoken to a representative of Finland. She says their country would take you. I know this for sure. She said they'd take your wife and your son as well. Amelia's parents could probably move there later on, if they so wished."

Finland?

"I know nothing about this country," Maka said. Besides, wasn't the USA the land of the free? It could be like Hilmo had envisioned it: maybe they didn't care about your name and, as long as you were prepared to work, anybody could get a fresh start.

"I know you want to work," Jean Klauser offered. "But imagine the war starts weighing down on you and you can't?"

He told Maka he had seen it before, with all the wars and prisons he had worked in since the Seventies. He'd witnessed how the burden sometimes became too much for men who'd fought in the trenches and languished in detention camps.

"I don't want to discourage you, but the mind and the body are not inexhaustible. What if you got sick and became unable to work? The US social security is paper-thin. Almost nonexistent, I might say. But Finland is an advanced country that cares for its residents."

Maka blew smoke and watched it disperse. *Finland?* A flat and cold country? It sounded just as opposite from home as he could think of. Then he remembered the dream he'd had in that ruin near Jadar, about the strange house and the snow-covered fields, and how he'd felt that intense, warm happiness for being there with Amelia. He guessed it didn't matter where it was, as long as she was there and Dino was there with them.

"I'll think about it. How should I proceed?"

"That immigration officer from Finland will visit here soon. Laura is her name. I've already spoken about you, tentatively. I'll tell her that you're seriously considering. The Serbs want to close down this camp anyway."

Back in his room, Maka opened the letter Jean Klauser had delivered. Amelia said it was cold in Munich. They were all good and her father had bought a car recently. Dino had been angry with Amelia because the boy had missed seeing his dad in the telly. Now the poor tot had been calling him daily from his toy phone. But Amelia had seen him and she was so happy. She thought Maka was very handsome, even with the moustache.

Laura, the lady from Finland, visited Šljivovica a week later. She came with an IOM delegate. She said she worked for the Finnish immigration service. She was very fair-skinned and looked fragile and nervous, but she told Maka frankly that he would be accepted as a refugee in Finland, should he choose to apply.

Maka tried to bring back into his head what he had learned about Finland in school. It was a small country that had fought the Russians. Outside of that, he knew nothing. Was it true they got six months of darkness in the winter, then six months of daylight, as the sun didn't set?

"Not really," Laura said. "In the very north, perhaps."

"Is there any summer at all?"

She smiled. "Yes. A short, but good one."

That evening Maka wrote a letter to Amelia. Hilmo lay in the bunk, like most of the time now, reading a book. It was an English–Croatian dictionary his aunt had sent from Zagreb. They were out of firewood and the room was cold.

I can't come to Germany, Maka wrote. *But I've applied for asylum in Finland. I know they will take me. They will take you and Dino, too, if you want to come.*

He lit another cigarette and thought of what to say. He felt good about having reached a decision, but lousy for wanting to disrupt the life Amelia had built in Germany. She must also be tired of always starting everything from scratch.

He put the pen back to the paper.

I've given your number to Laura. She will call you. She has promised to help us and fast-track your papers. Will you come?

The first Finland-bound group left Šljivovica in March. Maka was still waiting. He was waiting to hear from Laura. He was waiting to see Amelia's reply. Spring was coming on fast. The snow had all melted from the roofs and the camp yard was clear, and sparrows dusted in the sandy ground behind Maka's barrack. Wood anemones bloomed in the hazel tree copse on the little hillock. Sitting there, in the young weeds, and studying the Finnish-language leaflets Laura had left him, he could see the hills across the valley. Their round tops were still covered in snow, and white as sugar.

The Finnish language seemed odd and intricate. Everything had been very intricate and convoluted, Maka admitted. He hoped there wouldn't be any more complications. He'd had his share in life, he supposed.

THIRTY-TWO

IT WAS RAINING hard and a film of water flowed down the windshield in ripples. The street outside was dark, though it was early afternoon. These were the kind of heavy clouds that engulfed the whole city and would keep pouring down all day.

"Amelia, what does that sign say?" Her father was trying to see through the rain. He had the map of the city folded open on the dashboard.

She looked at the street sign. In the backseat, Dino was sleeping, buckled into a child's safety seat.

"Hausener Weg?"

They both scanned through the map until her father found it. It seemed they had driven too far on the motorway, and gotten off at the wrong interchange.

They had started in the morning. It was over four hundred kilometres from Munich, and the car was an old Fiat Uno that did not take the autobahn well. They had to stop twice on the way to let the engine cool down. Then it commenced raining, and the speed dropped in the poor visibility. When they finally crossed the Main on the motorway, the river had been flat and grey and wide in the rain. It was an early spring storm.

They stood parked on the long residential street now. The townhouses, trees and blocks of flats along the street all looked blurred in the rainfall. It was getting late. The Finnish consulate would close at 2pm.

"Looks like we're five, six kilometres off," Amelia's father said. "We better try to take these smaller streets."

"Do you know how to get there?"

"Maybe, if you read the map for me."

"Dad!"

"Difficult to see anything in this downpour…"

"Dad! It's already twenty past!"

Amelia had been told it would take at least three months before everything was ready. But Laura, the Finnish immigration lady, she'd really gone to bat for them. It was the beginning of April when, unexpectedly, Amelia got the phone call. Their visas were ready. The IOM had already booked the airline tickets for her and Dino. They would fly to Finland in four days. That would land them there a day ahead of Maka, who would come in from Serbia. Everything happened so quickly. They would just have to visit the consulate to sign another set of paperwork. That was something that needed to be done *today*.

"Let's get moving, then," her father said. He passed the map to Amelia and started the engine.

A taxi pulled over in the rain ahead of them. Someone in a trench coat got out and, with a newspaper for an umbrella, dashed into the nearest building.

"No, wait. I've got an idea." Amelia quickly unbuckled her seatbelt and handed the map back to her father.

"Where you going?"

"Just wait a sec," she told him, and stepped out.

She was gone for only half a minute, but when she got back into the car her hair was wet and dripping and her shirt all glued on her chest.

"Okay. Follow that taxi," she said, wiping her hair back.

"Now, that was clever."

"Isn't it? Like in the movies."

They saw the yellow sign on the taxi's roof go out and the brake lights flash. The car started into the rain, and Amelia's father put his Fiat into gear and went after it.

THIRTY-THREE

M AKA GOT OFF the plane at midnight in Turku in the south of Finland. A corpulent, middle-aged social worker from the immigration office met him at the arrival gate. He was bald and cordial, and he had a younger Bosnian man with him to do the interpreting.

They drove him from the airport through a dark landscape into the suburbs. The interpreter, demure and in a German football shirt, told him from the backseat it was the suburbs. Staring into the obscured night, Maka could not tell.

The apartment was old but clean. It was in a block of flats, in a bleak-looking prefab tenement area that must have been constructed in the Seventies. All the lights were on and the flat was bright and lonesome.

The Finnish man explained to him about the water. There was no boiler; you just turned the tap to red, and the hot water flowed. See? He flushed the toilet. This button, see? They had brought shampoo and toiletries, and the bed linen was new. On the bed was a set of clothes. A pair of brand-new sneakers had been placed in the vestibule.

"Hopefully they're your size," the Bosnian said.

Maka asked him where he was from. "Prijedor," he said.

The Finn told Maka there was milk and cold cuts and such in the fridge, and a bag of bread on the kitchen table. "Just to get you by overnight." He was talking in German. He said they'd come for Maka in the morning. They'd need to take him to the immigration office. There was plenty of paperwork to fill out: social security applications, employment agency forms and so forth, plus the medical check-up. In the evening they'd go back to the airport.

"There's been some delay and your relatives haven't arrived yet," the man said. "But their flights have been sorted, and they'll fly tomorrow from Frankfurt."

"Who are they, your wife?" asked the man from Prijedor.

"Yes," Maka said. "My wife. My son and my wife."

"Here's the keys to the apartment. Opens the downstairs, too. Don't go out without it, as the doors will lock. You know, normally you'd stay at a reception centre first. We're lending you this apartment because you've got family with you. You'll begin from here."

The Finn set the keys on the kitchen table and with his thick fingers pulled a banknote from a manila envelope.

"Here's fifty marks. It's yours, in case you need anything."

Maka signed for the money. The Finn and the interpreter put their shoes on and went out.

"Well, have a good night," the man from Prijedor said from the doorway. "Welcome to Finland, and see you in the morning."

Maka was alone. Sitting on the mini couch, he looked around at the apartment: a small living room, two bedrooms and a kitchen alcove. There was a little balcony. He was on the third floor of a four-storey building. From the window he could only see darkness. Some basic flea-market furniture had been installed already. A bed in both rooms. Good, he thought. Dino could have his own corner right away. He'd turn four in the summer. He was a big boy now.

Maka stood up and went into the kitchen. He opened the fridge door. The light came on.

The groceries looked different from what he remembered in Bosnia. Then again, he had not seen groceries for four years. One was a carton of milk, for sure. It was white and blue, with an illustration of a pasturing cow on it.

Another, an orange one, had a picture of juice-oozing tangerines.

He pulled open the drawers. Plates and cutlery. It was all very basic and clean.

Back in the bathroom, Maka turned on the tap by the sink. He felt the water with his hand. Warm, warmer. Hot. He shut it off. He turned it on again, cold now. He took some in his cupped hand and tasted it. It was clear and fresh.

Wiping his chin, he looked at the man in the mirror. A bit skinny, as you'd expect. Three years of guerrilla warfare. Eight months in a concentration camp. He turned his head to see himself sideways. He hadn't had a chance to keep company with this face for a long, long time. They'd never had a mirror in the camp. But it certainly looked familiar. He had shaven the moustache already. Something else had changed, though. The eyes were more settled than what he remembered. More composed and less quick to rush. They were slightly sad eyes, he supposed. Sad but undefeated.

He had travelled two days. They had taken him and four other Bosniaks from the camp in Šljivovica and driven them, handcuffed, into some town where they spent the night in a police cell. The next morning they were loaded on again, hauled to the airport in Belgrade and put on the plane.

It was his first time on an airplane. He had travelled abroad twice, in Germany and Croatia, both times by bus. Now, he could still relive that heart-stopping moment when the machine took off, his back and head pressed into the seat, then the soaring feeling as the plane climbed and, looking through the round little window, the Serbian suburbs and factories and hills dwarfed and flattening. Then the sun shifting, smoothly and impossibly, as the plane rolled to take its course to the north.

They flew to Gothenburg in Sweden. There, the other Bosniaks transferred onto a plane bound for northern Finland. Only he, Maka Delić, had travelled to this city in the south. It was as if a giant hand had picked him up from one reality and dropped him off in another. He'd been rocketed into the future. He'd left his home behind. This time for ever.

Maka looked at the man in the glass.

"Again, why only you?" he said into the mirror.

Because you were so concerned about the snow and the lack of summer, the man replied. Maybe that lady, Laura, had remembered just that.

He smiled, then started to laugh. It sure looked dark here, too. It was April and the winter was supposed to be over, but, coming from the airport, it had been like driving into a solid blackness that the occasional streetlights and gas station signs merely attempted to penetrate. And it had been a long two days. God, he was tired. An alarm clock in the bedroom showed 1am.

The time in Munich was probably one or two hours behind. Suppose he could call her? Maybe she was still packing.

He went to the vestibule where he thought he had seen a phone line. Yes, it was there, plugged into a jack in the wall, but it was just the cable, without the phone.

The sneakers were parked by the door. Next to them stood his old army boots, all shrivelled and the leather worn and broken as if someone had worked them over with a grater. Looking at them, one had to wonder how it was possible they were still intact, after everything.

He put on the new shoes.

It was very dark outside. The yard between the blocks was barren, and in the shadows of the buildings were white blotches of melting snow ploughed into heaps. The buildings were long and dark. From what Maka could see, only a couple of the flats still had lights on. He guessed one was his.

He went walking down the empty street. Driving in, he had seen what had looked like a phone booth. The air was cold and his new shoes felt comfortable. There were streetlamps, but they didn't illuminate very well. What a strange country, he thought. The wet, black ground sucked all the light.

After having gone on for a while, in the dark without seeing anyone, Maka spotted the phone booth. It stood like in vigil, a sad, lonely block of light in the distance by the street side, illuminating a patch of wet grass and asphalt around it.

It felt warm inside the plexiglass cubicle, with the wind cut now. Maka dug the money from his pocket and examined it. It was a crisp banknote coloured like the autumn foliage. It had some irritable-looking old gentleman on it.

He lifted up the receiver and heard the dial tone. That was when he saw the coin slot.

Okay. Of course. He wasn't thinking.

Peering through the marker-scribbled, spray-paint-tagged plexiglass, Maka made out a building up ahead and what looked like the front of a grocery store and a pub. Both had their lights out. Farther up the street was the yellow sign of a taxi stand. A solitary cab stood parked there.

He slipped out of the booth and advanced over to the car. Somebody was sitting inside, reading a newspaper in the dome light. Maka knocked on the side window. It rolled down. An elderly, rotund man looked at him enquiringly.

"*Minne sinä haluat?*" the man spoke.

Maka displayed the banknote. "Could you break this up, please?" he asked in Bosnian.

The driver looked at him. He had a thick, pale moustache and sorrowful eyes.

"*Okei. Sulla on rahaa. Mutta minne sinä haluat?*"

Maka looked back at him. How would he communicate if he only knew Bosnian?

"*Sori, en ymmärrä,*" the man said. "*Non comprendo.*" Then, in what sounded like English: "Get in? No? All right. Good night."

The window went back up, smoothly and without any effort from the driver. Maka watched it rise, bringing back the reflection of his own mug. A power window. He had not seen one before, only heard of them. He was very impressed. With a simple push of a button, the man had shut him out of his world.

Maybe he should've used body language? Cut the bill, he thought, with his fingers like scissors? But this was not his country. He'd arrived barely an hour ago, and it was a strange country, and he didn't know their ways or the language. He'd had a lot of luck. It wasn't good to push it. He backed away from the car.

Back in the tenement quarter, Maka saw the buildings with their rows of black windows spread out in the night. The moon had come out. The only light on inside seemed to shine from his apartment.

He fished the keys from his pocket, opened the front door and went in the hall and up the stairway and into the flat. He shut the door. There was a security chain inside and he attached it. He took a long, hot shower.

The bed linen was incredibly soft and smelled like lilies. Maka wrapped himself in the duvet. Oh, he was tired, all right. Where did he put the gun? He didn't have a gun. He had a son and a wife in Germany. He'd pick them up at the airport. His son and his wife. They were asleep now. Everyone resting. He felt the sleep taking over.

THIRTY-FOUR

Amelia sat in her seat in the steady, droning hum of the turboprop engines, looking out and seeing the tops of the clouds that extended to the horizon. They were dark with a hue of orange-grey from the dying glow of the sky. The aircraft had climbed up, then climbed more. Then, minutes after it came free of the cloud layer, there was an announcement saying they had started the preparations for landing.

It was that short hop from Stockholm to Turku.

She looked at Dino, strapped in next to her. The boy was asleep now, his head fallen forward. He had still cried when they took off. Barely four, Amelia thought, yet already so much he'd had to let go of.

First came the morning drive from Munich to the airport. It was beautiful spring weather. Her parents were in the front. She sat in the backseat with Dino in the safety seat.

The boy was unusually quiet.

Amelia ruffled his hair, saying they were going to meet his dad finally. "He's your father, don't you remember? He's been waiting to see you for such a long time, you know that?"

Dino went quiet, then asked, "Why so long?"

"Your dad's been busy taking care of some things. *Very* busy. But now you're going to meet him. How do you feel about that? Aren't you excited?"

The boy looked at his feet.

"Are we going to fly in an airplane?" he asked.

"Yes, we're going to Finland! What do you think about that?"

The boy put his fists up like a champion. "I want to fly!"

"Good! And what do you wanna do when we get there?"

"I don't know," he said, swinging his feet that hung down from the seat, staring at the tiny sneakers. He was wearing the little leather jacket which Amelia had bought him for spring and held the toy phone against his belly. Outside, the other cars were zipping past on the autobahn.

"Don't you want to see your dad?"

The boy nodded quietly. "I want an ice cream."

"Oh, we'll get ice cream. They say the Finnish ice cream is *so* good. But what else? Don't you want to meet Daddy?"

Squeezing the phone, the boy said, quietly, "I'll call him."

Amelia had two suitcases checked in. Two times twenty kilos. That's what they'd have to start a new life with. Better than when she had left Srebrenica, when she'd had a handbag with her identity documents and a few dinars in it. Still, forty kilos wasn't much when you needed to begin everything again. Dino had wanted to pack all of his toys. There simply wasn't room, and Amelia had to put her foot down. Only the favourites made the selection. The phone was too precious to even put in the luggage.

But the boy had not understood they were going alone. She'd told him, of course, a few times. Even so, it only really dawned on him at the security gate in Frankfurt.

Dino's grandmother stood there, waving at them. They hadn't found a parking space and Amelia's father had stayed with the car.

"*Baba!*" the boy called, tears in his eyes.

"But *Baba* and *Deda* can't come with us," Amelia said. "They don't have their passports."

"*Baba!*" Dino cried. "Go get your passports! I'll wait for you!"

But they could not wait and the boy had cried for a long time on the plane. Then, as they waited for three hours for the connecting flight in Stockholm, Dino called from the toy phone, for the first time, not Maka but his grandparents.

Now they were flying again and the boy had fallen asleep and he looked so peaceful. He must be so tired, Amelia thought. Good, he'd only sleep better. But she could not help feeling worried about him. How would he react to Maka? The poor tot had always been on the shy side.

And how would *she* react? Suppose the war had changed him? What if she had changed? It was four years now.

Maybe it didn't matter. Not now that it was finally coming to an end.

It wasn't all like that, though. She knew she had no clear picture of this future she was flying into. But why did it make her so mixed up and silly? Maybe it was the altitude.

A woman in a snug, blue uniform was coming down the aisle, her lips in a reassuring, professional smile, one hand in a measured pose as she walked by, checking the seatbelts. Amelia felt the nose of the plane pitch down. Slowly and smoothly, they started descending into the clouds.

The plane taxied close to the terminal. Stepping out of the aircraft and going down the steep boarding stairs, Amelia held Dino's hand. It was dark and cold and windy outside. She looked at the large terminal building ahead. There were bright lights inside, and behind the tall glass walls she saw distant shapes of people. One of them she noticed, a man standing close to the glass, his face and hands pressed against it, peering outside.

It was just a black silhouette against the lights, but she knew that shape, that posture. He looked very lean, but she knew it was him.

I doubt if he can see us, she thought. It was very dark and windy on the tarmac and, looking out, one could probably only discern the obscured shapes of the passengers getting off the plane.

THIRTY-FIVE

MAKA WAITED IN the small arrivals hall. It was not a big airport, and the flight from Stockholm was the only one. From what he had seen, looking through the glass wall, there were not many passengers on that plane. Now he stood behind a guardrail facing the exit. Every time those metallic double doors slid open he felt some odd, deep emotion. A woman with a young child had just walked through. For a second, just before they waved at someone else, Maka thought it was them. The exit had already delivered a couple of dozen passengers, sleepy, happy, dour, tired, all very neat-looking and clean.

He had always believed he would meet Amelia again, but that it would happen in Srebrenica after the war was over, when there were no more troops and guns in the hills and the town was being rebuilt. He'd dreamed of that moment, God knew for how long. Now he was in this strange country and it was happening, and it had all happened so fast he hadn't even had time to think about it. He simply waited, keeping his eyes on those metal doors. The Finnish social worker and the interpreter had stayed at the other end of the hall, allowing him privacy. It was very quiet and his body was calm.

The doors opened again and it was Amelia. She was coming through, holding a little boy by the hand, them both towing luggage, both looking a little lost, tired perhaps; she just a little older but still the same beautiful girl from Bratunac. She looked around, scanning the lobby, then saw Maka and her eyes began to shine. She gave a quick wave of her hand and pointed him out to the boy. They started running towards him. Maka, stepping out from behind the rail, embraced Amelia; they collided softly and Maka felt her hands around him, her hair on his face, soft, sweet-smelling, her hands slender and holding him tight. Something flashed through his mind. The war had just started. They were on the seaside and it was not real but then there was the artillery fire, like the bounding of his heart. He could feel Amelia's hands searching on the back of his head, going through his hair, feeling his face, and amidst the memory of the incoming shells he could hear her cry, "Oh, Maka!" A little hand touched his leg. "Oh, Maka!" cried Amelia. But he was somewhere in the hills. *We don't have much time*, he thought he heard someone say. With his face pressed against Amelia's hair it was dark, and he felt like he was submerged in water. But suddenly it was so cold it hurt him.

"Maka! Why did you send me away?"

Then, in a second, the war was over and he knew it. He was in the arrival lobby of an airport in Finland, holding his wife. Yet something was hurting him. Amelia had grabbed his ears, with both hands, pulling on them painfully. Anger was twisting her face and she had tears in her eyes.

"Why did you send me away? Why did you leave me like that?"

She let go and collapsed against his chest. She was crying.

"Oh, Maka, why did you do it?"

"It's all right now," he whispered, holding her. "Everything's all right." He kissed her head. It felt so sweet and familiar.

"Oh, never mind what I say," Amelia said, sobbing. "I'm just so happy you're alive. I don't know what I'm saying. Please don't mind what I'm saying. Oh, I'm so happy you're alive!" She looked him in the eyes.

"I know. It's all right."

"I'm just so happy and I missed you so."

"I know, honey. It's over."

"Oh, Maka!" She laughed now, wiping her eyes.

Remembering the boy, Maka looked down and saw him hugging his mother's leg. In his other hand was a yellow toy telephone. He had a little leather jacket on, and he looked very modish in it.

"Hi there, young man. Who've we got here?"

Maka kneeled, smiling. Dino hid behind Amelia's legs. Amelia laughed and put her hand on the boy's shoulder. "But Dino, this is your daddy, remember? Say hi to him, will you?"

The boy pressed the phone against his chest and stared at his feet, then said, shyly, "*Hallo…*"

"That was German, was it?" said Maka. "Great. You speak so many languages. I'll just say *zdravo*. You can call me Daddy or Maka, or anything you like."

The boy retreated further behind his mother's legs.

"Well, it'll come," Maka said. He ruffled Dino's hair. "Never mind, buddy. It's good to be a little careful with strangers. You'll be just fine."

They were at the apartment. The lights were out except for the small lamp on the nightstand. Dino was asleep in the other room. They lay in the bed under the duvet, still talking. There was so much to talk about and they had to take it slowly. It wasn't just covering and getting back the four lost years. These were years that had been anything but ordinary, and they knew such years were long and complex, like one's lifetime.

"How did you get these?" Amelia noticed the scars on Maka's back. She ran her fingers over them, feeling the minute unevenness.

Maka told her about the thorn bushes by the Drina. He said some were from the prison camp.

"Can you tell me about it, one day?"

"I'll tell you anything you want me to," Maka said.

"We've talked about such miseries. I don't want it to make you feel lousy."

"It doesn't make me feel bad anymore."

"But I don't want you to talk about anything unless you want to."

"I'll talk about anything," Maka said. "It's important. But it doesn't have to be tonight."

They had gone through all the relatives and friends they could remember, tried to figure out what had happened, to whom and how. It was a long list of mostly dead people, and it was quite late at night.

"No, it doesn't have to. We're starting in a new country tonight and I want it to be cheerful. I know this will be a good country for us and Dino."

"It's a strange country," said Maka. "I hope it won't stay this dark always."

"It's going to be the opposite in no time. I once saw a show on German TV about their summer. There were many empty lakes and people having barbecues, and they had saunas by the lakeside and they went swimming straight into the lake from those saunas. It was midnight, but it looked like late afternoon because it was so bright."

"Sounds like Bosnia. I mean, there's something Bosnian about that."

"The way they enjoy nature?"

"Yes, what we do with the rivers. And it seems like a peaceful country."

"Oh, you said that about Serbia, too."

"How do you mean?"

"You said it on camera. Remember?"

"Oh, did I? Yes, I remember now. Funny I said so."

"I know you had to. But it wasn't funny that you had to."

"No. But we're here now."

He had waited for this day for four ruthless years. He'd waited, hoped, fought for it. There had been moments, he knew, when he'd lost his hope. Now that it was here, he almost couldn't feel it. It was too much. The emotion was too much, so he killed it like one killed fear in combat. Sometimes you weren't able to kill the fear, and then it was like being in a dream where your legs were heavy as lead, and it was hard to move under the fire. But most of the times he'd managed to kill it, and he'd killed other emotions, too. What good had emotions ever done to him?

He held Amelia against him and knew it wasn't all true.

He had this love, and nothing could ever kill it. It was pure, tiny, unremarkable love and such love kept you moving, little by little, always moving and staying afloat. Even the house and the land that had been lost didn't mean so much now. He held her tight and felt her body. No, maybe there was no need to kill anything anymore.

"Maka. Where do we go from here?" whispered Amelia.

"I don't know. But we'll get there. The three of us."

He told her how that morning he had been to the immigration office and talked with someone from the employment agency. There seemed to be jobs that the Finns did not want but which sounded like perfectly decent work to him. He was sure they could both get jobs. He might become a farmhand, or take up cleaning.

"Cleaning is hard work," Amelia noted.

"So is being a farm drudge. Maybe I'll become a fisherman."

"They have the sea, that's true. It looks beautiful, too."

"I know I could do it."

"Will you bring me fresh catch every day?"

"Of course. Big *komarča* and lobsters."

"I don't think they have those. Oysters either."

"I'll bring what they have."

"Will you?" she asked teasingly.

"I will."

"Then what will you do in the winter when the sea is all frozen?"

"I haven't got it figured out that far," Maka said, remembering old Foric. "They told me I should learn the basics of their language. I've already started. I can say *moi* and *moi-moi*. Means hello, and bye-bye."

"That doesn't sound difficult," said Amelia. "Cute, too, for a foreign language. I want to learn it, too."

"It gets trickier from there," Maka said.

He reached towards the bedside table to switch off the lamp, then saw Amelia's blouse that was lying on the table and touched it. It felt satiny under his fingers.

"Do you remember that one?" Amelia asked.

He picked it up and looked at it. It was a simple, white silk blouse.

"That's the one you got me for my twenty-third birthday. Remember? You bought it from that fashion boutique in Sarajevo. Still like new, but it's my favourite shirt. You really always knew what I like."

"Is that so?" He set the shirt back on the table.

"I was wearing it under my winter jacket that day when your brother came running to the house. Can you realise, it's the only thing we've got left from Srebrenica? I didn't want to leave it in Germany. Because you got it for my birthday and because nothing else remains from our home. That winter jacket's gone. But this is the shirt I wore when I got on that bus."

"Is that so?"

"I remember looking through that wet window, seeing you stand there, on the street. You looked so sad and resolute. You were looking back at me until the bus drove off. Do you remember that? It was raining, and there was sleet on the ground and my feet were cold and wet. Do you remember? Can you remember how that same street was in the old days, when Auntie Jasmina had a flower shop there and the art nights in August and watching the fireflies dance from that little bridge over the spring creek?"

Maka switched the lamp off. Now, in the darkness, he noticed how the room smelled new though the apartment must have been over two decades old. The light of a streetlamp in the yard came through the window blinds and cast pale, horizontal stripes on the wall.

He held Amelia. Her body was warm and solid and incredibly familiar. The night was very quiet now and the bed and the duvet were soft and comfortable. Maybe it would all turn out to be all right. Maybe he wouldn't have to kill anything.

"Yes," Maka said. "I remember. I remember everything."

ABOUT THE AUTHOR

Jani Anttola is a Finnish novelist and a medical doctor. In the 1990s he served in Rwanda with the French military and fought in Bosnia as a soldier of the Bosnian army. His prior works have been published in Finland. He has spent most of his adult life abroad, working in Africa, the Middle East and the Asia-Pacific.